The Suicide Society

Book Four

Resurrection of Death

A Novel by

William Brennan Knight

Published by Altron Services
Copyright © 2021 by William Brennan Knight

Printed in the United States of America
First Printing, 2021
ISBN: 978-1-7339698-2-6
Published by Altron Services

www.authorwbk.com

To: Bill Benoist. Thanks for being a friend and making a decision that changed the life of a young, cocky, wet-behind-the-ears kid.

Books in the Suicide Society Series:

Chapter One

Winn ducked from behind a burned-out car and sprinted toward the entrance of a storefront whose doors were wrenched open and torn off their hinges. After just three strides, the automatic weapons fire traced his path, and he dove into the building as a bullet whizzed past, narrowly missing his left shoulder.

With a cacophony of sounds that confirmed a nasty fall, he crashed into a rack formerly used to hold bagged snacks and pastries. He slid across the floor until a refrigerated beverage cooler stopped his momentum. Panting heavily, Winn frantically looked for an exit. Time was short, and they would enter the store in just a few seconds. The brass knuckles on his right hand were no match for automatic weapons, so flight was the only realistic option.

After another deep breath of foul, rancid air wafting out from the dairy case, he got to his feet and ran to the back entrance as the Corporate's security squad entered the building. He hit the back door with such force it slammed into one of the regulars just as he was trying to open it from the outside. The fortuitous timing sent the man staggering backward as Winn collided with him, and they both tumbled to the pavement.

It took the regular longer to recover from the shock and surprise of the impact, and Winn used the security

1

man's momentary disorientation to his advantage. He grabbed his adversary's throat with one hand while the other ripped off his helmet and faceplate. Down and exposed, the "skanker" as the Krens called them, tried to raise his AR-15, but the combatants were too close together. Without a conscious thought, Winn brought the brass knuckles down on the man's visage, crushing the cartilage and sending a spray of blood in a 90-degree arc. Before the skanker could react, Winn punched him in the face several more times until he was sure his adversary was incapacitated. Just around the corner, he could hear another soldier approaching.

Rising to his feet, he started running up the alley until he found a fence low enough to climb. Two more skankers reached the back of the store just as Winn hopped the fence. Several rounds of bullets passed harmlessly overhead as he ran through a yard that led to a residential street. Out of the corner of his eye, he saw a van coming around a corner, its tires squealing as it accelerated towards him. Another screech of the tires as it stopped suddenly, and the side door swung open. An older woman in a burka leaned out and motioned him inside, and a younger man next to her extended a hand.

"Quickly," she said. "We have a cellar where you can hide." With only a slight hesitation, Winn jumped into the van.

A large man, also much younger than the woman, deftly maneuvered the vehicle through the neighborhood, taking a zig-zagging course that eventually brought them out to a main road. Two stoplights later, he slowed down, which Winn assumed meant they were clear of immediate danger. He tried to keep track of the street signs and stop lights the best he could, but the driver was clearly alert to the possibility of being tailed.

It must have been at least half an hour before they pulled up in front of a nondescript brick bungalow on an average suburban street. The driveway ran past the house up to a garage, but the driver stopped and parked close up to a side door. He got out and ran over to the slider, opening it quickly. The old woman almost fell on him as she stepped down while fumbling with her house keys.

"Hurry, damn it!" she said as they went inside through the kitchen. Winn's eyes swept around the room, but it looked pedestrian. The woman walked up to a China hutch sitting on a throw rug, and with the help of the larger man, pushed it to the side. This exposed a door with a swinging handle similar to what was found on the side of a metal garbage can. She used a key to disengage a lock and then opened the door and motioned him to enter.

"Hurry, and watch yourself on the stairs; it's dark. But there's no time; they'll be here soon."

Winn nodded and moved through the doorway into the inky, black abyss. He could see the first couple steps, but he'd make most of the descent into the cellar in darkness. Just before he reached the bottom, he heard a pounding on the front door from above that gave him all the motivation he needed to scurry down the remaining stairs. *Did the skankers find me that fast?* As he reached the floor, he heard the hutch being pushed back in place. There was silence, and then footsteps walking to the front door.

The basement smelled damp and musty, and with his first step, he could taste the dust thrown up into the air. He waited a moment to allow his eyes to adjust to the darkness. A few feet away, he could make out a thick support beam in the middle of the room, and he felt up and down the rough-hewn wood until his hands came upon a light switch. When he flicked it on, there was nothing, and the room remained pitch black.

From above, he could hear multiple sets of footsteps walking through the various rooms with a sense of purpose. Several muffled voices talked over each other, but he couldn't make out the words. Still, their inflections conveyed the tension between the woman and what Winn assumed were skanker shock troops. Finally, the conversation reached a fevered pitch before subsiding.

Winn looked around as his eyes continued to adjust to the darkness. He found an old wicker chair and sat down, rubbing his temples to ease a horrible headache.

What can I do to help her, anyway? There's probably a whole squad of skankers up there. Why would that woman sacrifice herself to save me? He looked up the stairs toward the door, expecting it to burst open at any moment.

Inside the house, the conversation resumed between a man and a different woman with occasional input from someone else. After a few more minutes and another search, one last argument ended before the footsteps ceased, and the front door and the house fell silent. Winn waited a minute to ensure they were gone before cautiously climbing the stairs. He hadn't reached the third step before the distortions clouded his eyesight, and the pounding in his head worsened. After a brief stumble, he fell backwards onto the hard dirt floor. He clutched his head as the mental fog rolled in.

Not now. Not another one of these Goddamn visions.

***

"Speaker Randall is in deep trouble, Sasha, I feel it," said Marshall Beiner as he sat behind a desk in a small room that now served as his office.

Sasha Simone nodded in agreement. She occupied a chair on the other side of the desk. "It's been several months, and there's been no word. Worse, although he's not entirely absent from my mind, he's not really there either. I sense he's in a kind of mental purgatory."

"Yes, that's exactly how I would describe it," said Marshall, turning to the caretaker, Juan Gustavo Ricardo Pena, who sat in the other visitor's chair.

"Pena, we've waited long enough. You've got to tell us where Speaker Randall went. We can't just sit here without knowing what happened to him."

Pena looked at the floor and shook his head. "Please stop questioning me about this. I am not at liberty. You are the last two overseers, and your safety is paramount. His instructions were specific; you were not to search for him."

"Damn safety!" said Sasha. "We are directionless without the speaker. Tell us what you know, or I'll take it out of you." She squinted and clenched her jaw.

"Sasha, relax," said Marshall as he extended his arm to stop her. "It would be wrong to force him to give us the information against his will, but we can reason with him." He turned back toward Pena. "You understand the important role Speaker Randall plays in rebuilding the Suicide Society. Without him, as Sasha says, we are aimless. If there is any hope of finding him alive, we must at least try . . . Please, Pena, help us."

"But my promise . . ."

"You gave that promise under duress. You don't have the capacity to resist the Speaker's directives, but we are telling you we need him. The chance we might find him alive is worth the risk."

Pena stood up and walked to the door. As he lingered in the threshold with his back to Marshall and Sasha, he shook his head. In a low voice, he said, "Speaker Randall went to Desolation. He knew he would find Mr. Cox there."

Marshall stood up and turned to Sasha, who was biting down on her knuckle and fighting back tears. "He is probably dead then," she whispered. "No one can face Cox alone."

"Sasha, you know only one of us can go after him. If we truly are the last overseers, then one must remain to carry on."

"And why should it be you, Marshall? I think I should go after him. You're better suited for organizing and administering, anyway."

"You know why I'm the one who needs to go. With the growing chaos and despair out there, the number of people choosing to end their misery is staggering. The visions overwhelmed you just traveling to Sedona. Could you even imagine what it would be like in a major city? If we encounter Cox . . ."

" . . . If we encounter Cox, we're probably both dead. Neither of us has his capacity for psycho-encephalic destruction. We don't even understand the nature of his power."

Marshall walked over and took Sasha's hand. Instantly, they made a mental connection, and the warmth flowed through them.

Sasha, please let me do this. I don't know why, but I sense this is part of my destiny. If you let me go, I promise

I'll find him and bring him back. Communication transcended words and thoughts, and emotions transferred instantly between them.

Sasha smiled. All right, Marshall, you're right. You bring the Speaker back. We'll need both of you if we're ever going to repair the horrific damage Cox has caused.

Marshall let go of her hand and patted her arm reassuringly. He wished this was the hard part. Telling Wanda he was leaving would prove far more difficult.

Later that night, Marshall sat with his new bride at a table in one of the eight dining rooms in the Sedona facility. The sanctuary was teeming with people from across the globe, drawn by the mysterious noospheric force. Inexplicably, the influx of migrants stopped when the population reached 996. Like a beacon suddenly extinguished, whatever attracted the gifted transcendents from all over the world ceased to call when the facility reached four short of full occupancy.

"I have something to tell you," said Marshall as he took a bite of cherry cobbler. The dinner had been a delightful blend of seafood soup and scallops, and now they lingered over their dessert.

"I have something to tell you too," said Wanda as she laid her fork on the side of the plate. "But you go first."

"Okay... I'm leaving to find Speaker Randall," he said. "I—I'll probably be away for a while." He paused and watched her expression morph from a soft glow to a hard frown. Marshall, who was a high-functioning autistic person, had become much better at sensing changes in attitude and emotion, especially when it was Wanda. "Someone has to go after him because he's the key to everything. We won't survive without him, so I've got to do something."

"Why does it have to be you?" she said with a note of desperation. "Everyone senses the loss of connection with the Speaker. No one wants to say it, but there's a good chance he's dead."

Marshall shook his head. "Maybe, but I sense there's something still there. The connection is very weak, but Sasha and I feel it."

She just looked down and didn't reply

"So, what was it you wanted to tell me?" he said, hoping to change the subject.

"I—I don't want to talk about it . . ." Then, after a pause and a deep sigh, she said, "Look, I can't hide this from you. They've assigned me to the first exploratory mission. We're leaving in two days."

Marshall leaned back, and his brow furrowed. "What? The awareness groups are not scheduled to enter the general population for more than a month. Planning and logistics need fine tuning before we're ready to start that program."

"No, Marshall, you're wrong. My section leader chose five of us who excelled in perception and influence development to take part in one of the first groups for beta testing. We're leaving as scheduled."

Marshall covered his mouth with his hand and looked away. "Where are you supposed to go?"

"Los Angeles. We're going to establish a position in a place called 'Skid Row'."

Marshall spun back to face her. "Los Angeles? You can't be serious. That's a cesspool of destruction, especially the Skid Row district. That place is a war zone, Wanda. I—I forbid it."

"What?" she said with more than a hint of defiance. "You *forbid* it? Okay, then how about I forbid you from going after the Speaker?"

They sat in silence before Marshall muttered, "Let's go home."

***

As the mists parted, the pulsing within the orb grew weaker, and the color changed from blood red to yellow until the energy dissipated completely. Mr. Cox looked around the room and then at himself to ensure he had sustained no physical damage. The location he telepathically transmitted to the orb positioned him exactly where he intended. Centuries may have passed, but the underground bunker in Desolation remained intact, although it appeared deserted and abandoned.

For decades, during moments when he was immersed in the orb's mysterious power, he forged a plan to transform the future into a world where he reigned supreme. Throughout the ordeal, he never doubted his grand plan would succeed because the orb assured him it would. Not that it communicated directly, but whenever a session with the enigmatic object ended, Mr. Cox had great confidence that everything would work out exactly as he envisioned.

Certainly, he had some doubts along the way. The Suicide Society was an unforeseen rogue element that nearly derailed his plans. But somehow, whenever an unanticipated event posed a threat, the orb made certain the situation resolved itself. That's why Mr. Cox instinctively knew it could transport him into the future, although there was no science to back up his belief. The sphere told him he only needed to visualize a time and place, and the transfer would happen.

Mr. Cox assumed the immense transmutation of reality could open up a wormhole of some sort. The ability to alter matter and energy gave it limitless power to make reality malleable and transform the fabric of space-time itself.

After waiting for some moments to collect his thoughts, the Benefactor walked over to the façade that blended perfectly with the stone wall. He felt along the grouted edges of the rough surface until he found a minor indentation and a small button inside a metal faceplate. After pressing it, a section of rock opened to reveal a vault embedded into the granite itself.

He stood in front of the device to complete a retina scan, and the locking mechanism disengaged as the door opened. This action would send a signal to his people that he had arrived. A jeweled box was the only item in the safe, and he took it out carefully and opened it. Gently cradling the orb, he placed it inside the box and put it back in the safe before closing the door. With its own compact nuclear power source and multiple levels of security, including a holographic cloak and two lethal defense mechanisms, compromising the vault was highly unlikely.

If everything proceeded as designed, a contingent from HUGE would be arriving within the hour to escort him to his headquarters in Detroit. These instructions were part of a detailed agenda Mr. Cox arranged for delivery to Xavier Watts immediately after he left for the future.

After replacing the rock façade, he walked over to a large refrigerated wine cellar just off to the right of the parlor. Mr. Cox gasped as he looked at the broken glass that covered the floor. The room was no longer climate controlled, and no doubt hundreds of priceless wines were ruined; their taste and bouquet gone forever. At that moment, he realized something wasn't right. How could his surrogates have ignored his explicit instructions and allowed the facility to deteriorate like this?

Just as he was preparing to leave the room, he noticed a single undisturbed bottle occupying a space on the third row of the rack. Pulling it from its berth, he fingered it gently and blew the dust off the label. Krug Blanc de Noir, 1996.

A vintage merlot, perfect.

The Benefactor shook with anticipation as he pulled off the wrappings and popped the cork, filling an unbroken Bordeaux glass three-quarters full.

The liquid washed over his taste buds, but the wine had soured, and he spat it out in disgust and threw the glass against the stone wall. This lack of respect for his property was unacceptable, and he vowed the incompetent responsible party would pay dearly.

The tardiness of his escorts only added to his irritation. While he had no watch, he knew over an hour had passed since his arrival, perhaps closer to two. He made a mental note to double the punishment for such an egregious transgression.

As more time passed, he was beginning to wonder with some urgency how he would proceed if no one came to greet him. It was at that moment he heard a low hum from some distance away. Within minutes, the loud whoosh of the airlock in the outer chamber signaled its opening, followed by the sound of a flurry of footsteps. Mr. Cox looked up just as the first person came through the door.

"Prevus Cox, it is indeed an honor. I offer great apologies for the lateness of our arrival. Traveling long distances is. . . difficult." The man stared at him with wide eyes before bowing deeply and moving to the side so that others could enter the room.

"Who are you?" asked Mr. Cox with a sense of impatience. "Where is my attendant, Grovus Hus?"

"Er, we have no one at HUGE by that name that I am aware of. I am Turkus Plints, I have trained to be your primary attendant for many years now. Your return was the stuff of legend. No one actually thought it would happen."

"I see," said Mr. Cox. "And who are these others with you?"

"They are all part of your greeting contingent. Like me, they have been on standby, awaiting your arrival. Of course, when your signal came through, there was some momentary disorganization due to the excitement, and as I said, hasty travel arrangements are nearly impossible. I hope you forgive us for the delay."

"Actually, I do not. Now, once more, tell me who these people are."

"Of course, please excuse me. The one to my left is Slagus Froid. She is in charge of your living arrangements. Next to her Klantus Tam, she will be your personal chef. To my right is Minkus Term. He is your personal concierge. Finally, Hlatus Roy is the head of your security detail."

Cox looked around suspiciously. "Where is Tampus Lan? She should be the current CEO of Gehenna and Chairman of the HUGE corporate conglomerate. I am surprised she did not come here to greet me personally."

Plints dropped his head and in a low voice said, "Tampas Lan was extinguished 17 years ago."

"Extinguished?" For a moment, the irises in Mr. Cox' eyes glowed red. "Then who is in charge of the Corporates?"

"Uh, Dantar Llross is in charge, naturally."

"Dantar Llross? I have no idea who that is."

"She comes from the Amrosia Corporation, your excellency."

"Amrosia . . . *Amrosia?* My instructions were explicit that no one but a direct employee of Gehenna was *ever* to be in charge of HUGE. Gehenna is the primary shareholder. The succession directive was very clear, and Tampus Lan was to be groomed to become CEO of Gehenna and Chairman of HUGE in anticipation of my return."

"Prevus Cox, please come with us. There is much you need to know that we are not privileged to discuss," said Plints.

Cox regarded his new attendant with suspicion. "I want to be taken to Gehenna's headquarters in Detroit. You will call a meeting of the other three Corporate CEOs for later today. I do not care if they are inconvenienced; just make sure they are there."

Plints looked at his shoes and shuffled uncomfortably. "I am afraid not, sir. You have a meeting scheduled with Dantar Llross. She will explain everything to you."

Mr. Cox smiled widely, and his eyes flashed a deeper shade of iridescent red before he quickly regained control. "Fine. Take me to this Dantar Llross. But I want you to understand that you will probably burn alive in a vat of acid before the day is over."

"Yes, sir, I understand," said Plints in almost a whisper. "But we need to be going."

Chapter Two

The man sat alone in a large basement, staring at a dead TV screen with no picture or power. He clutched a small framed photo in one hand, but Winn could only see the backside of the picture. Judging by the man's weeping and moaning as he held it to his chest, Winn imagined it was a picture of his loved ones.

Within the fog of the vision, he understood what came next. Since these conscious nightmares began, he learned the outcome was already predetermined, and there was nothing he could do about it. The day the bullet passed through his chin, tongue, sinus cavity and the left front quarter of his skull, his life changed forever. These strange delusions now bubbled up in his mind with increasing frequency.

As Winn expected, the man reached over and gripped a handgun of some sort, raising it slowly until the barrel rested against his temple. He closed his eyes and grunted while fighting against his survival instinct. Sometimes, these fictional characters agonized for several minutes before taking the final solution, but this guy was quick. He pulled the trigger, and brains and blood exploded from the other side of his skull and splattered against an adjacent wall. The man slumped over and dropped the gun as lines of blood ran down his chin and dripped onto the floor.

Winn recoiled at the sight of the carnage, but a sense of relief followed as the fog started to dissipate. The twitching corpse faded as Winn slowly became aware of a damp odor. He blinked several times while trying to figure out where he was and what he was looking at. His buttocks and head felt clammy, and he realized he was lying on his back. In the background, he thought he heard loud breathing and a wheezing noise.

Winn sat up and looked around the cellar. The breathing stopped, or perhaps it was another manifestation of his mental deficits. He listened to the old woman upstairs talking to someone again in a much less agitated tone than before. There were more footfalls and the sound of a door closing. Silence followed, broken by a long wail that came from someone in great pain. *My God, they're torturing her, and it's because of me.*

After getting to his feet and setting the wicker chair back upright, he took a deep breath and tried to collect his thoughts. Focus was made far more difficult because of the mental chaos, visions and overwhelming depression he struggled to contain ever since his own suicide attempt.

The doctors told him he should not have survived. In fact, they declared him dead before he inexplicably started to breathe again just as they pulled the sheet over his face. With the lack of proper equipment and medication at the hospital, they had no explanation for his survival, let alone full recovery.

Although it took nearly a year and seven surgeries to repair his tongue and skull, he regained full movement in his right side and eventually recovered his sense of spatial equilibrium. The only permanent effect of the self-inflicted shooting was trouble enunciating the "k" consonant. When Winn used words like kettle or kite, there was just a hint of a clucking sound.

However, inside his mind, there were many changes. Not only were his senses dulled, but his response to emotional stimuli was muted as well. In some ways, it was an advantage, but in the deep recesses of his diseased brain, he couldn't help but believe it was only a matter of time before he finished the job he started. After all, what was the point of living in this piss-hole reality, anyway?

"You're not getting out of here." The voice was deep and gravely. Winn turned around so quickly he almost knocked the chair over again. He got the first whiff of tobacco smoke just before he saw the glow of a lit cigarette from the dark recesses of the cellar.

"Who are you, and what are you talking about?" Winn paused a moment, but there was no answer. "Don't you know it's against the law to smoke?"

That elicited a chuckle, and the man took a deeper puff. "You think I give two shits whether it's legal to smoke? Do you have any idea what a pack of cigarettes costs these days?" The voice was a bit ragged, and the accompanying cough rattled with phlegm.

"Who are you?" asked Winn.

"Never mind that for now. How did you end up here?"

"I'm being tracked by Corporate security for no reason at all. They showed up at my work a week before my last scheduled day. Somehow, I just knew they had come for me. Not sure how or why, but I saw four of them standing with my supervisor, so I just ran. Now, they have the skankers after me.

"The skankers, huh? That's pretty much a death sentence. But I hate to tell ya, this ain't gonna be any better."

"Why? The old lady saved my ass . . ." The door from above the steps opened just as Winn finished talking.

"New guy. What's your name?" The woman who saved him stood at the top of the landing.

"I'm Winn. Winn Mathews. Thank you for sheltering me."

"Don't thank me, you cretin. Dinner is in half an hour. If you're not ready, you don't eat. And get your irons on before you come up from the cellar." In the light from the doorway, Winn saw her swing her arm and toss something down. When the object hit the ground, he heard the familiar clank of metal and feared the worst.

"Now wait just a minute," he said. "I — I thought you wanted to help me. If the skankers are gone, I need to get back on the road." She slammed the door, and the cellar plunged back into complete darkness.

"You believe me now?" The voice from the shadows returned, as did the red glow of the cigarette.

"What the hell is going on here?" The pitch of Winn's voice rose a bit.

"Hell is a good description, my man. A very good description."

Winn took small steps forward, feeling his way as he moved toward the glowing ember. "I want to see your face.

"Don't come any closer, or you might not like what you find. I told you this place is hell."

17

"Why is she doing this? How long have you been down here?" Winn stopped moving and reached out to make sure there wasn't something in his path he might fall over.

"I—I have no idea anymore. As for the why part, you'll have to figure that out for yourself. What brings you to Phoenix anyway, Winn?"

Winn shuffled his feet and shrugged his shoulders. "I'm not sure, really. My wife took off after our daughter was murdered in a robbery at a convenience store. We lived in a bad neighborhood in Chicago. She said I shouldn't have taken her with me . . ." Winn shook his head. "She was right, of course. After that, I had an—accident, and when I was able, I decided to travel to Arizona."

"Uh, huh. And how did you attract the attention of the Corporate's elite guard?"

"I swear I don't know. When they released me from the hospital, I had the strange suspicion I was being followed. It's never been unusual for the police to track an African-American man, but this was different. Then they broke into my apartment, and when they came to my work, I knew they were after me. I was fortunate to escape alive. Off and on, they've tracked me all the way from Chicago to here."

The ember lit up one last time before it disappeared, and Winn heard the sound of a heel grinding the butt into the dirt. "You called it an 'accident.' What does that mean exactly?"

"I'd rather not talk about it."

"Did you try to kill yourself, Winn?"

After a long pause, Winn spoke, choosing his words carefully. "Why would you ask me that?

Does it have something to do with why they're after me?"

"It has everything to do with it . . . Are you having visions of other people committing suicide, Winn?"

Winn stumbled backward a couple steps and grabbed onto a metal pipe that felt cold and rusted. "How—how would you know that?"

"Because that's the only plausible reason the skankers would track down one person. It's also the only reason you would be drawn to Arizona. You crave something you can't quite explain, and that's what brought you here."

"I don't know what you're talking about."

"Oh, I think you do." There was some shuffling in the dirt before the man emerged, but his features remained mostly hidden in the long shadows.

"My name is Nicholas," he said. "And I know a lot about you."

A small sliver of light coming through a well window briefly touched the man's face, revealing craggy lines, large blackheads and a thick, oily sheen. He looked tired and haggard, and it could have been months since he bathed. His hair was brown and matted, and even at this distance, his breath stank of cigarettes and the buildup of sulfurous bacteria.

The light from an outside street lamp illuminated a seam between two pieces of plywood that covered the window. At that moment, Winn realized escape would be difficult if not impossible. "I don't understand," he said.

Nicholas twisted his head around as multiple footsteps shuffled across the floor before they converged just behind him. Winn looked over at the sullen faces of five additional people, and he wondered if there were even more hidden in the far corners of the basement.

"Who are all of you?"

"We share something in common with you, Winn. We all tried to commit suicide and survived. I don't even need to ask how close to death you were. They declared you legally dead, but you came back. Isn't that right?"

Winn swallowed hard and ran his hand through his hair. "There's no way you could know all this about me."

"It's not that hard, really. I've heard the same story nine times already." Nicholas turned and grabbed the arm of a slight woman who was so damaged she might have been anywhere between her mid-20s and late 40s. With sunken eyes, and deep black circles under each eyelid, her premature aging looked accelerated and unnatural.

"This is Renati. Go ahead and tell him," said Nicholas.

She looked at the ground while speaking in a soft voice. "The anarchists cut off my husband's head and forced me to eat his intestines. As soon as they left, I sliced my throat." She lifted her chin to reveal a long, angry scar that ran from ear to ear. "Someone found me and took me to a roadside clinic, but the practitioner said I lost too much blood and was going to die. Don't ask me how, but the next thing I knew, I woke up with an IV in my arm. When the doctor found me conscious, she looked shaken and said I had come back from the dead."

She pointed at her head. "That's when the crazy dreams started. I see other people trying to kill themselves, and it's like a dream, but I'm awake. The skankers came after me, and I was trying to get help before this crazy bitch and her son talked me into getting into their van. Just like you, they brought me here."

"We all have similar stories, Winn," said Nicholas. "Suicide, death, and unexplained revival followed by the visions. Then, the skankers came looking and seemed to funnel us right into Norma's clutches. That's her name, by the way, Norma."

"Okay, so we all have a suicide attempt and bad dreams in common. Why does that matter?"

Nicholas opened his mouth to answer, but the squeaking of the door caught his attention. He stole a worried glance at Winn and brought his forefinger up to his lips.

"It's seven o'clock, so it's time for you filthy cretins to eat. You come up the stairs one at a time. If anyone tries anything, we'll blow your heads off."

Nicholas leaned over and whispered in Winn's ear. "You better put those handcuffs on quick."

Winn went back over to the stairway and picked up the handcuffs and snapped them on his wrists. The group began a slow procession up the stairs in single file. Each person had their heads bowed, and no one made eye contact with the old lady as they passed by her. When Winn reached the top of the stairs, he raised his eyes, which triggered a hard slap to the back of the head.

"You don't look up unless I tell you to, you freak," said the woman. "You look down at the ground when you're around me. Now, keep walking."

Winn trudged behind Nicholas with his head bowed. He shifted his eyes in both directions and saw two sets of legs on either side of the line and two rifle barrels pointing at the floor. They were led into a room with a long dining room table, and the first captive took

21

his place behind the farthest chair as the rest lined up accordingly.

By looking at the table settings and counting, Winn figured out which seat would be his and followed the lead of the others and stood behind his chair. Places at the head of the table and to either side were empty. The captives remained standing for almost five minutes before the old woman walked in with her sons following. The bigger one carried a kettle full of a steaming slop that smelled terrible while the other brought in three plates filled with steak, mashed potatoes and vegetables. Allowing another few minutes to pass, the woman finally said, "You miscreants can sit down now."

Besides the three captors, Winn counted seven people at the table, including himself. Every one of them looked malnourished and abused. Rashes and open sores covered their faces and arms from the infestation of insects and bugs that feasted on them. Winn imagined he could tell who had been there the longest by the condition of their skin and clothing. The smell in the room was overpowering, and he fought back against a rising nausea.

The three captors sat down, and she slapped the hand of the smaller of the two as he grabbed his knife and fork and began cutting away at the meat. "Darryl, you know better than to start eating before we praise the Lord." Darryl lay down the utensils and bowed his head sheepishly.

As if on cue, everyone followed suit and bowed their heads. "Oh, Lord," she said, "thank you for this bounty. And give us the strength to deal with these abominations spawned by Satan. I'll do your work, oh Lord, and I'll make sure they feel your might and glory before we send them back to the bowels of hell . . . Amen."

"Amen," everyone repeated.

The taller and bigger son used a ladle to scoop out equal portions from the kettle into bowels placed in front of the captives. Stirring up whatever was in it only added to the awful stench, and Winn wrinkled his nose as the steam rose from the bowl and offended his olfactory senses. He looked down at what appeared to be three rotted vegetables and a small piece of meat bathed in a cloudy broth.

While he looked at the food in disgust, the others were already diving into theirs with an enthusiasm that reflected their level of starvation. Born of repeated practice, they handled their spoons expertly in spite of the handcuffs.

"In case any of you sloths haven't noticed, we have a new resident. His name is . . . What's your name again?"

"Winn Mathews."

"Yes, Winn Mathews. He's from…"

"I'm from Chicago."

"Yes, I see. But something brought you to Arizona, am I right? In fact, you were getting ready to go to Sedona, weren't you?"

Winn stopped staring at his bowl and looked up. "I—I don't really know. Phoenix just seemed like a good location. It's warm, and with fuel and power so scarce, I didn't want to spend another winter up north."

"Yeah, but you were debating whether to go to Sedona. Every time you considered staying in Phoenix, your mind gave you a push toward the red rocks."

"I'm not sure . . . Maybe."

"A random person is rarely important enough to attract the Corporate's attention except when they are one of the freaks."

"What does that mean? Why do you keep calling me a freak?"

"You have the devil's dreams, don't you?"

"No, I . . ." The unexpected impact of the metal ladle on the back of his head caused Winn to lurch forward and turn around with his hand raised reflexively.

"Don't raise your hand to me, boy," said the larger brother as he struck Winn in the head with the heavy ladle a second time.

The younger brother stood up and grabbed his rifle, pointing it at Winn. "Apologize to my brother."

Winn nodded as he leaned away. "Okay, okay, I'm sorry."

The assault momentarily stopped as the older brother said, "Now answer my Mom's question."

"Dreams. Yes, I have the devil's dreams." Darryl lowered the ladle slowly, and both brothers sat back down.

"Thank you, Darryl. You're a good boy," said Norma while smiling. "Now," she turned her attention back to Winn, "I want you to understand this was your last chance to speak freely. From now on, you will only speak when you're spoken to. Do you understand?"

"Yes," said Winn.

"My name is Norma, and my sons are Darryl and Simon. From now on, we'll call you . . . Doc. Understand?"

"Yes."

"Yes, what?" Darryl stood back up and raised the ladle.

Winn tilted his head slightly. "Yes—Norma,"

She smiled with satisfaction and looked down at his bowl. "You didn't eat your dinner when the boys took all that time to prepare it for you. It's got cabbage, greens and some meat they pulled out of the restaurant's dumpster down the street. That's fine, we'll see how hungry you are tomorrow." Then, turning her attention to her sons, she said, "Okay, boys, let's eat."

For the next half hour, Winn and the other captives sat silently while Norma and her sons ate their meal of steak and potatoes while chattering about the repairs the house needed and how the neighborhood was going to hell. After her last bite of ribeye, Norma folded her napkin and stood up. "Alright, back to the cellar for you misfits. You have a long day ahead of you tomorrow."

Chapter Three

Marshall walked into the classroom and slipped into one of the chairs at the very back of the room. The instructor closed his notebook and stepped from behind his lectern. He looked away for a moment as though he was gathering his thoughts.

"I was brought here many years ago in anticipation of this day. You will be the first group to go into the chaos outside this sanctuary and plant the seeds that will advance the concepts you've always known intuitively but now understand consciously."

He pointed at one of the students. "Jasmine, explain the difference between external power and authentic power."

Without hesitation, the girl replied, "External power is fear based and used to manipulate and control. It strives to create winners and losers, but any gains are temporary and will revert to equilibrium over time. Authentic power aligns the personality with the soul, which leads to cooperation, compassion and a deep reverence for life."

The instructor nodded slowly. "Achinike, can you tell us about the power of choice?"

"Yes, instructor Padilla. Every choice creates experiences for you and others who are affected by your choices."

"And why should we focus on our strengths?"

"Because focusing on our weaknesses ignores our strengths. We find ourselves defined by our weakness instead of our strengths."

The instructor nodded and pointed to a young Asian student. "Hui, what do we want to convey to those outside these walls that are suffering so much?"

"We want them to understand that to choose differently means they can create differently. Instead of anger, rage and jealousy, they can choose to think and act in a new way with much different consequences."

"Yes, that's very good. Finally, Wanda, explain more about the new scientific method you will use as you interact with others."

"The new scientific method involves becoming aware of our intentions, considering the consequences of those intentions and consciously basing our actions on the intention and result we most desire."

"Excellent." The instructor returned to the lectern and adjusted the microphone. "It's your advanced multisensory perception that brought you to this place. A directive from the universe you could not ignore. Your intuition will be your most valuable tool as you spread your knowledge to those thirsting for direction and meaning. Couple your abilities with awareness and intention to achieve your goals. I wish you success, and may your journeys be safe and prosperous."

A low murmur swelled from the room as the students got up from their desks and began applauding before they made their way to the exits. Marshall stepped outside and waited until Wanda saw him. Her warm smile made him glow.

"What I should have said, is that I'm proud of you for being chosen to go on the first pilgrimage. It's my fear that made me respond the way I did."

She leaned over and kissed him on the cheek. "I understand because I felt the same way. I know you have to find the Speaker. His connection to the universe is indispensable to us, and we will rely on his guidance as we look to create a new reality."

He leaned over and kissed her on the forehead. "Thank you for that," he said. "I needed to know I had your support before I left tomorrow. Do we still have a date tonight?"

"You bet we do, handsome." Marshall blushed as he still had trouble dealing with Wanda's cute comments.

They walked hand in hand, laughing and enjoy each other's company, but when they reached their room, they found Sarah standing in front of the door. She appeared agitated, as though she had been waiting for some time.

"Marshall, I'm going with you tomorrow." Her tone was forceful and challenging.

As usual, Marshall's approach was direct and honest. "No, Sarah, I can't take you. Speaker Randall would never approve."

"I don't give a damn what Zach would approve of," she snapped back. "I'm the one who caused all this, and it's eating me alive. Please, take me with you."

Marshall chose his words carefully. "I imagine this will sound insensitive, although I don't mean it to be. But what if Mr. Cox still controls you? He might have planted another Trojan horse in your mind."

For an instant, her back stiffened. "Zach probed my conscious and subconscious thoroughly and found nothing. You're welcome to do the same. You have my permission to dive into my mind without my knowledge if that will make you feel better." She stopped talking and sighed deeply. When she looked up, Marshall could see the determination in her eyes. "I'm going, Marshall. Don't make me follow you from the shadows."

Their eyes locked for a moment as Marshall considered his options. In the end, he realized he had no stomach for a confrontation with Sarah. If he didn't allow her to come along, he imagined she would try to follow him anyway, which might put her and the sanctuary in even more danger.

"I think it's only fair to tell you where I'm starting."

Her gaze didn't waver as she waited for an answer.

"Desolation. I'm going to Desolation."

Finally, Sarah's eyes softened as she took a step backward. "Why? Why that place?"

"Because that's where Speaker Randall told Pena he was going."

Sarah clenched her fists several times, and her breathing became deep and ragged. She paused to regain her composure, but when she looked back, her gaze was as steely and determined as before. "I don't care where you're going. I'll go to the bowels of hell itself to save Zach."

Marshall turned to Wanda, who just shrugged her shoulders. "Okay, Sarah, I'm leaving at six a.m. tomorrow morning. Meet me in the garage." Sarah nodded once and turned away, walking back to her room without answering.

That night, Marshall found it difficult to sleep. Even making love to Wanda, which always took him to a place far away from his troubles, didn't provide enough of a distraction to squelch the uneasiness that gripped the pit of his stomach.

With the dull, muted light of dawn creeping through the window, he got out of bed as quietly as he could and made his way to the shower, trying his best not to wake Wanda. As he slowly closed the pocket door in the bathroom, he heard her voice.

"Don't worry, I'm awake. Do you really think I'd be asleep when I know you're going out there alone?"

He opened the door back up and leaned out. "I didn't think you'd sleep any better than I would. You'll be leaving soon as well, and your situation will be a lot more dangerous than mine."

"I hardly think so," said Wanda as she moved the covers and sat on the side of the bed. "I'll be with a group, but you'll be all alone dealing with Mr. Cox. That frightens me, Marshall." Wanda began to absently twirl her hair.

"Wanda, stop doing the hair thing. It will all work out just fine. You'll have to trust me on this."

She tried to hide her nervous habit by smoothing her hair instead. "I know, Marshall, but we've been through so much, and now we're together in this safe place. It frightens me to think of what could happen out there."

"You know what we're facing, Wanda. If something doesn't change, eventually this place won't be safe either."

She nodded. "I understand it's necessary, but I'm less than thrilled Sarah is going with you. I mean, no matter what she says, there's no real way of knowing if she's still under Cox' influence."

"You know, Wanda, there's no real way to know if I'm not under his influence."

She followed him into the bathroom, standing with her hands on her hips while he opened the shower stall door. "That's not funny, Marshall."

"I mean it. Mr. Cox visited me several times. During each encounter, he tried to persuade me to join him. I experienced a richness of emotion that I had never known before. The offer was tempting, and I might have agreed . . . except."

"Except what?"

"Except you came along. I get all those wonderful feelings Cox dangled in front of me by being with you, and I don't have to sell my soul."

She smiled and rushed over to him, wrapping her arms around him before pulling him close and smothering him with kisses. "I love you, Marshall Beiner," she said as she leaned back and looked into his eyes.

"And I love you too, Wanda Beiner. And some day we won't have anything to worry about except where we're going to take our next vacation." He got into the shower and closed the door. As the hot water cascaded over his body, he hoped that his words would not ring hollow.

***

At 6 a.m. sharp, Marshall went into the garage and found Sarah already waiting near a Toyota FJ Cruiser parked near the roll-up door. He walked over to the attendant and nodded, autographing the sign-out form. Sarah got into the passenger's seat as Marshall approached the driver's side. A voice called to him from behind.

"Marshall, may I speak to you before you leave." Pena approached rapidly with a piece of paper crushed in his fist. "We've been monitoring broadcasts and internet activity from the outside. Four major corporations have merged under the leadership of the Gehenna Group, and governments all across the world are ceding control to them. Look at this feed from what's left of the Associated Press."

Marshall reached out and unfolded the paper.

The momentum for the reorganization of the world's government under a single corporate banner continues with the acceptance of Brazil, Poland and Kazakhstan into the conglomerate known as HUGE (Humans United for Global Equality). HUGE comprises four major corporations headed by the Gehenna Group. It's Chairman, Xavier Watts, has promised global stabilization, prosperity and equal treatment for everyone who joins the confederation. Leaders, journalists and employees have called them "The Corporates".

The paper dropped to the floor as Marshall looked up at Pena. "So, it's happening. Detonating the third nuclear device didn't prevent the rule of the Corporates, it assured it. Sixtus Maras was duped by Havas Zir. The Corporates will defeat the rebellion in the future, and their totalitarian rule will continue unchecked. It is a disaster."

Pena nodded. "You say Speaker Randall's life force is still active but very dim. Find him, Marshall."

Marshall nodded. "I'll do my best, Pena."

The caretaker squeezed his shoulder and smiled glumly before turning and walking back toward the facility. Marshall went to the vehicle and got in, looking over at Sarah, who was obviously irritated at the delay.

"What was that about?"

"Everything is unfolding in the worst possible way. Four major corporations are gaining control of the world and condemning its inhabitants to centuries of persecution. The press is even referring to them as the 'Corporates'."

She slammed her fist into the dashboard. "We're always playing defense, aren't we? Reacting to the next horrible thing he does. I fear Cox is simply too powerful even for people with your abilities."

Marshall didn't reply and stepped on the accelerator as the garage door rolled up, and the rock facade parted. He drove over the rocky terrain deep in thought, and it wasn't until they reached Route 89A that he was jarred back to reality. Just as they left the outskirts of Sedona, he spotted a woman standing over a man lying motionless on the ground.

Two children, farther off the road amid minor outcroppings and tall weeds, were motionless. Both were thin to the point of emaciation. The boy had a hardened look on his face that belied his age, but the girl appeared fragile.

"That woman is in shock; I think her husband is dead. We've got to stop and help them, Marshall." Sarah craned her neck as the SUV roared past the desperate family.

"I'm sorry, but it's not a good idea. We're going to encounter a great deal of pain and cruelty out here, Sarah. Every second we delay makes it less likely we'll find Speaker Randall."

She pursed her lips tightly and continued looking out the window but didn't reply.

Twenty miles later traveling on a deserted road, they reached Cottonwood where the devastation was much worse. A car full of decomposing bodies was flipped over off the side of the road, scorched with flames set intentionally or the result of a collision. The family was burned into a frozen pose that told the story of a desperate attempt to get out of the car before they were consumed by the flames.

Several more emaciated corpses lay haphazardly along the shoulder, and Marshall noticed a long smear of blood that ran from the middle of the road until it ended beneath the body of a man whose hands were missing. Killed and dragged away, dried black splotches traced his journey into a patch of nearby weeds.

About two miles outside of Cottonwood, a lone motorcycle roared past them. The rider didn't wear a helmet, and his tangle of long auburn locks swept back behind his head in resistance to the wind. He wore a black leather jacket with the gang name *Bedouins* emblazoned on the back just above a patch that read, *Paco*. He sneered at the Cruiser as it roared past.

"That biker looks nasty," said Wanda absently.

Marshall nodded. "Unfortunately, we're an inviting target for road bandits looking for gasoline, electricity and perhaps even a stolen identity. If anyone finds out we're equipped with dual tanks, we'll be attacked for sure."

As they drove past Jerome, the hum of the Cruiser's engine was only disturbed by the howling winter wind. The high plains desert was barren, except for roadside scrub and some low-level mountains on the horizon. Marshall reached into a cooler set on the backseat floorboards and pulled out two bottled waters. He offered one to Sarah, who took it and nodded thankfully.

"Speaker Randall says you don't like to talk about your time in Desolation." He made it sound more like a question rather than a statement.

"No, I don't," she said.

"But that's where we're going, and if you know something that could help us or give us an advantage, I'd like to know about it."

Sarah looked out the window and didn't speak for several seconds. Then, in a low whisper, she said, "What would you like me to tell you, Marshall? How that monster raped my mother every day and turned her into a depraved animal until she died terrified and afraid? Would you like to hear about how he turned me into his mistress against my will?"

"I—didn't mean anything like that. I . . ."

"How about I tell you how he starved the people in the town because one of them tried to get away, or maybe you'd like to hear the stories of how he left our neighbors lying in the streets screaming as blood poured out their eyes while he incinerated their brains."

"Sarah, that's enough," Marshall said softly. "I understand that you have suffered."

"But you can't feel it," she interrupted. "No one can."

He nodded slowly. "People can intellectualize, but they only hear words, they can't experience the emotion. As someone with autism, nobody knows that better than I do."

"I'm sorry, Marshall, it's just that I can't forget what he did to me."

"Sarah, what should we expect when we get to Desolation?"

She shrugged and finally looked away from the window. "I'm not sure. I don't think he'll be there, although I have no special insight like you do. If the

35

reports I see on the computer are accurate and the new government is in Detroit, that's where he'll be."

"I still don't understand why Speaker Randall went there," said Marshall.

"He shouldn't have. I pleaded with him not to leave, but he said he had to try to stop Cox even if the odds were against him."

"Do you think he's alive, Sarah?"

She turned away and looked back out the window. "No. I don't think anyone could survive against that monster alone."

They continued traveling along the deserted two-lane highway in silence, but Marshall noticed Sarah grew increasingly agitated as they came closer to Desolation. By the time they passed Route 97, she dug her hand into the padding on the door panel so hard her knuckles were white.

Marshall turned the SUV onto Lindal Road and drove slowly until he came to the juncture of the Burro Creek.

"The first time I was here, I didn't think my compact car would make it over that old rickety thing. I can't imagine trying it in this SUV," he said.

"Go ahead, you'll make it," she said. "No one knows the underside of the bridge is reinforced. They brought heavy moving equipment across this bridge when he built the underground bunker. They hid the support structure to make it look like the bridge is falling apart to discourage people from going any further."

Marshall put the vehicle back in gear, driving slowly onto the wooden planks. Even though his rational mind reminded him the bridge was structurally sound, the creaking and splitting noises the boards made were unnerving.

They crossed without incident and drove on until the pavement ended and the road turned into a dirt and gravel pathway. The keening wind blew through the mesquite trees, and the tumbleweeds bounced across Main Street until they were blocked by the many abandoned shacks that lined the road. Marshall stopped and looked around for a moment. A sudden inexplicable chill entered the cabin, but the temperature gauge held steady at 68 degrees.

Sarah's face turned ashen, and her eyes were wide as she blinked rapidly. She glanced over toward her old house, and then to the building where she was most recently held prisoner with Zach and Jarad Anston before the final confrontation with Mr. Cox. Marshall noticed her hand went over her mouth, and she retched twice but didn't vomit.

"Over there," she mumbled through closed lips. "That's where the underground complex is."

"I remember," said Marshall as he steered the SUV in the direction Sarah was pointing. He parked, and they got out of the car and walked together over to the nondescript building Marshall recalled vividly. He held the door open for Sarah as they went inside.

As he looked around, Marshall realized that virtually nothing was disturbed since his last visit. The same red velvet couch with the stuffing pulled out. The gooseneck lamp that sat on the desk and the various wall hangings were still in place. In fact, there wasn't a single footprint in the thick dust that covered the floor.

"The elevator is over there," said Marshall while pointing to one of the many unremarkable doors that lined the outer wall. Sarah nodded and followed behind him.

When they reached the threshold, Marshall hesitated for a moment as his hand reached over and felt around an area where the sheetrock was smooth and flat just outside the doorframe. He furrowed his brow and glanced around the room.

"The elevator button is gone," he said. "It's as though it never existed. Someone must have removed it and patched the wall."

"Are you sure you're not at the wrong door?"

"No, it's not possible. I have a photographic memory. The button was positioned exactly where my thumb is now. I am absolutely certain."

"Now what?"

Marshall took a step back and pondered. "I'm not sure. There has to be another way to get down there though. Look at the floor. The only sets of footprints are our own. If they moved out of this place, there should be footprints everywhere."

"Should we look for another way in?"

"We'll have to. Let's start with these other doors. Maybe they closed off this entrance and created another in one of these rooms. If that doesn't work, we'll have to look outside."

Marshall turned the knob and opened the door slowly. The room's interior was dark and smelled musty, but it was clearly not an elevator cab. He pulled out a penlight. The walls were bare and unpainted. Cobwebs strung throughout the space, and the only sign of life was found in the fecal remains of rats.

He closed the door and moved toward the next as Sarah went in the opposite direction.

"You won't find anything behind these doors." The voice from behind sounded tired but forceful. Marshall whirled and looked at the slightly hunched figure standing in the entryway.

"Don't try any of your mind tricks on me, young man. I know all about your capabilities. If you want to know what happened to your friend, you better come with me."

Chapter Four

Hidden scanners confirmed Turkus Plints' identity, and the door opened automatically. Accompanied by Hlatus Roy and Mr. Cox, the three men entered the large room together. Plints moved ahead of his companions, and chairs materialized as he approached. Mr. Cox and Roy followed as each took one of the seats. A long, thick slab of clear glass-like material descended slowly from the ceiling and stopped about 3 feet off the ground, seemingly suspended in midair.

A portion of a sidewall shimmered for a minute before a woman emerged and took a position behind the table. Another chair materialized, larger and obviously more comfortable than those afforded to Mr. Cox and his companions. The woman held out her hand, palm down, and the conference table lowered slightly to accommodate her short stature. When she felt comfortable, she sat down and placed both hands together, smiling at the Benefactor.

"Prevus Cox," she said. "It is indeed an honor. You are quite a legend in this time. Many of us wondered if you actually existed, but your documentation was very thorough and explicit, so we hoped you would contact us even if it is still extraordinary."

"I am pleased that I could embellish your day," replied Mr. Cox. "May I ask where we are? The transportation method was quite primitive. A space plane? Really? The Science Ministry was experimenting with teleportation when I left."

"I am afraid you will find much has changed. You are in Abuja on the African continent. This once was the capital of Nigeria when the world was divided into city-states."

"Why are we here and not in Detroit?"

She waved her hand dismissively. "Detroit has returned to the cesspool it always was and always will be. When Amrosia assumed control of the corporate conglomerate, the capital was moved. The transfer occurred during the Woke Movement of the mid-21st century."

"Mid-21st century? Xavier Watts was placed in charge of Gehenna. I made sure of it."

"He quickly lost control, and the Board of Directors removed him shortly after you left."

Mr. Cox shifted uncomfortably in his seat. "Exactly who are you?"

"My name is Dantar Llross. I am the CEO of the HUGE Conglomerate. My affiliation is with Amrosia. We are—grateful that you altered time to assure our ascendance to power."

Mr. Cox stiffened. "I did not alter time to accommodate Amrosia. My plans were perfectly calculated and designed to assure *I* would control the conglomerate in this time. Something has gone horribly astray." He paused and looked out the window absently. "Yet, no matter. I am the largest shareholder in Gehenna and thus, the HUGE conglomerate. I will exercise my voting rights now."

A single chuckle escaped Llross's lips, which were perfectly fashioned through genetic manipulation. Her eyes were symmetrical and rounded in an almond shape. Every follicle across her hairline hugged a precise plane created by nano-sculpting. From her bronze skin tone to her shapely legs, Dantar Llross was an exquisite example of science and artistic expression.

"You do not own any shares, Coxnotus. Shortly after your disappearance in the 21st century, by court order, your shares were transferred to your son, Alan Ziminski. History is not entirely clear, but apparently you were declared dead, or it was decided you never existed. In any event, a massive battle between Ziminski and Watts transpired, and Watts lost."

Mr. Cox slammed his fist into the transparent table. "Ziminski? That bastard child was not my son. This is utterly outrageous!"

"Unfortunately, the story gets much worse for you. Ziminski never really was in charge of anything. He immediately sold his shares of Gehenna to Amrosia, and we became the majority owner in the HUGE conglomerate. Ziminski went on an indulgent binge for several years until he was found dead in a rat infested motel in south Philadelphia."

Mr. Cox stood up and moved to a window overlooking a scenic courtyard. "If you have power and control over the entire world, why am I here? I would imagine you would want to eliminate any threats. After all, I will challenge the legality of all of this in the courts."

"Bah," said Llross with a dismissive wave of her hand. "The courts issue verdicts as they are instructed. Jurisprudence is as ineffectual as you remember, but the only thing that has changed is leadership." The words barely left her lips when a loud explosion rocked the building. Mr. Cox ducked instinctively, but the others remained steadfast as though they were used to such occurrences.

"What was that?"

Llross stood up from the chair and glanced at Hlatus Roy, who immediately bowed and left the room. She turned back to Mr. Cox. "We have rogue elements that we are dealing with. I wonder if you fully understand the unintended consequences of your actions in the past. In each instance when you altered the timeline, the secondary effect resulted in the creation of forces opposed to the Corporate agenda."

"Alterations in the timeline? I do not know what you are talking about."

"Please do not play coy, Coxnotus. We are aware of your unauthorized manipulations. Central became deluged with reports from frantic agents experiencing the deterioration and deviations in their own realities. Eventually, we lost them all to mob violence, disease or mental breakdown."

"Impossible. The precise changes needed to manipulate the outcome I desired were assured. There was no possibility of error."

"Well, whatever method you used to calculate the outcome was obviously deficient because here we are, and you are not in charge of the HUGE conglomerate. The cumulative effect of the small changes the Time Sculptors made did enough damage. Your rogue actions created serious complications."

Mr. Cox shook his head. "I—I saw the visions. I should be worshipped and exalted. This is not the future reality I created."

"Oh, it is indeed the reality you created," replied Llross. Another less intense explosion sounded in the distance. At almost the same moment, Hlatus Roy came back into the room and walked over to Llross, whispering something in her ear.

"I am afraid we must temporarily evacuate this building, Coxnotus. Certain terrorist groups pose a temporary threat. We will turn them back, but we must ensure your safety first."

"Take me to my headquarters in Detroit immediately," said Mr. Cox. "I do not believe a word you have told me. You must be some weak rebellious group."

Llross nodded to Turkus Plints, who moved behind Mr. Cox and firmly grasped his arm. "Sir, we really do need to leave now."

Roy led them from the room down a long corridor to a hyperloop transport access point. After passing a retina scan, the door opened to reveal the interior of the cylindrical pod. Llross got in first and waited for Mr. Cox to take a seat beside her. Plints and Roy followed, and the hyperloop hatch closed as a red light blinked overhead. With a sudden surge of thrust, the pod rocketed out from the docking station. Just before they pulled away, Mr. Cox thought he saw several men with weapons rushing toward them.

"Where are we going?" he asked as the unit continued though the tube at speeds exceeding 250 mph.

"We will rendezvous with a waiting space plane and travel on to a city known as Jaunde in what used to be called Uganda," said Llross.

"Farther south on the African continent? Why are you running? We are the Corporates. We rule, and the Kren obey."

Llross hung her head and snickered. "You truly do not understand, do you, Coxnotus? The Corporates only control the southern part of the continent that spans from what was Nigeria to old Ethiopia. Perhaps even Nigeria has fallen. We will find out in the morning."

"What? The Corporates rule the entire planet. How could this be possible?"

Llross extended her forefinger and pointed it at Mr. Cox. "It is because of you, Prevus Coxnotus." Her last words were drowned out as another explosion rocked the cylinder, and it contacted with the smooth wall of the tube before the safety mechanisms engaged and compensated for the unexpected burst of energy.

"You unwittingly inspired a resistance movement that continues to grow despite our best efforts to quash it. Previous chairpersons tried various methods, including coercion and extermination, yet nothing could stop its growth."

"Who are they?" asked Mr. Cox.

"Their name? They do not have one, and after nearly three centuries, we still do not understand much about them. They are a loose confederation of groups that believe in nothing anyone would value. We call them 'the pacifists'."

"What do they stand for? Who is their leader?"

Llross shrugged. "They never had identifiable leaders, or we would have killed them. The only thing we know for certain is they do not believe in using force to achieve their goals. It is extremely difficult to capture them because they blend in until they rise up. Anyway, those we have captured never reveal anything useful."

"Then . . . how do they grow?"

"The movement started in many of the old cities across the globe before it spread. Teachers of some sort, 'guides' they call them, started giving the citizenry hope by changing their perspective. When people lose their lust for greed, they become uncontrollable and very dangerous."

"And let me guess. These people defied Corporate authority, and the more force we used, the more the movement grew."

Llross nodded. "Yes, I suppose you could draw that conclusion. Our security teams killed tens of millions, but we could never identify those who were driving the movement. They are adept at stealth and traveling incognito, and they are extremely patient. Once it took root, their cartel spread to Paris, London, New York, Beijing, Moscow, and on, and on, until . . ."

"Then why are we under attack if they are not violent?"

"We also deal with a number of fringe groups that saw our weakness and splintered off from HUGE. In fact, the Irexx Corporation left the conglomerate several decades ago. They are the main source of the attacks. None of the violent groups have any association with the pacifists."

Mr. Cox stroked his chin and shook his head. "What do you intend on doing with me? I do not see what value I have to you."

"I will get straight to the point. We want the orb."

Undetectable to most, Mr. Cox' left eyebrow raised up ever so slightly. "I have no idea what you are talking about."

Llross leaned back and smiled. "Please, let us not waste time with games, Coxnotus. According to historical text, you once possessed extraordinary powers. When you left on your time sculpting mission, you had no such ability beyond traditional academy training. One can only assume the reports were correct."

"Reports? Who would have fabricated such nonsense?"

"Someone who was very close to you. A personal servant. I believe his name was 'Hefe'."

This time Mr. Cox noticeably flinched. "Ah, I see you recognize the name. He told us about the orb just before our interrogators pulled his limbs from their sockets. Others in your inner circle also relayed anecdotal stories of such an object."

"Bah. I tell you no such thing exists."

"Really? Then how did you get here? You know that penetrating the space-time barrier is impossible without creating a Casimir Vacuum. The technology in that era was too primitive to construct Kerr Rings, and they lacked the fusion sources required to create the plasma injectors. Even building a vessel to accelerate to the speed of light was beyond their capabilities. So, again, how did you get here?"

Mr. Cox was about to speak when the pod started to decelerate until it came to a complete halt with a soft whoosh. The door barely opened when a blast from a coil gun blew a hole in the far wall. Before Hlatus Roy could draw his weapon, a second shot tore away the front of his torso. He slumped over in his seat as a deluge of blood splattered the round cylinder and splashed on the other three occupants. A second volley came from a different direction, barely missing Dantar Llross and hitting Turkus Plints in the arm.

Following a brief interlude, two helmeted men with shaded faceplates and black combat gear entered the cab, their weapons trained on the stunned passengers.

Wiping blood from her face, Llross looked up at the assailants. "You have assaulted the Director of the HUGE conglomerate. This is your opportunity to surrender. If you continue, I promise you will be crushed."

The leading helmeted assailants looked at one another before the taller one spoke. His voice sounded altered and electronic. "Dantar Llross, you are under arrest under the authority of the Irexx Corporation for crimes against the people of the world. You will offer your surrender and sign an armistice that transfers global governing power from Amrosia to Irexx. Step out of this cylinder, or we will eliminate you."

Looking at her companions, Llross stood up slowly and straightened her blood-stained pantsuit. Mr. Cox and Turkus Plints followed as the second attacker waved his weapon and motioned them out of the pod. When they reached the platform, Mr. Cox quickly counted three more in the squad dressed identically. Each one carried the same type of weapon held in the ready position.

For a moment, Mr. Cox considered going along with his captors, but this group was also insignificant, and even if they succeeded, they would ultimately suffer the same fate as Amrosia. He stepped forward and smiled, revealing his perfectly aligned and unnaturally white teeth.

"Does anyone have a fine cigar? I prefer an Arturo Fuente, but a Cuban brand will do." The squad leaders exchanged puzzled glances while Llross and Plints gave him odd looks.

"Move forward or we will kill you."

"Excuse me. I forgot there is no smoking allowed in this century. Perhaps a fine wine then? Surely, that is still permissible?"

The assailant raised his weapon and pointed it directly at Mr. Cox' head. "This is your last chance. Raise your hands and walk forward." Llross and Plints began moving toward the rest of the squadron with their hands extended as instructed.

"Stop," said Mr. Cox in a tone much lower than his normal voice. He turned to Llross and looked at her with eyes that smoldered.

"I—I do not take orders from you, Prevus Coxnotus," she said

"I said, do not move." As he finished speaking, she stopped abruptly, and Plints did likewise. Mr. Cox turned his attention back to the assailants.

"You may leave us now and nothing more will come of this. However, if you insist . . .

The squad leader looked at his companion incredulously before tightening his grip and steadying his aim. For a moment, everyone froze in anticipation of the coming lethal blast. The assailant grunted but his finger remained frozen on the trigger until it began to quiver. Noticeable tremors moved up his arm and spread until they affected every part of his body.

His companions didn't notice the squad leaders' physical impairment until it was too late. In a single swift motion, he swung the weapon toward them and opened fire. The coil gun erupted and sprayed rounds of munitions that detonated into multiple fragments, tearing apart his subordinates' protective armor and slicing deeply into their bodies.

The other soldiers couldn't process the information quickly enough to react, and by the time they raised their weapons, it was too late. With flame from the gun belching instant death, the others in the assault team danced like marionettes as their flesh was shredded, and their lifeless bodies fell to the ground.

When the shooting finally stopped, the soldier dropped the weapon, ripped his helmet off and threw it against the wall. He held out his hands as though they had betrayed him, and he looked over at Mr. Cox with an expression of abject fear.

"You—you made me do that. How? You are inside my mind. It . . . burns."

The soldier stumbled around as he began clawing at the sides of his head. A long, guttural sound of pain grew in volume until it morphed into a scream. He fell to the ground and thrashed about in obvious agony, grunting and groaning while he gouged the flesh on his face. The disoriented reeling and lurching continued until it became uncomfortable to watch, and finally, Mr. Cox ended the soldier's suffering. The rebel exhaled a final ragged breath as twin streams of blood trickled out of his nose and ran down the side of his face.

Mr. Cox surveyed the scene of barbarous butchery. Complete silence allowed him to merge with the exquisite flow of death and malevolence. The smell of fresh blood was like an aphrodisiac, and he breathed deep and shuddered in delight. He closed his eyes for what seemed an eternity as he immersed himself in the dense, dark energy.

" . . . Coxnotus . . . Prevus Coxnotus, can you hear me?

Mr. Cox disconnected himself from the stream and turned to Dantar Llross. "Yes, I am here."

"How did you . . . What did I just witness? This was a Burleuvian death squad. No one survives an encounter with them. Yet, they are all dead."

"Yes, they are dead. Is it not wonderful? They could have a hundred soldiers, but it would have ended the same way."

"Then it is true," said Llross. "Many believed you successfully manipulated the timeline solely because of the inherent advantages of being from the future, but that is not it. You have an even greater advantage, and we need it. Give us the orb."

Mr. Cox regarded her for a moment as he stroked his chin. "Why would I share anything with you? Your corporation has appropriated HUGE and arrested me."

"We know of the sphere, Coxnotus. Our people are searching for it as we speak. Give it to us or . . ."

" . . . Or what? You will kill me? Do you think I am a fool? You have experienced a fraction of my power. I can lobotomize you where you stand if I so choose."

Llross took a step back and sat down. Her shoulders slumped, and her head drooped as she spoke in a low voice. "Our forces are crumbling as we speak. The pacifists are encroaching from all sides . . . We must have that orb. Please, help us." She looked up with eyes brimming with tears.

A smile spread slowly across Mr. Cox' face. "That is much better," he said. "First, we will return to Detroit, the rightful capital of the world. We will reclaim Gehenna headquarters. You say the city is a cesspool. Perfect."

"I am afraid that is not possible," said Turkus Plints, who held pressure on his right arm to stem the bleeding. "Gehenna headquarters is now occupied by the pacifists. They have transformed it into a housing development for the people in the city. It is an ancient relic. Very low tech."

Mr. Cox started to shake, and when he spoke, it was in a measured voice through a tightly clenched jaw. "We must get to the space plane and go to an area where we can operate in safety. I will need a complete assessment of where all your assets are located. Most importantly, I want you to bring someone to me. I do not know his full designation, but he will most likely have a surname of 'Lars', and he will serve in a security capacity. I do not care what it takes, but you must find him."

Chapter Five

Winn woke up with a start and squinted in the dim light of a bulb positioned directly in the middle of the basement. Getting up to his knees, he blinked rapidly as a sudden pounding in his head caused him to reflexively start massaging his temples.

"The headaches will become more severe as time goes on." The voice and glowing cigarette were unmistakable.

"You all have headaches down here?"

"Every morning." Nicholas stood up and walked over to where Winn remained kneeling. "It took us a while to figure out she puts something in the food that causes the headaches and a feeling like you're hungover. It's a sedative of some kind, but there's more in it."

"And there's no way to avoid eating the food unless you want to starve, so . . ."

"Exactly," said Nicholas. "We get two meals a day and a snack in the afternoon." He pointed over to an area near the stairs. "There's a pot over there. Just ladle it in your bowl and don't look at it or smell it . . . And you better hurry. She gives us an hour of light in the morning, afternoon and evening, and we're about ten minutes from the blackout."

53

"It was dark in here all last night," said Winn.

Nicholas gave a half smile. "Anytime there's a new person, we're in blackout for the day."

Winn went over and looked inside the pot. Despite his best efforts, he couldn't ignore the smell of the food. There was no question the concoction was spoiled. He picked up the ladle and scraped the bottom until he filled a wooden bowl with the swill.

The first spoonful was so disgusting it made him gag, but somehow, he forced it down. With the consistency of spackle, the mixture was oily, and it had a strong taste of fish. Hard bits of something thin, hard and smooth caught in his teeth and throat. Based on the acidic taste, Winn suspected he was eating ground up fish heads, tails and entrails.

Three spoonfuls was all he could manage to swallow before his stomach seized, and since there was no trash container, he set the bowl down next to the others. Seemingly before he had it out of his hand, someone emerged from the shadows and snatched it, greedily spooning the fetid porridge and finally licking the bowl clean.

Winn recoiled as the man grinned and cackled before skittering back into the darkest corner of the room.

"Please, forgive Brandon for his rudeness," said Nicholas. He took a drag on his cigarette. "He's been down here the longest. Actually, he can't remember how long he's been here. His memory is pretty bad. Eventually, whatever she's giving you will eat away at your memory too."

"How could she do this? I mean, how could she outmaneuver the Corporate's intelligence apparatus?"

Nicholas shrugged. "Who knows? A few of us think she has someone inside the GSD who's feeding her intel. Others think she's got the same 'gift' that we do, only she chooses to use it to help the Corporates. Maybe she's on the payroll or something."

Just as Nicholas finished speaking, the lights went out. Almost simultaneously, the door creaked as it opened. "Okay, Bashful, get your irons on. I don't have all day."

A voice over in the corner of the basement moaned pitifully. "No, not me. It's not my turn . . . It's Dopey's turn. Take him. Please . . ."

"Git you ass up here, Bashful. You make one of the boys come git you, it's gonna be that much worse."

The one who answered to the name "Bashful" continued to whine piteously as he crawled out and over toward the staircase. When he reached the first step, he looked back at Nicholas and Winn. "It's just not fair. It's Dopey's turn, not mine. It's not fair."

Tears started running down his cheeks as he stayed on all fours and moved slowly up toward the landing. The chain between the handcuffs made a scraping sound as he moved.

"Get up here, Bashful. goddamn it. I swear you'll pay if you waste any more of my time."

With a cry of anguish, Bashful started climbing more quickly until he reached the top of the staircase. Norma uttered something profane and slammed the door.

"What was that all about," said Winn, and what's with the 'Bashful' thing?"

"His real name is Paco. Norma gave us all names of the seven dwarves. Since there were six of us, you got the name 'Doc' by default."

"What happens when the next person gets here?"

"We don't know," said Nicholas as he raised eyebrows. "We've talked about it. So far, seven is the most we've ever had. Who knows . . ." Nicholas pulled a cigarette out of his pack and counted how many he had left before lighting up.

"How come you get cigarettes?"

Nicholas put the pack back in his pocket. "She gives me one pack a month. It's my reward for looking after everyone. I always used to smoke them all right away, but I've learned to discipline myself to one a day. Unfortunately, when someone new arrives, the discipline goes out the window."

"Do you share them?" asked Winn.

Nicholas shifted uncomfortably. "No, I don't share. In this rotten miserable place these smokes are all I have. Sorry."

Winn grinned slyly. "It's all right. I don't smoke anyway."

Nicholas beckoned for Winn to follow. "Come on, it's time you to formally meet everyone." They walked over to the thin ray of light streaming through the gap in the boards. Nicholas motioned over to a dark corner, and the same pale and gaunt people he saw last night at the dinner table emerged slowly. While most of their features were hidden, Winn could see enough to sense their anguish and confusion.

"You met Renata yesterday." Pointing to each one in order, he continued, "This is Felicia, Brandon, and Bahati. Brandon's been here the longest. He was the one who ate your breakfast."

"It was good," said Brandon. "The food was good. You didn't eat yours, so I took it. How come you didn't eat it? I hope you're not mad at me because I ate yours."

"Well, I—I don't mind if you eat my food. If there's anything left, you can have it."

"Good, good food. I like the food here." Brandon cackled once and shuttled back into the corner.

Nicholas looked away and shook his head. "Brandon's endured the most 'therapy' sessions. There's not much left of him."

"There's not much left of any of us," said Bahati. "I came all the way from Cameroon to get to Arizona. Without knowing why, I felt compelled to come to this place hoping it held the answer to the horrible dreams." She brought her hands up to her face. "But instead these terrible people abducted me. Every day my mind slips further away. The sessions are so painful."

"Yes, me too. I came here from Belgium," said Renata. "The ones called skankers apprehended me, but there was a riot in the holding facility, and two men broke me free. I thought they were there to help me, but they handed me over to her." She raised her head and looked up at the basement ceiling.

"The only good thing is the dreams have stopped," said Felicia, "but the cost is very high. You will see that soon, Winn. The first time is the worst."

As if on cue, a scream erupted from above and then a second followed the sounds of thrashing and more panicked shrieks. Although he couldn't make out the words, Winn could hear moans and a loud, pleading voice.

Everyone turned their faces to the ground except Winn, who looked up to the source of the distress. "What the hell are they doing to him up there?"

"I'm afraid you'll find out soon enough."

Winn looked around the basement with eyes full of panic and desperation. "We need to get out of here. This is just a house, not a prison. It can't be that secure."

"Actually, it is," said Nicholas. He pulled out another cigarette, his third today. "The boards are ramset into the bricks, and even if you could pry them off, there are metal bars on the windows."

"We've got to try something . . . We can't just sit here and . . ."

The basement door opened interrupting the conversation, and the beam of a flashlight illuminated the steps. A man's voice came from above. It was one of Norma's sons, but Winn didn't know them well enough to distinguish one from the other.

"Darryl's bringin' Bashful down the stairs. Any of you freaks try anything, you'll get both barrels." Not waiting for a reply, heavy footfalls descended accompanied by dragging sounds. When he reached the bottom step, the larger son pushed Paco to the floor before scowling at the group and climbing back up the stairs.

Paco rolled over on his back and started moaning and talking incoherently, but Winn could make out enough to know they had tortured him. "No, not inside the brain," Paco cried out. "Don't stick them into my brain again, please, oh God please. Oh, aggggh, it hurts. My brain is peeling apart. Oh God, please stop."

Winn stood up and started toward Paco, but Nicholas grabbed his arm. "Not until she closes the door. Sometimes, she . . ."

"Doc, get your irons on and get your ass up here." Norma's voice was unmistakable.

Nicholas let go of Winn as though he might have leprosy. "God help you, my man. Remember, it'll end, eventually."

The SUV pulled up to the corner of south San Julian and east 6th street. Trucks and cars of all makes and models passed through the intersection daily, so the vehicle didn't draw much attention until the doors opened and five relatively young people dressed in brown utilitarian jumpsuits stepped out and walked to the back and waited for the tailgate to rise. After they pulled out a number of large backpacks — the full-length variety made for extended camping trips — the driver unloaded several aluminum cases before returning to the SUV, exchanging goodbyes, and driving away.

Activity in the general vicinity stopped for a moment as the local squatters looked on with interest ranging from mild amusement to overt suspicion. An endless string of portable tents lined the pavement in front of the abandoned buildings on the corner and stretched down San Julian as far as the eye could see. This was what used to be known as L.A.'s "Skid Row," but the scene was so common throughout the country and the world it lost any special distinction.

Wanda pointed to a spot about half a block down the street, and they moved their gear to an open space between two soiled and torn tents. Besides garbage and some human waste, the small area looked clear except for a large cardboard box tipped on its side that leaned against a roll-up door.

Wanda looked around for a moment, nodded to her crew, and they took off their backpacks and began pulling out and extending metal framing pieces to construct their own housing. Just as they began to remove the tightly condensed tent material, two deafening gunshots rang out nearby. The sound was so loud Wanda thought it came from the next block over.

Her companions ducked down, but everyone else in the area seemed oblivious and continued on with whatever they were doing.

With the help of two of her associates, Wanda began constructing the tents while the others donned gloves and started picking up the trash and scooping human feces into organic bags. She was about finished snapping the framing pieces together when she heard a voice from behind.

"You can't stay here."

Wanda turned to face a woman wearing soiled rags who looked to be in her 70s. Still, everyone out here looked 20 years older than their true age. "Is there a reason? This spot looks unoccupied."

"Well, there's two reasons," said the woman as her mouth worked like a cow chewing its cud, an involuntary motion caused by an absence of teeth. "First, you can't settle in front of a warehouse door. The Pocks won't allow it. They haven't been here for a month, but when they do come, they'll smash all your gear and drive you out."

"What's the second reason?"

"Because there's a body in that big box over there up against the door. He's been dead for a while, so if he's not stinkin' now, he will be soon. You can catch some nasty stuff from the stiffs."

Wanda whirled around and looked at the box. It once held a refrigerator, so it could easily hold a dead man. She turned back to the woman. "I—I appreciate the information. Has someone notified the authorities about the body?"

The woman laughed before starting to cough in deep phlegmy spams. She pulled a dirty rag from one of her pockets and wiped at her mouth.

"The dump truck comes once a week to pick up the stiffs. Everyone knows that. You and your friends aren't from around here, are you? People get nervous when they see someone who doesn't fit in."

"Don't worry, we don't mean anyone any harm. We only want to help."

The woman leaned back and laughed. "Help? Are you kidding me? No one is here to help anyone. They'll kill you if you look at them the wrong way. I hope you brought guns because you won't last here through the night without them."

" . . . Can I ask your name?"

The old woman brought a hand up to her chest. "My name? You want to know *my* name. It's . . . it's Iris."

Wanda walked over with her hand extended. "Hi, Iris, my name is Wanda. It's so nice to meet you."

Iris regarded Wanda before slowly raising her grimy hand. The permanent look of suspicion etched into her features remained until she touched her new acquaintance. For just an instant, her eyes lit up, and she drew in a sharp breath.

"You—you're not part of this," she said.

"No, I'm not. I belong to a different collective. But mine is based on love instead of fear. I don't say this to judge you or anyone else, but rather, to offer you an insight into a different way."

Iris looked off, and when she turned back, tears filled her eyes. "This is a horrible place," she said. "It was always bad, but it's become a true hell on earth. I've watched so many people die in the most terrible ways. No one can preach to this neighborhood if that's what you're here for. A few religious people have tried, but they're killed quickly. You all should leave before they find you."

Wanda smiled. "If that's my fate then I must accept it. I am at this place and time for a reason. My physical body may be destroyed, but it won't be anything more than a learning experience. My soul will endure."

" . . . Hey, Iris, these cabrones giving you trouble?" From about 20 feet away, a young Hispanic man yelled at the old woman while eyeing Wanda suspiciously. When he had their attention, he began moving toward them with a gait that expressed aggression and dominance. As he grew closer, it became clear his only interest was Wanda and her four companions.

With intimidation tactics honed through years of training and experience, the 20 something man displayed the vigor of youth by strutting in an exaggerated manor while wrinkling his brow and turning down the corners of his mouth. His body was covered with tattoos, including his face. Three inked teardrops fell just below his right eye, and an intricate mosaic of text and images depicting scenes of intense brutality covered the upper half of his forehead.

"Lady, what the hell are you doing here? You're not wanted; you get it, bitch? Move your dumb ass out of here before someone sticks a knife between your eyes." He looked over at the other four still busy raising the tents. "But you leave the shit you brought here. That's mine now."

Wanda watched the man making bellicose gestures with a sense of sadness. *All this posturing, and for what? His bravado just brings him more misery.* "Arturo. That is your name, right?"

He looked around uneasily. "Bitch, how do you know who I am?"

"I don't know, lucky guess?" she said while sticking out her hand.

Arturo looked her over from head to toe with disdain. "I'm not touchin' your hand you dumb bitch. Maybe you didn't hear me. You need to get outta here, *now*." He moved closer and invaded her personal space. His face was no more than two inches from hers.

Wanda kept her eyes locked on his. "You can only intimidate those who are fearful, Arturo. I do not fear you. Past the bluster, your soul is pure love like all others and can only project that love. That is the level I choose to communicate with you on. Everything else is personality, which is meaningless."

Arturo's expression morphed from aggression to confusion tinged with fear, and he backed off a step. Once personal space was reestablished, he pointed a finger at Wanda and said, "You're crazy, lady. You talk that bullshit around here you're gonna be dead soon." He turned around and began to walk off, twisting his head around to snarl and point at Wanda as he retreated.

"You talked down Arturo," said Iris as she watched him gesturing wildly as he walked away. "That's not an easy thing to do."

Wanda continued to watch the angry young man retreat. She yelled after him, "There's much work to be done here, Arturo. You're always welcome to come and help." He extended his middle finger without turning around, and Wanda smiled.

"Iris," she said while keeping her eyes on Arturo, "would you like to stay near us tonight? We'd enjoy having you. In fact, I think we have an extra tent if you're interested."

Iris's face lit up, but for only a second. "I would love the chance to sleep in a real tent, but I'm afraid you won't be here long. They won't let you stay. The odds are you won't survive a single night." As if to confirm Iris's statement, a burst of automatic weapons fire sounded so close Wanda checked herself to see if she was hit.

For an instant, she felt shaken and prayed the instructors back in Sedona were as wise as she believed they were.

Chapter Six

Marshall turned and regarded the man cautiously. "Who are you?

"I'm a simple guide and outfitter who worked in this area. There are a few of us left in town, but we keep a very low profile. Bob Tingle, Isabelle Lopez, Raul Fuentes . . . a few more. But most have died. This place is the epicenter of hell on earth. I was here when your friend showed up. He should have known better."

"Delgado?" said Sarah as she tilted her head and walked over to where the man was standing. She grabbed him by the collar and swung him around in a 360-degree circle like a rag doll. "Why the fuck are you here? You tell me where he is, you son of a bitch."

The man's eyes grew wide, and he gasped as she began to shake him violently.

"My name... My name is Harry Krause."

"No, you're Delgado, and you're a psychotic killer."

"Sarah!" Marshall pried her hands off the man's shoulders as he fell backwards once relieved of her iron grip.

"Goddamn it, Marshall, it's Delgado, the Benefactor's head of security. I'd recognize his face anywhere. This butcher has murdered countless innocent people. He needs to die." She charged forward again and took an assault stance with her fist raised and cocked.

The man calling himself Jerry Krause cowered and held up his hands in a feeble attempt to defend himself. "If you kill me, you'll never know where Randall is. I'm the only one who can take you to him."

"How would you know where he is?" said Marshall. "He may not even be alive . . ."

"Because she is right. I am Delgado..."

He slowly got to his feet, eyeing Sarah the entire time. "I wondered if she would recognize me," he said. "I was the head of security for Gehenna until the feds exploded a bomb at our headquarters in Detroit. Mr. Cox, he—he demoted me, and worse, cut off our telepathic connection. I wandered aimlessly for months and ended up here because it was the only life I knew before serving the Benefactor."

Sarah looked over at Marshall. "Don't believe him," she hissed. "He's third in the chain of command, second only to Watts. You're talking to the Benefactor's version of Josef Mengele. We should just kill him now."

Marshall stood between them and held out his palms to keep them apart. "No, Sarah, we're not going to kill him. He may be the only connection we have to find the Speaker." Looking at Delgado, he said, "Where is he? And what do you want out of this?"

Delgado's face hardened. "I want revenge, nothing more than that. My life was wasted in the service of the Benefactor, and he threw me out of the organization like yesterday's trash. I was banished to a remote post in the Middle East. Without his direction, I roamed the streets and contemplated suicide many times. Every minute of every day I feel a crushing sense of loneliness that is oppressive, and my depression is so severe it's only a matter of time before I kill myself."

Marshall regarded him for a moment. "Frankly, I have little sympathy, and I promise you, Sarah has none. If you don't tell me where he is, I can extract the information."

Delgado shook his head. "You can't. One of the last 'gifts' the Benefactor bestowed on me was severe short-term memory loss. I can remember events, people and places from the past, but anything significant within the last 48 hours usually escapes me. Tomorrow, I'll remember we met, but I probably won't know why. In fact, right now, I have no idea where Randall is."

"What the hell good are you to us?" said Sarah. Then, turning to Marshall, "Let's kill him and move on. Maybe someone else in town knows where Zach is."

"No," said Delgado. "They were all too afraid to call the ambulance from Phoenix, but I am still somewhat connected and pulled strings to get someone out here to pick him up."

"But you can't remember where he went?" said Marshall.

"No, I can't." Delgado rubbed his temples as though he was battling a severe headache. "But I have it written down."

"Alright, enough with the games. What is it you want from us?"

Delgado stepped forward, and his eyes widened. "I want to become a part of your effort. It is the only path I can take to seek my revenge."

Sarah let out a short, high-pitched laugh. "That's impossible. You are a mass murderer."

Silence followed as all three exchanged long looks. Finally, Marshall pulled Sarah off to the side and spoke to her in a low tone. "We have no choice in this, Sarah. There is no one else who knows where Speaker Randall is."

She sighed in irritation and turned away. "I don't trust him. You have no idea what he did to innocent people. He's a monster."

"I'm aware of what he did, Sarah. But if we turn him away, we may never know where the Speaker is or what happened to him."

Sarah hung her head and rubbed her eyes with her forefinger and thumb. When she looked up, Marshall saw the tears welling up. "I—I guess I'll do anything for Zach."

Marshall nodded and walked back to Delgado, who looked back anxiously. "I can offer you this much: if you lead us to the Speaker, I will allow you to talk to him about your, ah, situation. It will be up to him to decide what happens after that."

Delgado nodded. "Fair enough. Yes, I can live with it. The Benefactor largely destroyed my mind, so I pose no threat to anyone except him. Each night, I have to write a note to remind myself where I hid the other note that recalls what I saw when they took Randall away."

"Let's not waste any further time. Where have you hidden this note?"

Delgado reached into his pocket and pulled out a crumpled piece of legal pad paper. He unfolded it and read the contents. "I hid it in the back room of the laundromat inside the old Mayor's desk. There hasn't been a mayor here for years, so no one would ever discover it."

"Then lead us to it," said Marshall.

They walked the short distance to the laundromat. Inside, a single machine creaked and stuttered, filled with someone's tattered rags. The rest of the machines looked like old, rusted junk that hadn't worked for years. Delgado made his way down the aisle until he reached the door that led to a small back office. A desk and chair covered in thick dust sat towards the back of the room. A yellowed print of the Grand Canyon hung crooked on the wall, the sheet of glass protecting it cracked in several places.

Delgado opened the top drawer on the right side of the desk and pulled out a second note written on the same type of paper as the first. He opened it up and read out loud. "Two guys in a red van came and led Randall out of the grocery store. He walked like a blind man, one hand covering his eyes and the other feeling out in front of him. I overheard one attendant talking about where they were taking him. The name is Overland Behavioral Health Center in Phoenix."

Delgado handed Marshall the note. "I remember now," he said. "I think Randall was blind. At least that's what it looked like to me."

"Blind?" Sarah grabbed Delgado's arm and swung him around. "What did that son of a bitch do to Zach?"

Delgado flinched and reflexively brought his hand up to shield his face. When he was reasonably certain she wasn't going to hit him, he continued. "I'm not sure. I told you, he severed his connection to me and probably didn't even know I was in Desolation. When they left with Randall, the Benefactor was already gone. A few people looked for him, but he was nowhere to be found. He just disappeared."

"How many people are there in Desolation," asked Marshall.

Delgado shrugged. "About 15 or 20... I don't know. Maybe he did slip out without anyone noticing. I can't say for sure."

Marshall was already walking back to the SUV as he turned around and said, "C'mon, let's go. We need to find the address for the Overland Health Center and get the Speaker.

As they drove down the dirt access road, Marshall searched for the address and sent it to the GPS. At least the satellites were still orbiting the earth, unaffected by the chaos below. The drive to Phoenix would take about three hours, but with Delgado in the vehicle, meaningful discussion was impossible.

The tires hummed as the SUV drove along a deserted stretch of Route 96. "How could you do it?" Sarah broke the silence without looking at Delgado. "At least you were scratching out a living. Most of the people in Desolation were fighting starvation. I was a child, but I remember you from back then. It's nauseating to think I had a crush on you . . . I actually thought you were handsome."

Delgado starred out the side passenger window. "My life was in shambles back then. The business was failing, my fiancé left me for another man; it felt hopeless. I was waiting for an excursion that took me somewhere remote so I could kill myself. One day, out of nowhere, Cox showed up and wanted to go deep into Upper Burro Creek, and that presented the best opportunity for me to end it all. But somehow, he knew what I had planned. He taunted and ridiculed me until I had the gun to my head and was about to put the trigger. And then . . ."

"And then, what?"

"He offered me a job. A way to get Lupita back . . . God help me, I said yes. And as you're aware, once you agree to join him, there's no going back. The next day we went deeper into the canyon until he found something important, but I can't remember what it was. He erased that memory from me. My mind is like a redacted government report. Big portions are missing."

***

Some two-and-a-half hours later, they pulled into the parking lot of the Overland Behavioral Health Center on Van Buren. Marshall looked at the decaying building and wrinkled his nose. Clearly, this was a state run facility for those without other recourse. If Speaker Randall ended up in such a place, he must be suffering from a significant impairment. Marshall felt a sense of foreboding as wisps of tainted energy laced with pain and agony oozed from the building.

Together, they walked up a flight of crumbling concrete stairs leading to a lobby that looked like it hadn't been updated since the 1950s. A variety of people experiencing serious health challenges occupied every inch of wall space. Marshall imagined those in the dirty bedclothes were patients, and they actually looked worse off than the others who appeared to be trying to check into the facility.

Marshall pushed up against a throng of people gathered in the center of the waiting area, shuffling around aimlessly and looking at him with either fear or loathing. The ammonia smell of fresh and dried urine was overpowering, and it mixed with strong body odor, which forced him to fight the urge to vomit.

A faded stenciled sign over the check-in station reminded visitors they should not smoke in the facility.

There were several examination rooms and a separate part of the building isolated by a door with multiple locks and a sign that read, *pharmacy*. Marshall slipped through the crowd as Delgado and Sarah found a spot at the rear near a sagging, stained couch. A man, whose skeleton was warped by decades of drug abuse, shuffled over close to Sarah and began sniffing her clothes. She recoiled in disgust and slid over, but he followed, smiling and repeating "lovely" over and over as he took deep breaths.

Marshall knew he needed to find answers quickly.

"Excuse me," he said to a balding woman with hard features sitting at an old dented metal desk behind the counter. She held up a finger and kept typing on her computer for several minutes before looking up and making eye contact.

"Yes, what do you want?"

He looked at her nametag. "Nurse Spalding, my name is Marshall Beiner. I need to check and see if someone we know is a patient here, please."

"I can neither confirm nor deny the existence of a patient at this facility," she said flatly and started typing again. Ten seconds later she stopped and looked up in annoyance. "I can't help you, so please leave. I'm ready to process the next patient."

Marshall stared at her and collected his thoughts. Even though he was considered high functioning, as someone with autism spectrum disorder, he still found body language, sarcasm and insults difficult to interpret.

"Look," he said with some sense of exasperation, "it is extremely important that we find this person. We believe someone picked up our friend in a town called Desolation and brought him here. Can you please check for me?"

She again stopped typing and peered over her clouded glasses. "As I said, I can neither confirm nor deny the existence of a patient in this facility . . . Do I need to call security?"

Marshall sighed. "Sorry, I didn't want to have to do this." He simultaneously launched a telepathic incursion into her mind that loosened up her tight passive aggressive personality. After a few seconds, her posture relaxed, and she looked up and smiled.

"I'm sorry, I'm just having a bad day, but I shouldn't take it out on you." She paused and sighed. "It's against hospital policy to reveal patient information, but for some reason, I feel like I should bend the rules just this once."

"Thank you, I appreciate it," replied Marshall. "Our friend's name is Zachery Randall."

She nodded and typed on her keyboard. As her eyes followed lines of text, she shook her head. "No, we have no one here by that name or from that city of origin. I'm sorry."

When Marshall turned around to say something to Sarah, he saw her hands wrapped around Delgado's neck. "You lying bastard," she said. "I'll kill you."

The admittance specialist recoiled and picked up the phone, but Zach implanted a suggestion, and she placed the receiver back in the cradle.

"I'm not lying," croaked Delgado as he tried to pry her hands loose.

"Sarah!" Marshall made his way back through the crowd and separated the entangled pair, once again prying her hands from Delgado's neck. When she finally let go, Sarah stepped back and panted with a crazed look of vengeance in her eyes.

"This isn't going to work, Sarah. Stop trying to find an excuse to kill Delgado."

She turned away, and her breathing finally slowed. "I—I understand, Marshall, but I have a rage that's almost uncontrollable . . ."

"Do you want to find the speaker? Because if you do, this isn't the way."

Sarah nodded and looked at the ground as Marshall walked back over to the admissions agent, who was preoccupied with processing the next patient. His head drooped in frustration, and he leaned up against the wall, listening to the wretched soul interact with the nurse for the next 15 minutes. Finally, she handed the man a packet, and he shuffled away while picking his nose. Marshall wasted no time getting in front of her again.

"I know I seem cold, but the only thing I see every day is misery," she said absently. "And what can I do? We have 15 people in rooms designed for two. The only thing I can do to help is give him a couple packets of fentanyl and hope he overdoses. That's what it's come to."

Marshall shook his head in genuine sympathy. "I'm sorry. I can only imagine what it's like for you." He paused a moment. "Please understand I don't want to seem insensitive, but it's very important I find my friend. You said you had no one here named Zachery Randall, is that right?"

"Yes, no one with that name," she replied uneasily. As her stress level rose, Marshall found it more difficult to nudge her to cooperate.

"Can you check for patients who were brought here within the past three months without identification?"

Her smile faded even more as she typed in new search parameters. "Yes, there were 56 patients admitted during that time without any ID. 12 of them are dead or were discharged. 44 are still here."

"Were any of these patients blind?"

"I'm sorry, but we don't have time to do a preliminary examination or keep charts. We do the best we can, but . . ."

Marshall looked away for a moment. "I guess I'll have to see each one of them. Give me a print out with their room numbers."

"I — I could lose my job, and jobs are so hard to find," she said with a note of desperation.

"Look at me." She peered up and their eyes locked. "I promise you will not lose your job. You have my guarantee of that."

She nodded and hit the print button on her computer. "I don't know why, but for some reason, I believe you." After the sound of the printer stopped, she walked to the back of her small cubicle and ripped off a piece of computer paper at the perforation.

"Here you go," she said as she handed the page to Marshall.

"Thank you, Nurse Spalding," he said while smiling. In about an hour, she would begin to wonder why she cooperated with the strange young man earlier in the day. By tomorrow, she would believe he had slipped a drug into her ice tea.

"44 people are on the list, but you can see in this column, they marked 28 of them with an 'f' for 'female'. 11 others are either Hispanic or African-American. We need to find the other five men," said Marshall as he passed the list to Sarah.

The floaters standing around them were becoming increasingly agitated, and one man in a 1970s-style mod suit coat with wide lapels began stabbing his forefinger into Marshall's chest.

"You're a big shot, aren't you, Bubs?" He repeated the phrase several times in succession, jabbing with more force every time he said the word "Bubs". Marshall took Sarah's hand and started toward the stairs at the back of the reception area as Delgado and the disturbed man trailed behind.

The stairs presented an additional obstacle as a throng of patients sat together in tight groups, occupying every step up to the second floor. They looked at the threesome with collective malice, and those closest made no effort to move.

"Excuse me," said Marshall. "We need to get up to the second floor. Could you move just a bit so we could get by?"

The patient on the left ignored him, but the one sitting on the right smiled through decayed, yellow teeth. His striped bed clothes were so soiled the garment almost appeared as a single, grayish-black color. "I'm the gatekeeper," he said. "Cost ya a buck ta get past me."

"Ya got a buck, Bubs? Big shot like you should at least have a buck." Marshall felt the man's finger poking in his back.

On the next step up, a woman with tangled hair and bulbous acne stood up with her hands on her hips. She was shaking badly from either a neurological disorder or advanced opiate withdrawal. "Then you'll get to my step, and it'll cost you another buck," she said.

"Yeah, it'll cost you a dollar to get by me too," said a disheveled man on the third step. Soon a cacophony of voices from the different steps leading up to the landing and second floor loudly expressed their monetary demands.

"Ha, it's gonna cost you a few bucks, Bubs. Big shot like you better be carrying some serious coin, or you ain't going anywhere."

Marshall knew money wasn't the issue. The facility in Sedona had a vault full of cash, jewels and precious metals, and he had a thousand dollars in his pocket. Even though currency was losing value in favor of "credits," a cryptocurrency issued by the HUGE conglomerate, there were still many places that would only accept greenbacks, gold or silver.

The problem was one of scale. If he paid his way up the 27 steps he counted, it would attract an even greater throng of floaters looking to be paid. These days, one could never underestimate the herd mentality.

Anticipating the question Sarah was about to ask, he said, "It's difficult for me to influence more than one of them at a time. As soon as I get one to move, another will take his place." Instead, Marshall backed up, reached into his pocket and pulled out a large amount of cash and folded it in the center. He grabbed Delgado's hand and put the money in it and wrapped his fingers around it.

"This man," Marshall shouted while turning back to those blocking the stairs, "has about 50 twenty-dollar bills. He'll give one to everyone on the stairs, but you have to come down to get them."

The response was instantaneous and as a mad rush swarmed an unprepared Delgado, Marshall grabbed Sarah's hand and started climbing the staircase. Meanwhile, Delgado threw the money in the air and ran in the opposite direction back toward the lobby.

Once they reached the landing, Marshall checked the paper the admittance nurse had given him. Two of the five men were in room 204, which was only a short distance from the top of the stairway. As he pushed the door open, the overpowering odor of necrotizing flesh mixed with spoiling bodily fluids invaded his nostrils and caused him gag involuntarily. The environment was stifling hot and overcrowded with at least a dozen or more men in soiled bedclothes groaning, babbling or sitting in a catatonic silence.

As he scanned the area, Marshall saw one wretch bent over in a corner licking open scabs on his left arm. Across from him, another with long hair and a bald crown sat on a bed while running his hands through a dark malleable material that appeared to be fresh feces. He was trying to fashion an object of some sort and kept muttering, "I made this. I made this." Another took deep breaths and shot snot out of his left nostril and then walked over and licked it off the wall before it could slide down to the floor.

Fighting a rising panic, Marshall took tentative steps forward while looking for any signs of Speaker Randall, but the room was filled with so much suffering it was hard to focus. After about a minute, his anxiety reached a crescendo, and Marshall felt as though he might suffocate if he didn't leave the room. Just as he was about to turn, he heard a voice off in the distance.

"Oh my God, it's Zach. Marshall, help me. Come here quickly."

Chapter Seven

Deep inside a subterranean bunker in Jaunde, which was once called Kampala in Uganda, Mr. Cox poured over countless maps, and every one of them told the same unpleasant story. The reach and influence of the HUGE conglomerate was shrinking at a shocking pace. In the vacuum created by its absence, a pacifist movement continued to fill the void.

While the concepts of peace, love and eternal life were nauseating enough, the most maddening aspect of the self-righteous crusaders was their lack of structure. The armed forces of HUGE lashed out on many occasions, massacring millions without any appreciable effect. Murdered pacifists were always replaced by others, and the dead instantly became martyrs. This only served to help the movement grow, and it transmuted negative energy into purity that was twice as potent.

The Corporates were fighting a war without a definable battleground and an enemy who struck back without firing a single shot. As a result, the orthodox tactics developed through centuries of Corporate oppression were ineffective. Perhaps worst of all, areas that HUGE vacated were no longer governed in the conventional sense. Communities organized in a way that provided for the needs of everyone without coercion or the promise of greed and profit. Once people became part of the pacifist movement, they seemed to lose all of the characteristics Mr. Cox exploited.

Now, separated from the orb, the Benefactor recognized his power would slowly weaken, and he knew he must retrieve it from the vault in Desolation soon. In the meantime, he needed to learn more about these pacifists, and the only way to do that would be to visit them in person. They must have a weakness, and whatever it was, he would discover it and use it to crush them.

He looked down at the map and scrolled across the screen until he found what he was looking for. In an area formerly known as the Central African Republic, a small incursion of pacifists pushed south to a city near the southern border. While still surrounded by Corporate forces, the area of control was receding in the same pattern that repeated itself throughout the world. This would prove to be a perfect microcosm to study the pacifist phenomenon.

Mr. Cox minimized the map and pressed another icon, which opened a video chat request. Moments later, the image of Turkus Plints filled the screen. The assistant hid his wounded arm inside a long-sleeve jumper, but he moved with obvious discomfort.

"Yes Coxnotus? How may I assist you?"

Mr. Cox moved his face closer to the screen. "You can start by removing that irritating disingenuous smile from your face. There is nothing to smile about here. This era is in utter disarray, and the ineptness of you and your colleagues has ruined everything I so meticulously planned for." Plints sat up straight and his smile instantly faded.

"Good, that is better," said Mr. Cox as he sat back. "I need you to arrange transportation to a city farther north and east. I believe it is called, 'Nzoni'."

Plints looked down at his tablet for a moment, and when he came back to the camera, his expression transformed to one of alarm. "We cannot go there, Coxnotus. That area is under contention and falling to the pacifist rebels as we speak. It is very dangerous."

"It is precisely because the town is about to fall to the pacifists that we must go there. I need to learn more about these people. They cannot hide their motivations from me." He looked at Plints, and his gaze hardened. "And by the way, why do you access a physical device when your implant is so much more effective?"

Plints swallowed uncomfortably. "The pacifists shut down the Ark mainframe in the early 23rd century, Coxnotus. Unfortunately, the research I need can only be done in the physical realm."

"Must everything in this time be so disappointing?" Mr. Cox paused and looked away. "Make the appropriate arrangements for the excursion. I want to go there as soon as possible."

"It is highly irregular. I must contact Dantar Llross."

Cox moved so close to the camera his features distorted. "Listen to me, Plints. Llross is no longer in charge of HUGE. I will ask for her resignation to be on my desk within the hour, and I will then set up an emergency holographic conference with the remaining Board of Directors. I want their names and contact designations within the hour. By tomorrow, I will take my rightful place as head of the HUGE conglomerate."

"I. . ." Plints struggled for words. "Unfortunately, the pacifists have control over all the Vernox dishes and the Benton inverters. We—we have no holographic capability and can only communicate through radio waves. Still, I will try to contact the Board, but I must warn you, none of them may be alive, future Chairman of the Board Coxnotus."

"Fine. All the better if that is the case. I will also need an assessment of the assets we have near Nzoni. We must organize an overwhelming show of force to intimidate these people, but I don't want to exterminate them unless it is necessary."

"Of course," said Plints. "We have around 200 regulars still in that area, and there are about 20 members of the elite security guard with them."

"200 troops? That's the total of our force in a contested area?" Mr. Cox shook his head in exasperation. "Leave me, and arrange for the air car. My frustration and disappointment makes it difficult to look at you."

Plints nodded in deference as he signed off, and Mr. Cox leaned back in his chair. These accommodations were miserable, and for just a moment, he considered using the power of the orb to return to the Gehenna center in Detroit and resume his life of luxury in the 21st century. Yet, just as quickly, he dismissed the idea. That era was so culturally primitive he would certainly be driven mad by their ignorance and stupidity.

He stood up and walked over to a cart that held a small selection of fine wines and selected a '27 Villa Raiano Chianti. The cork popped, and he poured half a glass, swirling the deep red liquid and reveling in the bouquet. With time for only a single sip, he heard the hydraulic doors swish open and his personal concierge, Minkus Term, entered breathing heavily, his eyes wide with fear.

"Coxnotus, we must leave immediately!" Term panted and tried to catch his breath.

"Your name is Minkus Term, correct?" asked Mr. Cox as he set his glass down. "What is the meaning of this intrusion?"

"They are coming for you, Coxnotus. Turkus Plints revealed your plans to Dantar Llross, and she dispatched the elite guard to capture you. I fear that if they succeed, you will be shut away in isolation, and no one will ever hear from you again."

Mr. Cox folded his hands together. "But Llross asked for my help. They would not dare try and apprehend me. They know I can neutralize them all."

"I am unaware of the nature of your power, but she is sending the entire security detail here. There will be 20 heavily armed men arriving in less than four minutes. They have been ordered to shoot you with a high-powered sedative. Please, Coxnotus, come with me now!"

It took Mr. Cox less than a second to verify the information Term conveyed was authentic. Of course, there was always the possibility someone placed a telepathic suggestion in his mind, however, Mr. Cox followed his instinct, which told him the threat was real and imminent.

"Lead on, Term," he said.

Without a reply, Term ran out the door and down the hallway with Mr. Cox in close pursuit. "Quickly, in here," he said as he opened a utility closet.

As if the experience in this time was not humiliating enough, the Benefactor found himself in a small, darkened room standing next to cleaning robots and janitorial supplies. Seconds passed, and he was about to ask Term why they were crouching in this claustrophobic room when he heard multiple footfalls.

83

Llross's security detail walked past the janitorial closet on their way to his quarters. There was some shuffling and loud talk at a fevered pitch as the squad leader soon realized the Benefactor's room was empty. They retreated back down the hallway at a much faster pace than when they arrived.

As the sound of their footsteps receded, Mr. Cox whispered to Term, "Where is it we need to go?"

"This is an underground facility. We must get to the surface, but there are only two exits, and they will have both of them covered."

"Which exit will the leader of the security force secure?"

Term paused and stroked his chin. "He will take the majority of the force and guard the main east exit. There will only be a small detail at the west auxiliary exit. But what does that matter? Both exits will still be guarded." Term lowered his head and spoke in a low voice. "I have failed you — Benefactor."

In the darkness, Mr. Cox still expressed surprise. He wondered where Term heard the moniker his loyalists used to refer to him. "Term, lead me to the auxiliary exit. I will handle our escape from there."

Term nodded and opened the door slowly. In anticipation of their flight, he had disabled the surveillance feed from this corridor, so they made their way down the hallway without being detected. The purposeful malfunction might last a couple more minutes before it would self-correct.

Two turns and three flights of stairs brought them up to a staging area where the facility received supplies. From a crouching position, they watched as a five-man contingent of security personnel blocked the service entrance and two dock roll-up doors.

"Is that the one in charge?" Mr. Cox asked while pointing toward the soldier projecting the most bravado and conceit in his temporary command.

"Yes, he is the second. You can tell by the patch on his right arm."

Mr. Cox nodded. He wouldn't be able to compel the weakest-minded soldier to kill the others since the explosions from the coil gun projectiles would create enough noise to draw attention to the area. Plus, the entire sector would be under constant camera surveillance. A much more subtle approach was in order.

For a few moments, Mr. Cox appeared to have fallen asleep as he lowered his head and closed his eyes. Almost instantaneously, the unit leader jerked upright as though a wasp had stung him. He whipped his head around and looked in all directions with alarm as he raised his rifle.

One of his men walked over and grabbed his arm. "Chief, are you well?"

"There was something . . . I felt it. Like pin prick or a cactus needle. Someone is watching us."

The other soldier put his arm around the Chief's shoulder. "Grontus, there is nothing here. We have guards thoroughly covering the exits. If there was something, they would have seen it."

Clearly agitated, Grontus pointed at the entrance on the opposite side of the staging area. "Over there. I think whoever it was went into the food consumption area. Get everyone together, we must search that room."

His companion shook his head. "No, we cannot do that. We have orders to guard these doors. Why would anyone hole up in there of all places?"

"They are not coming this way, Nilus," snapped Grontus as he pulled away from his subordinate. "We are not qualified for this sort of thing. One minute we are figuring out how to pass the time to relieve boredom, and the next minute we are supposed to protect the Chairman of HUGE. I am telling you, I know they are in that room. We need to go after them."

Before Nilus could reply, Grontus turned to the other three security guards mulling around the doors. "Keep your weapons at the ready," he said. "They are in the eating room. Come with me."

He beckoned the other guards to follow, and everyone but Nilus obeyed. Grontus stopped and pointed his weapon at the subordinate. "I gave an order, Nilus, and I expect it to be followed."

"I am going to radio, Frothnor Kants." He reached over to touch the button on his lapel, which triggered Grontus to shoulder his weapon in a firing position.

"Our instructions were to stay radio silent, Nilus. If you touch that transceiver, I will have no choice but to kill you on the spot."

Nilus' hand dropped to his side, and he looked despondent. "Grontus, I have children at the collective. One of them is scheduled to return home this week. Please, do not kill me."

"Then pick up your weapon and join us on the search."

Reluctantly, Nilus reached down and grasped his coil gun and shuffled forward. Several of the men exchanged worried glances as they moved to the cafeteria, exiting the warehouse shipping area as a group.

"Did you do that, Coxnotus?" whispered Term.

"Yes, planting suggestions takes longer than simple commands, but in this instance, there was no choice. Now, how do we exit this facility?"

"Come, this way." Term entered the staging area and motioned for Mr. Cox to follow. They moved swiftly to a service door positioned next to the larger dock doors. Term swiped his keycard and placed his finger into the DNA scanner before receiving confirmation and hearing the lock disengage. Once outside, he scoured the surrounding area before pointing at a fleet of air cars. "There," he said. "He is waiting for us. Let us go."

About three quarters of the way to the waiting air car, the service door behind them swung open a second time, shoved hard by someone trying to exit. Within seconds, the security agents assigned to the west exit filed out of the building and stood for a moment until they located the fleeing pair.

"Prevus Coxnotus!" yelled Nilus, who was standing in the middle of the group. "You must surrender or we will terminate you and Minkus Term."

Instantly, Term slowed and raised his hands over his head. Once he realized his concierge was surrendering, Mr. Cox stopped and glared at him.

"Term, why are you stopping?"

"It is over, Coxnotus. Their weapons are accurate up to two kilometers. They would cut us down before we reached the air car.

"I see. Well, then let us walk to them." Mr. Cox raised his arms over his head, and together, they slowly moved back towards the building. About twenty yards separated them from the security forces when Mr. Cox stopped as a wide smile spread across his face.

"Coxnotus, why are you smiling?" asked Term.

"You will see . . ." The words were barely out of his mouth when the service door opened a third time, and Grontus ran out with his weapon drawn and firing from behind at the main group.

"Defy my orders, you deserters? I told you they were in the eating room!"

The plasma bursts from Grontus' weapon exploded on contact and fried two of the guards before their minds even registered that something was wrong. Nilus took a shot to the head just as he was turning around. The last remaining guard managed to fire her weapon, and the shot hit Grontus square in the abdomen. Despite his protective gear, the coil gun was set to kill, and it shredded the titanium plastic composite and tore into his insides, incinerating his heart, lungs and liver.

The remaining guard lowered her weapon and took off her helmet as she continued to stare at the carnage that surrounded her. She paused for only a moment before pulling a pistol from a holster and firing a kinetic slug into her own brain.

It took almost a minute for the sound, smell and smoke from the slaughter to dissipate. When the impact of the shock abated a bit, Minkus Term trembled and looked at Mr. Cox. "You—you made them do that to each other, did you not?"

Still smiling, Mr. Cox looked at his assistant. "Yes, and it was wonderful. The fear from the ones who knew they would die was intense. Could you feel it?"

"Ah, no . . . I was too stunned to notice anything."

"Listen, Term," said Mr. Cox as his eyes flared. "If you want to be an integral part of my inner circle, you must let me enter your mind and connect with me."

Term shook his head enthusiastically. "Yes, yes, I want to be a part of it. The Gehenna Corporation and the HUGE conglomerate under your guidance are legendary. Please, let me be a part of our return to glory.

"Good, then I will make it happen. But now I think it would be prudent to leave here before Llross organizes another group of her loyalists to apprehend us."

Term started back to the air car with Mr. Cox following closely behind. When they reached the vehicle, a man with a weathered complexion greeted them with an expressionless nod. He ran a hand through his jet-black hair before powering up the nitrogen fuel cells and driving down the service road out to a larger artery.

Once they were clear of the building, a pair of retractable wings emerged from the sides of the vehicle, and he engaged the gyros and guidance computer. With the push of an icon, the electrogravitic booster created an anti-gravity field, and the vehicle lifted off the pavement and steadily gained altitude until it cruised at a comfortable 500 feet.

After a few minutes airborne, Mr. Cox looked over at Term. "Where are we heading?"

"We are going to the rebels' stronghold just outside of Nzoni, the latest city where the pacifists have taken over. They are all that is left of the Gehenna Corporation resistance."

"Good. I will enjoy meeting with some of our loyalists." Turning to the driver, he said, "I assume our chauffeur is with us?"

Term nodded. "This is Hinsus Malconus. He has served in the front lines of the struggle against both Amrosia and the pacifists." Term paused and his shoulders dropped. "It is a battle that has persisted for over centuries, and it has taken its toll on us."

"You are all sniveling rodents," said Mr. Cox, "and yet, we will ultimately prevail in spite of your cowardice. My perfect plan will not be foiled by foes, either external or internal." He glanced at both of them before continuing. "Open your minds to me, and you will experience a sense of fulfillment you could not have imagined."

Term closed his eyes while Malconus continued staring at the Benefactor. He reached out with two tendrils that were dark, deep and dripping with malevolence. Once the filaments entered their minds, both stiffened, and their backs straightened as their eyes glazed over. Mr. Cox flooded them with images and snippets of the suffering and pain he caused through his many travels. With every new horror he revealed, their pleasure centers were rewarded with stimulation so potent an opiate would seem like a mild sedative by comparison. Within the context of the bombardment, their minds were saturated with a sadistic and feelings of loyalty and sacrifice toward the Benefactor.

In one sense, they underwent a psychological transformation accompanied by a physiological conversion as well. The tendrils split into millions of micro strands, altering the flow of neurons and rerouting synaptic pathways. For their part, Term and Malconus shook and frothed at the mouth as their ability to reason and think independently was transformed forever. Term's eyes rolled into the back of his head, and for a moment, Mr. Cox wondered if he swallowed his tongue.

Unfortunately, there wasn't sufficient time to carry out a protracted conversion. Every matter became one of urgency, and he needed new lieutenants to help expand his influence more efficiently. They would either survive to serve him with unwavering loyalty, or they would die from neural overload. While Mr. Cox hoped for the former, he could live with the latter. Neither Term nor Malconus was a suicide survivor, and those who never faced the isolated black hole of despondency and hopelessness could not receive the Benefactor's full communion.

Term was choking and crying out in agony as he tried to rise up from the floor of the vehicle. "I have never felt such terrible pain and depression before. And yet, these heinous thoughts exhilarate me at the same time. I—I am so confused."

By now, Malconus had taken his place back in the operator's seat. He checked the dashboard and stared straight out the window. Just before they began their descent, he said in a low voice, "I serve the Benefactor."

"Excellent," replied Mr. Cox. "Excellent."

Chapter Eight

All the windows in the room were covered with three-quarter inch plywood nailed into the studs. The walls were lined with old mattresses attached with stickpins and washers, and someone had tacked up nine-inch fiberglass batts to the ceiling. It didn't take much imagination to figure out why the room was soundproofed.

If Winn needed any more evidence as to the purpose of this place, the physician's examination table bolted to the floor and outfitted with arm and leg shackles left little doubt. Darryl pushed the barrel of the gun into Winn's back to prod him to move forward.

"C'mon, Doc, get your sweet ass up here on the table. It's time for your exam."

Winn stopped cold and turned around to run, but Darryl raised the rifle and brought the butt end down hard into Winn's forehead. Stunned, he staggered back and brought his hands up to his head, which gave Simon the chance to grab his right arm and stick him with a hypodermic. Almost immediately, Winn felt groggy, and a smoldering heat spread from his arm through the rest of his body. He was vaguely aware of the boys pushing him over to the examining table and forcing him down onto it. The chains rustled as they fed them through the loops and secured them with locks.

The next sensation Winn would remember was a scorching feeling in his groin that grew in intensity until he screamed his way back to consciousness. His throat was tight, and he struggled to breathe. Certain they had burned off his genitals, Winn continued shrieking in a primordial way. He looked down as Norma administered yet another shot, and just as quickly as it came on, the burning sensation abated, and his throat loosened, leaving him weakened and panting.

Even before he opened his eyes, he smelled Norma's foul breath. "So, Doc, I hope you understand the seriousness of your situation. Me 'en the boys ain't foolin' around here. We know all about you freaks and your mind games. You see other people when they're about to die, don't you?" It was a statement rather than a question.

"I—I'm not sure what you're talking about. I—agggghhhh!" Norma smacked him with a leather belt across the bare skin on his stomach. A second lash followed and seven more after that. The leather was roughhewn, and the belt was at least four inches wide. Each blow tore skin as fresh blood crept to the surface.

"Listen, you freak, the more you try to disobey me, the worse you're gonna get. Now, again, you see people when they're ready to kill themselves, don't you?"

Winn nodded feebly. "Yes . . . I have hallucinations."

"Good," said Norma as she backed away. "I knew you were one of them freaks. You tried to kill yourself, didn't you?"

Again, he nodded.

"Why? And why didn't you get it done?"

"I lost my family in the eradication in St. Louis," Winn said while swallowing hard. " . . . Can I have some water? My throat feels like sandpaper."

Norma smacked him hard with the belt across the stomach again. "Keep talkin'. If you say the right stuff, I might give you a swallow." It came out sounding like, *swaller*.

"I left to make a deal trading gold bullion for supplies, and while I was gone, the floaters tore through my neighborhood. When I got back, I found my wife raped and beheaded, and the bastards dismembered my children." Winn struggled to get the last words out as he burst into tears. The pain was as searing and as fresh as the first time he saw the disfigured bodies.

"And you died, right? I mean, the doctors said you were dead?"

He nodded again. "Yes, I put a bullet through my head. The sound of the shot triggered a security system alert, and someone surveilled the house and saw me on the ground with the gun. At the hospital, I died six times on the operating table."

"But you didn't die. Instead, you lived. How?" Norma's eyes narrowed as she squinted at him.

"I don't know. It took an endless number of surgeries to correct some of the damage. None of the surgeons could offer a theory as to why my cognitive functions weren't affected.

"You mean your brain? Oh, actually, it was mutilated, Doc. In fact, you started to see people trying to kill themselves after that, am I right?"

"I had blackouts, and the dreams were about people killing themselves, yes. But they aren't real . . . There's no way they could be real."

Norma slapped him hard across the face. "They're real all right. Just like the other freaks downstairs. You're seeing these people as they're getting ready to off themselves, and I want to know how you do it."

Winn shook his head. "I have no idea. It just happens. I start to lose consciousness, and then it's like I'm thrust into their world."

"I want the names of the suicides. Tell me their names." She raised the strap over her head.

"Don't," said Winn with a note of desperation. "Please don't hit me again." She brought the strap down hard across his chest and arms as he howled with pain.

"I'm not messin' with you, Doc." Norma moved away from the table and turned to Simon. "Get another shot ready, and make this one twice as strong."

Winn squirmed and strained against the chains. "No, please, don't give me any more of that."

Too late. Simon jabbed him with the needle and pushed the plunger in with a cruel smile on his face. "Here you go, buddy," he said with a sneer. "Enjoy your breakfast."

Winn could feel the caustic substance traveling through his veins and passing through his heart until it was fully distributed throughout his body. His muscles seized, and he gasped for breath once again with a sensation similar to an extreme asthma attack. He wheezed and sputtered as his mouth grew dry, and his tongue swelled.

"Where were you going when I picked you up, Doc?"

"I can't breathe," Winn gasped. "Help me . . ."

"Simon, load up another shot."

"No, no please," Winn said between gasps for breath. "Who knows where I was going? Away from the skankers, I guess."

"Wrong answer," said Norma. "Go ahead and give it to him, Simon." Grinning, the younger son pulled another syringe out of the wrapper.

By now, Winn was in so much pain he could barely stay conscious. Yet, something in the cocktail wouldn't allow him to pass out, so he had to endure the scalding sensation inside his muscles without even the respite of insentience. His seared blood continued to pump through his body as the intensity of the pain kept rising. In between screams and moans, Winn rasped, "I was going to Sedona. I don't know why. Now please . . . I'm begging you to make it stop."

Norma held up a hand, which caused Simon to hesitate. "Now we're gettin' somewhere," she said. "The two important questions are why were you going there, and where *exactly* were you going?"

Winn groaned and tried to talk through lips that felt like they were sliding off his face. "I'm confused about where I was going. Just to Sedona. Something . . . something drawing me to that place. I can picture it in my mind. A red mountain. That's all I know."

Norma brought the belt down hard on his raw chest. "The whole damn place has red mountains everywhere, you idiot. That's no help. I need road names or signs or something."

"I have nothing like that," said Winn. "Nothing."

"Simon, jack him up with another shot. Burn his arteries up, I don't care."

Winn stopped convulsing long enough to say, "Please, just kill me. No more acid in my veins . . . Just kill me."

Norma grabbed Simon's hand just as he was about to give Winn another dose. "That's enough for today, Simon. Take him down to the basement. There's always tomorrow."

With a shrug and a roll of his eyes, Simon backed away and put the syringe in a sandwich bag to save it for the next session. Together with his brother, they unchained Winn and picked him up, dragging his limp body over to the basement door. After descending half the flight of stairs, Darryl pushed Winn roughly, and he fell down the rest of the way. Simon pointed his shotgun into the darkness and said, "Any of you freaks come over to him before that door is shut, en you're gonna get blasted."

There was no movement from the shadows as Darryl climbed the stairs while Winn lay motionless on the floor moaning softly. The door slammed shut with Darryl yelling "freaks" one last time as the light from upstairs disappeared, and the basement was thrust back into its usual state of semi-darkness.

Nicholas was the first one to help Marshall up, and together with Paco, they carried him over to his mattress. Winn continued to moan as he squirmed in a vain attempt to find some relief from the pain inside his body. He put his forearm over his forehead and struggled for breath. "I burn," he managed to mumble through swollen lips. "Can you make it stop?"

Nicholas shook his head. "No, it has to be processed and expelled through your liver and kidneys. I'll give you half my water ration." Nicholas held a plastic cup to Winn's lips and watched as the fallen man sipped. "Small sips won't help," he said. "You have to take large gulps." Winn tried to take in more water, but his esophagus was swollen and narrowed, and he spit up most of it.

"Time is the only cure," said Felicia. "The good news is you'll get a day off."

"Not always," said Brandon dully. "I was on the table three days in a row once. It's okay though because I don't have as many thoughts in my mind as I used to. Sometimes hours go by and I can't remember what just happened."

Winn rasped, "We've got to figure out a way to get out this hellish nightmare."

***

Wanda woke up to the sound of a low murmur from the crowd gathered outside her tent. As she sat up, she saw the silhouettes of multiple people projected against the thin fabric. The first egg had woken her, but the second *splat* against the side of the tent alerted her to the mood of the crowd.

She got to her knees, adjusted her jogging suit and unzipped the front flap of the tent, ducking below the crossbar and standing up. The first face she saw was an Asian man in oil stained gray pants, unmatched shoes and a T-shirt. It was chilly in L.A. today, and he looked uncomfortable.

"You take my spot," he said. "I want it back now, or I kick your ass right out of here."

She looked around and saw her companions were slowly emerging from their own tents to join her. In another life, Sam Simpson was an auto mechanic; Aisha Lemon was a hairdresser; Jerry Kent owned a plumbing company and Talie Jones was a prostitute. They all heard the call and sought sanctuary in Sedona, and they were the first group sent out to bring enlightenment to an area mired in hatred, anxiety and violence. The task presented extraordinary challenges, and while Wanda valued the education she received at the sanctuary, it was difficult to ignore the overwhelming hostility projected in their direction.

"I'm sorry, I wasn't aware we were encroaching on anyone's space. That wasn't our intent. Can you point out a place that isn't taken? By the way, my name is Wanda." She smiled and extended her hand.

"I don't think you get it." The man backed up and frowned at the cordial gesture. "There's no place here for you and your bullshit. This place is a fuckin' war zone. You trespassed into Pock territory. Everything east of Main is Pock, but the Crege think they own it up to San Julian. Either way, you don't just come here and settle in without asking permission."

"I see," said Wanda as she dropped her hand to her side. "Can you at least give me your name?"

He looked around from side to side as a half dozen gang bangers behind him grew more agitated. "Name's Ngo," he said. "Now that we've done the polite shit, why don't you get the fuck out of here?"

"Ngo, you do understand we can't leave before we talk to the people out here in the streets. We're here to help, and we don't want conflict."

Ngo smirked and looked back at his shock troops. "Are you fuckin' crazy, lady?" He glanced over at the other sanctuary people standing near Wanda and walked aggressively up to Jerry Kent, who was eating a protein bar and sipping bottled water.

"Who the fuck you lookin' at, Holmes?"

Jerry looked at Wanda, who nodded to convey encouragement, and then he focused his attention back on Ngo. "My name's Jerry Kent. It's nice to meet you, Ngo. I'd like a chance to talk to you about authentic power and what you're looking to achieve in this lifetime."

99

Ngo pulled away from Kent as though he had contagious leprosy. "What the *fuck* is wrong with you people, anyway? I told you to get away from here." Out of his left pocket he extracted a stiletto and popped the blade into position. "I'm not messing with you, fool."

Kent continued to stand in place, slowly chewing his breakfast. If he had any fear, it wasn't reflected in his expression. This only seemed to enrage Ngo, who closed the short distance between them and stuck the knife blade up against Kent's neck. "Maybe you didn't hear me. I said get the fuck outta here. I'll stick you, man, and I won't think twice about it. There aren't any cops down here anymore, Holmes. You'll die in the street, and your body will lay there until the truck comes on Wednesday."

Wanda walked over so she was closer to the two men. Kent's eyes had widened slightly, but he didn't move as he swallowed hard. "If you kill Jerry," said Wanda, "it's only his body that will die. His essence will move to a new reality of greater understanding and love.

"But you, Ngo," she said while wagging a finger at him, "you will draw extraordinary darkness into your sphere if you choose to end his life. To bring your soul and personality back into balance, you must experience the same hurt and pain you would cause by killing Jerry."

"What?" Ngo squinted at Wanda like he was looking at a lunatic. "Will you just shut up? I don't know what you're talking about."

"I'm not sure how that would play out exactly," said Wanda. "Perhaps you will be stabbed by someone else. Perhaps you'll have to experience the pain of watching a loved one die in an equally heinous way. You must be very careful with your decision. Make sure your actions reflect your intent."

By now, the scene had drawn an even bigger crowd than the one encountered yesterday, and Ngo looked over his shoulder uncomfortably as he began to sense the sentiment was turning against him. He lessened the pressure on the knife, and his shoulders sagged slightly. The subtle difference in body language conveyed a lessening in resolve. Wanda imagined that if she gave him a way to save face, he would take it.

"Let's talk, Ngo. Come into my tent, and we'll share some food we brought with us. If you still want us to leave after we finish talking, we'll go somewhere else."

"I don't know," he said as the knife dropped to his side. "The OG told me to get you out of here no matter what."

"And you're going to go back with a message for him or her. Is that fair?"

Ngo scratched his bald head with the edge of the blade.

"Do it, Ngo," said someone from the crowd. "Talk to the lady. See what she has to say. How can these people possibly make it any worse out here?" Several others in the growing crowd voiced their agreement.

Ngo swiveled his head around in all directions with an expression of confusion. Finally, he pushed a button on the knife, and the blade retracted back into the handle.

"Well, ok," he said with obvious trepidation. "I'll talk with you, but then you need to get out of here."

Wanda nodded and smiled. "Understood." She motioned to Aisha standing behind her. "Great opportunity to get closer to these people, Aisha. Why don't you and the others introduce yourselves to Ngo's friends and give them a sense of why we're here."

Aisha nodded and stepped forward along with Talie and Sam. Apparently shaken, Jerry remained stationary while rubbing his neck and fingering the half-eaten energy bar in his other hand.

Wanda beckoned for Ngo to enter her tent, and she invited Iris as well. They were just seated when yesterday's antagonist, Arturo, pulled back the tent flap. Ngo jumped to his feet and pointed. "Get that *lon* out of here. I'll kill him."

Arturo looked over at Wanda and shrugged. "I just came back to see if I could . . . well, maybe help you today."

Wanda smiled at him and nodded before turning back to Ngo. "Wait a moment, Ngo, why is it you want to kill Arturo?" She lightly touched his arm.

Ngo pulled away sharply. "He's stinking Crege. The only good Crege is a dead Crege."

"And naturally," said Wanda, "since you're a 'Pock', you suspect Arturo wants to kill you as well?"

"Yeah, I'm sure he does."

"The Pocks and the Crege are collectives, Arturo. Do you understand what a collective is and why they exist?"

"What the fuck, lady? Now you're speaking more weirdo shit. Collective. Jesus. . ."

"A collective is a group of people that band together out of fear. The greater the fear, the tighter and more restrictive the bonds of the collective will be."

"The Pocks fear no one. We rule the streets here. Anyone gets out of line, they get wasted."

"Which solves what, Ngo? How has that made this a better place? How has it made you or anyone else feel safer?"

Ngo looked down at his shoes. "That's just the way it works, lady. That's just how it is out on the streets."

"But maybe it doesn't have to be that way," said Arturo. "Listen to her, Ngo, she makes a lot of sense. There's no reason we have to keep fighting and killing each other. Think about it. We have our rumbles and people get killed. What does it solve? We just wait until the next rumble... I'm afraid, Ngo. There, I admit it. I'm afraid that my little sister will end up dead like my brother, uncle and mother."

"There's nothing that can be done to change it," Ngo said while shaking his head. "It's been that way, and as everything has gone down the shitter, it's only gotten worse."

"You're wrong, Ngo. Everything can change," said Wanda. "It can change with a single choice to do something differently today. If you want a more peaceful existence, you must align your actions with your intentions. As long as you're at war with yourself, you will not find peace."

Ngo sat back down on the floor. "This is some heavy shit lady. But changing how I think ain't gonna feed anyone."

"No, but it could change the way people interact with each other. Instead of allowing the personality to project its fear, imagine if there was some degree of communication at the level of the soul where there can only be love. What could be accomplished if there was that kind of cooperation?"

"I—I don't know. You really are crazy. But why . . . why does sitting next to you make me feel better? Why does this *place* make me feel better?"

"I get it," said Arturo with a smile. "I had the same thing happen yesterday, but I couldn't figure out why."

Wanda crawled over to her backpack and reached inside. She produced several packets of seeds she laid down on the ground. "There is a vacant lot over on Wall and 7th. We'll need to relocate some people who are living there, but it shouldn't be hard to find them a place that's not in the dirt or mud. Once we've moved them, we can plant these seeds and raise our own food."

"Jesus, you can't be serious," said Ngo.

"I'm absolutely serious," said Wanda. "We'll start renovating some of these abandoned buildings after that. The city repo'd most of them anyway since the owners walked away and couldn't pay the taxes. Who knows how the new laws will be written, but I can envision them being owned by no one and everyone."

Wanda started to speak again when the flap to her tent opened. Sam stuck his head inside and said, "Wanda, you better come out here."

Chapter Nine

"Nurse Zultz, is that you? Nurse Zultz?" The frail man sat on an old bench in the corner of the crowded room. He wore a tattered undershirt stained with a variety of liquids, dirt and what looked to be splotches of blood. His legs were bare and covered with open sores as flies and maggots perched on the edges of the raw flesh, feasting on the pus that oozed from the many lesions. With outstretched arms, he extended his fingers while seeking to touch the contours of the face of the woman in front of him.

"No, Zach. It's me, Sarah. Zach, it's me."

His hands began feeling her nose, cheeks and eyes. "You're not Nurse Zultz. Who are you?"

"I'm Sarah, Zach. I'm here with Marshall."

"Speaker Randall," said Marshall as he bent down to one knee. "What's happened to you?"

"Doctor Thorn? Thomas? Is it you? You haven't come around for a very long time. My legs and abdomen hurt, Thomas, and bugs keep crawling over the places where it hurts the most. I have an oily wetness down there. Are you here to examine me?" His voice was weak and unsteady.

Sarah leaned over and choked back tears. "He doesn't know who we are," she whispered to Marshall. "What did Cox do to him?"

Marshall shook his head. "I don't know, but I'm afraid that even Speaker Randall is no match for Mr. Cox' telepathic abilities. I fear he may be permanently damaged."

"Thomas, please help me. I—I don't feel well. I'm burning up with fever and vomiting every time I eat. Can you get me medicine? I think I need some, or I may die."

Marshall reached out, but his probe hit a telepathically impregnable surface and dissipated. There was nothing there. Zach's mind was like a lump of dead flesh, rotting and decomposing in real time. "I can't touch him. Even his memories are gone."

Sarah whimpered and shook her head while wiping tears from her eyes. "We need to get him away from here right now."

Marshall nodded. "What is your name?" he asked Zach.

"You know I can't remember my name, Thomas. My eyes. Are there any new tests scheduled for my eyes?"

Marshall took his hand and waved it in front of Randall's face.

"He's totally blind, Sarah."

Her body slumped as she reached out and took his hand in her own. "Zach, it's me, Sarah. Please, try to remember."

For just a moment, he tilted his head as a fleeting sliver of recognition flashed through his mind. Just as quickly, the moment passed, and he pulled his hand away. "Do I know you? And why do you keep

106

calling me, Zach? If you're not Nurse Zultz, then who are you?"

Marshall looked over at the pitiful wretch with sadness and exasperation. "Speaker Randall, please try and remember us. The Suicide Society. The facility in Sedona. You are our leader."

The mention of The Suicide Society caused Zach to fidget while fingering the blisters on his legs. "Thomas, stop talking about such things. They make my head hurt. I—I can't remember anything, you know that. I've tried . . . I . . . Can you help me feel better? Please."

"We're not getting through to him," said Sarah. "This won't work." She looked around the room and towards the stairwell. "We've got to get him back to Sedona."

Marshall nodded. "Yes, you're right." He moved closer to Zach and placed one arm over his shoulder and gently lifted his frail mentor to his feet. Zach extended his free arm and felt around for something solid. Sarah moved to the other side to support him.

"What are you doing, Thomas? Are we going to the treatment room? Are you getting me some medicine?" A severe coughing spell followed as a large wad of bloody phlegm dropped from his open mouth to the floor.

"Yes," said Marshall, "we're going to the infirmary for medicine." Zach smiled weakly and began shuffling his feet as they directed him to the stairs.

No more than 10 steps into the journey, a group of patients moved to block the exit. Their bodies were ravaged, and they had the fearful look of lost souls with one foot in the grave. A man with salt and pepper hair reached out and grabbed Marshall's arm. "Where are you taking John," he asked. "Do you have medicine? I have an abscess in my leg that's spread up into my groin. Here, look." He pulled back his gown to reveal an angry red streak that followed the path of a vein in his leg until it ended in his genitals, which were swollen and discolored. "There's blood in my shit," he continued. "I'm dying; I need medicine."

A woman took hold of his other arm and shook it. "Me, me. Look at me!" she shouted desperately. "I have a tumor in my throat and thyroid, and it's choking me to death. I was in Chicago when the bomb went off. Where is Doctor Lee? He hasn't been here in a really long time. We have no food." She let go of Marshall and began to cry.

"I'm sorry . . . Truly, I'm sorry, but I can't help you." He pushed past them and continued toward the exit, aware that those around him sensed he didn't belong.

"Hey, why does John get medicine?" said someone from a far corner. A buzz rippled through the group as more patients came into the crowded room.

Sarah looked over at Marshall and pointed at the door. "They're blocking us. There's no way we can get through that."

As the man standing closest continued to paw at him with a hand crusted in diabetic boils, Marshall reached out and probed his mind. He crawled through the frontal lobes that controlled judgement to the temporal lobes that held memories. Turning to the woman next to him, he repeated the process with the same result. He plunged into a third mind and then a fourth, each time with more desperation.

"Marshall, is there something wrong?" asked Sarah as she reflected his obvious concern.

"I can't influence any of them," he said in a tone that expressed his growing frustration. "Their brains have been so wasted by drugs, disease and trauma there's nothing there. It's like grabbing hold of a piece of ice."

"Then we'll have to try something else," she said. The woman with the throat tumor and thyroid cancer continued to brush up against her with hot breath that smelled of sickly sweet rot. Sarah leaned over and spoke in her ear. "Can you keep a secret?"

The woman pulled away and nodded enthusiastically. Sarah looked around as if she was making sure no one would overhear them. "Can you help us get down to the first floor? They've brought in medicine, food and new, clean hospital gowns they're hiding and hoarding for themselves. It's all in the pharmacy supply room. Why don't you follow us down there, and you can get some of it before they're all out? Just don't tell anyone, ok?" The woman shook her head and brought her fingers to her lips.

"Shhhhh . . ."

Still focused on finding a path through the throng of increasingly hostile and tightly packed patients, Marshall put his arm out and pushed, but every time he moved one person, another would take his place.

"Marshall, just wait."

"We have to get out of here, Sarah. I'm experiencing a high level of claustrophobic anxiety."

"Listen to me; just stand here a moment. When the crowd moves down toward the stairway, we must act quickly."

With a puzzled look, Marshall stopped and stood in place. He tried to prop Zach up, but the tousled invalid was mumbling and seemed to nod off. Just as he was about to remind Sarah of crowd's rising hostility level, the group ahead surged forward and began to thin. Within a minute, the entire gathering inside the hospital room cleared as people from adjacent rooms heard the commotion and joined in.

"Now!" said Sarah as she grabbed Zach, opposite Marshall. Sarah counted on the old woman to not keep her secret, and she didn't disappoint. There was a mad rush to the pharmacy supply room, and it provided the opportunity and space they needed to move Zach. Together, they kept him upright while shuffling toward the doorway, following the crowd until eventually reaching the hallway and staircase.

Somehow, they managed to get down two flights without falling, although they came precariously close at one point. At the bottom of the stairs, Marshall noticed a throng of angry patients over at the pharmacy beating on the door and shouting threatening demands. The admissions nurse and two other staff members tried to satiate the mob and diffuse their anger but to no avail.

Sarah pointed to an exit at the opposite end of the foyer, and they made it to the back of the building with little attention and only minor jostling from the stragglers at the very rear of the crowd. Once outside, they paused a moment to catch their breath.

The strain of walking down the stairs and through the lobby taxed Zach to his limits, and he leaned up against the wall, overcome by sickness, fear and exhaustion. He had no clue who these people were or what they intended to do to him. His doctor had abandoned him, and now he was being kidnapped by strangers who claimed they knew him.

During his stay at the hospital, Zach was physically assaulted and emotionally tormented by his fellow patients, and his small food ration was stolen almost every day. By the time Marshall and Sarah found him, he hadn't eaten in nearly a week and was reduced to drinking water from the toilet. His ribs showed through stretched skin and deep circles ringed his eyes. "Please," he said as he felt a hand on his arm, "don't hurt me. I can't take getting hit or burned anymore." He shook his head and began to weep.

Sarah stumbled and nearly fell to her knees as if she had taken a punch directly to her midsection. "This is too much, Marshall," she said while dabbing her eyes with a tissue. "I can't see him like this."

"Let's get out of this place." Marshall repositioned Zach's arm around his shoulder and started walking out into the parking lot. Once they were far enough away from the building, he helped Zach sit down curbside on an entrance driveway.

"Stay here," he said to Sarah. "I'll get the SUV." As he ran towards the largely empty lot, his eyes swept back and forth until he found the FJ Cruiser. When he located it, Marshall could tell something was wrong even at a distance. The vehicle was equipped with a variety of anti-theft measures, including bulletproof glass, tire puncture resistance, engine kill device, and an electric current fed into the body to shock would be thieves. Yet, as he grew closer, Marshall could see a huge dent in the driver's door and several long scratches running down the side panels.

Moving closer, he noticed the grilles over the taillights were ripped off, and the lights were smashed as the plastic shards lay on the pavement. Looking at the body, he noticed several large puncture holes in the doors and fenders. Someone took shots at the SUV from point blank range with a high caliber rifle. Holding his breath, he walked to the front of the vehicle, pausing for a moment to assess the damage. His heart sank as he looked at the mangled grille and the holes in the top of the hood.

The protective plate welded behind the grille saved the radiator, but as Marshall raised the hood, he saw the extensive damage the bullets had done to the engine compartment. Wires were sheared in several places, and a valve cover and the alternator took a direct hit. He punched a button on the key fob to start the engine, but the only sound was the clattering of a dead battery.

Dejectedly, he walked back to the parking lot apron where Sarah was still waiting with Zach. "They destroyed it, Sarah. Shot it full of bullet holes. I should have found a safer place to park."

She brought her hands to her forehead. "What the fuck are we going to do now? I don't know how much longer Zach can last. He looks like he's ready to collapse."

"It's my fault," he said. "I should have known that a new SUV like that would create an obvious target. I'm sure that when they realized they couldn't steal it, they destroyed it instead."

"None of that matters now," said Sarah. "We need to figure how we're going to get Zach out of here."

Marshall shook his head. "The chances of getting someone to give us a ride to Sedona are negligible, but that's our only alternative."

He looked around for a moment and then pointed down Van Buren. "Let's walk in this direction. The closer we get to downtown, the better our chances of finding a ride."

Sarah looked up and down the street. "I say we go the other way. Downtown in a major city is where we'll find the worst violence."

Marshall paused a moment and nodded. There was no point in arguing since the chances of making it back to Sedona were negligible, no matter which way they went. Turning slowly, they began moving toward Van Buren as Zach rasped, "Water. Please, I need water, Thomas."

With a sense of hopelessness, Marshall bore Zach's weight and stumbled down the road, covering ground at a painfully slow pace. Even though it was midafternoon, and Van Buren used to be one of the busiest downtown streets in Phoenix, he didn't see a single car for several minutes. So, when a late model Kia compact approached from behind, Marshall thrust out his thumb as he once read was the custom for hitchhiking. Half hoping the car would pass, he was surprised as the driver slowed and pulled up next to them. The only thought in his mind was to protect Sarah since the likelihood of a violent confrontation was high.

The dark tinted glass window slowly opened. Leaning over, the driver said, "Get in the car right now. There's a gang of floaters coming up from the west."

"Delgado!" Marshall fought against opposing feelings of gratitude and revulsion. In the end, gratitude won out. He looked up at Sarah who stood stoically with Zach's arm still draped over his shoulder.

"I—I still don't trust him, Marshall," she said.

"We have no choice but to trust him. Now get in the car." He opened the door to the backseat and motioned for her to get in. When she hesitated, he said, "Sarah, get in the goddamned car."

She was taken aback, and her eyes widened. Pausing for only a moment, she helped Marshall load Zach into the backseat before she got in alongside him. Marshall climbed into the passenger's seat next to Delgado.

"Where did you get a car?"

"You left me in there to die." Delgado stared straight ahead as they accelerated away from the building. "They nearly trampled me to death; someone tried to stab me."

Marshall looked away. "The only priority is protecting the Speaker. I'm sorry, but you are inconsequential. Sarah and I would sacrifice ourselves for his safety. Considering the horrific crimes you have committed against humanity, you must understand that your life has little value to us."

"Actually none," added Sarah.

"Well, you're welcome." Delgado's hands tightened on the wheel. "I escaped the crowd and got out of the building. My intention was to leave and see none of you again. However, I watched the street thugs destroy your SUV and knew you'd never make it out of here alive. I, ah, found this vehicle nearby and stole it."

"Unlikely," said Marshall with a dubious expression. "There aren't any cars just sitting around anymore, and with anti-theft technology, it is virtually impossible to start a late model vehicle without a coded key."

Delgado sighed and blew air out of his puffed-out cheeks. "Look, I have a master coded key that will start virtually any vehicle in North America. Remember, I was head of security for all of Gehenna. It was a perk of the job. There were several of them we took from the Department of Transportation right after the U.S. government fell. The CEOs from

114

the other corporations got one as well as Watts and I. There may be others, I don't know."

"Impressive," said Marshall. "It appears you covered every contingency."

"It's a trap," said Sarah. "I guarantee this car has a GPS monitoring device. He's leading us directly into danger."

Delgado reached under the seat and pulled out a harness with several frayed wires on either end. "Yes, this vehicle has a monitored GPS system, but now it is disabled," he said. "You can check it yourself if you like."

Marshall nodded and turned toward Sarah, who shook her head and looked out the window. "I still don't trust him," she said.

"Where to?" asked Delgado.

"Sedona," said Marshall. "Point the car toward I-17 north, and let's hope there aren't any road bandits."

"Sedona . . . Interesting." Delgado pressed the accelerator down further.

Chapter Ten

Just before noon, the air car began its descent into an area that appeared to be nothing more than densely vegetated Congo jungle. Just as the craft cleared the tree line, Mr. Cox could see an encampment below. Several pup tents dotted the landscape, and people in uniform walked back and forth across a patch of cleared ground that covered about half an acre.

The wings shifted and retracted before the vehicle settled gently down on the ground. The hydraulic doors opened, and the Benefactor got out as Term and Malconus followed. Looking around with expectations of a greeting befitting the head of the world's governing body, Mr. Cox saw a lone person in battle armor approach. His face was drawn and his eyes had the sunken look of someone under perpetual stress.

"Forgive me, Chairman Coxnotus," he said while bowing awkwardly. "I am Major-General Ignasus Cron. We only became aware of your arrival an hour ago. Our remaining forces are battle weary, and we suffer defections at a staggering rate. If this continues, we will not have anyone left to fight."

Mr. Cox looked around at the tents scattered around the moist ground. "How many troops are in this division?" he asked.

"Division? There was a time when we had that many soldiers, but we are down to a company. Last count, there were approximately 50 soldiers continuing to fight."

"50 . . ." said Mr. Cox while shaking his head in obvious disgust. "50 soldiers defending the empire I built... And the enemy, how strong are they, and what level of casualties have they taken?"

Cron looked down at the dirt and kicked at it with his worn boot. "This is an asymmetrical war, Chairman Coxnotus. We are fighting two fronts. Amrosia has us outnumbered, and the pacifists refuse to fight back. When we battle Amrosia, we suffer more casualties than they do. We have slaughtered the pacifists, but they have a seemingly endless supply of zealots. In the end, we have lost thousands by attrition as they convert to the other side."

"Traitors? Deserters? They must be killed. All of them."

"We have tried that during various conflicts, but it only seems to accelerate the process of defection."

Mr. Cox began to pace. "Let us start with the pacifists since this is the larger threat. Is there a front in this conflict?"

"Yes," said Ignasus, "but it is not a war zone as you might imagine. They just keep moving forward to the next town or village. Every day, they hold meetings that can only be termed as 'brain washing,' and eventually, most of the people convert. It has been happening all over the world for two centuries, but the pace has accelerated in the last 50 years."

"Brainwashing meetings? Is that what is taking place in Nzoni? If so, I must go there immediately."

Ignasus pointed toward a land crawler in the distance. "Nzoni is only a mile or so from here, so it will not take long to reach. I know exactly when and where these pacifist conversion meetings are held. I will give an order to get the troops assembled for battle."

"No," said Mr. Cox with emphasis. "As you said, this conflict is asymmetrical. There will be no fighting today, at least not with the pacifists."

"As you wish, CEO Coxnotus." Cron bowed and excused himself, summoning a driver and motioning him to retrieve a land crawler.

Within minutes, Mr. Cox climbed aboard with Cron, Term and Malconus, and the vehicle drove down a makeshift road, plowing through the dense underbrush of the encroaching jungle. The earth was soft and moist, and the land crawler struggled to get through the craters and over the mounds. The temperature was in the mid-90s, with oppressive humidity even for January.

After a mile or so, the driver veered off to the left onto a rarely traveled pathway. She elevated the crawler several inches to avoid the thickest vegetation, but the dense leaves and stalks still provided a steady drone of sound as they impacted with the metal hull. A hard right put them on a road paved with cernesium crystal, and the driver switched over to the grid for power as they approached the city.

With a population just under 60,000, Nzoni was the largest metropolitan area in the south central part of the continent although it once was home to two million inhabitants. Over the three centuries since the Corporates assumed global control, world population plummeted to just over 300 million people. Famine, disease, pestilence, depression and strict child bearing laws drove the numbers down to a level where the earth's limited resources were in somewhat of a balance with its inhabitants.

Like most cities, Nzoni was a ghost of its former self when open-air markets dominated the streets, and vendors offered fresh produce and meats to a thriving, healthy population. Residents found an abundance of goat's milk, tender llama and other staples that kept the children happy and well fed. Unfortunately, those days had long passed, and rule under the Corporates was harsh. For those still living in places like Nzoni, Corporate-issued protein gruel was supplemented with native plant roots, insects and whatever game could be scrounged from the jungle.

The vehicle drove through several streets, turning sharply and stopping in front of an old building near the center of town. Unlike the mud huts that lined both sides of the street, this one was made of brick, and although it was in obvious disrepair, the architecture suggested it once served as a house of worship.

The driver opened the rear door while saluting as Mr. Cox stepped out and looked at the large crowd gathered outside the entrance. "We seem to have the good fortune of arriving during one of their 'brain washing' sessions, Cron," said Mr. Cox. He turned and faced the old church as a nauseating wave of levity and gladness washed over him. The sensation was so potent he nearly lost consciousness for a moment.

Whatever was happening inside the building elicited hope and a sense of optimism for these people, and their enthusiasm radiated outward. Term, Malconus and Ignasus may not have felt it consciously,

119

but they would be affected by it. Clearly, these positive feelings were the root cause of the defections.

Following the path of the Prana as it intensified, Mr. Cox identified the source of the emittance coming from inside. He walked toward the crowd without drawing attention, but when he started moving through it, his black energy signature briefly touched those within his sphere, causing them to instinctively recoil. Like water from oil, they separated while trying to shake the uncomfortable feeling. By the time he reached the steps with his companions, the crowd had parted and created an unimpeded path into the building.

Mr. Cox could barely hide his disgust as he went inside. The followers packed the pews so tightly there wasn't an inch of space between any of them. More people stood against the exterior walls, and he wondered how they could breathe in this stifling environment.

"You have such power within you," said the petite woman standing at what used to be the altar. She spoke in a voice that carried through the room, reverberating off the brick walls and high ceilings. Her blue jumpsuit must have been some kind of uniform, so it was easy to identify her companions dressed in identical garb standing behind her. "The power to change your reality is within your mind. There is nothing that anyone can do to you once you acknowledge the science of your soul. The secret is to understand how you were constructed." She paced behind the altar as though she was in a trance.

"Your soul is eternal, so no matter what happens to your body, you can take great solace in knowing you will endure. You have asked for all your experiences. They help you heal, and they bring your soul into alignment with your personality. By grand design, you were meant to live in love, not fear. You were meant to revere, not destroy. You were meant to help, not exploit. Every day begins with a choice of how you intend to live your life." She paused for effect and let the words sink in.

"Align your choices with your intentions. If you want to help someone, then do it. If you want to form a society where all share equally and no one wants, then do it." She pointed over to a skid full of burlap bags over in a corner.

"Inside those bags is the key to life. Seeds that can grow and feed everyone. When you grow and consume your own food, you nourish your body the way the universe intended. You will no longer need to wait for the trucks that show up less and less frequently with the unnatural poison they call 'protein porridge'." A murmur grew amid many heads nodding in agreement.

"All across the globe, communities have come together because they made the choice to love instead of hate. We have outlived the usefulness of governments. They never served the people; they only serve themselves. Whether it was democracy, tyranny, fascism, and yes, corporatism, in the end, it became all about control, oppression and external power. Well, our way is different. If you are with us, you will learn to exist for yourself and to help better the lives of others.

"The seeds we brought are designed to produce hearty crops in this climate. With our help, you will soon be able to feed everyone, and when that is accomplished, we will help you set up schools, workshops and trade centers. Soon, you will be self-sufficient, and you will be able to live your lives as you wish. For nearly two centuries our model has worked as we expanded throughout the world. We hope you join us . . . I look forward to questions if there are any."

The chatter rose as those native to the area buzzed with excitement and suspicion. For as long as they could remember, their families were forced to work in the harshest conditions under the cruel and merciless rule of the Corporates. They were exploited in the mines and forests, harvesting raw goods used to construct the increasingly complex machines the Udulates needed to pamper their already privileged lives. Most died before they reached 50.

"Does this mean we can stop working for the Corporates?" asked a frail older man in a tattered corporate-issue beige T-shirt and matching shorts. He was dressed like 90 percent of the men in the church.

The woman nodded. "Yes, that is exactly what it means. We brought enough food to feed your families until the crops grow and you become self-sufficient. There is no reason to endure the danger of working in unsafe conditions anymore. Those called the 'Corporates' no longer have influence here."

"But—but they will come to kill us," said a woman in a beige version of what the men wore, only cut to fit the different contours of the female body. "Many of our forefathers refused to work, and the Corporate elite guard killed half of them and left the corpses in the streets until the buzzards came to pick at their organs. Every time someone brought a story of salvation, the Corporates would kill them in heinous ways, and our lives would only get worse. What makes you any different?"

The woman behind the broken and crumbling slab smiled. "The difference is we are only marginally invested in our physical bodies. Once we accept that our immortal soul cannot be harmed or destroyed, the pain we experience on earth becomes far less important. Around the world, there have been horrible massacres of innocent people, and yet, our movement grows. The destroyers are the only ones who ultimately suffer because they must experience the same anguish they inflict on others before they can graduate from Earth School. It is tragic, really."

"I—I do not understand," said a woman from the back. "We have families to protect."

The woman nodded. "Yes, we are all concerned with our families, but when you join us, you will see that the higher power ensures that no one ever really dies. Instead, their energy essence is simply transmuted into a different form."

A silence fell over the gathering as those listening carefully considered her words. They knew of the legends of passive resistance that led to liberation. The movement was spreading to the south like an out-of-control wildfire, and yet, after hundreds of years of horrific oppression, did they dare hope?

"I will leave you to discuss this amongst yourselves. As you know, we are camped just outside of town. If you would like us to help you, send someone to contact us. Regardless of the path you chose, we will continue to assist in any way you deem appropriate. We hold more of these meetings daily, so you are always welcome. Thank you. I appreciate the audience."

A smattering of applause came from different quarters of the building, but the scene remained awkward. For a people used to backbreaking work and minimal comforts, the prospect of a life without restrictions was unnerving. The concepts the representative spoke of were alien and challenged the limits of their comprehension. Still, word was these "pacifists" were prevailing wherever they went, and they hadn't fired a shot or committed a single act of violence.

With the meeting dismissed, those looking for an early exit stood up and began making their way toward the aisles. Amid much talk and clamor, a strong voice spoke up from the back.

"Wait, before anyone leaves. Why should we delay any longer in making our decision?"

Those nearby the slight man with the pasty-white complexion, red lips, and gleaming teeth took notice first, but soon, the whole crowd stopped and looked at him. The woman who made the presentation was leaning over, replacing some papers in her backpack when she heard his voice. She stood up and faced him.

Mr. Cox' smile widened as he addressed her directly. "Ma'am . . . Excuse me, but I was a bit late. Could you tell me your name?"

She walked to the front of the altar and looked out until she placed him. "My name is Susan Keynes."

"Ah," he said while nodding. "Susan Keynes. So, you have abandoned your issued designation in favor of an ancient name. How . . . quaint."

She smiled. "My name is not a statement. It is simply something that pleases me. Of course, others are free to adopt names that please them. Some may continue to use the Corporate issued name. It is nothing of consequence."

"Oh, but I disagree," Mr. Cox replied as he moved closer to her. "Adoption of a name that is not a Corporate designation is a true act of defiance. It is your way of saying, 'I do not answer to the Corporates' is it not? I am not passing judgment. After all, every rebellion has to have its open acts of defiance."

She looked down for a moment, but her own smile never wavered. "So, we have a Corporate agent in our midst." By now, everyone who was leaving had turned back inside or sat down. "Please," she continued, "you have the floor."

Mr. Cox put his hand over his chest and mouthed an exaggerated, *Me?* He looked around at the crowd before turning back to the woman. "My friends," he said, "the year is 2364, and no one remembers the circumstances that ushered in the era of the Corporates. Perhaps it is best to look back in history at the tumultuous, dare I say barbaric, times that led to their ascension. Nuclear weapons were detonated in major cities; there was chaos in the streets. Brutality unlike any seen in history. The Corporates saved you from that."

"The Corporates instituted totalitarian rule that crushed the human spirit," said Susan Keynes. "Their harsh treatment of people resulted in the deaths of billions."

Mr. Cox raised his eyebrows and chuckled. "At seven billion, the population was unsustainable. Human beings were as plentiful as cockroaches, and their lives were about as meaningful. Loss of life is regrettable, but it did heal the planet."

"They forced countless people to work in squalid conditions for the pleasure of those few of privilege."

"And yet," said Mr. Cox, "those who worked were alive and not dying from street violence, military conflict or nuclear destruction."

For just a moment, a slight trace of anger was evident in Keynes' voice. "You distort the facts. The

Corporates caused more hardship and committed more genocide than Pol Pot, Leopold, Stalin, Kahn and Hitler combined."

Mr. Cox rubbed his chin in contemplation. "Interesting choice of historical figures, but you are grossly inaccurate. The Corporates brought peace to a united world."

"They ruined countless lives."

"They gave equality to the masses."

"They exploited people for their own gain."

"The established peace and ended war."

"They altered time . . ."

The steady undercurrent of low chatter stopped, and an uncomfortable silence descended like a heavy blanket. Mr. Cox' eyes grew wide, and he took several steps forward. "Who told you such a thing?" he asked.

"No one," she blurted. "I—I was speculating, that is all."

"No, you were not speculating. Tell me what you know."

Keynes backed up several steps as Mr. Cox closed the distance to ensure his mental probe would strike her with maximum potency. When the tendril reached her skull, she staggered back and nearly lost her balance as her associates rushed forward to help her regain her footing.

"My friends," said Mr. Cox to the audience at large. "Solsus Purf, which is her true designation, has spoken eloquently and painted a wonderful utopian picture." He partially withdrew from her mind and slowly moved his eyes through the crowd. Momentarily relieved of the invasive assault, Keynes rigid body slumped, and she breathed deeply while trying to regain her composure.

"I have to wonder just how much 'Susan Keynes' actually believes in her words. He whipped his head around and plunged back into her cerebrum, rifling through her prefrontal cortex while stimulating her pain receptors.

Despite her training in mind discipline, Keynes was not prepared for an incursion from someone so powerful. Her head pounded with horrible pain, but she was unable to scream since Mr. Cox disrupted the synapsis between her brain and vocal cords. He assumed control of her autonomic functions, so she appeared perfectly normal. In fact, he sent a message to the areas that controlled her facial muscles, and she smiled.

After a few moments, Keynes walked out from behind the altar and assumed a relaxed posture with her hands clasped in front of her. No one in the audience could have guessed that she felt as if her brain and internal organs were being seared by an acetylene torch.

"Well, do you have something you want to say to us?" Mr. Cox asked.

She nodded slowly. "Yes, I do."

"Certainly, but just a moment . . . You see," said Mr. Cox to no one in particular but loud enough for everyone to hear, "the hypocrites are still alive and well even in this century. Solsus Purf, oh, excuse me, 'Susan Keynes,' is more than willing to sacrifice your lives to gain power, but her willingness to personally sacrifice only goes so far." He turned back to Keynes. "Is that not correct? Now, let us start fresh by having you tell everyone your true name."

Keynes swallowed hard, but his control of her mind was complete. Her free will was cast aside as nothing more than a slight distraction.

"Please, what is your designation?" he asked as his eyes burned with an intensity reserved for his most intense conflicts.

He forced her to widen her smile, and she said in a soothing voice. "I—I am Solsus Purf."

"I see," said Mr. Cox as the fire in his eyes dimmed a bit. "And what is the purpose of your visit here today?"

"I would rather not say," she replied.

"Come, come, Purf. Please, tell us the truth. If you do not, I will be forced to reveal certain documents that could seriously undermine your credibility. Would you not rather admit to your past transgressions and keep some shred of dignity?"

Her head tilted forward, and she mumbled in a nearly inaudible voice, "Yes, I suppose."

"Well then, do not keep us waiting,

"We are here to lead these people away from the protection of the Corporates so they become vulnerable and dependent on us. Once they have no alternative, they will serve. If they fail to comply, we will . . . we will kill them all."

A collective gasp went up from the gathering followed by a low-level murmur.

"That is not true!" said one of her colleagues as he looked at Mr. Cox with a sense of outrage. Purf stared out at the crowd impassively while Mr. Cox continued to manipulate her neural pathways.

"It is a terrible thing you are doing to these poor people. I hope our exchange has helped you to see the error of your ways," he said in a voice dripping with sarcasm.

"It has," she replied as he momentarily lessened her pain as a reward for the 'correct' answer.

"And what would you advise would you give these good people now that you have purged the poison in your mind and the truth has liberated you?"

"I would advise them to forget the foolish notions I was preaching earlier. In my arrogance and thirst for power, I lost sight of what matters most. The Corporates are the only entity that can provide any sense of safety and security."

"Susan, that is enough!" A man behind her stepped forward and grabbed her shoulder, but she pushed him away.

"But not the corrupt and illegitimate Amrosian Corporates," she yelled out. "Only Gehenna can save us all. And only if you are the CEO of Gehenna," she said while pointing at Mr. Cox. "I pledge my loyalty to you, Prevus Coxnotus!"

Mr. Cox smiled and immersed himself in the smells, sounds and sights of the chaos and betrayal he felt from the crowd as they reacted to her words. That's what made it all the more irritating when he felt the hand of Minkus Term on his arm.

"Prevus Cox, we are doomed. Dantar Llross's troops have arrived. They will take pleasure in killing us all."

Chapter Eleven

Winn's eyelids fluttered as he tried to clear the cobwebs from his mind. As the fog receded, he recognized the familiar gun barrel held to his head by a grinning Darryl. Instinctively pulling up against the restraints, he became aware of the surrounding reality. Another "session" with Norma and the kids. The injections had become so routine, he only occasionally screamed as the caustic substances flowed through his veins. He also learned that pleading just brought more pain as Norma assumed she was close to breaking him. Thus, he refused to beg no matter how much he was suffering.

Yet, the mental aspects of the procedure continued to erode his sentience and ability to reason. The deterioration of his mental faculties grew worse during each episode. The drugs that forced him to admit every lurid detail of his life and childhood were painful and humiliating, but the deliberate manipulation of his brain waves and electrical fields was so intrusive he found it unbearable.

Whatever technology she was using, Winn could feel his thoughts and memories changing as the drugs and machine did its work. With a subtle turn of a dial or input on her keyboard, Norma could alter his memory of an event, his belief on an issue, or his emotional response to a given stimuli. She might show him a video of a beheading and purposely influence his reaction. He might look at the unfolding tragedy and begin weeping, but within seconds, he would find the scene so funny he couldn't stop laughing.

The toll this took on him physically and emotionally was enormous. Always, the questioning focused back on Sedona. Why was he going there? Where exactly was he going? Who was he meeting there? When she couldn't elicit the desired response, Norma's already sour demeanor worsened, and that's when the pain ratcheted up.

"Look at the screen, Doc. What do you see up there?"

Winn squinted and looked at a projection on the wall of a man sitting atop another, his arms pinned down by the larger man's knees. The one in the superior position was pummeling the other with vicious blows to the face. Blood spattered from the man's nose as the cartilage tore and split. Winn could hear him begging for mercy.

"How does this make you feel, Doc?" asked Norma.

By now, Winn knew silence led to more agony. "Sad," he said. "It makes me feel sad."

As he was speaking, Norma adjusted the dials on the machine, and Win could feel the electrical current entering his head through the metal ring lattice attached to his skull.

His thoughts and emotions shifted as he continued to watch the brutal beating. In a few moments, a sadistic smile crossed his face, and his eyes widened as he leaned forward.

131

"What do you think about it now, Doc?"

"It's good. I like it. I hope he beats the shit of that guy. Probably deserves it."

With a twist of the dial and a few more keystrokes, Winn was sobbing like a baby. His empathy for the victim was overwhelming, and he began to sputter and moan. "No, no . . . make it stop, Norma . . . please. I can't watch anymore. The brutality is too much."

The scene ended abruptly, and Winn slumped over, his head hung low. "Tell me, Doc, where were you heading when we saved you from the skankers?" Norma walked in front of him and grabbed his hair and pulled up, forcing him to make eye contact.

"Sedona . . . I've told you I was going to Sedona thousands of times. For the love of God, why do you keep asking me the same questions?"

Darryl stepped forward and shoved the barrel of the shotgun directly against Winn's temple. "Don't you talk to my mama that way. You apologize, or I'll turn your brains into wall splatter."

Winn shifted his eyes over to Darryl and back to Norma. "I'm sorry, Norma. I'll answer all your questions."

"Good. Where were you going once you got to Sedona?"

Winn shook his head and began to weep because he knew what would happen next. He would say he didn't know, which was the truth, but Norma would become enraged and inject him with another searing chemical to inflict more pain. He knew without a doubt that whatever was in the syringe was killing him. Two days ago, he felt a dull throbbing in his abdomen that was getting worse, and he noticed that his urine had turned orange.

"I don't know," he stammered while continuing to shake his head and cry. "I really don't know. I've thought about it a lot and tried to remember, Norma. I mean, I really, really tried to remember, but I don't think I ever knew it in the first place. But . . . but my mind is playing tricks on me sometimes. My emotions change so quickly even when I'm not in a session. My memories are getting all jumbled up."

"You having any more of those visions of people killing themselves, Doc?" she asked as she lit up a cigarette.

"No, no, I swear. I haven't had one since I came here. I swear."

She sat back. "Okay, Doc. I sort of believe you. But I've got to give you the tonic to keep the bad thoughts out of your mind." She reached over and grabbed a hypo, tied off his bicep, and jabbed the needle into a protruding vein in his left flexor. By now, Winn's arms were full of ugly red track marks. At least he wasn't being injected in his feet like Brandon.

"No, no, no," Winn whined piteously as the familiar fire spread through his body. Simon shoved a stick between his teeth to keep him from biting through his tongue as Winn went rigid. His muscles bulged while he pulled against the restraints and flopped around uncontrollably. As the seizure began, his heart rate topped 220 beats per minute, and he groaned in agony. In the ultimate act of humiliation, his bowels released as his body tried to purge itself of the poison.

Simon undid the straps, and together with Darryl, they dragged him into the shower, where a long hose was attached to the showerhead. After washing him off with cold water and rinsing out his underwear, they dressed him in his filthy clothing and brought him back to the basement. As always, they threw him down the last few steps before retreating into the house.

Nicholas crept over and watched as Winn's body shook and lurched with convulsions. "Get him some water," he said to Felicia. "They gave him too much juice this time. His eyes are rolling into the back of his head." Felicia pulled a cup of water out of the rusty pot. Without washing the water bucket, the boys merely filled it back up every day, so a thick green slick of algae grew around the rim. No doubt crawling with bacteria, every one of them had spent multiple nights with the shakes, diarrhea and sweats. Still, this was all they had to survive on, and Winn had it bad.

Felicia raised the cup to his lips. He gurgled and spit most of the rancid water out, but a few drops made it down into his stomach. Winn's breathing was labored, and he smelled like an unflushed toilet. The others, except Brandon, who remained huddled in a corner studying his forefinger, gathered round with looks of concern and worry.

The door from upstairs opened, and they collectively recoiled. Who had the next appointment with Norma and the boys?

"Dopey, get your ass up here," yelled Darryl in his deep, distinctive voice.

"He can't," yelled Nicholas. "The last session was all he could endure. He hasn't said a word since, and he spends all day looking at his finger and mewing like a cat. You've fried his brain, Darryl. There's nothing left."

There was a pause, and another shadow appeared in the doorway. "Dopey's not having

134

another session. He's leaving," said Norma as the distinctive foul smell of her exhaled tobacco wafted down into the basement. "He graduated from the academy. Now, get his ass up here, or the boys will come down there and cut his graduation short."

Nicholas motioned for help, and Paco and Bahatti followed him over to where Brandon sat in the corner, following his forefinger. Even though the drugs, electrical contouring and beatings had destroyed his capacity to think coherently, Brandon still reacted to primal threats.

He held out his arm and skittered farther up against the corner, shaking his head and whining in a singsong voice, although he didn't speak any specific words. With little resistance, Nicholas picked him up, and with help from the others, led him over to the stairs as Brandon's fear and droning protestations grew louder with every step. About halfway up the stairway, Darryl grabbed him roughly and pulled him the rest of the way. Brandon only offered token resistance by grabbing weakly on to the handrail.

"Say goodbye to Dopey," said Norma as she leaned her head through the doorway. "We got too many mouths to feed as it is. He's free now. See, I told all you freaks we was gonna set you free someday." She began laughing until the thick mucus in her lungs made her cough in deep bronchial spasms. The door slammed abruptly and plunged the basement back into darkness.

Several hours later, the group was still tending to Winn, who regained some degree of consciousness and was sitting up on his own. Felicia gently mopped his brow with a wet rag while Paco rubbed his shoulders. They collectively cringed when the familiar squeak of the hinges signaled Norma and the boys were back, confirmed by the sound of a body tumbling down the stairs. Winn thought Norma must have had a change of heart about Brandon. Nicholas got up and cautiously walked over to the stairwell and he stooped down for a moment, engulfed by the darkness.

"It's not Brandon, it's someone new!" he said in an excited but hushed tone. He reached down and put a hand on the new man's shoulder. "My name is Nicolas," he said.

Winn heard some shuffling before a weak voice replied, "My name is Lars," he said. "Where the hell am I?"

***

Wanda came out of her tent and looked at a small group of about 10 locals standing out in the street. Dirty, malnourished and desperate, she detected the smallest, dimmest glimmer of hope in their tortured eyes. From somewhere, they gathered a number of rusted, old, and in many cases broken garden tools. Shoulder to shoulder, Iris stood out in front of them with a smile on her face and a hoe in her hand.

"We're ready to go help plant them seeds you talked about, Wanda," she said while stepping forward. "But, how are we gonna water 'em? The water's been shut off for months now, and there's barely enough to drink when the Corporates drop off the barrels. That's why they don't let new people into the area. After the Pocks and Crege steal from us, there's not enough food or water as it is."

Wanda nodded to signal her understanding. "Our science people developed the seeds we brought with us, and they are extremely drought

136

resistant. They grow faster than regular seeds and need little water to flourish. We're going to need to find some big barrels — there should be a lot of old 55-gallon drums around here. Sand will clean them out."

"Sure. We can even skim two food and water empties before the Corporate drivers come to pick 'em up. They're always in a hurry to get out of here anyway, so I don't think they'll give us a hard time about it."

Someone from the back spoke up. We can find all the empty drums we want about a block down. That used to be a chemical distributor, and they never moved the barrels. Take a lot of cleanin' though."

"Good," said Wanda as her smile grew. "We'll get the seed bags and some tools out of the storage pod and bring them over to the lot. Give me about five minutes, and we'll meet you over there."

Wanda turned and walked back into the tent where Ngo and Arturo were actually talking to each other.

"You know this shit all sounds great until the OG hears about it. Then all hell will break, and they'll smash the whole camp and kill these people."

"He's right," said Arturo to Wanda. "I get all caught up in your talk of how we can make it better, but that ain't gonna to sit well with Terrell at all."

"And I assume he's the head of the Crege?"

Arturo nodded. "And I can't imagine Papa Grande will sit there and let this shit go on either."

"Leader of the Pocks?" asked Wanda. Arturo and Ngo nodded simultaneously.

"Well, we'll cross that bridge when we come to it. For now, we're going over to the lot on seventh to plant some lettuce, Brussels sprouts, broccoli, onions, peas and spinach."

"I—I gotta get back, Wanda," said Ngo. "They're gonna be wondering where I am. What am I supposed to tell Papa?"

"Tell him to come and talk with me. That's all I ask. The same with Terrell."

Arturo and Ngo stood up and prepared to leave before Wanda stopped them. "You know, a hug is a way to gain and transfer strength and love from each other. As humans, we're drawn to hugging because it's the closest we can get to our souls actually touching in this realm."

Ngo turned around and looked at Wanda. "Oh no, you must be fuckin' with me. There's no way I can hug him. Before I came here today, I would have killed him if we met out on the streets."

Instead of responding, Arturo simply held open his arms. Shaking his head, Ngo hesitated before moving closer and returning the embrace with obvious reluctance. Their contact was very brief, but when they separated, Wanda knew they experienced what she called, "the jolt." As a result of her training, she knew how to serve as a conduit between two people. With her involvement, their connection would be deeper and more fulfilling than either would be willing to admit. She almost laughed, watching Arturo and Ngo awkwardly waving to each other as they walked away with an obvious sense of conflict and confusion.

Sam and Jerry already pulled several sacks of seeds out of the pod and hoisted them over their shoulders as the group made its way over to 7th and Wall. The air was cool and crisp, a perfect Southern California day. Aisha and Talie stayed back at the camp, walking among those in the immediate area who lay on the sidewalks and streets. Regrettably, many of these people were addicted and hopeless, so providing salvation and rehabilitation would be a long and difficult process. Some were so damaged, they would probably not survive.

Wanda surveyed the lot before she spoke, carefully calculating the man hours it would take to prepare the area for planting. "Obviously, the first thing we need to do is clear the surface of debris. Let's get all the glass, metal and other garbage and make a pile on the sidewalk. Since there's no trash collection, we'll find a place to bury it."

They split up into different areas of the lot, picking up debris with their bare hands and putting it into old bags and sacks. The work was difficult and frustrating since so much was half buried, but after a few hours, they had cleared everything man made down to the fertile California soil.

"Now we need to form the rows," Wanda said. "Figure about two inches apart. Mark the placement and then make a furrow at about the depth of the hoe. Sow the seeds thick since many of them will die or get eaten by birds. When you're finished, cover them up and pack the soil with the back of a hoe."

She grabbed a pick and hoe and began to demonstrate the proper way to create a furrow. "Since we've had a fair amount of rain recently, I expect the seeds will germinate almost immediately. With any luck, they'll begin to sprout in a few days."

With time and more backbreaking effort, they slowly transformed the vacant lot into an agricultural field with a number of perfectly spaced seedling rows. Just a couple inches below the surface, the soil began to instantly provide the nourishment the seeds would need to germinate. Wanda turned her nose up and took a deep breath. She smelled more rain in the air.

The mood of the group was upbeat, and she made sure that Jerry and Sam continued to project the kind of optimism these downtrodden people needed to remain buoyed and optimistic. Iris sang a little tune as she worked, and Wanda noticed a sense of courtesy and civility she couldn't have imagined just a day ago. Of course, these weren't the gangs. They would prove to be a much greater challenge.

For now, Wanda would take every small victory she could. The work was just beginning, but the smiles, satisfaction and teamwork were all positive signs. Tomorrow, they would tackle the problems of waste disposal. She already had an idea where they could start digging natural latrines. After that, they would need to restore a fresh water supply by constructing a rainwater collection system.

When looked at in its entirety, the tasks were overwhelming, so it was important to stay focused on one objective at a time. As the group began to gather its tools for the return trip back to the cardboard boxes they called home, Wanda gathered them together.

"As a species, we invited misery when we deviated from our purpose. It was never about accumulating more things than someone else. Those are illusionary achievements that will only provide fleeting happiness. Instead, when we focus on working together for the common good, we gain a sense of satisfaction that is immeasurable."

She turned and gestured to the transformed lot behind her. "Today, you made a difference in your lives and the lives of those around you. This lot will provide fresh food for everyone in the area. Soon, we will politely refuse the chemical laced slop the Corporates give us. For now, that means they can feed others who need it more than we do. Eventually, everyone will grow their own food."

A man named Gus looked at Wanda for a moment and then dropped his pick and began to clap. Soon, others joined in until everyone was clapping together. It had been a very long time since Skid Row had experienced the emotion called hope.

Chapter Twelve

The trip back to Sedona was long and treacherous. Gangs controlled the freeways, and the bandits grew bolder and more vicious by the day. This forced Delgado to take a circuitous northeast path to Route 87 and then to RR 3 into rural desert areas that were desolate and unforgiving. This detour added nearly two hours to the trip, and even then, they were still exposed and vulnerable.

Around Strawberry, a house burned in the distance as a woman and man tried desperately to flee, pursued by a gang of thugs. Marshall turned away because he already knew the outcome. They would kill the man before raping the woman, and both would be left to rot by the side of the road. The landscape in the rural areas was nearly as savage as the inner cities, and those without the means to adequately protect themselves were prey to the animals that looked to exploit and steal what people had taken a lifetime to accumulate.

When they were about half an hour from the junction with 89A, Marshall turned and looked back at Zach, who sat slumped over with his arms wrapped around his head. Sarah whispered words of encouragement, but they didn't seem to console him.

They drove another thirty miles before he finally spoke. "Where are we going? Who are you people, and where are you taking me? Am I going to see the specialist Doctor Thomas told me about?"

"There is a doctor where we're going," said Marshall. "You'll be taken care of properly, and they'll help restore your sight and memories."

Sarah's hand crept over and took hold of Zach's and squeezed it softly. "Am I supposed to know you?" he said without turning his head.

"Yes," said Sarah as the tears welled up yet again. "You know Marshall and me very well."

"I—I sense sadness in your voice," Zach replied. "I am very frightened. It's difficult when you can't remember who you are, especially when you're blind."

"Don't worry, Speaker, er, John," said Marshall. "We're going to get you the help you need."

"I hope you're telling me the truth. The people at the hospital were cruel, especially at the end. They stole my food and beat me. I didn't even know who was doing it." He paused for a moment. "I'm very hungry and thirsty. Can I please have some food and water?"

Sarah looked at Marshall, who shook his head. Unfortunately, all the supplies they had were in the SUV. "I'm sorry, but there is nothing in this car. But we'll be at the facility soon, and they'll give you water and food as soon as we arrive."

"Thank you. I don't think I'm well," said Zach, "and I think I soiled myself." The rank aroma of uric acid confirmed his confession.

About thirty miles past Mormon lake on Route 90, they encountered a pileup of vehicles blocking the road. Delgado slowed as they approached, creeping cautiously while surveying the scene. Marshall had developed the ability to assess a situation quickly using analytics combined with his telepathic abilities. The cars up ahead appeared carefully arranged to prevent a quick and easy escape, but even worse, there was energy from within the pile that felt aggressive and foul.

"Trap," he said just as two off-road motorcycles revved momentarily before pulling out from hidden spots behind the wreckage. Tires spinning within a cloud of dust, they leapt forward simultaneously as an off-road vehicle came over a hill from behind.

Delgado punched the accelerator and turned sharply to the left. Whether it was instinctual or planned, the decision was the correct one since it took the faster machine and more experienced operator temporarily out of the equation. The other bike accelerated on a path that would intersect with the Kia within seconds. In the backseat, Sarah leaned up and held onto the armrests. Marshall continued to look at the nearest motorcycle, and as it came closer, he could make out the black-clad rider more clearly. A woman hugged the frame of the machine, and she reached into her belt and pulled out a handgun.

The first jerk of the trigger yielded a loud crack and a puff of smoke. Marshall wasn't sure if she was firing a warning shot or just missed due to the erratic trajectory of the car, but when the underside of the Kia scraped against a small hill, he knew they wouldn't be able to travel off road and at this speed for very long.

"What's happening?" said Zach with urgency as his blank eyes opened wide. He grasped Sarah's hand tight as she tried to reassure him.

"Road bandits," yelled Marshall to the back seat. "We're trying to outrun them. Grab onto something."

The distance closed quickly, and Delgado started to brake, giving the impression he wasn't going to try to pass the biker. She kept her weapon pointed at them but appeared to slow as well while the buggy and second bike closed distance. Within 50 feet, Delgado hit the gas, surprising the woman, which caused her to hesitate. Unable to get out of the path of the car, she squeezed off a shot that hit the windshield, creating an inch-wide hole and a spider web in the glass. Marshall looked over at the slug embedded in his seat just inches from his shoulder.

Turning the wheel slightly, Delgado impacted the bike with the left passenger front bumper and fender. Clearly, he had previous experience driving a car in tense circumstances. The Kia struck the dirt bike in a way that protected the structural integrity of the frame while still mangling the fragile motorcycle.

For a moment, the rider's left leg was pinned between the bike and the car, and the intense pressure instantly crushed it. The bike jumped backwards and went airborne with the woman desperately clinging to the handlebars. After several spins in midair, it crashed to the ground and skidded several feet amid thick, dirty clouds of burning oil. The biker survived the crash, but she was underneath the wreckage, and with a pulverized femur, she wasn't going to be able to crawl very far.

While Sarah watched the woman's struggles, Marshall focused on her companion, who was approaching rapidly from the other side with malice. Delgado passed the blockade and steered the car back to the road. Just as the tires reentered the pavement, the man on the second bike pulled up next to them with a weapon extended, screaming at them to pull over.

"I need to stop," yelled Delgado. "He's got the gun pointed right at you, Marshall."

"Gun? Gun? Who's got a gun?" said Zach with the urgency of someone in full-out panic.

"No," said Marshall while keeping his eyes locked with the biker.

"I have to. He's going to pull the trigger!"

"I said, no. Just keep going and don't stop."

Delgado shook his head and floored the accelerator. The man on the motorcycle reacted and easily caught up, screaming a series of profanities as he lowered the pistol and took aim. Yet, instead of pulling the trigger, he inexplicably slowed and nearly stopped. Using his weight, he extended a leg and did a 180 degree pirouette. Sarah turned and looked out the back window as Delgado checked the rearview mirror, but neither noticed Marshall staring straight ahead. It wasn't until the biker opened fire on the approaching dune buggy that Delgado looked over at him with a confused expression.

The ORV swerved violently to the left, then over corrected to the right while the biker kept moving forward, emptying the gun until he crashed head on into the buggy. The sound of twisting and scraping metal was unnerving, and the flash fireball signaled that no one would need to worry about that band of marauders anymore.

"You did that, didn't you?" asked Delgado. "I've only seen one other with such capabilities."

Marshall remained stoic. "The difference is," he said, "I take no pleasure in ending a life. It poisons the energy, and a bit of me dies along with those who perish. Regrettably, there was no choice here. They would have robbed and killed us."

"How — how do you do it? Where does your power come from?"

"Just drive, Delgado."

"What just happened? It's so frightening to be blind like this. I feel helpless," said Zach.

Eventually, they followed several back roads until crossing the freeway at Kachina Village and connecting to 89A. Continuing south, Delgado drove them directly into Sedona. Moving slowly through the town, Marshall was surprised to see a community largely unaffected by the chaos that had overtaken nearly every corner of the world. While there were few cars on the road, bicycles were in abundance, and many of the local stores seemed to be open. It looked like the few chain stores that lined the highway were converted into shelters.

Even the artisan's market looked busy with a mixture of farmers from the local area selling fresh produce alongside painters, jewelry makers and carpenters displaying their wares. No one from the sanctuary visited Sedona since the excursion to find Marshall, and they were forced to turn back due to the overload of suicide visions. For whatever reason, only Marshall was immune, but he imagined that neither Zach nor Sasha would have any issues in Sedona. The people he saw appeared happy, and their energy flowed brightly in arcs of multi colors as they moved.

"Turn here," said Sarah as they reached Dry Creek Road and headed north. A few minutes later, Marshall saw the sign for Vultee Arch, and he told Delgado to stop. Without turning to face her, he knew exactly how the conversation would unfold. He only wished he could fast forward to its conclusion.

"We can't leave him here, Sarah."

She shook her head, and her eyes flashed with anger. "You can't be serious. He's a butcher. Just let him fend for himself."

"Look at him. He's falling apart. He saved our lives and the Speaker's. There are no other options, and we owe him."

"We owe him nothing," she hissed. "You have no idea what this man has done. His crimes against humanity surpass Goebbels. We might as well bring a ticking time bomb into the sanctuary."

"But we already did that . . ." Marshall regretted saying the words as soon as they left his lips. He didn't need to access his learned responses to instantly sense her deep pain and hurt. Sarah gasped and covered her face with her hands and began to cry in long, deep sobs.

"What's wrong with her?" asked Zach. "Did I do something wrong?"

"No," said Marshall as he hung his head and looked at the floor. "You did nothing wrong. I did. I am an insensitive dolt, and I fear I will never master the art of diplomacy."

He remained motionless for some time, finally speaking in a low monotone. "You've taken us far enough, Delgado. We'll go from here."

Delgado let out a small cry of grief. "Please, you can't do this to me. I'm directionless and have nowhere to go. When he severs the connection, one feels helpless and lost. Please don't make me go back to Desolation. There's hardly anyone one left there, and I'll die alone."

"I'm sorry," said Marshall, "but there's nothing I can do." With hesitation, Delgado opened the door and started to get out.

"No, Marshall. That is your name, correct?" the small voice came from the backseat.

"What? Speaker Randall, are you with us?"

Zach shook his head. "I—I don't know. There are certain things . . . This place has an energy of some kind. I can't explain why, but I think you should take him with you."

Marshall motioned for Delgado to get back in the car. "We need to drive down Vultee Arch some distance. I'll tell you where to stop." He turned and looked at Sarah. "I—I don't know what to say. If you still want to leave him, we'll send him on his way."

She shook her head and said quietly, "If Zach says we need him, then he goes with us."

Delgado slowly slid back into the driver's seat. He looked at Marshall and began to speak but was waved off, so he grabbed the key and started the engine. Shortly thereafter, the Kia was climbing over bumpy, jagged, unpaved road until the terrain became too rough, and he brought the car to a halt.

"We'll walk from here," said Marshall as he got out and surveyed the landscape. The others followed him, and they took a pathway that would have certainly cratered their vehicle. After some distance, they approached the entrance to the facility, and Marshall stopped in a gully just below the base of the mountain and pushed his hand into Delgado's chest.

"Take off your shirt," he said.

Delgado looked stunned. "What? Why do I need to take off my shirt?"

"Please. I'm not in the frame of mind for argument. Just do it."

Slowly, without taking his eyes off Marshall, Delgado removed his worn long-sleeved button down. He handed it to Marshall who immediately walked

149

behind him and wrapped it around his head amidst Delgado's protestations.

"What are you doing? Are you going to execute me?"

Marshall rolled his eyes and shook his head. "No, you're not being executed. I'm going to bring you inside the sanctuary, but I fully recognize the risk you pose. Right now, you have a general idea where the entrance may be, but it is well-hidden, and it could take ten people months to find it even if they started from here."

He finished tying the knot tightly and then checked to ensure the material completely covered Delgado's eyes. They set out on an indirect path that included several turns that would make mapping even more difficult. The trek took much longer than it should have, but with two blind people in tow, Marshall was content to proceed as cautiously as possible.

Finally, arriving at the security panel, he typed in the code and waited until the massive red rock entryway slowly swung open. Sarah led Zach inside while Marshall gruffly shoved Delgado. The facility's residents occupied most of the foyer, filling it with the excited energy of love, tranquility and good will. Some were on their way to classes while others were returning from leisure activities, but all had a look of contentment and serenity on their faces. It was sight Marshall never grew tired of.

Almost reluctantly, he walked over to Delgado and removed the shirt from his head. After blinking several times, Delgado began to scan the immense interior of the facility. "This is beyond comprehension," he said after some moments. "The

Benefactor would give almost anything to know its location."

A sharp, open-handed punch to his solar plexus caused Delgado to double over and gasp for air. "I'll see you splayed open, and your insides fed to the vultures before I'll ever allow you to reveal the location of this place to him."

"Sarah!" said Marshall sharply. "This is a place of peace, not violence."

"I was merely making a statement. It was not about intent; I hate Cox as much as you do." Delgado pointed at Sarah as he talked while gasping for air.

"This place is called 'the sanctuary'." Everyone looked at Zach, who was fingering one of the smooth rock crystals that sat on a pedestal near the entrance.

"Yes, Speaker, that is correct. You are in the sanctuary. Do you remember?"

Zach looked upward with the eyes of a blind man. He strained mightily but to no avail, and his shoulders sagged. "I'm afraid not. Some things seem familiar, but just when I'm ready to grasp onto a memory, it evaporates like smoke in the wind."

Marshall looked at the pitiful sight in front of him. *How can we ever succeed without our leader?*

Hopefully, we won't have to. Whatever has happened to Speaker Randall, together, you and I will repair the damage.

Marshall smiled. Even with his back to her, he knew Sasha was nearby. Turning, his smile widened, and they quickly closed the distance and embraced. The instantaneous exchange of essence and energy rejuvenated Marshall's spirit, but when he finally let go of her, he instantly felt Sasha's pain. In the moment they touched, Marshall transferred the entire experience of finding Zach to her.

"Blind?" she said out loud. "He can't remember who he is, and he's blind?"

Marshall nodded. "I'm afraid so." He looked over at the frail man, still feeling the smooth surface of the large crystal, staring absently into the distance.

"Oh my God," said Sasha while stifling a sob. "What are we going to do, Marshall?"

"I don't know," he said. "We're all tired. The experience was very stressful, and we didn't expect to find Speaker Randall in this condition if we found him at all. I'd like a chance to take a shower and change my clothes. I'm sure Sarah feels the same way. And then there's Delgado . . ."

"Delgado?" Sasha looked over at the Benefactor's former lieutenant and then back at Marshall. "Have you lost your mind? You brought Cox' third in command into the sanctuary?"

"I agree with you," said Sarah. "It's a terrible mistake."

Marshall looked at them both with annoyance. "What Sarah's not telling you is that we would never have found Speaker Randall without him. He also saved our lives; it's that simple. He says he was disconnected from Mr. Cox and expelled from Gehenna after the bomb went off in their headquarters."

"And you believe that lying scum?" said Sasha.

"Speaker Randall told us to bring him in here, Sasha."

Sasha looked over at Sarah, who nodded to confirm. She turned back to Marshall. "I don't like it at all. It's bad enough we have Cox' Trojan horse still among us, but now you bring in one of the highest ranking aides?"

"If you have a problem with me, you just say it," said Sarah as she took several aggressive steps toward Sasha, whose muscles flexed as she turned to confront the threat. Marshall stepped between them and was about to intervene when a voice spoke from behind.

"Please, please, this is no way for you to conduct yourselves amongst these new residents. Everyone turned and looked at Pena, who gestured to the growing crowd forming behind him. They had started to attract attention, and several people in the foyer were watching the unfolding spectacle at the entrance. The smiles were gone, and the energy had darkened considerably.

"You're right, Pena," said Sasha as she backed away. "I'm entirely out of line, and I want to apologize to both Marshall and Sarah. I'm afraid my nerves are frayed lately with all that has happened to us."

Sarah sighed, and her posture relaxed. "It's fine, Sasha. Let's move on."

Pena looked at Delgado and his expression hardened. "I do not understand why you are here, Mr. Delgado, but I accept the judgment of the overseer. You will be escorted to your quarters where you can freshen up. You will not attempt to leave your room without your escort. Do you understand?"

Delgado nodded, and one of the new attendants that replaced Docker, who was tragically killed in Sarah's berserker attack, walked up and ushered him away.

After Delgado was out of listening distance, Pena ambled over to Zach, who remained stationary by the crystal. Sarah took his free hand in her own as Pena regarded the blind man.

"You have lost your identity, and that is a very terrifying thing, my friend," he said.

Zach perked up at the sound of the voice. "Yes, it is terrifying. Yet, I feel familiarity in this place. It calms me and brings me peace."

"Excellent," said Pena. "That is a start. We will escort you to your room, which is equipped for those who are sight challenged. You will find everything is sound sensitive, so you only need to issue a voice command, and the appropriate item will provide an audible aid to help you find and use it. If you need further assistance, an attendant will be right outside your door."

"Thank you," said Zach. "It sounds lovely compared to the conditions I have been living in."

Pena looked at the rest of the group and said, "It has been a very long day. Please, relax, get some sleep, and we will address this problem tomorrow morning. Let us meet after breakfast at eight o'clock at the entrance to the courtyard. It is imperative that we make our way back to the vortex."

Chapter Thirteen

The sound of heavy machinery hid the screams from the gathered townspeople as they ran frantically in all directions looking for an escape from the death trap inside the former church. General Ignasus spoke frantically through his embedded communicator while Term and Malconus moved swiftly to either side of Mr. Cox.

"Prevus Cox," said Term in a voice that reflected his angst, "we must somehow get you away from here. If we stay, it will most certainly spell doom for you." He gently touched the Benefactor's arm, but Mr. Cox immediately pulled away.

"There is no point in trying to flee, Term," he said. "They will have all the exits covered. We will have to confront them here."

"The odds are very poor," said Malconus in a low voice.

At that moment, the people at the front of the church parted, and a woman clad in a military style uniform walked in flanked by 10 soldiers with their coil guns at the ready. Her demeanor was confident if not arrogant. She thrust out her chest and raised her nose in the air as she looked around the room.

"By order of the Amrosia Corporation acting on behalf of the HUGE conglomerate, I am here to declare this gathering is in violation of Corporate law 16:52-9 that states: 'meetings, congregations and assemblies for the purpose of criticizing or questioning HUGE conglomerate policies are expressly forbidden. Each instance is punishable by no less than five years in a reeducation camp and no more than death'." She walked slowly until reaching the middle of the room.

"Clearly, you have all broken the law. The question is what should we do about it?" Pointing to the front of the room, she said, "I see you have pacifists leading the illicit meeting. Anyone cooperating with a pacifist is subject to immediate execution without trial."

The remaining members of the pacifist movement stood stoically without responding. Turning her head to the left, the troop commander nodded to the soldier directly behind her, who raised his weapon and fired five bursts, one for each of the pacifists. They stumbled before clutching at their wounds and collapsing, huge cauterized holes in the middle of their chests and abdomens. Someone in the crowd shrieked, which set off another stampede toward the exits, but the remaining Corporate soldiers had them blocked off.

"I can kill everyone in this room if you like," their leader said, "but I will let you all live if you do not cause any further problems. We are only here today looking for one person. He is a small, slender man with very pale skin. Do not try to hide him. We will look through every part of this building and kill anyone who tries to conceal him."

"Unnecessary," said Mr. Cox as he stepped forward. "I have no reason to hide. My purpose here today is to help these good people. We were making significant progress before you showed up and ruined everything."

"Prevus Coxnotus. You are under arrest by the direct order of Dantar Llross. Will you come peaceably, or will we need to take you by force?"

"Well, it appears you have us grossly outnumbered, so I should probably go with you . . . er, I do not know your designation."

"Ziertra X," she replied.

"Ah, a member of the Director's vaunted X Specialists," said Mr. Cox as everyone inside the hall continued to become more agitated and anxious. "I hear you can kill five people in less than three seconds with a graphite writing instrument. Is that true?"

"You would not want to find out, Coxnotus. Now, let us be on our way."

Mr. Cox nodded, and along with Term, Malconus and Ignasus, he began walking over to the center aisle as the sights of multiple plasma weapons and coil guns were trained on them.

"There is no need for violence," said Mr. Cox. He stretched out his arms. "I want all you good people as witnesses. I am Prevus Coxnotus, the rightful CEO of the Gehenna group. Your misery results from an illegal corporate takeover that corrupted the HUGE conglomerate. HUGE was supposed to bring peace and prosperity to everyone. But these people," he said while pointing at Ziertra X, "were corrupted by power."

"That is enough, Coxnotus," said X while walking up to him aggressively. "Another word and I shall personally shear off your left ear."

Mr. Cox reached up and fingered his ear gingerly. "Ooooo, only if you allow me to eat it," he said. Almost imperceptibly, X raised an eyebrow and flinched, which was an unusual response from an operative intensely desensitized to even the most shocking cruelties.

One of her agents walked over and stuck his weapon into the small of Mr. Cox' back, pushing twice to get him moving. The Benefactor scanned the crowd, making eye contact and probing minds as he slowly walked forward with his aides right behind him. About two thirds of the way to the exit, he found the person he was looking for.

The man was younger and naturally assertive in his demeanor. Within Nzoni, he was a member of the ruling council, so his word carried much weight. In just an instant, Mr. Cox learned he was skeptical of the pacifists but hated the Corporates. Even though he displayed no emotion, the Benefactor's statements relating to the hostile takeover by Amrosia registered with him.

Mr. Cox focused on suppressing the man's feelings of doubt and strengthened his desire to believe. Increasingly agitated, the spectator looked at the X Specialists. He opened his mouth to speak but then closed it. Another mental push by Mr. Cox was all the stimulation he needed.

"We must not let them take this man," he shouted above the din of the crowd. "What they are doing is illegal." The room went quiet as he stepped forward. "I am Slinkus Marnse. Most of you know me from the ruling Council. You all also know the story of how Amrosia saved the planet by replacing Gehenna as head of the HUGE conglomerate. Every child is taught this in the enlightenment classes. But what if it was a lie?"

X's agents waited for instructions to kill the agitator, but none were forthcoming. Anticipating such a response, Mr. Cox left Marnse and jumped into Zietra X's mind, interrupting the synaptic pathway that controlled her vocal cords and motor reflexes. Her eyes bulged as she strained to give a command, but she could only stand there motionless and paralyzed.

"We should not allow these agents to take this man and his companions," continued Marnse. "We must let him speak and tell us more about who he is and what his intentions are."

There was stirring in the crowd and some nodding of heads.

"Look," said a woman as she pointed up front at the altar where the five dead pacifist bodies continued to bleed out. "These people," she was now pointing at the Xers, "are butchers. If we allow them to take these strangers, they will undoubtedly be tortured and killed." As she finished speaking, the pathway to the entry in front of the Xers and Mr. Cox closed.

"X," whispered an agent who rapidly shifted the sights of his plasma rifle onto different people in the crowd. "What should we do?" he asked. "It is imperative we act quickly. Do you want me to kill the instigator?"

"No," creaked X in a voice filled with torment. Mr. Cox took full control of her thought processes and she was now merely an observer inside her own mind. "We must leave them behind, or this crowd will become even more unruly. Lower your weapons and start walking slowly to the door."

"But, X, this is a violation of a specific directive. We will most assuredly be executed for such a transgression."

"I have given you my orders," she said with Mr. Cox' planted inflections. Slowly her security people lowered their weapons and looked around with uncertainty.

"We are leaving," Mr. Cox made her say to the crowd. "Please step aside so we may exit."

The crowd parted enough to create a small corridor that led out of the building into the courtyard, and X and her team pushed their way toward the exit. Once they were outside, Mr. Cox forced her to give an order to fall back. For several seconds, her subordinates looked at her with incredulity born of behavior that was shockingly out of character. In fact, Ziertra X was notoriously bloodthirsty and ruthless as were all the X Specialists. They obeyed orders to the letter, but if they sensed vulnerability in a superior, it wasn't out of character to issue a challenge or organize a mutiny.

"Your behavior makes no sense, X," said the second in command. "We have explicit orders to apprehend Prevus Coxnotus and take him to the capitol."

"Our orders have changed," she said.

The second was a hulking man with one eye and a long jagged scar that ran the length of his bicep. "I do not believe you," he said. "Therefore, I issue a challenge,"

X walked up close. "If you disobey my order, I will personally see that your family gets assigned to the Mongolian iridium mines."

Calssus X inhaled deeply. "You scent has changed. Something is wrong here." He turned to the X Specialist standing nearest to him. "Kill her on my authority."

160

Mr. Cox cursed and released Ziertra X from his mental vice grip. She would need to control her own motor reflexes to stand any chance of repelling an assault. Not that he cared whether she lived or died, but a battle between two Amrosian factions would give the Benefactor and his team more time to escape.

He turned to Term and said, "This is our opportunity to escape. They will come back for us within minutes."

Term nodded and whispered something to Malconus, who moved quickly into the crowd and returned less than a minute later. "There is an exit on the far side of the room. The crowd will push through the barricade to help us get out."

Term nodded and relayed the information to Mr. Cox. Allowing Malconus to lead, they moved back up to the altar and followed a path past what was once the vestibule toward a side door sunk into the ancient brick. Somewhere within 25 feet, movement stopped as they heard the sounds of scuffling and shouting from the front of the crowd.

"The doors will open at any moment. We need to be ready. The size of the mass will provide anonymity and shield us."

Just as he finished speaking, the rotted wood gave way, and the pack surged forward, temporarily overwhelming the five Xers standing guard at the door. The scene instantly descended into chaos as the agents struggled to train their weapons on the charging mass. When the first plasma blast hit a man trying to push through the small opening, the crowd became primal as people scattered in every direction.

Their attention drawn away from the Ziertra X, her agents regrouped and formed a defensive position outside the church, firing plasma bursts and coil gun projectiles indiscriminately. The rapidity of the weapons discharge thinned the crowd considerably, and the layers of human shielding around Mr. Cox' entourage evaporated.

A plasma burst hit someone standing in front of the Benefactor, and as the man fell, he could see the weapon was now pointed directly at him.

"Listen to me," said Ziertra X to the agents behind her. "Prevus Coxnotus is capable of extreme mind control. He is excessively dangerous. Our only mission is to bring him to the capitol. If I rescind or change that order in any way, kill me immediately and continue on with the mission. If the next person in the chain of command rescinds the order, kill them too."

Mr. Cox jumped from mind to mind until he located the agent with the weakest resolve and dove into the victim's cerebrum, sending a message to his prefrontal cortex, prompting him to open fire on his companions. The rogue agent was able to gun down three fellow Specialists before multiple weapons fired, killing him. Instantaneously, Mr. Cox moved into the mind of the next weakest agent and repeated the command. Two more Xers went down before she was killed.

Sensing the slaughter would continue until her entire squad was dead, Zietra X screamed, "We have no choice, kill Coxnotus!"

In that moment, Mr. Cox realized he didn't have enough time to corrupt an agent to neutralize the remaining soldiers, so he threw up his hands and fell to his knees. "I surrender," he yelled to Zietra X. "No more deceptions. I will go willingly."

X held up her arm bent at the elbow. Her troops, with hair triggers, displayed astonishing discipline

162

as they refrained from firing another shot. X slowly approached Mr. Cox, talking as she closed the distance.

"Keep your weapons trained on him. If any agent shoots another, immediately fire at Coxnotus and his companions." Once she was within five feet of the Benefactor, she said. "You are much more cunning and dangerous than anyone suspected. I wish I was given the option to kill you because you would be dead where you stand."

Mr. Cox kept his face turned to the ground. "Then I suppose I should be pleased with the restrictive nature of your orders."

"Get up," she said, "and move away from your associates. They must be executed."

"No, that is unacceptable," he replied. "I will cooperate completely if you allow them to live. However, if you kill them, I will resist your efforts to apprehend me and leave you no choice but to violate your orders and terminate me. I assume that would guarantee your own demise."

She looked away for a moment. "Fine," she said with bitterness, "but any subterfuge from any of you, and I will have you all shot. My personal safety is irrelevant."

"It might be when I make you believe your skin is being removed one layer at a time," Mr. Cox said under his breath.

"Go over to that transport near the monument," said X, pointing to a large covered ground vehicle in the distance.

After standing up and straightening his clothing, Mr. Cox motioned for his companions to follow, and they moved in lockstep under escort by the remaining X Specialists. The situation appeared increasingly grim, and escape seemed impossible. He had little doubt that when they reached the headquarters in Jaunde, they would isolate him and begin the "experiments" until he revealed the location of the orb.

As Mr. Cox desperately looked for any means of escape, he heard the crack of a gun as a kinetic projectile ripped through the back of the skull of the X Specialist closest to him. For just an instant, the other agents looked confused and disoriented, and Mr. Cox used the opportunity to reenter the mind of Ziertra X, stimulating her aggression so she turned and began firing on her own people.

With essentially no lapse in time, multiple precision shots slammed into the remaining agents surrounding the Benefactor before they had time to react. Fully expecting he was the ultimate target, Mr. Cox fell to the ground and his entourage followed. Several seconds passed with only the sounds of the frightened crowd scattered throughout the muddled scene. When he finally opened his eyes and looked up, he could see the prone bodies of the X Specialists lying next to him. Every one of them had taken a head shot from a high-caliber kinetic projectile.

There was no reasonable way Ziertra X could have killed all of her own, which left Mr. Cox confused as he searched for answers. Through the smoke of weapons discharge and the dust raised from all the activity, a figure approached slowly from the distance, an ancient, semi-automatic assault weapon at his side. He walked over to Mr. Cox and extended his hand, which the Benefactor grasped and used as leverage to get to his feet. The man looked at Mr. Cox with steely blue eyes.

"Prevus Coxnotus, I am . . ."

"I know who you are, Lars," said the Benefactor.

The tall, muscular man with long blond hair backed away. "Yes, I am Sinorus Lars, but how would you know that? I received a message originating from General Ignasus Cron that you wanted to see me, but I have no idea who you are besides the anecdotal stories I have heard."

"You are part of the resistance, I assume?" said Mr. Cox as he walked forward.

"Yes, we are part of a loose confederation that fights against Amrosia and its surrogates." Lars lowered his head and spoke more slowly. "Yet, our efforts have not yielded the results we had hoped for. For every gain we make against Amrosia, the pacifist's reach extends tenfold."

"I am aware. Amrosia has done substantial damage to a perfectly conceived plan. However, I believe we can change the narrative, and you will play a significant role."

A sense of confusion crossed Lars' face, but Mr. Cox turned and walked back to the church where the surviving townspeople remained frozen, crouching down behind trees, stones and other objects that might provide protection from the onslaught. When he reached a spot where he could be heard by most people, Mr. Cox began to speak.

"It is safe," he began. "The brutal assault by Amrosia's X Specialists is over." Several people stood up slowly, but the major remained in hiding.

"Today, I offer you a new way," he continued. "Not the way of the treacherous fascists at Amrosia or the ineffective methods of the weak pacifists. Under my leadership, Gehenna will take back the HUGE conglomerate and implement policies that will bring peace and prosperity to the world for the next 1000 years. Only *we* can fight Amrosia on its own terms.

165

Inside the church, the dead bodies of the pacifists convey everything you need to know about their strategy. If you join them, you will most assuredly die."

More people stood up and listened to the Benefactor as he motioned for them to reenter the church. As they filled the rows, he walked up to the area that once held the pulpit.

"We can expect to see more Amrosian soldiers and more pacifists shortly. This area is a flash point and unfortunately, a battlefield. We will need to mobilize in preparation. I need to know if you are with me?"

Mr. Cox sought out the councilman he used before and found him shaken but still alive. He entered the man's mind once again, soothing his fear and bolstering his confidence.

The man stood up and faced the crowd. "I reject the pacifists. My family is too important to allow them to be used as fodder for their feeble approach to defeating Amrosia." He turned and faced Mr. Cox. "No, I am supporting Prevus Coxnotus and Gehenna!"

The applause that followed was authentic and enthusiastic. Mr. Cox was pleased, and he smiled widely. He fed off the fear that wafted up from the terrified crowd. As he looked at their tired, worried faces, he was starting to believe he might actually be able to salvage his plan after all.

Chapter Fourteen

"Well," said Nicholas to the rest of the group, "at least we know what happens when the eighth person arrives."

"Yeah, one of the other seven gets sent away to die in the streets," replied Felicia. "Brandon was almost a vegetable. There's no way he'll survive out there."

"It looks like you're the new Dopey," said Paco.

"What?" said Lars. "What the fuck is that supposed to mean? *Dopey?* I'll kick your ass you piece of shit."

"Wait," said Winn as he held out his arm to keep Lars from advancing on Paco. "He meant nothing by it. That bitch gave each of us the name of one of the seven dwarves from Snow White. We wondered what would happen when the eighth one showed up. Dopey's real name was Brandon, and they lobotomized him and turned him out onto the streets just before you arrived. We're betting you get his name."

As if on cue, the door opened and the stench of Norma's cigarette wafted down. "Dopey, get your ass up here. It's time for your first session."

Lars looked around curiously. "What the fuck is she talking about?"

Before anyone could answer, they all heard the cock of a shotgun.

"Damn it, Dopey, get over here, or Simon will blow your fuckin' head off."

"For God's sake, Norma, he hasn't even been here a day. Give him some time to adjust," said Nicholas.

"You shut your ass up, Happy, or maybe you'll get the next session. Dopey, this is your last warning."

Nicholas grabbed Lars' arm. "You better go. Simon might not shoot you, but his brother will surely taser you, and your session with Norma will be that much worse."

Lars hesitated for a moment before standing up and walking over to the stairway.

"Get them irons on, Dopey, and don't forget the leggins'." said Darryl. Slowly, Lars picked the leg irons up and fastened them to his ankles. He didn't need to be told what to do with the handcuffs.

As the door shut behind him, Winn looked over at Nicholas. "We've got to get out of this place, or we're all gonna die. They chemically lobotomized Brandon, and look at Renata. She's next."

Upon hearing her name, Renata stopped rocking and looked over at Winn. "How do I look? I don't look like I'm dying or anything, right? I mean, I still look pretty, right?" She reached up and gently touched her face with her hands. "Sometimes I can't remember things . . . Like, I can't remember my sister, but I'm sure I have one. I think I have one . . . don't I?" Her eyes closed as she strained to remember, finally giving up and resuming her rocking motion.

"I know," said Nicholas to Winn. "You're right, but I can't see any way to escape. I've been here . . ." he stopped to think, "three or maybe six months, and they never have let their guard down, not even once."

"There are seven of us and three of them," said Winn. "We can overpower them."

Nicholas shook his head. "It won't work. They always have two guns pointed at us . . ." He paused as an agonizing, muffled shriek sounded from above. Like all of the basement dwellers, Lars would eventually adjust to the repetitive abuse, but the first session was so intense the victim could only cry out in pain and terror.

Nicholas waited until Lars screams subsided and the moaning began, which signaled Norma had injected him with the "juice." He sat back and sighed as he reached for a cigarette. "Even more than escape," he said, "I want answers. I still have no idea why we're here. Why do our dreams of suicide scare these people so much, and how could this woman and her two imbecile kids capture us when the skankers couldn't?"

Winn shook his head. "I can't say, and I really don't care, but I'm not going to sit here and let them turn me into a blubbering idiot like Brandon."

For most of the next hour, Lars' wailing reverberated through the basement, causing everyone to cringe in sympathetic response with each tortured scream. After nearly three hours passed, the door finally opened, and Darryl and Simon repeated the routine of hauling the victim down half a flight of stairs before letting him fall the rest of the way to the bottom.

Nicholas, Winn and Felicia went over to Lars, who lay supine, his body jerking amid spasms and small tremors.

"He's swallowed his tongue," said Nicholas with alarm. "Let's prop up his head and open his jaws. Don't let them close, or he'll bite off your fingers." Even in the dim light, Winn could see Lars' face turning purple, so he grabbed the bottom of the fallen man's lower jaw and pried it open while Nicholas firmly held his skull in place. This allowed Felicia to stick her fingers in Lars' mouth and pull his tongue out from the back of his throat.

With his airway cleared, Lars breathed deep until his color slowly returned to normal. Felicia brought the rusted cup up to his lips, and he sipped at the rank water, struggling to swallow. Once he regained a semblance of consciousness, he sat up and coughed until his throat and lungs cleared.

"Can't stay here," he said in a slurred voice. "She'll kill us all. Have to get away."

"I know," said Winn. "We're not sure how to do it."

"I'm trained in special ops. Tonight, just before dinner. When they open the door, we'll be at the top of the stairs. Surprise them. They won't be ready for it."

Winn looked at Nicholas. "Will that work? They're bound to get a shot off."

"That's too risky. I think we need more time to plan."

Lars reached up and grabbed Nicholas by the collar. "Can't waste another minute waiting. Find a mirror. You're dying. You all look like Dachau prisoners," Lars said in a raspy voice.

Nicholas shook his head. "I know you're right, Lars. I'm just not sure if I want to die today."

From the corner, Bahati called out in a surprisingly calm voice, "Renata is fading away."

Winn stood up while Nicholas remained with Lars. He went over to Renata, who was lying on her soiled mattress while Paco and Bahati kneeled over her. As Winn approached, he saw Renata shaking and digging her fingers into Paco's arm. Bahati laid a damp cloth on Renata's forehead as she moaned and thrashed from side to side.

As soon as Winn kneeled down, Renata reached up and grabbed him with surprising strength. "Come inside, Winn. Come inside with us." For just a moment, Winn hesitated. He looked at Bahati and Paco, but both were completely still and had an absent look in their eyes.

"What? I . . ." Winn never finished his sentence as a strong gust of scorching wind enveloped him and blotted out the sparse light. The wind blew harder and began to draw in a dark, dense fog, and as it spread, he slowly realized he was being pulled into a vision. For some moments the nausea rose in his stomach, and a sudden, pounding headache felt like someone was jackhammering his skull from the inside.

With his sense of time distorted, Winn couldn't tell how long it was until the fog finally began to recede. Through the lingering haze, he saw a man sitting on a sofa chair inside a large, well-appointed room. Just within his peripheral vision, Winn noticed Paco, Bahati, Felicia, Renata and Nicholas standing near him. The man on the couch looked off absently in a way that suggested he might be blind. He held a long, thin piece of fabric in his hand that looked like the kind of belt used to keep a robe together. Winn glanced at his companions, and their eyes all seemed to lock together simultaneously, yet no one was able to talk or produce any sound.

The strange man got up and moved stiffly and slowly across the room. He extended his hand as he felt his way over to a bedroom door. When he found the handle, he opened it and tossed the loose end of the scarf

171

over the top of the door before closing it. After wrapping the other end around his neck and tying it off, he backed up against the door and started breathing heavily. At that moment, Winn realized this wretched soul was about to hang himself.

Stop! Winn shouted, but the words weren't spoken. In fact, there was no sound at all, but his companions turned simultaneously as though they heard him. The blind man stiffened and looked around in multiple directions. Apparently, he also heard Winn.

"Who said that? Who's there?" he said.

I — I said it. Winn spoke again, but this time, he realized the speech was originating from his mind rather than his vocal cords.

"Who are you? Do you know who I am?" The blind man inflections conveyed a sense of curiosity tinged with fear.

No, I don't know who you are, but it seems you intend to do yourself harm. Am I right?

The man hung his head. He spoke again, but this time his words were conveyed telepathically. *I have lost my eyesight and my memory. The sensation is terrifying, and I can't live with it anymore. And now it seems I'm losing my mind and hearing voices.* He raised his head and looked in the group's direction. *How did you . . . How did we come to be in this space? I sense there are five, no, six of you, but I'm not sure if you're really here.*

Yes, said Nicholas. *There are six of us, but we don't have any idea how we got here either. Still, I can assure you, you're not going crazy. We all experience — visions of some kind. We assume that's what happening here. Except we have never had a collective experience, and no one has ever communicated with a victim.*

Victim? said the man. *Victim of what?*

172

No one spoke until Winn filled the awkward silence with a thought. *Our visions always involve those who are about to commit suicide.*

...The Suicide Society, said the blind man.

What? What do you mean 'The Suicide Society'?

I — I remembered something. I finally remembered something from my past ...

***

Wanda woke with a renewed sense of purpose and resolve. In less than a week, the efforts of her group were beginning to bear fruit. They now had three empty lots planted, and sprouts had begun poking up through the soil. Southern California was experiencing a welcome period of rainy weather, which helped nurture the seedlings and also provided the benefit of rainwater collection.

Organized crews began handling the problems of open waste, a major contributor to the ongoing diseases and pathogens passed on by flies, rats and other vermin. Wanda located an area between two abandoned buildings that was wide and private enough to construct two long latrines. The smell and sight of feces and urine disappeared from the living area on the streets as the inhabitants willingly made the two block long walk to eliminate and cover their waste with fresh dirt.

Perhaps most ambitiously, they began transporting water from the Los Angeles River back to Skid Row. Boiling the liquid and storing it in barrels cleaned with ash paste provided ample drinking water and surplus to fill a few of the toilet tanks in the nearby abandoned buildings. As word of the abundance spread, people from surrounding streets and neighborhoods started to show up looking for work, knowing honest labor would be rewarded with the promise of organic food and fresh water.

While they worked, but mostly after the day's chores were completed, Wanda and her companions from the facility conducted informal meetings where they talked about the purpose of human existence and the need to find harmony between the soul, personality and universe. As the inhabitants began to understand the futility of endless cycles of violence, a new attitude took root as sure as the crops on 7th and Wall.

She stretched and looked at her watch, which read 5:45. That meant there was less than an hour before sunrise when her day would begin. After groggily getting to her feet, she reached over and grabbed a jumpsuit that lay folded over a chair. Thanks to the division of tasks, Wanda's clothes were washed every other week, and although the action of rising and kneading in the river didn't remove all the grime, at least she smelled better.

With one leg in the jumpsuit, she nearly fell over as Jerry Kent burst into her tent with no warning. Wanda dropped the clothes and brought her arms up over her breasts.

"Ah, I'm sorry. I didn't mean to . . ." he immediately turned his back.

"Never mind, Jerry. You must have something important to tell me."

"Just come right away. You need to see this before everyone gets up." Jerry left hurriedly, and Wanda dressed quickly without bothering to comb her hair or brush her teeth. When she stepped outside in the cool winter air, she immediately sensed something was wrong. The sun was beginning to peak over the hills to the east, which cast just enough light so she could see the toppled water barrels in the distance.

"Someone shot holes in them, and that's not the worst of it," Jerry said as the other sanctuary pioneers joined them.

"I imagine they didn't stop there."

Jerry motioned for her to follow, and the group moved down the street toward 7th and Wall. Wanda wasn't surprised when they reached the vacant lot to find all the seedlings pulled from the ground and stomped underfoot or driven over by a vehicle. The thugs destroyed several weeks worth of effort in one night. Without having to ask, she knew the other two lots would be in the same state. The latrine was also despoiled, and raw feces were scattered everywhere. The stench was so overpowering, Wanda found it impossible to control her gag reflex.

She stood for some moments surveying the scene before turning and walking back to her tent as her companions followed sullenly. Once they were inside, she motioned for everyone to sit.

"I suppose we should have expected this," she said. "External power is never relinquished easily even if its hold is tenuous and counterproductive."

"The people worked so hard," said Aisha sadly. "They will be crushed when they discover the destruction."

"Can we recover from this? If we try to rebuild, they will just tear it down again," said Sam dejectedly.

"We have to tell the people and hope they're strong enough to persevere." While she felt discouraged, Wanda was taught that a leader must never show signs of defeat.

Sam stood up and poked his head outside. "They're starting to gather around the water barrels. We better address this before it gets out of hand."

Wanda nodded and walked out of the tent and over to where about twenty of the street people stood near the ruined barrels. When they saw her, they immediately turned and looked away. Despite reservations, Wanda smiled at them warmly.

"You see the effects of misguided souls in these destructive actions," she said forcefully. "Regardless of the inevitable futility, external power rarely surrenders to authentic power without a struggle. Look around you. Has external power made the lives of those who hold it any more secure than yours? They live in the streets like you do. They scrounge for food and water like you do, and yet, when shown a new and better way, external power lashes out. Does anyone know why?"

"Fear," said Iris from the front of the crowd. "They fear the consequences of losing power."

"Yes, exactly," said Wanda. "Iris is right. Fear motivates them and closes their minds to the possibility that their lives might be better and happier if they focused their efforts on raising consciousness instead of suppressing it."

"It all makes good sense, Wanda," said Gus from the back, "but it don't feed us or give us anything to drink. They're not going to let us do this. There's no answer except to take what they let us have and live out our miserable lives."

"I have an answer," said Arturo as he stepped forward. "We organize and go smash them. I don't care if it was the Pocks or the Crege, the only thing either of them know is force. I can get some knives and maybe even a few guns, and then . . ."

"No Arturo, that isn't the way." Wanda tilted her head and smiled, which seemed to diffuse the rage building inside him. "Our response must not be anger; it must be compassion and love for those who did this. We must understand that they will experience the same hurt and pain they created here before they can heal. This will be difficult for them since they have probably established a long pattern of such cruelty."

She stepped forward and projected confidence. "There will be much work to do today. We need to find new barrels for the rainwater. The lots must be cleared of debris and tilled again for the new seeds. A new latrine must be dug. To satisfy our immediate needs, we'll haul water from the river, and we'll need a team to scrounge for canned goods."

"And what if they do it again?" said a small man in a tattered red coat.

"Then we will rebuild again, Hasim. They won't be able to silence us or stop us because what we are doing is right and just. We are in an evolutionary phase, and the forces of nature and the universe are immutable."

Arturo turned to the gathering and said, "I swear I only understand half the shit she says, but something about the way she says it makes me feel good." He turned back to Wanda. "Okay, I'm in." Arturo's levity lightened the mood and elicited chuckles from the crowd. Wanda looked out and saw many heads nodding.

"Yeah, I'm in too," said Ngo. He picked up a shovel and began walking down the street towards the lot on 7th. Slowly, several people grabbed tools and started following him. It seemed that everyone understood the struggle would be long and hard.

From daybreak until noon, Wanda worked with the others on a patch of dirt in the 7th street lot, clearing the human waste and debris while trying to salvage some of the seedlings that were pulled from the ground but hadn't been crushed. She was gently placing one of the plants into a freshly dug hole when she heard a gunshot and a scream from back at the camp on San Julian. Instantly, she knew something terrible had happened, and her heart sank as her emotive perception foretold of a tragedy.

She dropped her hand rake and ran back to the camp as the others followed. Approaching the scene, she looked in every direction while trying to make sense out of the chaos in front of her. Her neighbors scrambled for cover as a man writhed on the ground, clutching his abdomen and crying out.

"Oh, fuck," said Ngo from behind her. "It's the OG. Oh God , it's the OG. We're all gonna die."

Wanda kept running, and as she grew closer, she saw the man on the ground was Arturo. He was bleeding freely from a bullet wound deep in his abdomen. "Call an ambulance," she yelled instinctively, but her subconscious knew there was no phone to make a call with. Cell phone service was down almost everywhere, and even if they somehow could get through, ambulances only served rich Corporate enclaves.

She kneeled down next to Arturo and cradled his head in her arms.

"Did you mean that shit?" he sputtered through bloody teeth and lips. "I ain't gonna die, right? I get to graduate this place and go to the next if I learned and am at peace, right?"

"That's right, Arturo," replied Wanda as she fought back tears. "You've made such incredible strides in such a short time. I'm certain you're going to get to graduate from earth school. But don't worry about that now. An ambulance is on the way."

"I—I didn't do no violence, Wanda," he said. "I just let him pull the trigger because I know that he can't really kill me. You taught me that. I feel cold... So cold."

Wanda's eyes spilled over, and she hugged him tight while rocking back and forth. She didn't need to look down to know he was dead. His essence rose and touched her with a deep warmth even as his body went limp.

Suddenly, she felt a hard impact to her ribs, and when she looked up, there was a large man in a pinstriped suit standing next to her. His appearance was such a caricature she might have laughed if the circumstances weren't so dreadful.

"Get up, bitch," he said in a thick, Latin American accent. "I want to see your face before I put a bullet in it."

Chapter Fifteen

Zach sat on a very comfortable sofa listening intently to the quiet that surrounded him. He couldn't recall when he experienced such a deafening silence. Although it was a dangerous, unsettling place, the hospital was always pulsing with activity. The sounds of the nurses frantically trying to keep order as the arguments, fights, gunshots and screaming patients created a constant din that Zach had grown accustomed too.

Sound was just one of the sensations that provided him with clues to what was going on around him. Smells in the hospital were overpowering and changed frequently. Some were ever present like the odor of human waste and body odor, but others were unique and distinctive like conjured up images of spoiled blood, infection, rotting flesh, disinfectant and fear.

As horrible as that place was, Zach found this environment even more unsettling and disconcerting. The long interludes between sounds created a great deal of anxiety, and he found himself focusing on the mundane movement of insects crawling along the floor and the soft hum of the fluorescents as electrical current coursed through them. The absence of odor was even more unnerving than the lack of sound.

While he sensed the facility was immaculately clean, there was no associated smell. No freshener, antiseptic, ozone or other telltale byproducts of the cleaning process. He could only sense a vague natural freshness.

When Sarah and Marshall left him at his insistence, Zach found a place on the sofa and sat in the same spot for several hours. Although Sarah offered to stay with him, he was uncomfortable at the prospect of having a woman he didn't know, or at least didn't remember, in the same room for the entire night. Based on her words and actions, he sensed they had a relationship of some sort, but Zach had no recollection of her at all. She and the one named Marshall seemed to know a great deal about him, but they were clearly holding back.

Somehow, he was connected to them and this place, but he just couldn't recall how or why. There was a tragedy of some sort, that much was certain. Sarah was near tears whenever she spoke to him; he heard it in her voice. Marshall was far more reserved and harder to read, but he sounded very young, and it was clear from the way he carefully chose his words there was a deep connection . . . somewhere.

In the hospital, there was always someone available to give him the time, and if that didn't work, he could feel the hands on the old wall clock out in the hospital lobby. This place probably only had digital clocks, so time passed without context. He remembered they told him he was in a room for the visually impaired with a personal assistant available at his request. He struggled for a moment to remember the trigger word.

"Er, Elva, can you tell me the time?"

A sweet sounding female voice said, "The time is 3:23 a.m."

3:23 in the morning, and I'm sitting here on a couch in some strange place with no idea who I am or why I'm here . . . As if that wasn't enough, I'm blind, and no matter what Dr. Thomas said, my eyesight isn't coming back. It's been too long.

"Elva, guide me to the closet." A beeping noise sounded in exactly two-second intervals, and Zach rose from the sofa and began following it, mindful to move slowly since he was unfamiliar with his surroundings. From below, he heard a softer beeping sound, and he stepped around it.

I'll be damned. The whole room is equipped with technology to keep me from stumbling over the furniture. How clever.

Once he gained confidence in the audible alert system, Zach made his way to the closet. He swiped his hand over the source of the beeping noise and pulled on the handle to open the sliding door. Moving the different garments along the closet rod, he noticed the high quality of the fabrics and weave. Rifling through the clothing, he found the thick terry cloth robe he was looking for at the back of the closet and reached down and pulled the belt out of its loops. After winding it around each hand, he made a snapping motion to test the strength of the fabric. Satisfied that the belt would suit his purposes, he walked back into the living room.

"Elva, where is the bedroom?" Another beep sounded to his left, and Zach walked in that direction, avoiding an end table and a floor lamp by following their lower distinctive beeps. When he reached the master bedroom, he grasped the knob and opened the door, throwing the robe belt over the top before closing it tightly. Once again, he pulled on the belt to ensure it was wedged in place between the door and the frame, and then he wrapped the other end around his neck and made a knot.

With his back up against the door, Zach's breathing was heavy and labored. The decision to take his life was spontaneous, but he knew it was better to finish the deed before doubt crept in. He just couldn't live like this. The lack of an identity and history was an unimaginable hell he refused to endure.

Every morning he woke and spent the first five minutes unsure of who he was. The exercise never varied; he would remind himself of yesterday's events and try to remember his new name. *John Doe*. Never at the forefront of his mind, he had to search for it before finally remembering.

Every-single-day.

He took a deep breath and began sliding down the door. Once he was in a sitting position, there would be no way to get back to his feet again.

His pulse quickened and his breathing became shallow as the pressure on his esophagus increased. *Don't think about it. Just do it*, he said to himself. With one last rasping breath, Zach started scuttling further down toward the floor.

Noooo!

He stopped and used his feet and the support of the door to keep from sliding down any further. Zach whipped his head back and forth to find the origin of the voice.

Who said that? Who's there?

He realized he wasn't actually talking, but instead projected speech through thought.

I – I said it. The strange voice reverberated inside his head once again.

Zach paused a moment to gain his bearings. Without sight, he couldn't tell if there was someone in the room. He pondered the distinct possibility he was hallucinating.

Who are you? Why are you here?

The voice spoke with a mixture of curiosity and fear. *It seems you intend to do yourself harm. Am I right?*

Zach shook his head as a single, short sob escaped his lips. *I have lost my eyesight and my memory. I don't know who I am. The sensation is terrifying, and I can't live with it anymore. And now it seems I'm losing my mind and hearing voices.* He raised his head and looked in the direction of the group. There were several shimmering outlines of human forms standing inside the panoramic blackness that defined his window of vision.

How did . . . How did we come to be in this space? I sense there are five of you, but I'm not sure if you're really here.

Yes, said Nicholas telepathically. *There are five of us, but we don't have any idea how we got here. Still, I can assure you, you're not going crazy. We all experience — visions of some kind. We assume that's what happening here. Except we have never had a collective experience, and I have never been able to communicate with a victim.*

Victim? Victim of what? Although he asked the question, Zach already knew the answer.

Our visions always involve those who are about to commit suicide.

The Suicide Society . . . Zach stopped to ponder his thoughts for a moment. In his mind, a distant sphere of glowing energy gained speed as it approached. He watched it become larger and brighter until it slammed into him with such force that he recoiled. In that moment, a distinctive piece of his memory was restored.

What? What do you mean "the suicide society"? asked Winn from afar.

After untying the belt from his neck, Zach went back over to the sofa. *I – I remembered something from my past.* He sat down and rubbed his hands together. *It may be significant. I'm not sure . . . Where are you now? Are you all together?*

Yes, we are all together, but we're in a horrible place where we're tortured daily. Our captor feeds us drugs and beats us to dull our senses and get information.

But you are supposed to be here in Sedona, aren't you? said Zach.

Yes, Sedona. We were all drawn to Sedona for reasons we can't explain, but something compels us to go there . . . But how could you know that?

Zach leaned forward and focused intently. *Listen to me carefully. You must free yourselves and come to this place. I can't say why, but it is imperative that you escape and come here.* He shifted his head to the side. *You must be very cautious. There is something wrong with the flow, but I'm uncertain what it is.*

What do you mean? We . . .

Yes? Are you there? Are . . . Zach stopped projecting and slumped back onto the sofa. The twinkling outlines grew faint until they dissipated into wisps of smoke. For several minutes he sat and contemplated the encounter.

The Suicide Society. I am part of it . . . No, I am its leader. Another sphere of energy amassed in his peripheral vision and collided with his medial temporal lobe. *I am . . . I am Zach Randall. They call me "Speaker Randall", but . . .* He brought his hands up to his head. He knew he did something important but couldn't quite capture it. Finally, exhausted and frustrated, he fell asleep on the sofa.

***

185

The chime sounded at 6 a.m. sharp, and Zach sat up with a start. By the second chime he regained enough of his senses to follow the beeping sound until he reached the front door.

"Who is it?" he said suspiciously.

"It's Sarah. Can I come in?"

Sarah . . . The name had familiarity, but it frustrated him that he couldn't remember how. He reached down to confirm he was clothed and said, "Ah, yes. You can come in. He twisted the knob and heard the door open. When she walked past him, he inhaled and recognized her distinctive scent.

At that moment, another massive sphere of crackling, molten thought plasma emerged from the periphery and exploded in his mind, creating a bright flash that reverberated for several seconds before dissipating.

"We are acquainted," he said while turning and following her over to the living area. "Your name is Sarah."

"Yes, Zach, that's right. My name is Sarah. Do you have memories of us?"

"Fleeting memories," he replied. "I have single frame images of you. One has you in a red dress at a dinner table. In another, you're in a bed reading a book. Then there are others . . ." He shook his head.

"Are any of them—more intimate?"

"Uh, yes," he said with a short, uncomfortable laugh. "All of them are joyous except one. It's very disturbing and unlike the others."

"I see." Her voice was soft with a hint of darkness. Zach knew in that instant that their history together was deep and complex. If the image of Sarah covered in blood while wielding a fire ax was any indication, something tragic had taken place in their collective past.

"Zach," she said, drawing him away from his thoughts. "It looks like you slept in your clothes. I've picked out a nice shirt and a pair of pants. Why don't you shower and we'll meet Pena and the others in the dining room?

He nodded and said, "Elva, where is the bathroom."

The first beep sounded when Sarah interrupted. "Elva, cancel that." The beeping stopped and Zach stood silently until he felt her hand slip inside his. The stimuli created more memories and images. By the time he finished showering, he was convinced they were intimate, and visions of her naked body gave him a partial erection he hid beneath his bathrobe. To avoid embarrassment, he declined Sarah's help and used Elva to get to the bedroom.

Dressed and refreshed from the shower, he walked with over to the dining area with his arm intertwined with Sarah's. Along the way, Zach responded to several greetings of good will from people they passed. Every salutation was addressed to "Speaker Randall".

Sarah led him to the table and helped him with his chair. Zach realized he was dining with several other people based on the sounds coming from different place settings. The distinctive scent and sighing told him Marshall was sitting directly to his right. The low mumbling from the end of the table came from the person he met yesterday, Pena. Another female voice sounded familiar, but so many things were familiar without being clear. Sarah reached over and touched his hand.

"I ordered you a ham and cheese omelet with a side of country potatoes, extra crispy, just how you like them. Is that ok?"

He nodded. "Is that what I like? At the hospital, we only had potato soup with some bits of meat occasionally. Everyone said it was dog, but there was no way to be sure. Sometimes they gave us those freeze-dried packets."

"Well, don't worry, everything here is healthy and fresh."

"Excuse me," said Pena as he rose from the table. "It is wonderful we are all back together again. Speaker Randall, we thank the heavens you are alive, and even though you have experienced great difficulty, I am sure you will recover completely."

Zach sensed everyone was looking at him, so he smiled. "Thank you. I have started to remember certain things since I arrived here. My depression ebbed last evening, but there is buoyancy in this place I can't explain, and the longer I am around, the more optimistic I become."

"Yes, that is good. It seems the healing powers of the sanctuary are helping restore your memories. Can you tell us what you remember so far?"

"Well, my name is Zach Randall. I am part of an organization called 'The Suicide Society,' whatever that is. There are also memories of Sarah, and I know I'm close with Marshall and the woman named Sasha, who I believe is sitting next to you, Pena."

Sasha gasped. "Speaker Randal, I . . . I am so glad you are recovering."

Again Zach smiled. "I am certain we are close, Sasha. I wish I remembered more."

The servers brought out the breads and juices, and thereafter, much of the talk centered on the food and the daily tasks at hand. Sarah was prescient in describing the cuisine, which was so delicious Zach's mouth watered even as he ate. He fought the urge to shovel the food in his mouth and made it a point to place his fork on the table between bites to avoid appearing gluttonous. Despite his best efforts, he completely cleaned his plate but respectfully declined seconds.

When it appeared everyone had finished eating, Pena said, "It is time to make the trek to the heart of the facility. As you all know, the energy from the vortex is exceptionally pure and pristine. Perhaps direct exposure will help hasten Speaker Randall's spiritual, emotional and physical healing."

"That's fine," said Sarah, "but there's something else that we must address first."

"Delgado," said Sasha.

"Mr. Delgado is in an isolated room near the infirmary right now," said Pena, not allowing for debate. "He is being monitored closely on a security feed, and there are two attendants in front of his door. There is no reasonable way for him to escape."

"That's acceptable for now, but what are we going to do with him long term?" asked Sasha.

Pena shrugged. "That is for the Speaker to decide." All eyes turned to Zach, who appeared befuddled.

"I have no idea who he is. I just met this Delgado yesterday."

Sensing the need to end a moment that had become awkward and contentious, Pena rose from the table with his attendants in tow and led the small group down the winding corridors toward the center of the facility. The buzz amongst the tightly knit community was electric. By now, word spread that Speaker Randall had returned, but the residents knew he was blind and without memory. A glimpse of his smile gave them hope and something to talk about with their friends.

"Pena," said Marshall as he caught up to the caretaker, "I need to ask you. Wanda. Is she . . ."

"She left on her mission as scheduled, and right now, she's in the Skid Row district of Los Angeles."

"That area is like a war zone."

Pena clapped his hand on Marshall's shoulder. "Empaths are needed where people are suffering the most. I know you understand that. Wanda is our most advanced student."

Marshall hung his head and nodded slowly. While his intellect agreed with Pena, his emotions did not.

After several twists and turns they arrived at the threshold to the courtyard. Without hesitation, Pena pushed the doors open, and he stepped outside the building. The area was exactly as Marshall had grown accustomed during his stay at the facility except everything seemed even brighter and even more alive than usual.

Pena hurried through the grassy areas, following the brick path as it took the group further into the center of a courtyard that seemingly had no boundaries. Due to his memory loss, for Zach, this was the first time he experienced the mystical nature of this place, and he took in the pleasant sounds and smells as he struggled to establish spatial boundaries.

"So, this is a courtyard in the center of a building?" he asked Pena.

"Yes, Speaker. The courtyard is circular. There are several entrances spread out around the perimeter."

"I—I get a sense that it is vast. It's like standing in the middle of a forest that stretches out endlessly."

"Your intuition is correct. Outside, there are very measurable and finite dimensions, but once you step inside this place, there is a limitlessness that is inexplicable."

Zach walked with his hand on Pena's shoulder, and he felt the gentle touch of the caretaker as he guided him out of the grasslands and into the forest area. He sensed the change immediately and experienced the presence of the large trees and their canopy high overhead. The fragrance of fresh moss, pine and accumulated mulch filled his nostrils, and he breathed deeply. After months in the hospital smelling nothing but rot, decay and waste, his nose celebrated the delightful odors of abundant and thriving vegetation.

They continued on a path through the dense woodlands, stopping only briefly for rest and refreshment. Zach had no idea how far they traveled, but his ability to gauge the passing of time was honed, and he knew they were in the courtyard for just over an hour before Pena and the rest of the group stopped. He heard a slight hum coming from a few feet away, and his spirits soared for reasons he could not explain.

The first wave of crisp, clear and unfettered energy enveloped him like a babe in swaddling clothes, washing over his body and cleansing his psyche and emotional core. The second wave began to clear cerebral blockages while healing his physical embodiment. A third wave converged with the first two until he was immersed in a single continuous stream of ectoplasmic energy so pure he felt intoxicated.

As he stood motionless, Zach let the streams carry out specific tasks to repair damaged synaptic pathways, and restore his memory patterns. He experienced a bright flash of light, and when it passed, he was more alive, alert and perceptive than at any other time in his life.

Sensing and experiencing Zach's psychic awareness and renewal, Marshall said, "Welcome back, Speaker Randall. It is good to have you with us once again."

"Marshall, Sasha. I remember everything . . ."

Chapter Sixteen

Inside one of the tents surrounding the encampment on the outskirts of Nzoni, Mr. Cox sat at the head of a long table. To his right was Minkus Term with his hands folded neatly in front of him. Hismus Malconus sat next to him fidgeting with a laser writer. On the other side of the table, General Ignasus Cron sat near Lars, who looked at them all with suspicion.

"So," said Mr. Cox as he sat back and evaluated a large digital display board at the back of the room, "our forces are fractured and depleted. We have no formal leadership structure, and we wage a battle on two fronts. Is that right?"

"Yes, Benefactor," said General Cron. "We have lost most of our assets and manpower. Amrosia has systematically eliminated our followers over time. Perhaps worse, the pacifists continue to make huge gains worldwide. No one, including Amrosia, has found a way to deal with them."

"I am afraid we have lost the war," said Malconus. "There is no clear path to victory. Our best option might be to negotiate a surrender with Amrosia."

"Bah!" said Mr. Cox. "We will not negotiate with an illegal entity that has stolen what is rightfully ours." He got up from his seat and walked to one of the small plastic windows set into the sides of the command tent.

"You see," he began, "Your approach in dealing with these pacifists is entirely flawed and counterproductive. They come into an area offering ethereal concepts that make physical coercion irrelevant. You threaten to kill them, but they believe death will only lead to a better existence. If you do kill them, the dead become martyrs, which only hardens the resolve of the survivors."

"Then what are we to do? How can we possibly combat this movement?" asked Term.

"Today was a glimpse of how we will defeat them. We will kill their leaders, but covertly and one by one. There will be no massacres that create martyrs and legends. We will combat them with alternative ideas and try to create doubt in the minds of those they hope to convert."

"And just how will we do that?" asked Cron. "Resources are scarce."

"We start here in this place," said Mr. Cox as he turned back and stabbed his forefinger into the table. "Right here in this city, and then we push them back. And we train whatever leaders we have left in other areas to do the same."

"And Amrosia, how will we deal with them?"

"Amrosia will die of its own accord. They continue to pursue a failed strategy, which makes them an easy target. We will consume them and use their resources for the larger struggle with the pacifists." He looked up at Cron. "As such, I will need a complete intelligence report on Amrosia's remaining strongholds, key personnel and assets."

Mr. Cox looked around the table but no reply was forthcoming. "Well, what is it?" he asked.

No one would make eye contact except Lars, who gave them all a look of disdain. "The resistance has a leader. I do not imagine he will give up his position easily."

Mr. Cox smiled. "Is he near Nzoni?"

"No," said Lars. "The resistance is only here to harass Amrosia. The main force hides in the desert in North America near the place once known as Las Vegas. They remained holed up and impotent, desperately hoping for the pacifist movement to collapse under its own weight."

"It sounds like you despise him."

"Yannus Hern is a dishonorable faslone." In modern vernacular, faslone was a degrading, comprehensive insult that suggested the person had artificial DNA, brain deficiencies and Kren class roots.

"When we depose Dantar Llross, this Yannus Hern will become irrelevant. He will request a meeting to negotiate, and we will kill him. We can carry out the deed when we return to Detroit."

Malconus finally lifted his head and said, "Sir . . . Benefactor, we must face reality. We have no army and few followers. Gehenna is a footnote in history. You have no influence anymore. This is all hopeless. We must get away from this area and any place where Amrosia can find us. They believe you possess the key to their resurgence. It is essential you stay hidden."

Mr. Cox slammed his fist into the desk. "We will not run and hide like dogs. We will press on until we succeed. Do you all understand me?" His eyes blazed a simmering red as he looked around at the nodding heads, all except Lars who remained stoic. "Please, I wish to speak to Lars alone." Without hesitation, the others rose, bowed and left the tent

When the tent flap closed as the last aide left, the Benefactor turned and faced Lars, who ran his hand through his long blond hair. "Do you take issue with my plan?"

Lars looked away for a few seconds and then said, "Honestly, you disturb me, Prevus Coxnotus. I sense that you know me, but I do not recall meeting you or even being in the same proximity with you. And yet, there is a familiarity that unsettles me."

Mr. Cox' smile widened. "Perhaps we have met before. If so, it will occur to one of us with time."

Lars shook his head. "No, this is a different sensation. It makes me wonder why you sought me out. I do not come from privilege, and I am not part of an upper echelon command structure. How did you even know I was a rebel, and what do I have to offer you?"

"You have much to offer, Lars. When the time comes, you will be an integral part of our resurgence. For now, I want you to take a leading role in planning the defeat of Amrosia in Jaunde."

Lars rose and nodded, but did not bow. As he left the tent, Term entered with a concerned look on his face. "Sir, the leader of Amrosia's forces is outside the gates and wishes to see you. I fear they have our camp surrounded and are preparing an attack."

Mr. Cox sat back down. "Fine, fine. Show them in but continue making the arrangements to travel to Detroit."

Term paused at the tent. He opened his mouth several times but said nothing.

Mr. Cox looked up. "What is it now, Term?"

"Sir, traveling trans-continentally is not as simple as you might remember. Sub-orbital vessels are in extremely short supply due to the collapse of the Corporates. They are only available in the protected cities."

Mr. Cox rolled his eyes in exasperation and said under his breath, "I swear, I should have stayed with the primitives."

"Excuse me, sir, I missed that."

"Never mind. I assume Amrosia has such a vessel in Jaunde?"

"Yes, but . . ."

"Then, at the appropriate time, we will take theirs."

"Ah, yes, but . . ." One glance from Mr. Cox, and Term understood further discussion had ended. "Uh, about the leader of the Amrosian forces . . ."

"Yes, yes, send them in."

Seconds later, a tall, slender woman with penetrating eyes and an air of confidence ducked under the tent flap held open by Zietra X, the X Specialist he encountered in Nzoni earlier. X stood behind the leader, but it was clear she could barely contain her contempt.

"Prevus Cox," said the woman, clad in shiny black battle fatigues adorned with many war decorations. "I am Tox Mulcus. On behalf of the Amrosia Corporation, the HUGE conglomerate and its Director Dantar Llross, I am here to discuss the terms of your surrender."

Mr. Cox gestured expansively to a seat at the conference table. Brusquely, she waved him off. "I see," he said with a trailing inflection. "I am certain your Xer told you what transpired in Nzoni yesterday."

"We were caught unprepared. It will not happen again," replied Mulcus.

"I imagine you are referring to the slaughter of your troops." He launched an inter-mind probe, but she

197

easily deflected it. *Interesting. Superior mind discipline. This one will be more difficult.*

"Do not try your mind manipulation on me, Prevus Cox. I have advanced training and superior development of my cerebral cortex, parietal lobe and occipital lobe. Your incursions will have no effect on me."

Mr. Cox' smile widened. "If you insist on initiating a conflict, I think you understand that I have no choice but to see how effective your training may be. Still, I would rather negotiate."

"There is no room for negotiation, Prevus Cox." Her stern expression hardened.

"You do realize that I am the majority stockholder in the Gehenna Corporation, and therefore, I am the rightful Director of HUGE."

She shook her head. "None of those things are meaningful any longer. The courts gave your interest to your son, Alan Ziminski, two centuries ago. He sold his shares to Amrosia, which has had controlling interest for two centuries."

"An illegal transaction I will challenge in court."

"You have no standing in the courts, Prevus Cox. Dantar Llross has already denied your claim. Further discussion on this issue is pointless. I am only here to see if you are willing to surrender?"

Mr. Cox chuckled and shook his head. "No, there will be no surrender. Instead, I ask if you are willing to defect and join with the legitimate shareholders of Gehenna?"

Muclus' eyelids fluttered a moment, and he realized she was transmitting instructions to her subordinates through brain implant technology. Despite her boast of superior mental discipline, Mr. Cox suspected that most of her protection came from hardware. She might have experienced some mild probing in the past, but she could never imagine the strength and depth of the assault he was about to unleash.

Her head snapped back with such force it appeared as though she might have broken her neck. As her arms and legs splayed and flopped around spasmodically, Muclus fell to the floor and began writhing and gasping for air. Mr. Cox intensified the assault as he accessed the hardware that strengthened her synaptic pathways. She rose to her knees while trying to internalize and focus on her Chi to lessen the impact of the attack. A second jolt slammed into her with such violence she bit deep into her tongue, and a quantity of blood and saliva erupted from her mouth as she spit to clear her throat.

To his consternation, Mr. Cox was having some difficulty disrupting the portions of her brain fortified by the implants. Her defenses were stronger than he expected, and the distance from the orb continually weakened his influence. To make matters worse, this time period lacked the kind of suffering he had fed on in the past. Yes, these people were wretched and hopeless, but their emotions were so numb that even death or severe physical pain produced very little fright or terror.

Muclus grabbed the side of the conference table, sputtering and heaving with extreme effort. She looked at Mr. Cox through bloodshot eyes and said, "Is that the extent of your power, Coxnotus? I am disappointed."

Mr. Cox shook with rage, and if he had more energy to use against her, he would have. Yet, he was having a difficult time maintaining the intensity of his assault, and as she started to rise, he felt a sense of panic stirring in his loins. He needed the power of the orb, but it was in a vault on another continent.

Unsteadily, she rose to her feet. Her hand trembled and shook as it tried to grasp the kinetic weapon in her belt. The Benefactor backed up several steps as he realized she intended to shoot him. He froze, but just as her hand touched the weapon, she screamed and stumbled backwards, falling to the floor and grabbing her head. A torrent of blood gushed from her nose as her face swelled grotesquely, and a large, wet bloodstain formed near her hips and spread slowly up through her abdominal area. With a whimper, the taut muscles in Tox Mulcus' body relaxed, and she let out a long, labored death rattle.

Mr. Cox looked up at Zietra X. His cerebral assault hadn't killed Mulcus, but the strain on the implant had apparently caused it to malfunction. The device superheated and burned through her brain and down through her sinus cavity before embedding itself in her esophagus.

"I am not afraid to die, Coxnotus," said X as she backed up toward the door with her hand out and arm extended. "I only ask that you refrain from rupturing my implants as you did to Mulcus. My family would appreciate receiving my body in one piece."

Mr. Cox walked toward Zietra X. "I have no desire to kill you, X. In fact, your training and command of your troops would be very valuable to me as we negotiate these difficult situations. If I have your loyalty, I will spare you. If not, your death will be quick and painless. You are an honorable warrior, and I respect that."

"I—I cannot betray Amrosia."

"How can you betray an illegal and illegitimate entity? Right now, you are disloyal to the HUGE conglomerate, although I can forgive your transgression because of your ignorance."

Zietra X turned away and looked contemplatively at the gray canvas tent cover. "So much death and Amrosia has accomplished nothing. You have such raw, unbridled energy. I feel it as the byproduct of your assault on Mulcus surges through my body. Anyone with your power was meant to rule . . ."

She turned back toward Mr. Cox and her eyes narrowed. "Still, the thought of treason. I..."

Mr. Cox held up his hand and interrupted her. "If you join me, I promise you a seat on the HUGE corporate board of directors. You will have unbridled influence."

Zietra X's eyes widened ever so slightly, betraying her carefully cultivated emotionless veneer. "Truly, what have I to lose? I believe you offer the best chance to defeat the pacifists." She closed her right hand into a fist and placed it over her heart. "I will pledge my loyalty to you and Gehenna, Coxnotus."

Mr. Cox smiled. "Good. Your ruthless killing skills will prove very beneficial to our cause. Please, let Minkus Term familiarize you with the encampment. Let us know how many of your troops will join you, and we will make the appropriate accommodations."

Zietra X looked at Mr. Cox with a hardened gaze of steel. "My entire platoon of 20 X specialists will join me. Their loyalty is beyond reproach."

"Then it is settled. Please consult with General Cron and help him develop a plan to attack to neutralize the Amrosian force in this sector. I want to take the facility in Jaunde as soon as possible. You must know the layout and vulnerabilities."

"Yes," said X, "I know every inch of the compound. It will not be easy, but they are weakened, and their forces are spread thin. I suggest we first confiscate the weapons cache in the encampment outside Nzoni. They have about 50 dynron cluster bombs there. These will prove very useful in the fight against Llross."

"Agreed. The first task is to eliminate the forces that surround our camp. I am sure whoever is in charge has an order to attack if Muclus does not return?"

Zietra X nodded. "Indeed. We have a little more than an hour to respond. That is when the General Cortus has instructions to eliminate you and your followers."

"Then we must act with haste," said Mr. Cox while walking to the entrance to the tent. He said something to one of the security people standing outside, and in minutes Lars entered. He stopped suddenly and went for his side arm as Zietra X did likewise. They stood staring at one another with small, triangulated sight beams locked on their respective foreheads.

"Zietra X. What a surprise," said Lars.

X's expression hardened considerably. "Sinorus Lars. I was told you died in the Zencon offensive on the European continent."

Lars smiled sarcastically. "A pity for you that I escaped but returned later to destroy the Amrosian stronghold."

Mr. Cox enjoyed the scene playing out but decided to interrupt. "Well, well, I see you two know each other."

"Lars was part of the X project, but he could not endure the physical and mental demands of the program and quit."

"Entirely inaccurate," said Lars as his jaw muscles flexed. "I left because of the indoctrination. I am suspect of anyone or anything that spews propaganda and demands I continually pledge my loyalty. That is what prompted me to investigate the Amrosian takeover of HUGE to begin with. When I realized the entire effort was an elaborate coup, I left to join the Gehenna rebels."

"You are a traitorous parasite," said Zietra X. "I should drop you where you stand."

"Please, try it. Your brains will be splattered against the back wall before you can squeeze the trigger."

"Oh, you have no idea how badly . . ."

"Ahem . . ." said Mr. Cox. Ordinarily, he would have helped inflame their anger until one killed the other. In this case, however, he needed both of them, so it was imperative he diffuse the situation. "So, how long were you two users?"

Instantly, they both lowered their weapons while looking at him with stunned expressions. Mr. Cox sighed. "Oh, come, come. I do not need to invade your memories to tell you two were using each other. Was it emotional or purely physical? Please, do tell."

"You told him, you bastard." Zietra X raised her weapon. Lars held both arms out, palms up. "I—I did not say a word."

"Actually, no one told me or needed to. Obviously, passions such as these can only be elicited from an intimate relationship that soured. Personally, I do not care who the guilty party is. I am only interested in knowing that you both can work together for the common good. The enemies are Amrosia and the pacifists. Is that clear?"

X lowered her weapon and shook her head. "I agree, but he cannot be trusted."

Lars let out a forced laugh. "Ha! How ironic coming from the traitor herself. I suspect she is nothing more than a plant put here by Llross. When the time comes, her stalwarts will kill everyone in our camp."

"No, I believe Zietra X when she pledged her loyalty," said Mr. Cox. "Regrettably, we must take chances to achieve our goals in this weakened state. That is why you two will have to work together despite your loathing. No individual is above our cause. We must defeat Amrosia and eliminate these pacifists."

He looked at each one individually. "Can I count on you to put aside your differences and help me raise Gehenna back to its rightful place as the controlling entity in the HUGE conglomerate?"

For a long moment, they continued staring at each other. Finally, Lars looked away and said, "I can work with her."

Zietra X exhaled and said, "Yes, I can tolerate this dog."

"Excellent," said Mr. Cox. "Now, let us get to work. You will both assist General Cron in developing a plan to thwart the forces surrounding us. And based on our time frame, I would suggest you start immediately." Mr. Cox turned away and walked from the tent as he wondered how long it would take before his two new subordinates would become intimate again.

Chapter Seventeen

They collectively snapped out of the vision with such ferocity the nausea sent each of them scurrying for the waste bucket. Unfortunately, Nicholas made it first, so the others were forced to purge in different corners of the basement. All except for Renata, who was still prone and vomited on herself. When they finished rinsing their mouths to remove the awful taste, they reconvened around Lars.

"Wow," said Nicholas, "that was intense. Did everyone experience the hallucination the way I did?"

"If you saw a blind guy who was getting ready to hang himself, then yes, we saw the same thing," said Winn. Paco, Bahati and Felicia all shook their heads in agreement. Renata lay on her mattress with her eyes wide open, staring absently at the ceiling and blinking occasionally as Felicia scooped remnants of vomit out of her companion's mouth.

"So, we all experienced a common vision. I didn't know that was possible," said Paco.

"Neither did I," said Winn. "The more pressing question is what did it mean, and who was the person we saw in it?"

"I have no idea," said Winn, "but he was very troubled. Still, I wonder if we were part of a mass hallucination brought on by the drugs Norma gives us."

Nicholas stood up and absently grabbed for the cigarette package he discarded two days ago. "I don't think so. It just didn't feel that way. He gave us some very specific information about himself and encouraged us to come to Sedona."

"Speaker Randall? Did anyone hear him refer to himself that way? And who is 'the Suicide Society'?"

Lars sat up and grabbed Winn's arm. "Zach Randall? The Suicide Society? Is that what he called it?"

"Yes," said Winn while carefully removing Lars' hand. "Does that mean something to you?"

Lars lay back down with his forearm across his eyes. "No, for a moment I thought I remembered the name, but I was wrong."

"But Winn didn't mention the man in the vision was named Zach, did you?"

Winn shook his head. "I—don't think so . . ."

"Yes, you called out his name when you were in your trance. I heard it clearly."

"You know," said Winn while furrowing his brow. "It's odd that you were the only one who wasn't in the vision, Lars."

Lars moved his arm and looked up at Winn. "I just had my brain fried by Auntie Norma up there. Could be I was so heavily sedated that I missed your mass delusion."

Nicholas looked at Winn and shrugged. "Yeah, it probably explains why he wasn't in it. When I come back from a session, I have trouble even forming thoughts."

"I still think the whole thing was a hallucination courtesy of Norma. Maybe Lars wasn't in it because he hasn't had enough injections yet."

"It could be," said Felicia. "I was wondering the same thing about Norma. She might believe that if she can get all of us to experience the same dreams, we'll reveal something important."

"Like the man in the vision saying we should go to Sedona?" asked Winn.

"Yes, exactly like that."

"But why would he ask us to come there without giving us a specific location? It makes no sense."

"Who knows? Maybe that will be the next vision," said Nicholas.

"There isn't going to a 'next vision', at least not here. We need to get the hell out of this place, or we'll all be permanently damaged if not dead," said Lars.

Winn and Nicholas looked at each other. "All right, Lars," said Nicholas. "It'll take a while to recover from the drugs and beating. Let's see if you think of something when your mind clears."

"Fine. Now please, let me alone. I feel agitated and unsettled."

Just as Lars spoke, the light clicked on. Everyone shuttered their eyes against the glare. For the next hour, they would get a chance to see how much they deteriorated from the day before. Winn walked over to his mattress and sat down, hung his head, and began to cry.

Inside his mind, he realized his brain was slowly being destroyed by the toxic drug concoctions Norma injected in him every other day. His thoughts were becoming increasingly violent and desperate, and he often had no memories of hours or even days that passed. Lost in a debate as to whether it would be better to kill himself or die while trying to escape, he was jarred back to reality when he heard Felicia stifle a shriek.

"Oh my God, Renata is dead."

Winn opened his eyes and looked over at the lifeless, pale corpse lying on the mattress in the far corner. Nicholas was holding her limp wrist as he checked for a pulse while Bahati and Felicia held onto each other. Paco walked to the darkest corner of the room and started banging his head against the concrete wall.

For an instant, Winn considered taking off his shirt, tying a sleeve around his neck and fastening the other end onto the stairway railing. In the midst of what he would later recall as a psychotic episode, he began to undress when Lars sat straight up and said, "That's it. That's how we're getting out of here. Who are they coming for next and when?"

Everyone looked at Bahati, and she began to weep. "Yes, it will be me," she said. "I will be next, I just know it."

Lars nodded. "When they come for you, you must not say anything about Renata's death. Do you understand?"

"But the drugs are so powerful. I don't remember what I say."

Lars turned toward Winn and Nicholas. "Listen to me. We all have to focus on Bahati now, and we must project one thought into her mind. She must not reveal any knowledge of Renata's death to Norma or her boys."

"Lars, that sounds . . . silly," said Felicia.

"No, it's not silly at all. In fact, all of our lives may depend on it."

Winn looked over at his companions, who seemed as puzzled as he was. Lars continued pointing at Bahati. "Now, just do it . . . goddamn it, do it!"

Slowly, Felicia, Winn, Paco and Nicholas joined hands with Lars and projected the exact same thought at Bahati, who stood motionless, looking frightened and confused. For some moments she turned her head in multiple directions and muttered sounds that conveyed her distress.

"I don't like this, Nicholas. What are you all doing to me? I can feel you inside my head. What is this?"

At that moment a smile spread slowly across her face as her eyes grew distant. She began talking in a monotone that signaled she was in a kind of trance. "Yes, I understand. I know nothing of Renata's death. She is alive and well, and she was singing when I left her."

They remained connected for several minutes until Bahati started mumbling about her dead brother.

"It's done," said Lars as the collective dissolved. "Now, we'll see just what kind of power we have. Gather around me, and I'll explain my plan. And bring me those handcuffs . . ."

**

Even without a clock to guide him, Winn knew exactly when Norma and the boys would fetch them for dinner, and they didn't disappoint. The ritual quickly became a habit. They affixed their restraints and waited at the bottom of the stairs for the door to open.

As soon as the sliver of light grew, and the door creaked, they shuffled slowly up the steps with their heads lowered in deference. They made their way to the table to take their usual spots, and as they grew closer,

209

Winn touched Lars shoulder and glanced at the third chair on the left side of the table. It had been Brandon's seat, but now it belonged to Lars.

"Good boy, Dopey," said Norma. "Yer getting' used to sittin' where yer s'pposed to." She looked around the table until her eyes found an empty chair. "Hey, where the fuck is Bashful?"

"She can't make it up the stairs, Norma. She's crapping herself and can't keep anything down. You need to call a doctor." said Nicholas.

Darryl continued unlocking the handcuffs and fastening them to the bar bolted into the table. He already secured Paco and Nicholas and was heading toward Bahati.

"Doctor? She needs a doctor? I'm the goddamn doctor around here. If she needs another shot, I'll give it to her." Norma turned to Simon. "Go down there and bring that damned freak up here. And if she gives you any trouble, beat her senseless." Simon nodded and grabbed the shotgun and began walking down the steps with the weapon at the ready.

Winn counted 13 footfalls, which meant the kid reached the cellar floor. After looking at Lars, who gave him a quick nod, he jumped up and ran to the basement door, slamming it shut and engaging the bolt. Almost simultaneously, Lars grabbed Darryl and slammed him against the wall. Startled, Norma's eyes widened, and she picked up the handgun on the table and swung it over in Lars' direction.

By the time she saw someone coming at her from the left, it was too late. Felicia grabbed Norma's wrist and swung her arm upward just as the Machiavellian woman squeezed off two shots. One slammed into the ceiling as shards of drywall floated down on the table.

Almost simultaneously, Paco slumped over and grabbed his abdomen. "My God, I'm hit," he screamed.

***

Wanda carefully laid Arturo back onto the street and stood up to face the man who killed him. He sneered at her and pushed the gun forward while making a motion with his arms and body as though he was preparing to assault her.

"You come and disrupt my business," he said. "We worked hard to get rid of the cops and soldiers, and now everything is set up right. But you come down here and now one of my *soldados* has defected. I had to kill that worthless Crege to keep everyone in line. You probably started a war, bitch."

"So, I take it you are the leader of the Pocks, right? Can you tell me your name before you shoot me?"

The man removed the fedora and wiped the sweat from his brow. "You can call me the OG or Papa Grande."

Wanda nodded and shaded her eyes from the bright sun. "Your supply chains are breaking down, and the flow of drugs is drying up, Papa Grande. One day soon, the trucks with the powdered gruel and barreled water won't show up. You get that, right?"

"Just shut the fuck up," he said as he pushed the gun against her temple.

"You know I'm telling the truth," she said. "The people living on the streets have been missing meals for a while, and this week, the food deliveries stopped. The same with those a few blocks away. This is your territory, isn't it? That means the trucks didn't deliver any food to you either."

"I can promise you we haven't missed a meal," said Papa Grande.

"No, I imagine you haven't missed a meal because you've stockpiled some food and water you stole from others. Good forward thinking on your part, I suppose. But what happens when the trucks stop showing up completely? And trust me, they will stop showing up. It's becoming as bad outside Skid Row as it is inside it."

"If that happens, we'll figure it out." He paused and stroked his chin. Then a broad smile spread across his face. "We'll just go outside our area and take someone else's shit." The gang members standing beside and behind him nodded, laughed and gave each other gang sign salutes.

"No," said Wanda as she shook her head, "that won't work. Are you going to take water and food from the Crege? Past their zone of control, there are other gangs who are more vicious and deadly than they are. Will you fight them all?"

Papa Grande looked over at Ngo. "So, this is the shit she's been putting in your head, *traidor*?"

"You should listen to her, Papa," said Ngo. "She makes sense. The fields you ruined could have fed a lot of Pocks. The trucks are coming less and less, and she's right, you know our stockpile is running out."

"Shut up, Ngo," said Papa Grande as he pointed the gun at the former Pock. "You're a dead man too. You violated your blood oath."

Wanda walked up and grabbed the hand that held the weapon and pushed it into her own stomach. "Kill me, Papa Grande, not Ngo. I'm the one who changed his thinking. After you kill me,

212

you can kill Sam, Jerry, Talie and Aisha too. And do you know what will happen?"

"What, bitch?" said Papa Grande with a strong hint of uncertainty.

"More will come to replace us, and those who witness these murders will become stronger in their beliefs."

As though he sensed something closing in on him, Papa Grande turned and looked around. While he was talking to Wanda, he hadn't noticed the area filling with floaters from the nearby streets. What started as a half a dozen had grown into a crowd of at least 50, and it was fluid and expanding. He looked into the faces of the people surrounding him. Their expressions were neither angry nor vengeful but instead, conveyed a strange sense of resolve that was unnerving.

He turned back to Wanda. "If I kill you, your people won't retaliate?"

"No, they will not. They will go out to the lots and replant the seeds and rebuild the rainwater collectors. If you tear them down again, they will rebuild."

"And what if I kill all of them?"

"More will come," said Jerry Kent. "Your soul will sicken before you run out of bullets."

Papa Grande lowered the gun and took two steps backward. "I—I don't understand you people. You're fuckin' crazy."

"No, we're not crazy," said Wanda. "We're just trying to heal." She made an expansive gesture with her hand. "What has your killing and intimidation gotten you, anyway? Maybe the Corporates give you an extra barrel of gruel. You might even have a few less rats to push away at night. But you're always looking over your shoulder, aren't you?"

Papa Grande stared at the ground without speaking.

213

"What's your real name, Papa?"

"You don't need to know anything other than I'm Papa Grande, the OG."

"Oh, come on. It's just your name. I'm not asking you something important like renouncing violence."

Papa Granda scratched his cheek with the barrel of the gun. "Tomas . . . Tomas Estevan."

Wanda slowly walked over to him and put her arm on his shoulder. "I can't imagine the kind of life you've been forced to lead, Tomas. Before you kill me, would you come inside the tent and tell me about yourself?"

Papa Grande glanced at Wanda and shifted his eyes to each side. There were now over 100 people gathered around them. He might have the chance to kill Wanda, but even with her assurance, there was no guarantee that the gathered crowd would maintain their peaceful demeanor if she was brutally murdered, especially after he had just killed Arturo.

"Okay, I'll talk to you," he said.

"Papa, are you serious?" said one of his henchmen. "I thought we came here to waste these people?"

Sam stepped forward and beckoned the Pock strongman toward his tent. "Why don't you and I talk while Wanda is with Tomas?"

"Get away from me you crazy twink," said the strongman.

"Edwardo," said Papa Grande sharply. "Talking costs nothing. Go with him. All of you, go with the others and listen to their words. What can it hurt? I will come and get you once we're finished, and if we need to, we can kill them all then. Anyway, we did what we came to do. That Crege piece of shit is dead."

He walked towards Wanda, and they disappeared inside her tent. After exchanging worried glances, the three other gang members followed Jerry, Sam and Aisha. Talie remained outside and started organizing the crowd to prepare a respectful farewell for Arturo. He would join three others who died the same day from either violence, drugs, starvation or disease.

Sadly, in this environment, death had grown so commonplace the Skid Row residents were completely desensitized, and they disposed of bodies as though it was just another part of their regular daily routine.

"Where did you grow up, Tomas," said Wanda while pouring him a cup of lotus tea. He accepted and sipped at it before raising his eyebrows to signal surprise at the pleasant flavor.

"I've been in East L.A. my whole life. I have no special story. My father left when I was five, and my mother raised us the best she could. She got cancer when I was 13 and my brother was 11. We went to live with my aunt who was a drug addict. It didn't take long for me and my brother to get hooked on dust and black tar. I was shooting before I was 16 and joined the Pocks that year."

"And your brother?"

Tomas stiffened. "The Crege killed him. I made a promise to him I would kill the Crege until they were all dead, and I would spit on their colors."

"What was your brother's name, Tomas?"

He paused. "Roberto. His name was Roberto Louis Estevan."

She reached out and gently took Papa Grande by the hand. His body appeared to shiver for a moment at her touch "It's a beautiful name. I'm so sorry for your loss, Tomas."

215

The gang leader looked up at her with tears in his eyes. "No one has ever said anything like that to me about Roberto. They killed him in the streets like a dog, and he was taken to the city morgue and cremated by the state. No one even told me, and I never got to say goodbye. There was no ceremony." He stifled a sob. "They gave me his ashes, and I climbed over the fence at Santa Rosa Country Club and spread them out on the golf course. It was the only place I could find that wasn't some dirty neighborhood stink hole."

"What about your aunt? Where was she?"

"Drunk and high. She kept asking me where Roberto was. She didn't get that he was dead until about a month later."

"And so, the pain and hurt you experienced ended up driving you to the life you lead now. No one ever showed you a different way. So many of the people out on the streets never learned there is a different way."

Tomas sat back and gulped his tea. "What's in this tea? Did you drug me or something? Why do I feel—better being around you?"

"Perhaps your soul is cutting through all the noise and you're finally listening to it, Tomas. Maybe it's telling you to consider a different way."

He shook his head. "It's too late. I've wasted so many people. I just wasted that Crege out there."

She nodded. "Killing is a terrible thing, and I know this will be hard to understand, but each person you murdered asked for that experience. They needed it to heal and align their soul with their personality. Perhaps Arturo killed someone and needed to have the experience of being the victim."

216

"You're talkin' crazy shit, lady. I . . ." Finally, the tears overflowed and fell down his cheeks. Once they started, his crying intensified until he somehow found himself in Wanda's arms as she rocked him back and forth for several minutes until his sobs gradually turned into whimpers before he went silent.

After some time, Tomas sat up and looked at her. "I don't understand what happened here today," he said. "You've filled my mind with a bunch of stuff, and I have to figure it out. It's not as simple as I come over here and start planting seeds. There's people who follow me. Very nasty people always looking for a weakness. They would kill everyone here without a second thought."

"You reflect on it, Tomas. You will always be welcome here. If anyone wants to destroy what we've built or kill us, others will fill the void. We are entering a new era of evolution and enlightenment, Tomas. I hope you choose to join us."

After exchanging awkward salutations, Papa Grande left the tent to find his three underlings waiting for him. They were chatting casually with Sam, Jerry and Aisha as well as several members of the community. When they saw Tomas, they looked at him and then turned away sheepishly. Together, the Pocks began walking down San Julian back toward their headquarters near Alameda and the river.

The neighborhood people watched as they retreated, and Iris and Ngo stood next to Wanda and the other pioneers.

"Will they come back?" asked Iris.

"I don't know," said Wanda. "Sometimes the hurt runs so deep the personality has lost any sense of connection with the soul. Tomas is a very damaged person."

"They all are damaged," said Jerry, "but I hope we can help them."

Chapter Eighteen

Zach turned toward his companions as the tears began to flow. Beyond the restoration of his memories, he could see them in extraordinary detail. The outlines of the corporeal bodies shimmered in a light whose brightness and intensity was beyond the sensory capacity of his ophthalmic system. Pulsating luminance could only be compared to perpetual lightening or the aura in an ocular migraine. The light shimmered and danced around each body, defining their features and expressions in such vivid detail Zach realized how much information he had missed with his limited natural eyesight.

The most remarkable aspect of his new vision was the ability to look past the outer layers of skin. A fluid mass filled each body, floating around and morphing into different shapes and shades of the color spectrum. Sometimes, the mass took on recognizable figures, and Zach watched in fascination as Sarah's mass formed a giant teardrop before changing into a pair of arms wrapped around the shape of a body that strongly resembled his own.

Of the group, Marshall's mass was the most curious. The complexity of the shapes was extraordinary. Geometric manifestations of higher mathematics transformed into a pinpoint so small Zach was certain the mass disappeared until it burst forth again and remade itself into a three dimensional representation of the Fibonacci Sequence.

The colors of Marshall's mass changed far more frequently than the others. Mostly purple, the mass transitioned to blue and then a bluish red before returning to the original color. If the mass reflected the person's state of being, Zach could only imagine the level of discipline it took for Marshall to remain outwardly stoic and keep his internal turmoil under control.

He walked up to Sarah and smiled.

She looked into his eyes and returned his gaze. "You remember," she said. "You remember, and you can see." The mass inside her instantly changed from purple to a deep, rich shade of blue.

As he glanced around, Zach noticed varying degrees of blue shading in each of them.

"Yes, I remember all of it." Sarah rushed over and leaned up against him, and he kissed her lightly on the lips. "And you are right," he said as they pulled away a few inches, "I can see all of you again in unimaginable clarity."

He appreciated the looks of relief and joy on the faces of his companions, his closest friends, as they walked over and hugged him. Even Marshall, who still found it hard to express his feelings, smiled and embraced him tightly.

"It is better than I had hoped," said Pena. "The purity and energy of the vortex has an infinite ability to heal, and it has made the Speaker whole again.

"Speaker Randall, what happened to you? Based on what you're telling us now, I assume you had a confrontation with Mr. Cox," said Sasha.

"Yes, a confrontation that turned out badly for me," said Zach as he nodded and arched his eyebrows. "Despite summoning all my telepathic and telekinetic abilities, I was no match for him alone. He draws his power from somewhere or something I can't identify."

"Perhaps if you connect with each other, the combined reach of the overseers will allow you to find him," said Pena.

Zach shook his head. "I—I've lost the gift, Pena. I can't connect with anyone, and I'm unable to read or influence thoughts."

Sasha looked at Marshall and then at Zach. "It's true. We've tried to join with the Speaker, but there's nothing there."

"Then, how can he see?" asked Sarah.

"Restoration of his sight, even if it is a different kind of sight, tells us he is still influenced by the dynamic energy of the vortex. Perhaps with time, the healing will continue and the more complex components of his mind will be repaired," said Pena.

"Except we do not have time," said Zach. "When Cox left, I had the distinct feeling he left for good. Has he emerged at all while I was in the hospital?"

"No," said Marshall. "There's been no mention of him in any of the news we've received. The new global conglomerate called HUGE seems to be running everything, and reports always refer to Xavier Watts as the Director."

"Then that is who we need to locate first. I've got to find out where Cox went."

A long silence ensued as everyone waited for someone else to break the news to Zach.

"Speaker Randall," said Marshall in a tone that conveyed uncertainty. "Visiting Xavier Watts may be unnecessary."

221

"Of course it's necessary. We must find out what happened to Cox. Watts is the organization's second in command."

"Perhaps Alfonse Delgado can give us that information."

Zach grimaced. "Delgado? He will be just as difficult to access as Watts and won't know as much. No, we need to go after Watts himself."

"But Speaker," said Sasha in a small, soft voice, "Delgado is here."

"What?" Zach snapped his head around. The auras in the room collectively darkened. He looked at Sarah, but she just shook her head.

"He helped us escape that hellish hospital, Speaker," said Marshall. "In fact, he saved our lives. We would never have found you or made it out of there alive without his help."

"That was Delgado? *The* Delgado? But he is a part of Cox' network. In our midst . . . Get everyone ready to evacuate."

"Speaker Randall, listen to the full story. We found Delgado in Desolation wandering around without purpose. He's been disconnected from the neural network Cox uses to keep his sycophants in line. Without the control he's been so dependent on for years, he's hopelessly lost."

Zach inflated his cheeks and blew air out. "Okay. Let's return to the facility. I need to rest, and then I want to talk to him."

Pena nodded, stood up, and began walking away from the vortex as everyone followed. After they returned to the facility, a meeting with Delgado was arranged for an hour later. Zach sat with Sarah in his room as the outlines of the shimmering digital clock slowly spun numbers. When he looked at her,

222

he noticed her mass kept forming into a dead person who most closely resembled himself. Her color was dark purple bordering on black.

"What's wrong, Sarah. You're troubled."

She smiled sadly. "I thought you couldn't read minds anymore?"

"I can't read your mind, but I can visualize something inside you. I'm not sure what to call it. Aura, maybe? Anyway, it's almost black, which I'm learning means anxiety and depression."

"I don't know, Zach. I just have a sense none of this ends well."

He walked over and wrapped his arms around her. "Look, an hour ago, I couldn't remember who I was, and I couldn't see. Now, I have the ability to get around, and I can feel my mind clearing. Every second, more of my memory returns."

"That's not what I mean," she said. "Mr. Cox, I believe he's won, and I think we need to accept it. How much pain, death and agony must we endure before we admit we're defeated? Let's find some remote island where we can live out our lives in peace."

He sat on the edge of the bed and fingered the blanket. His memories might be restored, but what he didn't reveal was that his feelings were not. He remembered Sarah clinically, but each memory imprint lacked a recollection of the sensation he had during the moment. He knew they were involved romantically, but he was emotionally numb.

"I don't have a choice in this, Sarah. You must understand. This monster has ruined so many lives . . . He must be stopped. It's the only thing that matters."

Her aura darkened further to black with a yellow tint. She hung her head and nodded softly just as the alarm chimed.

"Let's go see Delgado," he said.

"I hope the filthy pig dies," she answered.

Delgado was seated at the far end of a conference table inside the east wing library as two attendants stood directly behind him. When they entered, Zach found everyone was already there and seated. Zach purposely positioned himself directly across from Delgado at the other end table, and Sarah sat down next to him.

Upon seeing Zach enter, Delgado's eyes widened momentarily, and his back stiffened slightly.

"You look surprised," said Zach impassively.

Delgado moved around uncomfortably in his chair. "Frankly, I am. When I asked for assistance from my contact in Phoenix, I was fairly certain you wouldn't survive. You were convulsing, and I thought your mind was gone. Traveling with you only seemed to confirm what I suspected."

"And yet, here I am. So, you're claiming it was you who saved me?"

"In a sense. Once the Benefactor was finished with you, he left you to die. I intervened, but I don't ask for your thanks."

"Good, because I'm not giving you any." Zach leaned into the table. "It's too convenient you happened to be in Desolation at the same time as Cox, yet you want us to believe he expelled you from the network."

Delgagdo shrugged. "Believe what you want. I already explained this to Marshall and Pena. Mr. Cox blamed me for the bombing in Detroit. His girlfriend also wanted my job, so I was given the choice of going to some remote Middle East desert

224

city to rot or disconnect from the Network. I chose the latter.

"Once removed from Mr. Cox influence, I wandered amidst a deep depression and finally returned to Desolation, the last place I lived and worked before I met him. Since it's a veritable ghost town, I had no idea he would ever return there. Since I was no longer connected, he either ignored me or was unaware of my presence."

"What is it you're looking for, Delgado, salvation? I wonder if you'll find it even in this place," said Zach while gesturing expansively. "You were an integral part of the most horrific killing machine in history."

For just a moment, Delgado's mass turned blood red. "I do not seek salvation, Randall, only revenge. I am keenly aware that my place in eternal damnation is secure. All that remains for me is to help ensure Mr. Cox takes his rightful place in hell next to me."

Sarah stood up, and without facing him, said in a voice that smoldered with hate. "I believe none of it. He is a traitor in our midst. If given the opportunity, he will transmit our location to Cox. Kill him now. Kill him now!" she shrieked and climbed on the table, scuttling over to the far end before launching herself at Delgado. Her hands wrapped around his throat as his chair overturned, and they tumbled to the floor.

After recovering from the shock of the moment, Sasha and Marshall pulled Sarah away, struggling to restrain her as she kicked and screamed. After several minutes, she recognized the futility of continuing to fight and slumped over while panting heavily. Zach and the others walked her back to the other side of the table where she quietly took her seat.

For his part, Delgado coughed and rubbed his neck while trying to regain some sense of composure. Since he was removed from the network, he lost a significant amount of weight, and he lacked Sarah's youth and passion. Pena fetched him a glass of water, and Delgado slurped as he gagged and sputtered. It took some time before the chaos abated, and the room settled back down.

"I—I apologize for Sarah's outburst," said Zach as she immediately flashed a look of betrayal in his direction. "We've all been under a great deal of strain." He paused and spread his hands out on the table. "Let me get quickly to the point. Where is Cox?"

Delgado set his water glass down and cleared his throat. "I'm uncertain, but I strongly suspect he has left this reality. According to my few remaining contacts within the network, he's disappeared, and the telepathic connections with his followers have been severed. Business proceeds as usual because he left a strict blueprint for Watts to follow, but the essence of Mr. Cox has vanished. I imagine the only one who may know of his whereabouts is Watts."

"Do you think Cox is dead?"

"Unlikely," said Delgado. "Suddenly severing the connection would have sent a massive shock through the grid and seriously damaged his followers. Instead, his control was withdrawn gradually and imperceptibly. When he left for good, they only experienced a gentle nudge."

"You say you want revenge. What exactly do you have in mind?"

Delgado slid his chair up close to the table and looked around at everyone with shifting, beady eyes. "I can bring down Gehenna, and that will collapse the HUGE conglomerate. I have worked on this for months." He reached into his pocket and pulled out a number of folded handwritten pages.

"Unfortunately, I frequently forget the plan, so I have written it all down."

Zach looked at his companions and then back at Delgado. "Please, continue."

"Apparently, Mr. Cox never officially signed over his shares in Gehenna to Watts or anyone else. Therefore, they would revert to his next of kin in the event of his death. The only one with a possible claim would be his son, the idiot Ziminski, and he is easily corruptible. I have already been in contact with the CEO from Amrosia, one of the other corporations in HUGE, and they are extremely interested in litigating this if Ziminski is cooperative."

"Very clever, Delgado, but that does not answer the question of where Mr. Cox has gone to," said Pena. "If he shows up unexpectedly, our efforts to disrupt HUGE will have been wasted."

"If by chance he shows up to save HUGE and Gehenna, it will provide the opportunity you need to eliminate him." Delgado remained in control, but his eyes conveyed a deep rage.

"He won't come back," said Zach in a measured tone. " . . . I know where he is."

Marshall looked over and opened his mouth but thought better of it and said nothing.

Zach motioned to Pena's attendants. "Please escort Mr. Delgado back to his room. I will summon him later when we have decided what to do with him."

As the attendants moved forward, Delgado stood up voluntarily and bowed. "I will wait for your decision, but I'm sure you understand that time is of the essence. My memory continues to deteriorate, and I need to find Ziminski and appeal to his greed before I forget my plan completely.

"The lawsuit is already prepared. We only need to confirm his lineage through a DNA test. I have a sample of Cox' blood obtained from his penthouse after the explosion at Gehenna headquarters."

"We will discuss this with haste," said Zach as Delgado bowed again and walked slowly toward the door.

Once he was out of the room, Zach turned back to the table as everyone focused on him. The sparkling lights within his sphere of vision were so bright, and the colors so vivid, they were nearly blinding. Watching the shifting masses within each person was fascinating; Sarah's bright red of anger, unflappable Pena's deep blue, Marshall's agitated purple and Sasha's yellow tinged with green, an indication of her lingering sympathy towards him.

"What did you mean when you said you knew where Cox is?" Marshall asked.

"During my battle with him, I learned he was the missing Time Sculptor."

Marshall gasped, sat back in his chair, and slapped his forehead. "Of course, why didn't I see it? Sixtus Maras had a meeting with Mr. Cox arranged by Havas Zir. Obviously, Zir wanted to ensure Sixtus completed the detonation of the bomb, which would pave the way for Cox to return to a future where he would rule as Director of the Corporates."

Pausing a moment, he shook his head and grimaced. "But Sixtus assured me there was no way to return to the future. We didn't have the technology or the energy needed to construct a transport device in this century.

"You're right. That's the same conclusion I came to, and yet, there is more," said Zach. "When I was battling him, Cox tapped into an enormous reservoir of hidden energy from a different source I couldn't identify. An intense yellow light enveloped us that eventually turned red. I think it's what burned my retinas. It's all I can remember, and when I came too, I was alone, befuddled and blind."

Zach could see Pena's blue essence becoming darker until it bordered on black as it formed into a small, perfectly symmetrical sphere. His shoulders slumped, and he sank down into his chair. "Pena, what is it? Do you have something that might help us?"

Pena shook his head slowly. "Perhaps, but I am afraid the knowledge will do much more harm than good."

"Please, Pena, tell us."

"Mr. Cox possesses the Third Orb of Gehenna. It is the source of the power you speak of."

"The Third Orb of Gehenna?"

"It is an object of enormous influence but also the essence of evil. Ancient legend says that Satan placed six of the orbs in different places on the earth during the time of fire, and those who discovered them would become his servants and create a path for his escape from hell. Practically, there have been many theories of their origin, mostly extraterrestrial in nature."

"Who possessed the first two orbs?" asked Sasha.

"Genghis Khan held the first and Adolf Hitler the second. Both were merciless genocide killers who caused catastrophic death and destruction before they were stopped."

Marshall, who remained quiet, looked over at Pena. "Where are the first two orbs now?"

Pena paused, staring down at the floor. In a whisper, he said, "They are here, Overseer Beiner."

"What?" said Zach as he noticed the mass inside Pena turn to a rich shade of yellow. "Why would you keep that information from me?"

"You do not understand, Speaker Randall. The orbs are the ultimate evil. They will corrupt whoever holds them. The Suicide Society finally managed to defeat both Kahn and Hitler by compelling them to make fatal battlefield decisions, but victory came at a terrible cost. The assembly in the third epoch of the overseers had to terminate Speaker Xi because the power of the orbs corrupted him. That is why they were secured in a granite container and placed inside a vault with foot-thick steel, lead and concrete walls. They were never to be accessed again."

The group looked around at each other in stupefied silence, finally broken by Zach who said, "I want to see them."

"Speaker Randall, I strongly advise against it. You have no idea . . ."

"If Cox has one of these orbs, he will be unstoppable. There are only two overseers left, and I doubt they can defeat him even with their combined power. You saw what he did to me. I lost my eyesight, and he disrupted my brain, perhaps permanently."

"What are you suggesting, Speaker?"

"As Marshall says, there is no way anyone can travel forward in time with our current technology. Therefore, if Cox returned to the future, he used the orb to do it. If we can determine the year he fled to, maybe we can use the orb to follow him."

"But how can we possibly know what time and place he traveled to? It would be like finding a needle in a haystack," said Sasha.

Zach shook his head. "I don't know . . ."

A long pause ensued before Marshall said, "I do."

Chapter Nineteen

"Our plan is to outflank them to the east and north where they are most heavily concentrated. Our troops have already left the camp singularly and without specific patterns. The enemy will have a difficult task finding them as they reconnoiter at the rallying points. We will then launch a surprise attack and kill them all," said General Cron.

"And do you two, agree with that assessment?" Mr. Cox continued looking at the map spread out over the conference table.

"We — ah, we do not have an opinion," said Lars. "No matter what the scenario, it does not work out well for us. The rebels rely on stealth, and that advantage was neutralized when you showed up."

"So, what do you suggest?"

"We believe it is best to try and negotiate to buy time. Your persuasive abilities are quite impressive," said Zietra X. "We suggest you use them to convert as many of Llross's soldiers as possible."

"Precisely!" said Mr. Cox as he folded the map over and returned it to Cron. "General, move your people into position as you planned. In the meantime, Lars, X and I will go to their encampment and speak to their leader."

"Coxnotus . . . Benefactor, I strongly urge you to reconsider. They have orders to apprehend you. You will either be captured or killed."

"Perhaps," said Mr. Cox, "but I still think negotiations will prove to be the prudent course of action." The general shook his head and turned away. "Cron, I appreciate your concern, but really, what chance do your men have against these superior numbers? You have sent 50 troops to surround a force of what, 200? You are outnumbered four to one. I do not see much hope for a positive outcome."

"Yes, but . . ."

"There are no 'buts'. Unless you can reasonably assure me of victory, we will proceed a different way."

Reluctantly, the general sighed and nodded. "The troops we have surrounding the enemy will remain in place until you give the order. Then they will attack from the flanks as our main force will launch a frontal assault."

"Let us hope it doesn't come down to that. After all, 50 troops . . ." Mr. Cox grabbed a plasma rifle and tied a white rag around it, the universal signal for surrender or approach without hostile intentions.

With Lars and X walking directly behind him, he summoned a driver and went over to the ground transport along with Zietra X, Lars and General Cron. In seconds the vehicle was crawling through firewater swamps and thick jungle, plowing down kaya and sapel. Within half an hour they arrived on the outskirts of the Amrosian encampment. Two sentries were guarding the entrance gate, and they looked confused as Mr. Cox stood up with the roof of the vehicle open waving the white flag.

"I come in peace," he yelled out.

One of the sentries nodded, and the other turned and scurried into the center of the camp and disappeared into a tent. The remaining sentry raised his rifle and pointed at them.

"Halt!" he said. "You have trespassed on territory belonging to the HUGE conglomerate."

"Yes, yes, I know," said Mr. Cox impatiently. "Please, take us to whoever is now in charge here."

"Tox Mulcus is in charge here," he said.

"Well, not anymore, I am afraid. Mulcus had an unfortunate accident."

The sentry's mouth gaped open, and he seemed confused. He was about to speak when a voice from behind caused him to stiffen, and he moved his weapon to the side and saluted.

"An unfortunate accident? Do you not mean you killed her?"

Mr. Cox smiled and lowered the flag while making a sweeping gesture with his other hand. "It is a matter of semantics," he said. "Mulcus is indeed dead, but it was not the outcome I hoped for. More importantly, I assume that puts you in charge, General . . ."

"My name is Dux Jolas, and I am the assistant to the Director of this Sector."

"Not anymore. Apparently, you are now the Director."

"Yes," he said. "If Mulcus is dead, I suppose I am."

"Good," said Mr. Cox as he got out of the ground crawler and walked forward slowly. "We are already off to a fine start. I helped you get a promotion."

"It seems along with your other attributes, you have a wry sense of humor as well," replied Jolas. Then looking behind Mr. Cox, he focused on Zietra X , and his eyes narrowed. "An X Specialist traitor is unheard of. You will suffer a particularly gruesome death."

"In fact, I might," replied X. "But before you arrange for my execution, I suggest you listen to Prevus Coxnotus first."

"What could he possibly have to say that would persuade me otherwise? We have our orders."

"Ah, yes, your orders," said Mr. Cox with an air of amusement. "And what good have your superiors done for you so far, Director? Look at your forces. You have, what, 200 troops left? This is one of the largest Corporate armies in the world and it numbers 200? How many were in your company 10 years ago? Twenty years ago? How about 100 years ago? Well?"

Dux Jolas hung his head for a moment, and when he raised it, his face was taunt and his muscles strained. "It is true that we are losing the war. You cannot fight an enemy who will not fight back. Despite all our efforts over two centuries, their movement continues to grow. I have personally participated in the sickening slaughter of thousands, and it disgusts me to kill those who put up no resistance."

"The war will be over soon, Director, and your side is going to lose. If you do not perish, you and the other survivors will scatter to the wind or have no choice but to join the pacifists."

"Never!" said Dux Jolas forcefully.

"Then, you only have one other choice, and that is to join forces with us. You do understand that you are part of a corrupt and illegal movement? The HUGE conglomerate was seized in a hostile takeover two

235

centuries ago. I am the majority owner in the Gehenna Corporation."

"Nonsense. Everyone knows Gehenna was dissolved in the 21st century."

"It is far from nonsense. I am the one who founded Gehenna," said Mr. Cox forcefully. "I was a Time Sculptor, and I conceived and executed a plan that demonstrated my genius, and it would have ensured the stability of the world under my leadership."

Mr. Cox handed the rifle to Lars and stepped forward. "But instead I come home to this . . ." He waved at the countryside. "My organization was destroyed and these . . . these weak, sanctimonious, spineless ingrates are running things."

"A Time Sculptor? Impossible. That program was discontinued a century ago. Those who were part of it were abandoned or assassinated. No technology existed in the primitive past to allow anyone to return to their original time."

"Well, I did," said Mr. Cox. "You are welcome to compare DNA samples if you like. I have returned, and I intend to restore Gehenna to its place as majority owner in HUGE. I will live to see the conglomerate dominate the world as was planned."

Jolas brought his hand up and started rubbing his forehead with his fingers. "I suddenly have a massive headache. The effort has gone so poorly. Every day we lose more troops either defecting or disappearing into the jungle."

"There is nothing left for you, Jolas. You are going to die an ignominious death, unless . . ."

"Unless what?"

"You have only one option that might ensure your survival and the survival of your troops. You must join us."

"A traitor? No, out of the question. I cannot abandon my post." Jolas continued to rub his temples. "Can we — can we sit down? I suddenly feel very lost and confused."

"Jolas," said Z as she stepped forward. "You know my loyalty is unwavering. But we have been betrayed and led on a path to destruction by incompetents. This man offers the only hope. Pledge your loyalty and give us a chance."

"I — I do not know. My headache is getting worse."

"Yes," said Mr. Cox. "I can make it get much worse." His eyes began to glow as Jolas fell to his knees and clutched his head between his arms.

"Stop. The pain is unbearable."

"Alright, then let us try this."

Jolas rolled over and began scratching at his body, raking hard at his stomach and chest. "Insects biting and crawling all over me. Get them off. Please!" Just as quickly as it started, the headaches and insect bites abated, and he uncovered his head and looked at Mr. Cox.

"How do you do that?"

"It is not important. You have just witnessed a fraction of my power. We will use it to change the direction of the war." Mr. Cox walked closer so that he was within inches of Jolas. "We have troops stationed to your east and north flank. If we attack, I imagine you ultimately will prevail, but we will kill many before the last of us dies." Mr. Cox pointed at Jolas. "You will suffer the worst. I will make sure of it."

Rising to his feet, the Amrosian military man's back stiffened. "Threats do not intimidate me," he said, "but your power is undeniable. If you can authenticate your legal claim, I will consider your proposal."

Mr Cox nodded. "Do you have access to the NIN? I am sure I can piece together exactly what transpired that led to the hostile takeover."

"The neural network is unreliable and intermittent," said Jolas. "The available processing power is mostly used to assess pacifist and rebel movements. In every city the pacifists occupy, they have destroyed the network. The remaining core on this continent is in Jaunde."

"Take me to an access point. While I search for the documents that will confirm my claims, I want you to consult with Lars, X and General Cron to help develop a plan of attack on their facility. Once Jaunde is under our control, we will return to Detroit."

"Detroit?" said Jolas with a hint of incredulity. "That is a pacifist stronghold. It represents everything they despise about the corporate movement since it was the original headquarters. They would never give it up."

"They *will* give it up, and the Gehenna center will once again serve as the capitol of the world."

Lars squinted. "The Gehenna Center? The pacifists have converted it into functional housing for the street people. It would not be appropriate for our purposes."

Mr. Cox raised his upper lip into a sneer. "Functional housing... Yes, so I understand. We will see how much of a dormitory it is when we evict the squatters and move back in."

Jolas waved his arm and motioned for them to follow. Inside the main command and control tent, he led Mr. Cox over to a station set up in a corner with a single large display screen sitting on a small metal table.

"What is this?" asked the Benefactor. "I need a passkey to activate my implant."

Jolas shook his head. "Implant? No one has those anymore. The pacifists made the practice moot by destroying the global processing hub network, and any existing neural implants were disabled as a result. We can only access the NIN through terminals."

Mr. Cox stared at Jolas as though he was lying. "That cannot be true. Have we reverted to the 21st century?"

"Yes, I am afraid it *is* true. In many ways our regression has put us behind the 21st century."

Shaking his head, Mr. Cox picked up the cumbersome sensory array and fitted it over his head. Instantly, he felt the reduced computational power and reach of the system. He watched the screen as he called up the public Corporate database and rifled through several files, searching until he found the historical documentation that chronicled the hostile Amrosian takeover. Perusing several public information accounts and a few private ones he accessed with Jolas' password, Mr. Cox opened a series of legal documents. Unfortunately, every source he looked at was highly redacted.

Piecing together the course of events was difficult since most of the events surrounding the takeover were erased, altered or classified, but a single report by someone in a low-level Corporate legal office provided the majority of the source of information he could find.

DNA test results were presented in a Corporate authorized court today that confirmed that Alan Ziminski is the biological son of the sole shareholder in the Gehenna Corporation. Known legally as M.R. Cox, he was commonly referred to by those who knew him as "Mr. Cox." Plaintiff's lawyers contend that M.R. Cox disappeared over four years ago, and all efforts to locate him have been exhausted.

Xavier Watts, CEO of Gehenna, vigorously opposed the petition, but the plaintiff provided DNA evidence from a jacket recovered after the explosion at Gehenna headquarters that contained M.R Cox' blood. A sample of Alan Ziminski's blood verified the match, and the court ruled that M.R. Cox' shares in Gehenna should be immediately transferred to Ziminski.

To facilitate the transfer of the company, Amrosia has obtained the services of Mr. Alfonse Delgado, a former vice-president of the Gehenna Corporation.

Mr. Cox ripped the sensor array from his head and stared at the screen. His body trembled with rage, and he had a strong desire to kill everyone in the tent.

Those conniving scoundrels. I should have killed Ziminski and Patricia Johansen when he was in her womb even if the bastard wasn't mine. And Delgado . . . How?

The Benefactor tilted his head back and let out a long anguished wail that reflected his fury and anger. All activity in the tent ceased as an imperceptible cloud of doom hung over the room for several minutes.

Mr. Cox placed the sensor array back on his head and dove further into the system until he came upon the transfer of ownership documents.

On behalf of the Amrosia Corporation, (redacted) is hereby authorized to pay the sum of (redacted) to Mr. Alan Ziminski. As sole shareholder in the Gehenna Corporation, Ziminski agrees to transfer (redacted) shares in the Gehenna Corporation to the Amrosia Corporation.

The legal documents occupied volumes, but the crux of the transaction was summarized in a single page. Ziminski sold out, but it had to be Delgado who was behind the scheme. While great with coding and information technology, Ziminiski was a moron who lacked any sort of common sense or capacity for deception. He scrolled through a variety of other reports detailing the fall of Gehenna and the flawed policies of Amrosia that ultimately left the HUGE conglomerate weak and vulnerable.

Instead of dealing with the rising pacifist movement head on, Amrosia's CEO initially tried to appease them to avoid further violence. Their approach was exactly opposite of what the masses needed, which was an unrelenting demand for unwavering loyalty and subservience borne of severe hardship and pain. When that didn't work, Amrosia resorted to mass killings, which by that time was again the exact opposite of the correct strategy that still might have squelched the burgeoning passive aggressive rebellion.

One last report caught his attention as he stopped scrolling. Only a few lines long, it startled Mr. Cox.

The former CEO of the Gehenna Corporation and former Director of the HUGE conglomerate was found dead last night of an apparent suicide in a motel room in the Poletown East section of Detroit. Watts recently lost a bitter hostile takeover battle when Alan Ziminski was awarded the entirety of M.R. Cox' estate, which included 100 percent ownership in the Gehenna Corporation. Those close to him said Watts was despondent in his last days.

"Xavier, you were a fool," said Mr. Cox to no one in particular. "The solution was obvious. You had the resources to have Ziminski killed. He had no heirs. Yet, left to your own devices, you always preferred to find a non-violent solution, and look what it did to both of us. As for Delgado, that was my mistake. Any time I show mercy, this is the result."

Mr. Cox looked at the screen for several seconds, unsure of how to transfer the information. Corporates were always interconnected by their implant through the NIN system, so it was simply a matter of calling up the recipients on the overhead and downloading the information into their storage. Without it, he didn't know how the transference should take place.

"Excuse me," he said to a technician sitting in a cubicle nearby. "How do I transmit information from one person to another?"

The man looked over to a corner opposite his desk. "Uh, unless the other person is wearing a sensor display, you will have to send it to their inbox. Just call them up at the bottom of the screen. All the command personnel have theirs marked," he said.

"Inbox? Seriously?" The man nodded. Mr. Cox turned back to the screen, hardly able to contain his frustration. It wasn't bad enough that he spent decades in the late 20th and early 21st centuries living with ignorant primitives who were barely conscious. Now, he returned to a future where everything was supposed to be arranged to accommodate his preferences only to find people received information in an "inbox".

Grumbling under his breath, he looked over at the bottom of the screen and sent the documents to Dux Jolas.

Once finished, he disconnected from the NIN and walked over to where the group was huddled around a screen displaying a geographical representation of the city of Jaunde along with troop positions and security details. They looked up as Mr. Cox approached.

"We have developed part of the plan to secure the facility in Jaunde," said Dux Jolas.

"Communications are still open, and I have told them that we apprehended you and your rebels. They have no reason to disbelieve me. If we approach with you, they will certainly open the secure doors and let us in."

"The issue," continued General Cron, "is what we do once we're inside. We can't arrive with our entire battalion. That would be unusual and unnecessary. However, if we don't have the firepower, they will defeat us quickly. The largest remaining division in the Corporate elite guard surrounds the facility to protect it. That is a force of almost 1,000. Our brigade would not survive odds that overwhelming."

"1,000 . . . I ruled over armies in the millions before I left. I was to return to a time where armies weren't required to maintain order and obedience. Instead, I come back to this . . ."

His companions stood silently. Their own lives were so miserable they found it difficult to find sympathy for Mr. Cox.

"Back to the problem at hand," said Director Jolas. "I see no way we can penetrate their defenses. We will be slaughtered if we try. They outnumber us five to one, and the buildings are heavily fortified."

"No doubt, this will be difficult," said Mr. Cox. "In this time, we must resist the temptation to use tactics that have failed miserably. We need a new strategy, and I think I have one."

"Please," said General Cron. "What is it?"

"I want Term and Malconus to return to Nzoni and seek out the city leaders. They will arrange another meeting with the locals. We want to conduct this gathering before the pacifists make another attempt at influencing their people."

"I am sure that can be arranged," said General Cron, "but I don't see how that is going to help us overcome the Amrosian forces."

"Asymmetrical thinking, Cron," said Mr. Cox. "We need to take a drastically different approach."

"I will have the troops at the ready and awaiting your instructions. My company will join this camp later today. It will be challenging to maintain order at first. These people have fought against each other for generations."

"My X project team will also coordinate with the main force in preparation for the coming battle."

"Fine, let us get to work," said Mr. Cox. "Director Jolas, I have sent you the documents you requested. After reading them, you will understand exactly how my organization was stolen from me." Turning, he continued, "Lars, please remain behind, I need to speak to you privately."

The others looked at Lars suspiciously before moving away from the conference table and engaging in their respective assignments. When he was certain they wouldn't be overheard, Mr. Cox said in a low voice, "I have a very special assignment for you, Lars. Everything I planned may hinge on your success. Listen carefully . . ."

Chapter Twenty

Lars and Darryl struggled fiercely to reach the rifle propped up against the wall. Lars had his hands around Darryl's neck while Norma's older son had Lars in a crushing bear hug. They danced around in a small circle in the space between the table and the wall.

Almost like a child's contest to see who could hold their breath the longest, the color in their faces drained as they continued squeezing each other with all their remaining strength. Every fiber in Winn's body told him to help, but he remembered Lars' admonition that he must not leave the basement door unattended under any circumstances. He fingered the metal serving plate and hoped Lars knew what he was doing.

Over on the other side of the table, Felicia's weight toppled over Norma's chair as she sputtered and screamed out profanities. Felicia held Wanda's gun hand by the wrist, and they both pulled hair and scratched flesh with their free hands. Norma was somehow able to knee Felicia in the groin, which caused her to grimace and pull back. Recovering momentarily, Felicia responded by punching Norma directly in the face, and fresh blood instantly poured over the rim of her mouth.

"You bitch!" Norma cried out. "You worthless, filthy bitch. I'll kill you." The struggle for the gun intensified as Norma tried to twist her wrist so she could point the barrel at Felicia. She pulled the trigger, and another flash and bang followed, which stopped the struggle as they were both momentarily stunned by the deafening blast. The errant bullet tore up a section of the wood floor, landing about four inches from Felicia's head.

Cocking her fist, Felicia rained punches down on Norma as the old woman tried to shield herself but to no avail. After grabbing the gun barrel, Felicia twisted it down toward Norma, who howled like a wounded Coyote. Instantly, her other hand grabbed at the gun to counteract Felicia, so all four hands were struggling in opposition.

The barrel changed direction several times before another shot went off, but this time the recoil ripped the gun away from Norma. This proved to be all the advantage Felicia needed. She unleashed another series of punches into Norma's bloodied face, and the older woman cried out in pain and frustration. A crooked hand reached up and clawed at the air, but that left Norma even more vulnerable, and Felicia's surprisingly strong hands gripped her head and slammed it twice into the floor. Whether she was unconscious or dead, Norma's eyes closed and her body relaxed.

Lars and Darryl were grunting and rolling around in a death struggle. Unable to gain a significant advantage, both men abandoned their chokeholds and wrestled while throwing punches. Winn finally decided that he had no choice but to help Lars, but just as he prepared to move, he heard footsteps rapidly ascending from the basement.

"Ma . . . Darryl?" yelled Simon. "It's a trick. This whore is dead down here. It was a trick. Be careful." He reached the top of the staircase and tried the knob on the door, twisting it frantically until he realized it was locked.

"Goddamn sumunabitch," he yelled out before backing down the steps. Winn braced as a loud roar accompanied an impact that shattered the wood and turned the knob into shrapnel. Simon raced up the steps and kicked the broken door so hard it separated from the hinges. The barrel of the gun emerged first with Simon following closely behind it.

Out of the corner of his eye he picked up Winn standing to the side of the doorframe, but the heavy stainless steel platter impacted with his skull before he could aim the gun properly. Staggering forward, Simon's eyes briefly fluttered before he started to regain his senses, but the second blow with the platter hit him square on the forehead.

The shotgun fired a second time and tore a hole in the ceiling, but the recoil caused Simon to stagger backwards, and he missed the first step and went tumbling down the basement stairs as the shotgun flew over the side rail, hitting the ground with a dull thud. Winn briefly considered going down to check on him, but Simon's head was twisted and stretched in a way that looked grotesquely unnatural. Instinctively, Winn knew he was dead.

He turned back in time to see Lars with his hands yet again wrapped around Darryl's neck as the sadistic kidnapper gasped for breath while his limbs flailed futilely. A few seconds later, his body began to heave with spasms until he choked out a final breath and lay still.

For a long moment, no one said anything until Bahati came out from under the table and tended to Paco. She held his head with one hand as his eyes stared absently with a glassy look. Bloody foam spittle leaked from the corners of his mouth.

"Help me," she said. "I think Paco is dying." Winn ran past Lars, who continued to choke Darryl's dead corpse. With his shirt plastered to his stomach, Winn could see Paco's wound was deep in his abdomen.

Bahati tried to put pressure on it with her hand, but the blood quickly seeped through her fingers like running water. She looked up in desperation and said, "Help him."

Winn looked at Paco and then back at Bahati. "I can't. He's not going to make it." At that moment, Paco turned to Winn and smiled, revealing teeth covered with fresh blood. "Sedona. You must go. But beware there is—" He never finished his sentence.

From the head of the table Felicia straightened up, looking down at Norma while still straddling her. "Bitch," she said before spitting in her face. She pulled Norma up from the floor and set her into the chair, pulling her arms behind the high back and fastening them with a set of handcuffs.

"Is she dead?" asked Winn, who was still attending Paco.

"Hardly," said Felicia. She reached over to the table and picked up a glass of water and threw it in Norma's face. The old woman sputtered and shook her head before opening her eyes, twisting her body in every direction as she tried to gain her bearings. By now, Lars stopped assaulting the dead body of

Darryl but kicked it before walking over to Felecia and Norma.

"Just a minute," said Felicia. She disappeared down the hall for a moment and returned with two syringes filled with a brown fluid.

"Listen, bitch," she said, "you'll tell us what we want to know, or I'm gonna give you a big shot of this juice you're so fond of." Felicia held the syringe in front of Norma, who was only now returning to full consciousness. She scanned the room until she saw Darryl lying on the floor.

"Darryl," she screamed. "My boys. What have you losers done to my boys?"

Felicia slapped her hard across the face. "Who are you working for," she asked. "Give us your contacts. How did you find us, and how did you learn about the visions?"

Norma looked over and sneered. "Fuck you. Fuck you all." Her words provided all the prompting Felicia needed, and she plunged the needle into Norma's veins. Almost instantly, the old woman went rigid and began to shake as her skin changed color and became a deep shade of red. Short gurgling sounds came out of her mouth as the corners turned down, giving her the look of a sad clown.

"Norma, who do you work for?" said Winn. "What is it they want from us?"

She looked at him with torment in her eyes. "You're dead. All of you. They'll make you into lab rats and burn out the part of your brain that's you."

"Who is it, Norma? Tell us."

"You want to know? You are all so stupid. The answer is right in front of your loser noses. You're just too . . . Agggh!" Norma recoiled as Lars plunged a second needle into her neck and unloaded the contents into her bloodstream. Within seconds, her body seized and her hands curled into claws like a severe arthritis victim.

"Lars!" yelled Winn as he pulled the syringe from her neck. "What the fuck did you do that for?"

Lars turned toward Winn and flashed a threatening look. "I'm tired of that bitch lying to us and delaying. Maybe that second jolt will make her talk."

Norma strained against the chair, and as her neck swelled, bright red welts about the size of baseballs protruded through her skin. She gagged and then vomited as her head swung from side to side. "My boys, my boys," she groaned piteously. The others looked at her thrashing about, realizing that asking more questions was fruitless. Finally, after expelling a huge wad of thick, yellow phlegm, she slumped and exhaled a long, ragged breath.

"Lars, Norma was our only chance to find out what this is all about. What the hell were you thinking?" asked Felicia.

Lars stepped back and shook his head. "I—I'm not sure what came over me. There was a moment where I felt such rage for what she had done . . . I'm sorry."

Nicholas interrupted the awkward silence that followed and threw up his hands. "Well, what's done is done. We need to get out of here as quickly as possible. "Bahati and Felicia, why don't you start gathering supplies and load them in the van? Winn, Lars and I will search through the house."

The women nodded as the two men climbed the stairs to the second story while Nicholas moved into the "session" room.

Based on the decor and the pictures on the bureau, Winn realized he was in Norma's bedroom. The space had a strange, unpleasant smell that Winn couldn't place. A sickly odor of decomposition mixed with something that wasn't strong enough to mask it. *Lavender*, he thought. He rifled through clothes stuffed in her dresser but found nothing. Walking over to the nightstand, he opened the drawer and looked inside.

"Nicholas, Lars, come here," he yelled out. "I think I've found something."

***

Wanda woke up the next morning feeling refreshed. She stretched, yawned and began the morning ritual of sponge bathing and brushing her teeth. Acceptable hygiene was always a challenge, and every day they worked to keep the germs and diseases at bay. As she picked up the rough cloth and started to brush her teeth, she was reminded of the pressing need to find a doctor and dentist. Simple things like toothpaste and toothbrushes were only available to the Corporates. At some point soon, they would need to return to the factories and start manufacturing essential products.

One day at a time, she reminded herself.

"Wanda? Come out here as soon as you're dressed." Jerry Kent had a distinctive tone to his voice when there was a matter of urgency. She quickly stepped into her jumpsuit and brushed out her hair.

The morning sun was brilliant coming out of the east, and she squinted as she looked at the outlines of several people silhouetted in front of her. When she shaded her eyes, the first one she recognized was Papa Grande, the leader of the Pocks.

"Tomas?" she said with a hint of surprise.

"I'm not making any commitments," he said. "We're here to work today. If that works for you, we'll do what we can to help." Behind him, Wanda counted seven other Pocks, a mix of men and women.

She nodded. All of Pocks carried a variety of tools, including shovels, picks, screwdrivers, wrenches and hammers.

"That's fair enough," she said. "As you're aware, the fields are torn up, the latrines are spoiled, the water barrels and collection system are damaged, and we have three new bodies to bury. Please use your expertise to help in those areas.

Papa Grande nodded and turned to his people, directing them to join different groups assembling for the morning chores. He walked back to Wanda and said, "Most of us are going to the lots to replant and salvage whatever we can."

"Thank you, Tomas," she said.

"Remember, one day, Wanda. That's all we're signed up for."

The Pocks joined the regulars and put in a hard day's work, and they returned early the next morning without explanation to help finish the new planting. On the third day, they stayed past five o'clock and ate with the others. By the end of the first week, they attended the evening meetings held around a barrel fire where Wanda and her sanctuary companions explored purpose, essence and the reason for existence. Throughout the period, Wanda noticed Tomas would always return with one or two more Pocks than the day before.

Unfortunately, Wanda knew they were fighting against the clock. When the Corporate deliveries of food and water stopped completely, the genetically engineered crops were still a week away from ripening. On a particularly bleak night, she sat on a milk crate with Sam, Aisha, Talie gathered round in a circle inside her tent.

"We're out of food, Wanda, and we've used up whatever we could save," said Jerry. "We won't have enough gruel to serve for breakfast."

"How long before we can harvest," asked Wanda.

"About a week, maybe a week and a half," said Talie. "And even then, the radishes will still be a little ripe."

"Were the scroungers out today?"

"Yes," said Sam. "I doubled that detail, but every day they bring back less and less, and the missions are growing more dangerous. Two of our people ventured outside Skid Row, and one of them was beaten so badly he didn't make it. There's just no food left out there."

"Or anywhere for that matter," said Aisha.

Wanda sighed. "Well, we'll have to give everyone half as much tonight and try to stretch the supply out for the morning."

"But what then, Wanda," asked Jerry.

"Honestly, I have no idea. Remember, we need to plan for the future, but it's just as important to live in the moment. We have food for this evening, and we should be thankful for that. Tomorrow, the circumstances may be entirely different."

Her assistants nodded but without conviction. As they rose and walked out of the tent, Wanda noticed Papa Grande with a broom absently sweeping up the sidewalk and street.

"I drew latrine and sweeping duty today," he said with a shrug. "Being the OG doesn't carry much weight around here."

Wanda laughed. "We're the ultimate democracy, Tomas, but make no mistake. That you would clean the latrines and sweep the streets sends a powerful message to everyone." He shrugged, smiled back at her and then started sweeping again.

They cut the rations of gruel in half, and the scavengers returned with six cans of food, which wasn't enough to feed more than a dozen people. The sanctuary group's sphere of influence was spreading and now encompassed four-square blocks in the Skid Row neighborhood. With such growth, supplying food became paramount, and the rations given to each block in the Pock controlled area grew increasingly scarce.

When the evening's rations were served, Wanda braced for complaints, and she readied herself as a group of about ten residents approached her. As they grew closer, she saw that Iris was leading the way.

"Wanda, we want to thank you for the food. We know how hard you're working to keep us fed. We—we understand the strain this puts you under. Don't worry about us, we've survived much worse."

Wanda started to speak, but the tears welled up in her eyes, and her voice cracked. "Thank you, Iris. Thank you all."

After the evening meetings, Wanda bid everyone goodnight. She wouldn't sleep well knowing what faced her in the morning, but as she lay quietly in her small tent, she noticed the gunfire sounded more distant and more sporadic than usual. There may not be enough food, but there was always hope.

***

Wanda may have dozed, but it felt like she was up throughout the night. The familiar din grew steadily as the neighborhood began to stir in the early morning, and the challenge of dealing with a hungry crowd without any food waited just outside. She breathed deeply and stood up, dressing as she rehearsed a speech that still lacked conviction.

With a projection of purpose, she walked through the tent flap and found the crowd as expected, but they weren't looking at her. Instead, they were fixated on something down the street off to the right on the sidewalk. Wanda moved closer to the center of the commotion, trying to see past the residents. As she made her way through the crowd, many smiled, and a few patted her arm reassuringly.

Upon reaching the front of the gathering, she saw the source of their delight. Packed together in a group were 10 barrels.

"What is this?" Wanda looked around but couldn't make the connection. Sam and Talie were inspecting the 55-gallon containers when she approached.

"Three of them are full of gruel and seven have fresh water," said Talie with a wide smile.

"We'll have enough food until the crops are ready to harvest," said Sam.

"Who would have . . ." Wanda stopped, shook her head and smiled. In that instant, she realized exactly where the bounty had come from. "Where is Tomas?" she asked.

"He's at the lot on 6th working the field," said Talie. "His people got here very early this morning."

Wanda nodded. "Okay, let's get everyone fed. I'll be back in a while."

After making the short walk to the 6th avenue lot, Wanda saw Papa Grande cleaning the rows and tending the healthy new sprouts. She noticed he had dropped some weight since he started showing up every day to work. His T-shirt was stained with sweat, a telltale sign he was working the area hard.

"Tomas, can I talk to you a minute?"

The big man laid his hoe down and walked over to her, mopping his brow with a handkerchief he pulled from his back pocket. "Sure, Wanda, what can I do for you?"

"Ten barrels of food and water mysteriously showed up this morning. Do you know anything about that?"

He carefully parsed his words. "No, I can't say that I do. But that's a really great thing, isn't it? Now everyone will have food until these crops are ready."

"Tomas, I know you have people who depend on you. I hope no one is going hungry or thirsty because of us."

"No, everyone in Pock territory got their allotment," he said. "Could be the Corporates finally made a delivery. Maybe that's where it came from."

"Uh huh. You think the Corporates would deliver a shipment five times bigger than we've ever received in the middle of the night out of the kindness of their hearts?" She looked down and said softly, "Tomas, you gave us your reserves, didn't you? I—I hardly know what to say."

He neither confirmed nor denied. "Wanda, I'd like you to come to our camp after we're done working today. It's time you minister to all the Pocks at one place and time. I talk to them, but it's not the same. You give off something that I can't explain.

Something positive." He slapped his forehead. "Now I'm sounding stupid."

"Nothing you say is stupid, Tomas. I'll go with you to your camp if you think that would help."

"I do," he replied. "Now, I—ah, better get back to work."

Later, once everyone had their evening meal, Wanda walked down Alameda with Papa Grande and the other converts to the Pock headquarters. The Pocks occupied what used to be a self-storage facility that had natural protection from the river on one side and the railroad tracks on the other. The exposed area in the front was isolated by a 10-foot iron bar fence the Pocks had reinforced with barbed wire.

While the automatic locks weren't working, the front gate was secured with a heavy chain and a combination lock. Standing in front of the stronghold, Papa Grande flipped the numbers to open the lock and moved the gate enough so he and Wanda could slip inside.

The area looked more like a warehouse yard than a gang hideout. Different articles of value were grouped together, including food, water and a variety of electrical, plumbing and auto parts. In a corner of a lot they had assembled huge piles of different kinds of scrap metal and broken tools.

They walked together toward the main building as Wanda felt multiple eyes following her. When they went inside what once was the lobby, all activity stopped. A man covered in sleeve tattoos got up from the chair behind a broken desk in the front office. He came up close to Wanda, invading her personal space.

"Papa, why you bring this bitch here?" he said as a snarl crossed his face.

"She's here to talk to the group, Vlad. Get everyone together in the lot while I show her around."

"What? You fuckin' this bitch?" asked Vlad with a hearty chortle.

Papa Grande's face contorted, and he charged Vlad, grabbing the muscular man's throat and pinning him against the wall.

"Watch it, Vlad. You disrespect me like that again and I'll smear your face on this concrete wall."

Vlad spread his arms and said, "Okay, okay, Papa. I was just making a joke. A bad joke, okay?"

Slowly, Papa Grande released his grip. "Get everyone together in ten minutes, Vlad." He turned to Wanda, and his expression softened considerably. "I'm sorry, Wanda. Please, let me show you around."

Chapter Twenty-One

"How could you possibly know the date Cox traveled to? He provided no clues about his intentions."

Marshall looked up. "Remember when we were in Portales, and we were visited by the old man? The old Sixtus Maras?"

"Yes," said Zach, "but I don't know what that has to do with Mr. Cox' whereabouts in time."

"Before he expired, Sixtus whispered a number to me. It was puzzling, and I've spent many hours trying to figure out the significance. 2132364. I looked at geometric postulates, theorems and quantum physics equations, but nothing made sense . . . until this moment. Sixtus wasn't giving me a number; he was giving me a date. February 13, 2364. That's the year Cox traveled to, and that's the date where you can find him."

Zach stopped to consider the theory. "Quite compelling, Marshall. If Sixtus Maras came back from the future to warn us, it would make sense he would provide the year we would need to intervene."

"Now wait a minute," said Sarah as she stepped forward. "You're all sounding slightly unbalanced. First, you're assuming Mr. Cox has left for the future. What if he's just hiding? You're relying on some mysterious 'orb' that you speculate provides the ability to travel in time. Finally, because some old man who resembled a younger Sixtus uttered a number, you make the assumption it denotes a date and year. Do you know how absurd this might sound to a disinterested third party?"

"To a disinterested third party, maybe," said Zach, "but we are about as interested as you can get. I know Cox is the second Time Sculptor, and he's disappeared. Imagine for a moment that he was sent back and quickly found he hated our primitive culture. Then, he discovers the orb and unexpectedly possesses the power to change history and create a future world that bends to his will and accommodates his every whim."

"Yes," said Marshall. "And just as his plan reaches its apex, he returns to take his rightful place as the leader of an empire in the time of his choosing."

"There is only one person on the planet who can confirm this theory," said Marshall.

"Yes, I know," said Zach. "Xavier Watts. And there is only one person who can get us in to see him."

Pena stepped forward and looked at Zach with eyebrows arched in a way that gave him the appearance of pleading. "Speaker Randall, I beg you not to do this thing. It is extraordinarily dangerous, and you have no assurance of a favorable outcome. You — you no longer . . ."

"I know. I no longer have 'the gift'." Zach paused and looked at everyone in the room before continuing. "If we don't stop this madman, he might continue to race endlessly through time changing history to accommodate his own psychotic ends.

"Remember, the only thing he truly values is pain and suffering. He will use whatever means available to inflict as much misery on humanity as possible. Can we ignore such evil? Is the Suicide Society closing shop and turning a blind eye?"

The lack of a response, even on Sarah's part, gave him the answer he was looking for.

"Good. The first step is to talk to Delgado and see if he can get us a meeting with Watts. If we learn enough to further confirm our suspicions, Pena will take me to the orbs."

***

Delgado sat with a headset attached to a landline telephone set in the middle of a small table. He was surrounded by Zach, Marshall and the others, and they looked at him intently as he dialed the number printed on a small crumpled piece of paper he carried with him for some months. He swallowed hard and put his hand over the microphone. "They're putting me through . . ."

"Watts, it's Delgado." The pause on the other end of the line spoke volumes.

"Delgado? . . . How did you get through?"

"You've gotten sloppy, Watts. No one changed the private extensions after I left."

"Well, thank you for pointing that out. We will take care of it when we're finished here. So, what is the purpose of your call, Delgado? I'm a very busy man."

"First of all, don't bother with a trace. The call is being rerouted through India, and I can assure you I'm not in India."

"Then where are you?"

"Unimportant. The only thing that matters is that I have the information you want. The exact location of the

261

Suicide Society, and I'm willing to hand it over to you on a silver platter."

Delgado could picture the irritating smirk on Watts' face. "Assuming I believe you actually have such information, which I don't by the way, I imagine there is something you would want in return?"

"Naturally, Watts. Do you really believe I would provide something of such value for nothing?"

"Of course not. So, what is it?"

Delgado paused as the anticipation grew. "I will tell you that tomorrow when a private corporate jet picks me and my associates up at the Phoenix airport. You still have the ability to schedule a flight, am I right?"

"I see your poor sense of humor is still intact," said Watts dryly. "Obviously, I can charter a flight, but how do I know this isn't some subterfuge? After all, word has it you were wandering around homeless on a beach in Southern California."

"Your sources were wrong. I have been in Desolation, and I witnessed the confrontation between Mr. Cox and the leader of the Suicide Society. I saved Zach Randall, and that's how I know his exact location."

Watts didn't hesitate. "I'll have a plane at the airport at 6:00 a.m. your time. Be ready in the executive terminal, and by the way, who are your 'associates'?"

"Two people who helped me track down the Suicide Society. Since I left the Network, it has been my obsession."

"Fine. I will see you tomorrow around 10:00 . . . Oh, and Delgado?"

"Yes?"

262

"If this is some sort of ruse, I will have you killed immediately, as I wanted to do when you were disconnected. Only the Benefactor's compassion saved you."

"Until tomorrow, Watts."

Delgado hung up the phone and looked up at Zach and Marshall. "It's done. We leave at six o'clock."

"What if he recognizes us?" said Marshall as he fidgeted with his thumbs.

"He only saw us once for a short time from a distance, and it was under some very unusual circumstances," said Zach. "I'm counting on the fact he won't remember, or it will take him some time to recall."

The following day, Zach, Marshall and Delgado arrived at the virtually abandoned Phoenix Sky Harbor Executive terminal, where a corporate jet emblazoned with Gehenna Corporation sat on the runway with its engines idling. Two men waited at the departure doors, and a woman behind the counter ushered them through the metal detector, which wasn't turned on.

One of the men smiled and greeted them while the other one remained aloof and hidden behind mirrored sunglasses. The skies were clear and the runways deserted, so after a brief period of inspection to ensure there wasn't debris on the pavement, the jet took off and smoothly ascended to 30,000 feet. The flight itself was comfortable, but Marshall despised airplanes, and he spent the entire three and a half hour flight skirting the edges of a panic attack.

Mercifully, after what seemed like an eternity, the wheels touched down, and the plane taxied up to the nearly deserted corporate terminal at the Gehenna airport in Detroit. As usual, Marshall vowed to a nebulous deity that he would never fly again. Two members of Watt's security team stood off to the side of air stairs as they extended outward, and the group was escorted quickly through the terminal.

After a brief introduction, they were checked for weapons and led out to a well-appointed waiting Mercedes SUV limousine. The ride over to the Gehenna center was only a few blocks, and entering Building #1, they were passed off to a different set of security people.

During the elevator ride, Zach saw Delgado's eyes widen as they passed the 73rd floor and began slowing at the penthouse. The doors opened, and the escorts beckoned for them to follow as they walked down a wide corridor. At the end of the hall, they reached an office with a sign over the threshold that said, "Xavier Watts, CEO."

"Watts has moved into the Benefactor's penthouse. We need no further confirmation that Cox is gone permanently," whispered Delgado to Zach.

"I understand. Let's see what he has to say."

At that moment, the door opened, and an executive assistant gestured for them to enter.

"Good morning. I am Albert Lenzie, Mr. Watts' personal assistant. Please follow me."

The office was large and spacious as expected. A sitting area complete with a sofa, chairs and coffee table were set up in the middle of the room with a huge crystal chandelier centered directly over a Gehenna logo emblazoned into the carpet fiber. A full-sized wet bar occupied a corner of the room, and an eight-foot-wide flat panel video screen was mounted on the east wall across from an enormous stone fireplace. Off in the distance, Xavier Watts sat behind the massive mahogany desk formerly belonging to Mr. Cox.

Zach noticed Delgado's jaw muscles working as they approached the desk. Watts continued writing on a tablet and waved to the seats in front of them. Without looking up, he said, "Delgado, you are like a fungus one cannot clear up. I was hoping I would never have to see you again. Honestly, it would be better if you were dead. You claim you have information about the Suicide Society's location. Reveal it and let us be done with this meeting."

Delgado sneered. "I see you have wasted no time in assuming the Benefactor's position, but his penthouse? That you occupy his personal residence tells me what I came to find out, but I will ask anyway. Where is he?"

"It is none of your concern, Delgado. He is attending to business elsewhere and will return at the appropriate time." Watts laid the pen down and finally looked up, spending more time on Zach and Marshall and almost ignoring Delgado. "Your companions, they — they look familiar."

"You don't recognize them, do you? Well, it's understandable considering that we sat a considerable distance away from them in Desolation."

"What are you talking about? I . . ." In that moment, something triggered Watts' memory, and he rose from behind the desk and leaned forward with his arms stiff and palms on the smooth surface. "Zachery Randall!" he called out. "The Suicide Society's leader delivered right into my hands." He smiled broadly. "Delgado, this is so huge I might actually reinstate you."

"You don't seem to understand, Watts. They are not here to surrender. They're here to learn the whereabouts of Mr. Cox."

Zach leaned forward and said, "He's in the future, isn't he?"

Watts' facial muscles grew taunt for just an instant. "I—I don't know what you're talking about."

"Of course you do. He wouldn't have left abruptly without telling you where he was going. And you certainly would never have been so bold as to move into his penthouse if there was any chance he was returning."

Watts moved his arm under his desk but stopped suddenly as his hand returned to plain sight and slammed rather loudly on the desktop. He looked up in alarm and opened his mouth to speak, but no words emerged.

"No security people," said Zach. "We're not here for a confrontation. We just want to confirm what we believe we already know. Cox is a Time Sculptor, and he's returned to his native time in the future. Isn't that right?"

Watts' features conveyed the strain he was under as his hand began to tremble. "You mutant freaks," he hissed. "Release me."

Zach glanced over at Marshall. The mass inside him was an iridescent red, and the shimmering glow that defined his outline was so bright that Zach was forced to turn away. While he couldn't sense the surge of mental energy Marshall was projecting, the change in his aura and the reaction of Watts provided enough evidence to confirm what was happening.

"Watts, you are a fool as always," said Delgado while glancing at the two attendants out of earshot near the door. "You check us for weapons, but invite two members of the Suicide Society into your inner

266

sanctum. Before they boil your brain, I suggest you answer the question. Where is Cox?"

Watts sat straight up in his chair, gnashing his teeth as small beads of sweat bubbled up on his forehead. "Yes . . . yes, he's in the future."

"How did he get there?" asked Marshall as he intensified the mental assault. "This era lacks the technology and energy needed to construct and power a teleportation device. How could he do it?"

Watts' face grew so flushed and red that Zach wondered if he might stroke out. "He has something that gives him power. I saw it twice when he was passed out after drawing energy from it. It's a sphere . . . glows yellow. I think that's what he used . . . Now, leave my head."

"I will," said Marshall, "but we'll remain close by. If you try to signal anyone, we'll stop you and inflict great pain. There will be a vehicle charged or gassed up waiting for us in the driveway, and you'll accompany us out of the office and down to the lobby. Do you understand?"

Watts nodded robotically. After he called down to transportation for the car, Marshall signaled for Watts to rise as Delgado and Zach did likewise. With Watts walking stiffly in front of them, Marshall maintained a presence inside his mind, forcing him to cooperate and probing Watts' memories for information that could prove helpful in bringing down Gehenna and the HUGE conglomerate.

The elevator ride back to the lobby was tense. The security people seemed to sense something was amiss but couldn't quite figure out what it was, and Watts' orders were explicit. When they weren't looking at the flashing floor lights, they were exchanging awkward and suspicious glances.

Walking out into the lobby, Zach made eye contact with Watts and motioned toward the main exit. Watts nodded, which meant the transportation was waiting. An attendant stood by the door while holding it open, and as his dull, gray, muted mass slowly swished around, Zach knew she was under Marshall's influence.

Without pausing, they walked outside as a group, leaving Watts, the woman and the two guards at the door. The security people were talking and using animated gestures, but Watts simply held up his hand and gazed out at the shuttle.

Zach couldn't drive and Marshall was overly cautious, which left them in the hands of Delgado. As soon as the doors were locked, the former third in command squealed the tires and pulled away from the Porte cochére out onto Jefferson. A lack of gasoline, electricity and parts kept most cars off the road, so Delgado had little trouble maneuvering down what was once a 24-hour downtown traffic jam. Instead, he easily made it to the freeway and turned onto I-375.

"My sphere of influence has ended," said Marshall. "Watts has free will again." Without saying it, they all knew that meant the Corporate enforcement division would soon be in pursuit.

"The elite guards will be after us for sure," said Delgado. "They have patrols all over the city. I imagine they'll be converging on us quickly."

He made the turn onto a mostly deserted I-75 North, which was both a blessing and a curse. The lack of traffic allowed Delgado to drive at speeds exceeding 90, but it also meant their car would be an easy target to spot. All across the country, roads that weren't blocked or barricaded by bandits had turned into American autobahns, and the lack of law enforcement meant every driver took their lives into their own hands.

In Detroit, floaters were kept away from the Gehenna Center, but became more abundant the farther west one traveled. By now, those who were still alive could be found collapsed on or around the road from the fentanyl the Corporates distributed freely throughout the local neighborhoods. Sometimes they stopped in the middle of the pavement to defecate because the shoulders were covered in so much waste there was nowhere else to squat.

A loud bang thundered through the cabin as Delgado swerved sharply before recovering. A second whizzing sound followed. "Someone is shooting at us," said Zach.

"It could be anyone," replied Delgado. "Lots of guns on the streets these days, and cars are a prize. If you have a vehicle, you probably have something else of value."

They were just past the Fisher Freeway overpass when Zach saw the bright flickering outline of a car speeding down the on-ramp in the side mirror. "I think we have someone following us," he said.

Delgado looked in the rearview mirror and nodded. "Based on their rate of speed, we have to assume so. Can one of you do your mind thing and slow them down?"

"They're keeping a distance that's too far for me to reach them," said Marshall from the back seat.

"Good," said Zach, "that works out perfectly for us." He pointed at the Mack Avenue exit. "Pull off here, but wait until the last possible moment."

Delgado glanced over at him briefly, but Zach continued to stare straight ahead with a single-minded purpose. At the last second, Delgado jerked the wheel, and the car pulled onto the off ramp and continued speeding at 60 mph.

"Take a right on Mack and then a left on DeQuindre. Again, Delgado did as he was instructed while continuing to look for the trailing car behind him. When they reached Canfield, Zach signaled for Delgado to turn left yet again, and as they approached the park, he grabbed the driver's arm.

"Slow down, this is where we're going to stop." He pointed to a parking lot next to a church. "Turn in there."

Delgado looked back at Zach and squinted. "Why are we stopping here? This is a massive floater camp in the worst neighborhood in Detroit. We're likely to be killed instantly."

Zach rolled his eyes and said, "Just get out of the car, Delgado."

The air was crisp, and the wind blew as Zach zipped up his jacket and started walking down the street with Marshall following. Delgado kept a distance as three people from the park side crossed over, clearly preparing to intercept the new arrivals.

Once they were within speaking distance, Zach's face lit up, and those approaching smiled and waved enthusiastically.

"Speaker Randall; Overseer Beiner. It is such a joy to see you."

"Taj Mang, it is truly a pleasure," said Zach as he hugged the slight woman. More hugs were exchanged among the arrivals and residents, along with warm greetings. "I wish our meeting was under more favorable circumstances. How goes it here?"

She smiled and nodded. "The progress is slow, but steady. Our reach extends out three blocks now, and the violence in the park has lessened considerably. We have two fields planted over on Farnsworth, but water and sanitation are still problems. Power and food are scarce, and since they represent control, the Corporates guard them closely."

Zach looked around and surveyed the area. "You're doing wonderful things here, Taj. You and your crew are bringing the joy of Sedona to these people. I wish we could stay to help, but unfortunately, I'm afraid we have little time to visit."

"Of course," said Mang. She reached into her pocket and pulled out a key and handed it to Zach. "Our SUV is parked in the church garage. The lock is open."

Zach took the key and clasped her hands. "Thank you. We've got to go."

After exchanging more hugs and handshakes, Zach and his companions turned and walked toward the detached church garage. They passed Delgado, who looked at the floaters and then back at Zach.

"I—I don't understand," he said to Zach while trailing behind the group.

"Seedlings, Delgado. We're planting seedlings in hopeless places. Our people from the Sedona facility are here amongst the most downtrodden, teaching and helping to restore their dignity and self-respect. They drove out here in one of our SUVs from the facility, and we're going to use it to get away from here. Please get the Corporate car and park it inside when we pull out."

Marshall opened the garage door, and they climbed into the waiting F4 cruiser. Zach had to motion for Delgado to hurry as he walked slowly, still looking puzzled and dumbfounded.

They exchanged vehicles and pulled out of the parking lot, turning down Canfield. The overseers looked back at Forest Park and the endless rows of tents and cardboard boxes. The area was crowded, but neat, and the lack of litter and refuse conveyed a certain sense of civic pride. The effect produced an energy that was bright and hopeful, and it sent a chill down Marshall's spine as he tapped into it.

At the corner of Canfield and Mack, they passed the car that was trailing them. Marshall stole a quick side-glance, but the driver never bothered to look in their direction. Delgado merged back on the freeway, but no one bothered to tell him where they were heading.

Chapter Twenty-Two

Mr. Cox leaned over and poured Lars two fingers of the cheap whiskey he took from the desk of Dux Jolas. "Drink up, Lars, this may be the last time we can indulge in such pleasure, although I will say whiskey is so . . . primitive."

"You're lucky he has something so refined. The only alcohol we see comes from the hill people with their homemade stills." He picked up the glass and drained the liquid in one gulp. Mr. Cox sipped at his and then refilled Lars'.

"I have an assignment for you," he said with a hint of intrigue in his voice. "It will not be easy, but it is essential."

"I am listening," said Lars while attacking his second drink with the same gusto as the first.

Mr. Cox drummed his fingers as though he was trying to figure out how to broach the subject. "You seem to prefer the direct approach, so I will be blunt. I need you to travel back to the past."

Lars lurched forward and spit half his drink back into his glass. "The past? Have you lost your mind? The last Casimir Vacuum was destroyed by the pacifists a hundred years ago. They wanted to prevent anyone from altering history ever again. They have very few precepts, but eschewing the timeline is one of their most fundamental principles."

"I suspected as much," said Mr. Cox after another small sip. "Still, I know there is a functioning apparatus somewhere. In all likelihood, there are several."

"And what makes you so sure?"

"Because I knew you in the past. I sensed it all along but could not be sure. That is why I made the effort to locate you when I arrived here in the future. Once I found out you existed here, I knew exactly why I sent you back. This reality is far from what I envisioned, and I apparently have confidence that you can correct certain — defects in the plan."

"Assuming a Kerr Ring setup actually exists, and you can somehow generate the power to drive it, why would you not simply go back yourself?"

Mr. Cox shook his head. "Impossible. I would have to arrive during a time when an imprint of me is already there, and to make the necessary changes, I would have to come in contact with the earlier version of myself. You know the theoretical implications of such an interaction."

"A collapse of space-time into an instant black hole . . . theoretically,"

"Yes. I imagine that was my rationale behind sending you."

Lars finished his drink and set his glass down. "And should I make it back to the past, what am I to accomplish?"

Mr. Cox clenched his teeth and hissed, "Elimination of The Suicide Society. A damnable organization that has thwarted my plans at every juncture. As I look at this so-called 'pacifist' movement, I cannot help but believe they are

274

responsible for it. I used every method at my disposal, but I could not completely eradicate them."

"Yes, your plan worked out brilliantly," said Lars with more than a hint of sarcasm. "Where are they? I mean, in the past. Where do they assemble?"

"I do not know, exactly," said Mr. Cox, "and I am reluctant to give you too many details for fear it will influence your actions. We cannot allow the same reality to play itself out again. I can only tell you that when you arrive, they will be in Portales, New Mexico. Approach them with extreme caution. They are extraordinarily cunning, and they possess the capacity to affect your mind."

"I see," said Lars as he rose from the table. "I will remember that in the unlikely event any of what we are discussing comes to pass. In the meantime, you will excuse me as I have a battle to prepare for." He turned on his heel and began walking away as Mr. Cox said from behind, "Ah, I do not recall dismissing you."

Lars stopped, and his back stiffened noticeably. He was about to speak when the tent flap opened and Minkus Term walked in. "Sir, word has been spread throughout the city. You are set to speak at the old church at 3:00 p.m. We should begin making preparations.

"Yes, yes, of course." Then, looking up, Mr. Cox said, "You are dismissed, Lars. Carry on with your task." Lars' sneer was hidden as he exited the tent.

"They have arranged quarters for you," said Term as he led the way over to a series of tents in the center of the camp. "In fact, they are giving you the VIP tent."

"Yes, but it is still a tent and not what I am accustomed to." As he stepped inside, Mr. Cox surveyed the interior of the space. The contrast with his penthouse in Detroit was startling. Over in the corner sat a bed with a conventional mattress. A desk sat on the opposite side with two unpadded chairs. Someone set a pipe rack near the shower, and several sets of clothes hung on it.

"I know the accommodations are Spartan, but they are much better than what would be afforded in the rebel camp," said Term.

Mr. Cox walked over and fingered the garments. The 3-D printed clothing from this period was far more comfortable than the stitched fabrics of the 21st century, but he found more of the handmade garments in his wardrobe every day.

"Term, why is my attire so full of hand-sewn clothing? These materials irritate my skin. Please find more seamless articles. That is what I prefer."

The attendant hung his head and shifted his eyes up uncomfortably. "Pacifists believe that 3D printing spoils the environment. The raw materials must be mined, and they do not engage in such activities. That means only recycled natural-fiber clothing is available."

Mr. Cox stood silently for a moment before letting out a low growl and pushing the clothing rack over. "I know these pacifists are the spawn of that accursed Suicide Society. My plan was foolproof and ran through thousands of simulations when I was connected to the NIN system. I am living my worst nightmare."

Minkus Term stooped down even lower. "I hardly know what to say . . ."

"Suicide, Term. Why do I not sense anyone committing suicide here? Before I left, suicide among the Kren class was an epidemic."

"Pacifists never commit suicide, sir. It is not forbidden, but they just do not engage in it. I assume it is because most of them claim they are content knowing a better existence awaits once they die."

"Utterly maddening," said Mr. Cox as he undressed and stepped into the shower, muttering loudly as the lukewarm water cascaded over him. When he finished bathing, he leaned over and picked up a loose fitting orange Henley and stepped into a pair of white cotton trousers. In short order, he turned to Term and motioned him over, pointing to his dark canvas shoes. "I always receive assistance with my footwear . . . Oh, I do miss Hefe."

Term stooped over and carefully fitted a shoe onto each foot, respectively. When he was finished, he stood up and bowed awkwardly, unsure of protocol. Finally, he leaned down and kissed each foot.

The Benefactor rolled his eyes and pulled his feet away. "It is 2:30, Term. Let us make our way over to the old church."

A ground crawler was ready and waiting as they walked out to the gate. Malconus was already behind the wheel, so Mr. Cox and Term got in the backseat. Once they were situated, Malconus turned around and said, "General Cron suggests we take an armed escort."

Mr. Cox waved him off. "No, we do not want to intimidate these people. In fact, we want to appear as non-threatening as possible."

Malconus nodded, turned back, and engaged the thrust, and the vehicle responded by moving at a moderate pace along a pathway cut through the theta. Even though it was the dry season, excessive humidity hung in the air, and the temperature approached 90. Mr. Cox could not help but curse his poor luck. As if everything in this time wasn't bad enough, he had to be in a place that was hot in the winter.

Since the tropical rainforest had long ago been cut and processed for commercial gain in the 20th and 21st century, the ground crawler moved swiftly through the resulting grasslands, completing the drive to the old church in less than 15 minutes. As they rounded a bend and the land flattened out, Mr. Cox could see a large gathering outside the church. If the size of that crowd was any indication, the church itself would be standing room only.

He waved to those who watched the vehicle pull up next to the building, but they did not wave back. Instead, he was greeted with stares that ranged in intensity from blank to hostile while the majority simply looked on with mild curiosity. Mr. Cox waited for Malconus to open his door, and the Benefactor stepped out with the panache he felt was befitting for the leader of the world. With his head held high and eyes peering down his nose, he walked with great purpose, gesturing with his hand as though he was tipping a cap.

Inside the church, the pews were packed with people who strained to get a glimpse of Mr. Cox as he strolled up the nave to the wall of brick that once supported a table for the sacraments. Instead, only rubble lay strewn across the floor. A person he assumed held some position of authority in the city walked up and introduced himself as Jan Mabatus, shaking hands while transferring an abundance of sweat.

A small filament of dark energy entered Mabatus' mind, so subtle he couldn't notice it. Yet, a tremor rippled through his body, and he shook slightly before turning away and slinking into the background. By the time the gathering ended, he would be an advocate for joining with Gehenna.

Mr. Cox smiled and licked the man's sweat from his palm before turning toward the crowd, allowing fear and trepidation to flow from their bodies and release through the heat their heightened sense of awareness generated. He stopped to enjoy the moment and inhaled deeply to absorb the full effect.

Finally, he held out his arms to quiet the buzz in the crowd. "My friends," he said while smiling widely, "I come to you today to finish our discussion that ended so, uh, tragically yesterday. I extended my condolences to Mayor Jan Mabutus. Unfortunately, it is a dangerous world, and it is important to choose your allies carefully." Mr. Cox paused for effect and then began pacing across the makeshift stage.

"You have been told there are only two paths. Either the way of the pacifists or the Corporates, led by Amrosia. Until now, perhaps those were your only two choices. One would give you peace, they say. Of course, you lose all sense of self as you join their cult, er, I mean commune. You will break your back working every day to provide enough for your family to eat, hopefully. All the while, you are told that your rewards will come after you die. My, isn't that convenient?"

There was much head nodding and some grumbling as neighbors turned to whisper to each other.

"On the other hand, Amrosia offers the same misery they have delivered for two centuries. They lack ingenuity and creativity, and the result of their incompetence is stunningly obvious." Mr. Cox wiped his brow as the ambient energy combined with his intensity.

"Amrosia was never meant to lead anything, let alone the HUGE conglomerate. In the 21st century, they were run by a second-rate CEO who came to power in an illegal corporate takeover. With your help, I intend to take back control of my company and provide the kind of prosperity intended for Gehenna and HUGE."

A smattering of applause followed. Mr. Cox walked over to a small table and poured himself a glass of water.

"I am a Time Sculptor," he said as the crowd gasped. "I am the first Time Sculptor to traverse the centuries back to the time from which he came. Yes, I returned from the past to rectify the horrors you are experiencing." He waited for the din to die down.

"I am the one who founded the Gehenna Corporation. This is documented. I am the one who founded the HUGE conglomerate. This was done to help improve your lives and the lives of everyone in this era. By now, if my plan had not been corrupted, you would all be living in perpetual prosperity. The Kren class was to be eliminated. With my leadership, everyone was to become an Udulate.

"My dream has been subverted by the evil ones at Amrosia. Dantar Llross represents the futile past. Even now, her forces camped around your town have defected and joined us. Soon, we march to Juande, the last Amrosian stronghold on this continent. However, we need soldiers to defeat them."

He waited for the low frequency hum of the crowd to crescendo and then die down before continuing. "Under my leadership, you will keep your identity. There will be greater prosperity for your families, and you will be able to preserve your unique culture and identity. Do not join the hive mentality of the pacifists and become lost in their collective.

"This is your place and time to make a difference that history will remember and thank you for." His eyes were blazing, and the perspiration rolled off his forehead as he paced the floor like a preacher in the midst of a revival. "So, I ask you, are you with me?"

Heads nodded and several people clapped. A few shouted "yes" from the gallery. Mr. Cox shook his head. "People, this is an opportunity to seal your place in history. Your time to secure the future of all mankind." His voice echoed off the walls as he shouted, "I ask you. Are you with me?"

The crowd erupted and stood on its collective feet, clapping and shouting. The energy grew dark as the vengeance and hatred Mr. Cox projected saturated the room before diving deep into the hearts of those gathered in the church. Mayor Mabutus fought his way through the crowd and grabbed Mr. Cox' hand with his sweaty palm. As the Benefactor looked out over the crowd, a chant started, small at first, but it quickly grew in volume.

Kill the Amrosians . . . Kill the Amrosians . . . The tone of the chant grew malevolent as it shook the rafters of the building. Mr. Cox stepped back and soaked in the bouquet of the primitive emotions and smiled before coming forward and asking for quiet.

"We need people willing to fight and die. Mayor Mabatus will give you our departure time. Bring vehicles and any weapons you may have. The trek will be arduous, but ours is a righteous cause. Now, you are all part of the HUGE conglomerate!"

Amidst much shouting and mayhem, Mr. Cox made his way back down the nave as people reached out hoping to touch the charismatic leader. Just before he reached the exit, a small, bony decrepit man stepped from the crowd to block his way. He looked up and pulled his cracked lips back to reveal bleeding gums and a single rotted tooth in his upper palate.

"Voodoo," he said. "I am Abidemi of Kabye, and you come from the depths of the darkest place in infinite space. We wish to align ourselves with you, Prevus Coxnotus. You are the Dark King, and your power is strong. Much stronger than I have ever experienced before, but not strong enough to defeat your enemies. He comes for you Prevus Coxnotus." He extended an arm crippled by advanced arthritis, a knobby finger pointed at the Benefactor.

Mr. Cox stopped and looked at the old man. When their eyes met, he experienced a depth of emptiness and coldness he rarely felt in anyone else. "Who comes for me?" he asked.

The old man's eyes widened. "You know who he is, Prevus Coxnotus. Even here, he haunts your dreams, and he will come for you. We have used all our magic to protect you, but it is not enough."

"Where do you reside, Abidemi of Kabye?"

"The villages in Cameroon, Nigeria and many of the other old places. We have survived the brutal oppression of the interlopers as we knew for generations that you would return. It is foretold in the stories and fables that you would lead us to the place of ascension, *Petro loa.*"

Mr. Cox whispered to Term, "Voodoo? How does this man openly profess his other worldly beliefs without fear of reprisal?"

"The pacifists strongly encourage spiritual belief. Religion and philosophy have flourished in the areas they control."

Mr. Cox' face tightened, but he paused for a moment as a smile spread slowly across his face. "I assume that means all types of beliefs and philosophies."

Term nodded. "Yes. Belief is varied and abundant."

"Does that include Satanists? They existed in significant numbers in the past."

"Yes, I have heard they exist in this time as well, although they are fragmented under a variety of different names. Their numbers are not large, but they have a presence."

Mr. Cox turned back to the voodoo shaman. "I appreciate your coming today. I want you to organize your followers and come to the encampment on the outskirts of town. You will accompany me as we seize Jaunde. Prepare your spells and bring your dolls. We must rain misery down upon our enemies."

"Yes, yes, Petro Loa, we will gather and be ready. Those who practice voodoo in West Africa, Central Africa, Haiti, America and the rest of the world will be ready for your orders." The man fell to his knees and wrapped his arms around the Benefactor's legs.

Mr. Cox placed a hand on the old man's shoulder and sent out a thread of dark energy laden with just enough pain to make him gasp. He looked up with tears in his eyes. "It is true," he gasped. "You have come back for our salvation."

With both arms, Mr. Cox helped the man to his feet. "Go now and organize your followers. I will be waiting."

The crowd gathered in the aisle in such a way that Mr. Cox could not leave easily without stopping to interact with his recent converts. With their arms stretched out, they tried to make eye contact, or if they were lucky, touch his garments. Term and Malconus struggled to clear a pathway to the front of the church, but the aisle was clogged with people, and it didn't help that sweaty-palmed Mayor Mabatus was doing everything in his power to further engage Mr. Cox in conversation.

When they reached the area that was once the courtyard, Malconus retrieved the ground crawler as Mr. Cox talked with the mayor. "I have laid the foundation here, Mabatus. I expect you to organize a force of at least 500. Tell them to bring whatever weapons they have. Clubs and stones if nothing else. We will need every people mover at your disposal."

"Sadly," said Mabatus, "we have no way to transport people. The pacifists offered us mass transit road crawlers. This was part of the appeal of allowing them to infiltrate."

Mr. Cox stepped inside the ground crawler. "This is maddening," he said to Malconus. "We have no way to bring the followers to the battle."

"Mabatus, how do you transport goods?" Malconus leaned over and spoke directly to Mabatus.

The mayor scratched his head. "Trailers are pulled by the beasts of burden. Donkeys and oxen."

"Gather them and bring them to the church area. We have 15 ground crawlers that can pull your trailers. We will fill them with citizen soldiers."

Mr. Cox nodded enthusiastically. "Superb idea, Malconus. Now, let us return to our camp to organize the incursion."

Once they were back inside the walled confines of the base camp, Mr. Cox felt the nervous energy of soldiers who knew a battle was imminent. Packs were assembled, uniforms washed and pressed, weapons cleaned and loaded. The mechanics made sure the plasma turbine engines were tuned. Although the trek would only take about seven hours, moving a mass of people over distance was never a simple task.

Mr. Cox walked into the command tent to find Zietra X, Dux Jolas, General Cron and Lars huddled over maps of the facility at Jaunde. He briefly looked over Lars' shoulder until Cron stepped to the side to make room for him.

"Well, we have the brightest strategic minds in Gehenna gathered here. What will be the plan of attack?" he asked.

"With just 150 troops, we will be significantly outnumbered. Yet, even with only 150, it will be difficult to transport that many people," said Jolas. "If we arrive in seven hours, we will be fortunate."

"What about the hyperloop tunnels?"

"By now, the stragglers will have migrated on foot from the defeat in Nigeria. They will sabotage the Hyperloop to keep us from being able to use them."

"So, what is our plan?" asked Mr. Cox.

"We do not have enough firepower to sacrifice our troops in a frontal assault, so we will have to be covert. Fortunately, this building is two centuries old, and there are two gray wastewater access tunnels that run about a quarter mile to a processing facility near the lake. They have not used them since we began converting waste to food, so they will not be guarded. From the east, we will get in through an old room they used to house the big heaters and air conditioners."

"I would feel so much better if we have a diversion," said General Cron.

"A diversion? How about 500 people storming the front gates? Would that help?" asked Mr. Cox while stepping away from the table.

"Why . . . yes, naturally it would," said General Cron. "But they would be massacred . . ."

"I will have them here in the morning. You just figure out a way to get them to Jaunde."

Chapter Twenty-Three

Nicholas and Lars came over and stood behind Winn as he looked down at an open book with handwriting scribbled in small tight letters. He flipped the page and continued reading.

"Well?" said Nicholas. "What does it say?"

"Norma was one of us. She had the visions, and her doctors turned her over to the skankers. According to what she wrote, they did thousands of tests on her and found her theta brain wave activity was much more intense than the average person. After the brainwashing process was complete, the Corporates used her to find and capture those with the same ability. Our unusual brains' wave signatures were like a tracking beacon. That's how she found us."

"Well, I'll be damned," said Nicholas. "So, Norma had the visions, and they forced her into becoming the caretaker of this house of horrors."

"Yes, but it seems like she came to like her work a little too much," said Winn.

"Did she know anything about Sedona?" asked Lars.

Winn shook his head. "It says early on in the journal that she was drawn to Sedona like we were, but like us, she just didn't know why, and it became her obsession to find out by torturing us."

"Probably lost the visions just like Brandon and Renata," said Nicholas. "That would explain why she became so sadistic. The visions made her feel special somehow, and they took that away, so she wanted to take it away from all of us."

"How could visions of despondent people committing suicide make anyone feel special?"

"I don't know, but there was something about them that made her feel better about herself. Important maybe. I . . ." Winn stopped flipping pages and focused on a specific passage.

"What is it?" said Lars as he looked over Winn's shoulder.

"She claimed we have greater abilities than just seeing visions of other people committing suicide. Norma claims the Corporate interrogators told her those with 'the gift', as she calls it, can do other . . . things."

"Like what?" Now he had Nicholas's attention.

"Things like reading minds, influencing the actions of others and causing pain. A combination of telepathy and telekinesis. She claims she used to be able to do those things before they experimented on her. They were looking for a way to neutralize her abilities, and apparently, they found it." He began flipping pages and reading other passages.

"This is gruesome," he said. "They gave her massive quantities of hallucinogenic cocktails that contained PCP, mescaline, LSD and bath salts."

"So, that's the shit she was giving us," said Nicholas.

"I imagine it was," said Lars. "I wonder if any of what she wrote is true?"

Winn moved over and sat on the bed. "There's something more. She claims the suicide visions are real."

Nicholas cocked his head. "Real? Are you kidding me? That has to be bullshit."

Winn shrugged and folded the journal before sticking it in his back pocket. "I don't know, maybe it's all bullshit. Or, maybe it's not."

"We were stuffed into a dark basement and tortured for a reason." said Nicholas. "So, there might be something to all of this."

"Well, one thing is for certain, we need to get the hell out of here right now," said Lars.

Winn nodded, and together, they made their way back to the kitchen where Bahati and Felicia were already waiting.

"We didn't find much of anything useful," said Bahati. "A handful of cartridges for the shotgun, rifle and handgun. Apparently, whoever was supplying the ammunition wanted them to have limited firepower. We also have the keys to the van."

"Did you find any food?"

"Yes," said Felicia. "We put all of the canned goods and nonperishables in a sack. There should be enough food for a few days. Norma kept several gallon jugs of water, so we're okay there."

"Is it all loaded in the van?" asked Winn.

Felicia nodded. "We're ready to go. There's a half-tank of gas, which hopefully will get us to Sedona."

"C'mon, let's get moving."

"One more thing," said Felicia. "We've got Norma's cell phone. No one has service, but somehow she did. There is one number in her call history."

"She must have a satellite phone. We'll look at it once we're clear of this place."

"We . . . I mean, I called the number. A woman answered, so I just hung up," said Felicia.

Winn raised his eyebrows while Nicholas groaned. "Felicia, no. They'll know something is wrong. Let's finish loading up and get out of here."

Winn had just finished placing the last of the supplies in the van when he heard a loud knock on the door. Lars grabbed the 30-06 while Nicholas picked up the shotgun. Bahati took the pistol and ducked behind the table. The rapping on the door became louder.

"Norma, open up. It's Jertron. I got a call to check on you. I need a progress report."

"He's probably not alone," Winn whispered to Lars. "Every time people come to the house I hear multiple footsteps."

"You're right. Let's get to the van."

"No," said Winn. "They'll certainly have a faster vehicle than that old van."

"Then we'll have to disable their car somehow. Getting into a firefight with them with these weapons and limited ammunition won't work," said Lars.

"Norma! Open up right now." The voice outside was growing more urgent and demanding.

Winn scuttled over to Felicia. "In your best Norma voice, tell him 'just a minute'."

Felicia looked at him strangely, but he waved his hand in a circle to emphasize the need for haste.

"Just a minute," she said while trying to emulate the same low drawl Norma used. "We just got the retards chained back in the cellar."

There was a pause. "I'm giving you one minute to open this door, or we're going to bust it down."

Lars put his finger to his lips and motioned for everyone to follow him into the garage. Once past the service door, they got into the van with as little noise as possible.

"When I give the signal, you start the engine. Once I pull the emergency release on the garage door, floor it. Leave the sliding door open and I'll jump in as you pass. Wherever they're parked, pull up next to them so I can get a shot at one of their tires. Things are going to happen fast, so keep your head about you."

Winn nodded and clutched the wheel with one hand and kept his other hand on the key. Lars started a countdown at five, and just as he finished mouthing "one," Winn twisted the key while Lars pulled the emergency release and flung the door open.

The engine caught spark, and Winn quickly surveyed the scene out of the rear-view mirror. Whoever was at the front door arrived in a large SUV, and it was parked in the middle of the driveway.

"Aw, fuck," said Winn as he locked eyes with a man sporting a large afro sitting in the driver's seat. Momentarily frozen, he gave Winn enough time to gun the engine and maneuver the van around the other vehicle, albeit with a sizable chunk taken out of the side of the garage door frame.

As they planned, Lars jumped in, and when they were parallel to the SUV, Winn slammed on the brakes. The driver started to duck just as Lars squeezed the trigger, sending a slug into the sidewall of the front tire, which instantly deflated it. Winn gunned the engine and slammed the pedal to the floorboards.

The van rocked from side to side as it bounced over the curb onto the street. As he looked in the mirror, Winn could see two men running toward them waving weapons. When it became clear they couldn't catch the van, they fired a series of shots that slammed into the back tailgate and tore a hole through the metal. Another volley followed as they turned onto 111th Ave, and two more slugs ripped through the side door.

"Oh, shit, I've been hit," said Nicholas.

Felicia moved over and examined Nicholas's arm. "Is it bad?" he asked her while grimacing and guarding his damaged appendage like a broken wing.

"No," said Felicia. "It just took a chunk out of your skin. It's a deep flesh wound, but I think I can get the bleeding stopped.

"I packed some gauze and bandages. They're in that backpack," said Bahati. "Pack it tight."

"Shit, Winn, look out!" yelled Lars.

***

As they walked down the corridor, Wanda looked into each of the storage units the Pocks converted into living areas. Every unit had a mattress on the floor, a waste bucket, bowl and pitcher. Some residents had taped pictures, magazine pages, sports images and erotica to the walls while other cubicles were stark and barren.

"Where do you live, Tomas?" she asked as they turned a corner.

"I'm in what used to be the living quarters for the manager," he said. "I have a toilet that flushes if you fill the tank with water. It's bigger than these, and it's the one perk I give myself."

"No doubt well-deserved."

He smiled, and they turned down another hallway as a woman approached from the opposite direction. She was balding badly and looked malnourished. "Papa, Vlad has gathered everyone together out by the wrecked cars."

Papa turned and looked at Wanda. "I guess you're on."

She nodded, and together they made their way back to the lobby where Vlad and two other Pocks waited. Vlad stubbed out a hand-rolled cigarette and motioned for them to follow. When Papa Grande wasn't looking, he shot Wanda a look that conveyed his contempt.

Wanda looked out at the Pocks gathered in the heavily fortified parking lot. While others might see a gang of vicious, unconscionable killers, she saw a group of tired, malnourished and frightened people. She understood the energy it took to maintain such a veneer of toughness and anger while suppressing the relentless guilt attached to the horrific crimes they committed. There were an equal number of men and women in the gang, probably numbering around 50. All of them were muscular and battle hardened. The world had truly reverted to a state of survival of the fittest.

Standing inside the bed of a broken down pickup truck, Papa Grande helped Wanda up before facing his legion. "This shit is hard," he said without an introduction. "We know that. Every day we fight and kill to protect our turf. We scrounge for shit to eat." He paused and made eye contact with several of the higher-ranking gang members.

"Now, we have to go outside our territory because we've used up most of the shit we have here. But the Crege and other gangs got the same problem. That means more fighting for less and less."

"We don't have no worries, Papa," said Vlad. "The Corporates come and give us food and water. The food is shit, sure, but it keeps you alive."

Papa Grande pointed to one of the bigger units near the front of the building. "That's where we keep the reserves," he said. "We were able to build them up because we stole food and water from the weaker people. But now, the Corporates have stopped coming around, and we've been pulling from the reserves. We won't be able to feed our own people soon, and the floaters outside these gates are getting restless. No good time to say this: we're gonna run out of food soon, and we're low on water."

Restless shifting, fear, and looks of anger greeted his words. After allowing them to digest the new information, Papa continued, "But we got hope, and it's this lady. I went over there to kill her, and I did kill one of her people." He hung his head and shook it slowly. "We tore the place up and destroyed everything she was doing. I'm ashamed of it. But you know what? She wouldn't back down. Toughest *mujer* I ever met, and I've known a bunch of tough ones. She ain't afraid to die. That's her edge. When we fucked up all her work, do you know what she did? She just started over."

He looked at Wanda and gestured. "She has a way that can lead us outta this shithole. I want you to listen to her."

Papa Grande moved farther back into the bed as Wanda stepped forward. She took a deep breath. "I'm not here to offer you much except a way to feel better about yourselves and your lives."

"Oh yeah, and how you gonna do that, lady?" asked a woman with raven black hair and a face tattoo of a skull with a dagger through it.

"By doing something positive." Wanda didn't skip a beat. "Take an action that improves something instead of tearing it down. It's as simple as that."

Many in the group either laughed or groaned. "We got it a lot better than other people out there," said someone in the back. "Why the fuck should we listen to you?"

Wanda shrugged. "You have it better . . . What does that mean, really? That you're only slightly less miserable than they are? You take from them because you're stronger, but how long before some group that's larger and armed with better weapons take what you have left?

"I saw where you live," she continued. "Your little cubicles have no windows. Great for safety, but you can't see the green grass or smell fresh air. Frankly, your building stinks. Urine stained mattresses, garbage, filth and human waste. Yeah, you're really living it up."

Subtly, they began edging closer to her. "A single positive act changes everything." She knew she had their attention. "A decision to improve something changes everything. When we work together for the common good, we can grow our own food and purify our own water. When people feel safe, they come out of the shadows. Who knows what we might accomplish? Maybe we find enough people with specialized skills we could get the power turned back on. Yet, it all begins here in this place at this time."

"So, you're plantin' beans and shit. That's what's supposed to save us?" Vlad leaned up against the building dragging on another home-rolled cigarette.

"We're raising a variety of crops. In a week or so, we'll have enough to feed everyone living on 6th and San Julian and several blocks out. If you help us, we would be able to feed double your number."

"Papa, this is crazy shit," said Vlad. "You can't be serious."

"Oh, he's serious," said a Hispanic man while fingering rosary beads. "I been with him the last three days. These people are onto something. It's not just growing shit and stuff. When I work with them I feel . . . better. I can't explain it."

"Same with me," said a thin woman in her 20s with a long, angry scar over her left eye. "Jerry, Talie, Sam and Wanda, they give off these vibes that make me feel good, so I started thinking different. I . . ."

The woman was cut short as a single shot rang out followed by several more as everyone in the lot ran for cover, an old 1990s Cadillac skidded to a violent stop, and two people on the driver's side unloaded their automatic weapons simultaneously. Most of the bullets were caught by the old mattresses the Pocks wired to the fence, but several more made it through and ricocheted off the building, abandoned cars and other objects in the yard. There was a pause as the shooters reloaded, and that was when Vlad rose up and fired back while screaming at the top of his lungs.

Three of his slugs impacted the side of the car, and one of them must have hit the guy in the backseat because he fell over sideways and hung out the window. Another gang member sporting Crege tattoos leaned over and pulled him back into the cab. With lead flying in both directions, the driver finally had enough. The tires squealed as the Caddy sped off.

Without checking for casualties, Vlad ran inside the building and came out with two more AR-style weapons. "C'mon, get your guns. Those were Crege. We have to track them down."

Several Pocks stood up to make sure the attack was over. Papa Grande held up his hand and said, "Is anyone hurt?" He scanned the grounds, but no one was laid out or seemed to be injured. "Good. Then let Wanda continue."

Vlad whipped his head around violently. "Are you fuckin' crazy? That was a hit. We can't let that go without responding."

"That's the second Crege hit this week," said Papa. "There will be plenty of time to hit them back, Vlad."

"And to what end?" asked Wanda as she got back on her feet. "They attack you, and you respond. More people die; more property is destroyed. I'd like you to tell me who prospers from that? Who is better off because of it? Who does it help to reach their potential?"

"Reach their *potential?*" said Vlad as his eyes widened and jaw clenched. "What in the fuck are you talking about? We don't respond they'll be back to finish us off."

"I don't think so, Vlad. They can never finish us off. There are too many of us. If they kill some, others will take their place. The loss of this temporary housing," said Wanda as she held out her arm and pinched flesh, "is a small price to pay. We transition from one form to another, and our sacrifice may save the world. If we show no fear, they cannot prevail."

Realizing the immediate danger had passed, the other Pocks started to assemble in front of Wanda, moving even closer than before. "What would we do? How would we begin?" said a man with an impediment that suggested he had lost part of his tongue.

"Can I ask your name?"

297

"Log . . . I mean, Err-ah." He struggled with the "l" sound and looked down sheepishly while those surrounding him tittered. "Friends call me, Log," he said finally.

Wanda smiled. "Sure, Log. If you or anyone else wants to join us at our camp on San Julian tomorrow, we'll put you to work. I noticed several empty lots just down the street a ways from here. You have a great location right next to the river. We could start planting on the lot next door tomorrow. The natural irrigation would cut the work in half."

Wanda looked at Papa as he extended a hand to help her down from the truck bed. "I'll take you back up to your camp," he said, and she nodded. After talking privately with several of Pocks on her way out, Wanda waved and began walking with Papa back toward Alameda.

"Wanda, why don't you move over here and stay with us?" he said softly while keeping his eyes focused on the ground. "You'll have a roof over your head, and it'll be much safer than living out on the street. The bigger you get, the more of a target you are."

She reached over and squeezed his arm affectionately. "I truly appreciate the offer, Tomas, and your concern is touching. But I wasn't put here to hide. Unless you have room for everyone on San Julian, that's where I belong."

Papa Grande nodded, and they walked for the next block without talking. "Wanda," he said as he stopped and gently grasped her arm, "who put you here? Was it… God?"

"No, not God," she said. "Someday, I'll be able to tell you that, but unfortunately, not right now. What I can say is that the people in the place I come from represent the greatest hope for the survival of humanity."

***

The following morning, Wanda rose and walked over to the bowl on the quarter table. She splashed water on her face and changed into a fresh jumpsuit. The old one went into a bag that would join a pile of other garments the clothes washing detail would take down to the river.

After stepping outside, she stopped short. A large group lingered around her tent with Papa Grande standing in front of them. "They're all here," he said. "Everyone except Vlad wanted to come. We're all in."

Wanda nodded. "We welcome you," she said to the assembled Pocks at large. "Divide yourselves into four groups. The first group will work with Sam; the second with Jerry; the third with Talie and the fourth with Aisha. And please, don't hesitate to ask questions." She pointed to the various team leaders who were organizing people and getting them prepared for the day's work assignments.

Talking privately with Papa Grande she said, "This is a big day, Tomas. Some of our crossbred radishes are ready for harvesting. Our people will be eating natural food for the first time in years. It's pretty exciting."

"It is exciting," he replied. "And it's all because of you, Wanda. You and your friends have taught these people to hope again."

"They only needed to open their minds to the possibility of a different way." As she was speaking, she saw Sam running up to them from the corner of her eye.

"Wanda, there is a Corporate vehicle coming up 6th. They stopped at the corner and someone got out. He's just walking around and talking to people."

Wanda turned to Papa, who nodded, and she hurried off down San Julian to the corner. A large SUV sat idling, producing the familiar high-pitched whine of an electric drive motor. The exterior of the vehicle glistened with fresh polish, and Wanda wondered if it was brand new.

Are they even making new cars anymore?

She slowed as she caught up with the Corporate representative, who was casually strolling down 6th toward San Pedro, looking through the dirty windows of a building that used to be a mission. When she was within 20 feet, he turned toward her and smiled.

"Good morning, Ms. Parsens. Isn't it a wonderful day? Just a hint of chill in the air. Ah, I love California winter weather."

"I'm sorry, I didn't catch your name?"

"Oh, how impolite of me. My name is Cameron Wintz. I am the HUGE regional manager for this area."

"I see. And what brings you down to Skid Row, Mr. Wintz? We rarely get visitors of your standing."

"Well, I'm always interested in the welfare of our residents. I've been receiving some very . . . unusual reports on your activities. Perhaps we could talk? I have a very interesting proposition . . ."

Chapter Twenty-Four

Zach instructed Delgado to get back on I-375, which eventually merged into I-94 heading east. They continued traveling about half an hour before clearing the outskirts of Detroit. The medians and shoulders lacked any sort of vegetation, and the landscape looked like everything along the route, scorched and burned even though there was no evidence of a fire.

"How come these freeways are empty?" asked Marshall. "Even the street people are gone. It's like we're the only ones out here. A few months back, we wouldn't have been able to drive down a major road without being assaulted. I saw an old movie when I was a child where everything was deserted like this. I can't remember the name of it."

"Mad Max," said Zach. "I remember watching as a kid. It scared the hell out of me, and now we're living it. Unbelievable."

"It's deserted because everyone is either dead or too afraid to come out of hiding," said Delgado somberly. "Many of the survivors are probably in a Corporate relocation camp."

"A Corporate relocation camp? What the hell is that?"

"The plan was to harvest these street people and use them to serve the Corporate elite. They even had a term for them. Watts called them 'Kren,' which is a mustard plant of some sort. I don't know who came up with the name, but Mr. Cox liked it. Clearing the streets of these people was a high priority since they were an embarrassment to HUGE. In the re-education institutes, they're taught menial labor and servant skills before they're relocated to one of the protected areas."

"How horrible," said Marshall.

"Well, it's either that or they die in the streets. There aren't any good choices."

The vehicle drove down south Rawsonville Road for another 10 minutes before Zach said, "Pull in here."

"What?" said Delgado as he slowed. "This is an abandoned airport. You have a plane?"

"Just pull in."

The SUV rolled slowly down the entry road, moving closer to the small, boarded up executive terminal. Just as they reached the end of the parking lot, a loud roar exploded from the runway behind the building.

"Let's go," said Zach as Delgado parked the car. They exited and ran in a pack to the runway where a sleek Hawker 900 XP stood with its engines at idle speed. The stairway was already extended to the ground, and Zach could see hot red infra signatures around each engine. He signaled for everyone to run toward the plane, and they covered the ground quickly, looking over their shoulders periodically to confirm they weren't being followed.

Once they reached the aircraft, Zach smiled as he looked up to see the pilot waving back. He climbed the stairs quickly with the others close behind. Without a wasted second, the pilot pressed the button to retract the stairs, and once everyone was strapped in, he returned to the cabin and began taxiing down the runway. Within five minutes they were in the air, and as Zach heard the landing gear retracting, he breathed a small sigh of relief. As the plane leveled out, and the seat belt sign flashed off, Zach unstrapped himself and walked over to the cockpit.

"John Simmons, I can't tell you how good it is to see you."

"Hi, Zach. I have to admit that I never thought we'd meet up again after I left you all in Salome."

Simmons referred to the abandoned airport where he set down after an abortive effort to crash his plane with the Suicide Society on board. Originally adversaries, he had formed a friendship with Zach and the others.

"Is your family safe?"

The pilot shook his head. "Yes, I hope so. I had to move them three times just to be sure, but I think killing me has become a low priority for the people who hired me to kill all of you."

"Good, but don't let your guard down, John," said Zach as he clapped the pilot on the shoulder.

"Don't worry, I won't," he said. "Anyway, when the SAT phone rang, I'll admit it startled me. It's about the only way left to communicate besides ham radio."

"Well, that was the number you gave me, and you did offer to help . . ."

"Absolutely, Zach. I owe you guys a great deal. So, where are we going? The good news is there are very few aircraft in the sky anymore, but finding fuel is like finding gold. I'm fortunate I'm part of an underground network, and we trade information, so I'm gassed up."

"What's the bad news?"

"Air traffic control is nonexistent. That means we only have visual. Needless to say, no one flies at night unless it's an emergency."

"Can you get us to Sedona in Arizona?"

He nodded while blowing air out of his inflated cheeks. "Yes, I can, but it's a long trip, and you should know that a mid-air collision is a distinct probability."

"It's a risk we're going to have to take."

The pilot nodded and began entering course data into the onboard computer. Under these circumstances, he wouldn't be using the autopilot and would instead rely on visual. Zach gestured at the co-pilot seat, and after receiving thumbs up approval, he sat down and strapped in beside John and looked out the window. With his enhanced visual perception, he could see for many miles farther than normal eyesight would allow.

A flock of birds several miles away gave off a distinctive heat signature as their wings fluttered and left pink and blue contrails. Zach wondered if John knew they were even out there. The clouds were large and fluffy, and they shimmered in a strange sparkling silver color so alive it felt like someone plugged them into high intensity stadium lamps.

Somewhere over Kansas, two distinct heat signatures bubbled up in Zach's visual spectrum coming from opposite directions. One was heading northwest and descending while the other was moving from the southwest and climbing. He looked over at the pilot and realized Simmons wasn't aware of either aircraft.

"John, there are two planes that look like they're going to come very close to us in a couple minutes."

Leaning forward and whipping his head around 180 degrees, the pilot replied, "What are you talking about? I don't see anything."

"I can't gauge the distance, but I imagine they're about two minutes away and closing fast. Unless they change course, I'm worried they'll collide with each other or us."

Simmons rubbed his forehead. "There's nothing out there . . . Are you using those strange abilities you have?"

"It's a long story. The condensed version is that I'm technically blind. Yet, I can see, but not in the way everyone else does. I visualize heat signatures that resemble those from a thermal imaging camera. It's much different, but it's the only reference that will make any sense to you."

"I see, Zach. So, what should I do?"

Gauging depth while traveling at speeds of 450 mph was difficult, especially when the other aircraft were traveling at similar speeds. Zach closed his eyelids, which gave him a clearer view of what was transpiring outside the cockpit. The plane on the left was plunging downward at a very rapid rate of speed while the one to the right continued to climb. They were growing closer, and there didn't appear to be much distance between them.

"We need to get higher, John. I think they'll collide just above us, and if that happens, we might get hit with falling debris. At that moment, a light on the console started flashing and an audible warning sounded.

"That's the ASAS warning us there's another aircraft within five miles. If either of them is equipped with the system, we'll get position data so we can adjust."

Simmons looked at the instrument panel for a few seconds and shook his head. "No, I don't see anything. They either have less sophisticated equipment or none at all."

Grabbing the control wheel and pulling back, Simmons raised the elevators while simultaneously increasing thrust, sending the aircraft into a steep climb. Zach imagined Marshall and Delgado would think a collision was imminent, and they wouldn't necessarily be wrong.

He looked over to say something to John when he saw the pilot's eyes widen as the color drained from his face. The two red heat signatures suddenly grew so large they merged and occupied nearly all of Zach's panoramic vision. A bright flash blotted out the sky, and the cabin shuddered as the plane was hit by the concussive wave of an explosion. The airplane bounced from side to side as the turbulence from the collision below shook the cabin.

Throughout the ordeal, Simmons kept his eyes directly ahead, working the pedals and thrusters. For a few, long seconds, Zach wondered if they would get drawn into the downdraft as the engines whined and sounded rough and uneven, but then the red heat signature slowly dissipated until they were once again in clean, undisturbed air.

"Poor bastards," said Simmons as he throttled down and leveled the plane. "There's just no way to know what's out there without traffic control." Turning to Zach, he sighed and shook his head. "You keep your eyes or whatever you used to detect those planes peeled until we arrive."

Some four hours later, and without further incident, the Hawker successfully landed on the airstrip at Sedona-Oak Creek. Like most of the other

306

small airports in the country, the facility was abandoned except for a single steward who came running out when the plane finally taxied to a halt.

"Holy smokers," said a man in bib overalls and a train engineer's cap. "What in holy hell are you all doin'? Nobody's flyin' anymore. There's no air traffic control. The collisions grounded everyone. Are you all crazy?"

Zach clapped the old man on the shoulder when he reached ground level. "Yes, we're crazy. Anyone who would fly from Detroit to Sedona is absolutely insane."

"Damn straight," said the old man as he looked up at the pilot and other passengers. "What are you all even doin' here? The airport is all but closed down."

"Yes," said Zach, "you told me that." He turned and pointed to a large pickup truck setting in the parking lot. "We need a ride. How about it?"

"No. I don't even know you people," the steward said while taking a step back.

"I'm Zach Randall, and these are my friends, Marshall and Delgado. We need a ride to the Devil's Creek trailhead."

The old man took off his conductor's cap and shook his head. "Naw, I can't do that."

"Oh c'mon . . . What's your name?"

"Dave Bledsoe. I was the mechanic here before all the planes left or were abandoned."

"Look, Dave, there's no one here. You won't be missed. Besides, I'll pay you handsomely."

The old man's eyebrows raised. "Pay me how?"

Zach reached into his pocket and pulled out a one-ounce gold eagle coin. "With gold, Dave. The only tender anyone cares about anymore. Get this melted and powdered, and you'll be able to buy food and supplies for a month."

Old Dave's eyes lit up, and he wiped his hands on his dirty overalls, a habit born of years of having them covered in dirt and grease. He reached out to grab the coin, but Zach pulled it away. "No, only after you drive us to Devil's Creek."

Dave nodded vigorously. "Sure. You got it. When do we leave?"

The others started hurrying toward the vehicle while Zach turned back toward the pilot standing at the bottom of the air stairs.

"John, I have no words. Thank you."

Simmons smiled and reached out to grab Zach's hand. "Travel safe, my friend. I hope we meet again in better times."

Zach nodded, shook heartily and turned to join his companions. When he reached the SUV, he opened the door on the front passenger's side and looked over at Dave Bledsoe. "I'm ready; let's travel." The steward nodded and put the vehicle in drive and pulled out onto Airport Road. The ride lasted less than half an hour before Bledsoe shifted into 4-wheel drive and crawled over the rocks on the pathway off of Vultee Arch. When they reached the point closest to the sanctuary that was still far enough away to avoid revealing its exact location, Zach signaled for the driver to stop.

"Hey, Dave, thanks for the ride," said Zach. "Oh, and here's your coin." He flipped the gold eagle to the old man who held it in his hand like it was, well, gold.

Bledsoe looked up at Zach and furrowed his brow. "There's nothin' out that way except more scrub and more mountains, you all know."

Zach patted him on the arm reassuringly. "We have a campsite set up over the ridge. Thanks for your concern, but we'll be fine." Unconvinced, the old man shook his head and stayed long enough to follow their movements until they finally slipped out of sight.

After blindfolding Delgado yet again, they walked the short distance to the entrance to the facility and soon were back in Pena's office just outside the foyer.

"So," said Pena while stroking his chin thoughtfully, "it appears Mr. Cox has traveled back to his own time. The damage he has done here will set up the empire he plans to rule in the future."

Zach nodded. "Yes, which is why we need to follow him. Pena, I want to see those orbs."

"I—I hardly know what to say, Speaker. They are consummate evil, and they haven't been exposed to the light of day in many, many years. If you handle one, it will possess you."

"We don't have a choice," said Zach. "Marshall believed we were warned by his friend from the future that Cox would return to the year 2364. The only way he could have accomplished such a feat is by using a technology or other-worldly phenomenon that could distort space time and create a wormhole he could travel through. The orbs provide the only explanation as to how he would get back there."

Pena sat with his head hung low, but he didn't answer.

"Pena," said Zach, "I'm not asking."

The caretaker removed his hands from the sides of his head and said, "Perhaps we should think on this and get a fresh start in the morning. It has been a long day."

Zach looked at the exhaustion on Marshall's face, and Sasha saw it as well. "Pena is right," she said. "I've been overwhelmed with worry. A night's rest might offer all of us a different perspective."

"All right," said Zach while nodding. "We'll meet down here tomorrow at seven. Make sure you've had your breakfast. There will be no delays."

Everyone nodded and split up, walking to their quarters with slumped shoulders and feet dragging. Zach went inside his room and started toward the shower, but the shimmering glow of a human form caught his attention. It was Sarah, and he remembered he had given her a passkey to the room. The mass inside her was an orange shade, which indicated she was both sad and angry.

"Were you even going to tell me you got back?" she said while shifting position on the sofa.

"I'm sorry. I was still caught up in our trip to Detroit. Watts confirmed what we suspected. Cox traveled to the future."

"Do you realize how absurd this all sounds? Time changes; time travel; telepathy; telekinesis . . . Has the world gone mad?"

"Look, Sarah, you know Cox better than anyone. He's an aberration, a mutant, and he represents the greatest threat the world has ever known. He has the advantage of knowing the future through the power of some supernatural or paranormal orb. Who knows where they came from? There are so many things happening right in front of us that ordinary people just ignore. We live in a strange reality. I am the leader of The Suicide Society, and somehow, I've got to make this right."

"You have no idea how to get to the future. Pena says that orb will possess you." She walked up and wrapped her arms around him. "Please, let's just walk away from all this. Cox is gone. We can go somewhere and make a life for ourselves. Let someone else save the damn world."

310

He tentatively returned her embrace and noticed her aura transitioned to dark yellow. She was overwhelmed with sadness. Still, no matter how hard he tried to will himself to love her, there was no way he could hide his indifference.

What has happened to me? I am emotionally numb. Did Cox destroy my ability to love?

"I need time, Sarah. Much has changed for me. I lost my eyesight and the gift. I feel — lost." She nodded and buried her head in his shoulder. He felt the warm wetness seep through his shirt onto his skin, and for just a moment, something stirred inside him.

He led her over to the bed and laid her down gently and crawled up beside her. There was something there, but was it pity, or . . .

***

The morning light crept in through the bay window and fractured into a rainbow of intensely vivid colors as Zach sat up and yawned. He didn't remember falling asleep, but the night passed without memory, so he must have dozed off. He gazed over at the other side of the bed, but Sarah was gone. In her place was a folded note. He picked it up and read slowly:

I can't do this anymore. Zach. The only thing I ever wanted was a happy, boring, normal life with you, but I guess that wasn't meant to be. Somehow, while chasing your obsession with Cox, you lost your love for me. I know the world is dangerous and cruel, but I'm leaving this place because it's not reality. I talked to Pena, and I've joined one of the missions leaving this morning. If you survive and ever find your way back to me, I'll be waiting. Love, Sarah.

He wasn't sure what color ink she used, but the writing glowed in a deep green as small wisps of sadness and regret floated away from her words before dissipating and fading away. For a moment, Zach experienced a sharp pang of deep anxiety. Almost simultaneously, he heard someone walking past his door.

I wonder if they're going to have eggs benedict today? Why does my left foot hurt? I need to get a valve for that boiler. I hope we have one.

Zach swiveled around quickly. There was no one in the room, and yet he was certain he heard the voice clearly.

Was I reading someone's thoughts? Just as quickly, the sensation abated.

He turned his attention back to the note, wishing there was something he could do for Sarah, who had suffered a life filled with nothing but pain. Yet, he had very little to offer her right now, and she was probably better off to move on. He knew she was right; his ability to love had been hijacked, replaced by an unrelenting drive to find and destroy Mr. Cox. He looked at the clock as the numbers flipped to 6:30. Just enough time to shower, dress and grab a breakfast sandwich.

Zach reached Pena's office at 6:55, but the caretaker was already there with Marshall and Sasha. He looked up and said, "Speaker Randall, I implore you."

Zach held up his hand. "I have made up my mind, so there's no point in discussing this further."

"There is one more thing we need to talk about," said Marshall. "There are two orbs. Who is going with you?"

"No one," said Zach while shaking his head. "I need to do this alone."

"No," said Sasha, "you can't take the chance that you're overpowered again. You might prevail with the orb, or you might not, but you stand a far better chance with one of us with you."

"I agree with Sasha," said Marshall. "One of us must go with you, and that needs to be me."

"No," said Sasha while shaking her head. "I should go. I am more expendable and you are needed here."

"Absolutely not," said Marshall, "I . . ."

"Sasha will go with me," said Zach. "She's right, Marshall, you're needed here. Besides, there is little choice in the matter. You remember the mind crushing effects the massive number of suicides had on the overseers when we left the building. You are immune to the misery, but Sasha is not. That's why she didn't accompany us to Detroit, and it's why you must stay here and make sure our plan succeeds."

"But . . ."

"The issue has been decided, Marshall." Zach's inflections made it clear the discussion was over. Marshall's head dropped, and while he said nothing more, his lips kept moving.

Pena nodded, rose from his chair and motioned for the others to follow. They went to a door off the foyer that was locked, and the caretaker used a passkey to open it. The corridor was small, narrow and about 20-feet long. At the end, there was a big vault door similar to what was found in large banks. With hesitation, Pena walked up and placed his palm on a flat scanner and motioned for Zach to follow his lead on a second reader across from Pena's. Two light bars flashed as they read the unique lines and crevices of the Speaker and Caretaker's hands. Shortly thereafter, a loud whoosh accompanied a stream of air, and the vault door swung open.

They walked inside where the walls were made of thick concrete impregnated with 6-inch iron and lead sheeting. The room measured about 20′ X 20′ square, and in the middle, a single table held a small box. Pena walked up carefully and handled it as though it was radioactive.

"Are you sure, Speaker?" Zach nodded, and Pena punched the number into a digital lock. He reached down and raised the cover, and an intense, focused yellow light leapt from the box with a ferocity that almost seemed angry and sentient. Pena screamed and stumbled backwards as Sasha and Marshall grabbed their heads and stumbled around the room moaning.

Zach's entire body felt like a highly charged electrical current was running through it. The intensity of the light was magnified a thousand times by his altered vision, and within the beams, he could see an infinite number of shapes morphing, converging and splitting again. They took form occasionally, and the ghoulish apparitions looked at him with malevolence and beckoned him to approach. A sense of dread and despair coursed through his psyche and soul, and in that instant, he understood the deep satisfaction and perverted beauty that came from inflicting pain and misery on others. He sought out Sasha and grabbed her hand, dragging her toward the orbs while she resisted and screamed for mercy.

"Focus Sasha," he said. "Focus on the date of February 13th, 2364. We want to find Sixtus Maras. Wherever he is, let the orbs take us there."

"No, no don't make me do it. Please, Speaker, let me die. Please . . ."

"Focus, Sasha." He grabbed her hand and forced it down on one of the orbs as his free hand closed onto the other. The light coursed with a mass of

314

energy that felt both thick and solid but also fluid and molten. The color emanating from the orb grew darker until it was a garish blood red. A low hum like a synthesizer playing a bass note at 100Hz grew louder until it became deafening.

The whole room began to shake until the subharmonic rumbling made it seem like the entire facility would shatter. Zach's enhanced vision was disrupted by the blinding light, and he heard a sharp crack as the wall split open. He looked around in a kind of stupor similar to anesthesia and thought he saw another pair of hands fighting with Sasha for the orb.

"Speaker Randall, find him. Find Sixtus Maras . . ." Marshall sputtered as he wiped blood from the corners of his eyes. The sound grew louder, and the light grew brighter until he was certain his skin would burn off and his head would explode. Struggling to remain conscious, he collapsed in a corner and screamed.

In an instant, the light and sound disappeared. The complete silence was almost as painful as the projections from the orb itself, and when he looked around, Marshall saw Pena writhing in a corner, purging as his back lurched upwards. His eyes traced a path around the room, but he couldn't find any trace of Zach. Sasha was lying on the floor next to the box that contained the orbs, moaning and nursing a contusion on her forehead that was growing larger by the minute. Pena got up and stumbled over to the box. It was empty, and Zach was gone.

Chapter Twenty-Five

At dawn, they gathered just outside the camp. Perhaps there weren't a thousand as Mr. Cox demanded, but there were at least 300 men and women armed with farming tools, stout tree limbs, rocks and other weapons. A few of the more fortunate carried ancient handguns and rifles. Jan Mabatus stood at the head of the group, and Mr. Cox flooded his mind with the kind of endorphins that would enhance his vanity and narcissism.

"Fine work on such short notice, Mabatus. They may not be much of a fighting force, but they will serve our purpose."

Mabatus beamed. "Their passions are inflamed, Coxnotus. A new band of pacifists came to town last evening, but they were shunned. The people are tired of their philosophical nonsense. You have stirred their thirst for possessions, the need to care only about themselves."

Mr. Cox was joined by Zietra X, Lars, General Cron, Malconus, Term and Dux Jolas.

"We are loaded and ready to move out," said Dux Jolas. "If we leave now, we should be ready for the attack by late afternoon."

Mr. Cox smiled. "Then let us commence. At all costs, we must take over that Amrosian facility. The only chance we have is to seize the remaining technology at their disposal. I sense the ever-expanding pacifist movement has reached a tipping point. If we don't stop them now, our future is doomed."

Inviting Mr. Cox to follow, Dux Jolas walked up to the lead ground crawler and opened the back door, motioning for Mr. Cox to get in before Jolas joined him. Lars pushed Minkus out of the way and got in next to the driver as the others went to a second ground crawler.

Using a digital radio, Jolas signaled to the rest of the convoy, and they began the long journey to the Amrosia Corporate headquarters in Jaunde. The roads were old and neglected, and the vegetation encroached from all sides. The ground crawlers were equipped with object removal capabilities, and the driver blasted rocks from the roadway. Two other vehicles drove parallel to the lead, and together they cleared the way for the others to follow.

While he sat in the back seat, Mr. Cox mourned the loss of the future he had so carefully planned for. The orb was never wrong, yet, here he was in a version of the future that was actually worse than the place he left in the past. How this could be possible was beyond him, but further tinkering in an already muddled timeline was out of the question. He would continue to try to change this reality, but the only real hope for altering the past lie with Lars, who now understood his destiny. And yet, he already knew Lars had failed. Something must be done differently, but what?

The pang of doubt was small, but its presence was growing. In that instant, Mr. Cox realized just how much the separation from the orb was eroding his will and his power. After securing the fortress at Jaunde, he must return to Desolation and retrieve the orb.

Although it was only a four-hour excursion, moving that many people and much equipment almost doubled the travel time due to breakdowns and other logistical issues. When they rounded a curve traveling on a set of steep slopes, Mr. Cox breathed a sigh of relief as he saw the city. The Corporate complex was just on the outskirts, and as the caravan rolled toward it, predetermined elements began to split off and move to the flanks as they planned.

The driver of Mr. Cox ground crawler pulled to the side and allowed the vehicles carrying the main force to proceed, and they crept forward slowly. Once inside the live-fire perimeter, those with kinetic or plasma weapons went to the front of the advancing force. About two hundred yards from the entrance to the building, Mr. Cox, Term, Malconus and Mabatus left the vehicle while Lars, Zietra X, General Ignansus and Dux Jolas joined their respective squadrons. From a nearby hilltop, Mr. Cox and his companions stood and looked toward the approaching troops through near-field glasses.

When the new conscripts from Nzoni were 50 yards from the main building, Mr. Cox braced for the coming onslaught, but not a single shot was fired.

Llross must be waiting until the last possible moment to inflict the greatest carnage.

The first wave of disorganized Nzoni townspeople approached the front gate to the complex. He watched as one of them pushed the gate open without resistance. The electronic locking mechanism was apparently disengaged.

"A trap," Malconus muttered. "They have prepared an elaborate trap."

"Do not worry," replied Mr. Cox, "It is of no concern. These foolish townspeople were only here to serve as a diversion, anyway. They are cannon fodder." This elicited a strange look from Mayor Jan Mobatus, but after he made momentary eye contact with Mr. Cox, he quickly looked away.

The first man from the advanced team reached the front door of the facility and set his weapon against a wall that defined the boundary of the courtesy area. Mr. Cox watched as he reached down, turned the knob and carefully opened the door while several of his colleagues waited with guns locked, loaded and pointed toward the adversaries they knew were waiting just inside. The point person walked through the door, but no shots were fired. Several seconds later, others followed. Soon, even more of the villagers cautiously went inside.

Mr. Cox lowered his field glasses. "Something is wrong here." He took a small transceiver out of his pocket. "Lars, respond immediately." The digital communicator was silent as it scanned the spectrum for a response. "Lars, X, Cron, Malconus . . . anyone. What is the status of the operation?"

More silence followed as Mr. Cox turned to the driver, "Take me down there, I need to know what is happening." He waited for Term to open the door when the communicator flashed with an incoming transmission.

"It is Lars . . . They—they left."

Mr. Cox stared at the commutator with a sense of confusion "Left? What do you mean, 'they left'?"

"There is no sign of Dantar Llross or any of the Amrosians. We have people searching over the facility, but there is no one here . . . They are gone."

"How — how is that possible?"

"We found a set of Kerr rings in an underground basement with an ancient fission generator next to it."

"What? Are you telling me they traveled to the past? All of them?" Mr. Cox' mouth gaped open.

"I'm not sure. Maybe some of them were left behind and scattered, but I imagine many of them used the Casmir Vacuum." He paused a moment. "We have another huge problem."

"As if I could not have guessed. What kind of problem?"

"They have sabotaged the fission reactor by over feeding the power supply. We have about 10 minutes before the place is incinerated."

"Is there any way to escape?"

"Yes, there is a space plane intact in the hanger, and our people are wheeling it out. Malconus can pilot the craft, but you need to come down here quickly because we are not going to have much time to get out of here."

"How many people know about the coming explosion?"

"Only a handful. These ignorant peasants you brought along have no understanding of nuclear reactors, and I disabled the alarms."

"Tell everyone who knows about it to exit the building immediately. They should understand that if they attempt to warn anyone else, they will be shot."

3"I understand," said Lars.

"Tell X, Cron, Term, Malconus and Jolas to meet me at the space plane."

There was a momentary silence. "What about me?" asked Lars.

"Listen carefully. While there is still power to the Kerr Rings, you must travel back to the time coordinates I gave you previously. This is the opportunity I hoped for; our chance to repair the damage. When you arrive, you shall seek me out, but you must not reveal the nature of your mission. The task will not be easy. Somehow you must uncover the location of the Suicide Society and destroy them. I know they are at the root of this pacifist movement. If we fail here, this future is not one worth living."

"Per your orders, Coxnotus," said Lars. "I will do it. But unless there are other Kerr Ring setups somewhere, no one will be able to follow me."

"I know," said Mr. Cox, "and perhaps it is for the best."

Rushing to get into the ground crawler, Mr. Cox instructed the driver to travel at maximum speed down to the Amrosian fortress. As he grew closer, he could see the space plane as it was being freed from the tow bar connected to the heavy equipment mover.

Mr. Cox looked over at the clock inside the ground crawler. He and Lars spoke exactly four minutes ago, which only left six minutes to board the plane and depart. The driver cut a path through the main group of villagers from Nzoni as they milled around the large yard in front of the building while looking confused and directionless. They came for a fight, and the Amrosians evacuation left them frustrated. Mr. Cox noticed several scuffles breaking out among the troops. While he enjoyed watching the hostilities, there was no time to linger.

The space plane's electro-aerodynamic ionic engines glowed bright blue and produced a chest-rattling hum as the spacecraft taxied slowly to the runway. When the ground crawler pulled up next to it, Mr. Cox joined his loyalists, and together they moved quickly to the air ramp. The driver looked at Mr. Cox expectantly, but the Benefactor just shook his head. "You wait here in case ground evacuation is required." The man nodded, but the concern for his personal safety was obvious.

As Mr. Cox walked to the moving ramp, his attention was drawn to a small group of people standing under the vessel. Their appearance was radically different from the other villagers as they all sported strange tattoos, piercings and other body modifications. As the leader came forward, Mr. Cox recognized him as Abidemi of Kabye, the voodoo priest from the earlier meeting in Nzomi. The old man's eyes bugged out and shifted constantly as he flicked his head around suspiciously. In his left hand he held a small cloth doll, and in his right, he held a large pin.

"Coxnotus, from the underworld, do you dare to leave us behind? It was our spells that caused the townspeople to follow you."

Mr. Cox walked up close to the old man and recoiled from the same muted, sallow energy as before. Confusion in Abidemi's mind caused his emotions to fluctuate from anger to joy and pain to ecstasy so rapidly they were impossible to read. Most notably, there was that same spicy, foul smell.

"We will come back for you. Unfortunately, we cannot take you right now," said Mr. Cox. "Return to Nzoni, but I promise you will share in the riches from this place."

The voodoo chieftain hissed, "You lie, Coxnotus. You know that death awaits us here. You lie, and we die." He reached back and thrust the pin directly into the doll. For just a brief instant, Mr. Cox felt a sharp stab of pain directly in his heart. Instantaneously, he released a potent charge of toxic energy so powerful it lifted Abidemi off his feet and threw him backwards, and he hit the ground hard as a sickening sound of shattering bones filled the air. His fellow voodoo practitioners let out a collective "Oooooo" as they looked down at their leader and then at Mr. Cox. As a group they backed up, regarding him with awe and fear.

The Benefactor stared at them as his eyes blazed a bright red while Abidemi writhed on the ground and moaned. A second vodouisant reached up with a pin and plunged it into his doll. Again, Mr. Cox noticed a stabbing sensation in his heart, twice as strong as the first. Responding immediately, he delivered a stream of black energy that caused the skin on the man's face to blister, and he screamed as he fell to his knees.

"Don't," said the Benefactor while pointing to a third man who was preparing to stab his own doll.

"Sir," said Term as he pulled on the Benefactor's arm. "Sir, we have to go now!" Term and Cron pulled him away, and the trio climbed up in the cabin where they joined Zietra X, General Cron and Dux Jolas. Jan Mabatus was left behind, ostensibly to organize the occupation of the fortress.

Once inside the spaceplane, Mr. Cox took a window seat and looked out at the voodoo group. They were gathered around their fallen leader, but the instant Mr. Cox found them, they turned as one and stared back at him. He could feel their venom and hatred as it wafted up and formed a dark cloud over the gathering. With a nod, he tried to penetrate the mist with a tendril and drink from the negative emotion, but once again, the taste was sour and curdled.

Down below, the vodouisants stabbed their dolls repeatedly with vigor and grimaced with each penetration. Every pin thrust into the doll's fabric sapped a little more of Mr. Cox' energy. He turned to Term and said, "We must go to Desolation; it is imperative."

The engines rotated, so the thrust pushed against the ground as the ship gained vertical loft. As they reached altitude and put distance between them and the vodouisants, Mr. Cox welcomed the relief as the pressure in his chest subsided.

Damned pacifists, he said to himself. *These voodoo people should not even exist in this reality. Their frivolous live and let live philosophy allows these Cretans to thrive.*

Dux Jolas leaned down over Mr. Cox. "Sir, there is a development. Reports are coming in from the other Amrosian strongholds in different areas of the world. Their loyalists have abandoned their capitals and headquarters just like in Jaunde. They have all disappeared. Every Amrosian facility across the globe is deserted."

Mr. Cox stroked his chin as he continued to look out the window. "Tell our people to keep away from these facilities. They will no doubt suffer the same fate as this one." Across the runway, rebel soldiers fled while the ignorant Nzoni townspeople continued to explore the interior of the building and the surrounding area.

As the engines rotated back to their standard position, thrust increased rapidly, and the spacecraft lurched forward, climbing up at an extreme angle. Mr. Cox stared out the window as a huge mushroom cloud ascended from ground level. Seconds later, the ship was rocked by the concussive force of the sound wave. Although he couldn't see through the clouds, he was certain the Amrosian capital lay in rubble, and everyone within a mile of the complex had been incinerated.

After roughly ten minutes of climbing, the light transitioned to darkness, and the brightness of a seemingly infinite number of stars intensified. The plane leveled off and seemed to slow, but Mr. Cox recognized it as an illusion. The modern version of this vessel, which had never been built in this reality, could make the trip in half the time. When he originally left the future, teleportation was a leading edge technology. He assumed with his rise to power, he would travel instantaneously when he returned. Yet, no one here was even familiar with the concept.

In an uncertain situation, there was only one thing he knew with complete confidence. Before anything else, he must recover the orb from the safe in Desolation. Something was adding additional strain on his connection and draining his power exponentially. The Vodouisants? He sensed a growing vulnerability that must be remedied soon.

The flight lasted roughly two hours, and the space plane descended in the same manner it took off but in reverse sequence. At one point, Mr. Cox heard the whine of the engines as they became perpendicular to the ground, and he could see the ruins of Desolation come into clear view as the plane cut through the low-level cloud cover.

Since the area was so barren, the pilot chose an area just outside of what used to be the town square and set the spaceplane down. Amidst puzzled looks from Term, Malconus, and the others, Mr. Cox waited until the air escalator extended down to the ground before riding it to the bottom where he took a step onto the hard, dusty and familiar dirt.

A cold wind blew from the east, and Mr. Cox pulled up the corners of his jacket as he walked toward the rubble that once served as his headquarters. By now, only remnants of the shanties and wooden structures remained in this centuries-old mining ghost town. Cracked and crumbling foundations served as the only real clue that anyone actually ever lived there.

"Over here," said Mr. Cox as he moved to the rear of what appeared to be a large concrete slab. Brushing off the dirt that had blown over an iron door set in the concrete, he turned toward his companions. "Please lift the doors open. We have a long walk down to the lower level." General Cron and Dux Jolas each grabbed a side of the thick plate steel doors, and with great effort, pulled them open. The light from the overcast sky illuminated the first few steps, but the stairway soon disappeared into pitch darkness.

Taking the point, General Cron fired up an illuminator and started down the steps with Jolas and Zietra X close behind him. Mr. Cox traveled in the middle of the pack. The walls were covered with moss, and the air had the damp smell of thriving fungus. Cron kicked away debris as he walked but stopped at one point and turned back to the group.

"People were here recently," he said while shining the light on several sets of footprints traveling in both directions.

Mr. Cox stopped and looked down at them for a moment. "There was much activity here when I arrived," he said. "I imagine the footprints are from the Amrosians sent here to apprehend me."

Minkus Term shook his head in agreement.

Cron nodded but didn't look entirely convinced. He continued his trek down the stairs, taking them two at a time. After several flights, his beam shone on a metal door set into the wall of the stairway, which ended at the bottom of a concrete slab with a drain in the middle. He grabbed the handle and pulled, and after a couple yanks it cleared the doorjamb and swung open.

He waited for the rest of the entourage before entering, carefully swinging the light from side to side. The place was as Mr. Cox remembered it, but now he had more time to look around. Dux Jolas went to the end of the room and turned on a large illuminator and placed another in the center of the room and a third at the far end so all the shadows were eliminated.

"So, this is where it all began?" asked Zietra X rhetorically as she looked around.

"Yes, this is where I was directed by a greater power to come and formulate the plan," said Mr. Cox. He slowly walked down a hallway towards the part of the building that once housed his office and quarter chambers. He held up his hand when the others tried to follow. Sessions with the orb were private, and he wanted no interruptions.

A long glance around the room where much of his planning had transpired brought back many memories. The old sofa still sat in the corner, its fabric and matting ripped out by rats so that only the springs and broken wooden frame remained. His desk still sat at the far end of the room. The wood was dirty and cracked, but remarkably well preserved from all the wax Hefe applied daily. He went over to the far corner where an old bookshelf was set into the wall and pushed on a very specific section.

The unit swung out on its hinges, which revealed a smaller room. Mr. Cox walked over to a safe embedded in the opposite wall, and he twirled the numbers on the combination lock until he heard the click of the tumbler. As he twisted the handle, he could already feel the power of the orb surging into his body. Carefully extracting the jeweled box, he picked it up with the tenderness of a parent handling a babe in swaddling clothes and took it over a small table in the corner. Lifting the lid, the yellow light enveloped him like an old familiar friend as the sensation of dark power coursed through his body. It was electric, and it reignited the smoldering embers of darkness within him.

The Benefactor cried out in ecstasy, but even as his reserves were replenished and his senses heightened, he felt something else . . . Something disturbing had entered this space, and for the first time in many years, Mr. Cox was apprehensive. A sharp pain stabbed into his heart . . . The vodouisants.

Chapter Twenty-Six

Just as he turned back, Winn noticed a group of floaters pushing an abandoned car into the middle of the road. He hit the gas and turned the wheel sharply, jumping the curb and running up on the sidewalk before slamming back onto the roadway past the derelict vehicle. While they avoided that obstacle, he had no doubt there would be many others to contend with.

Two random shots rang out as he turned onto Van Buren heading west. "We're going to be dealing with this all the way to Sedona," he said to Lars.

"I know. That's why I should drive." Lars stood up and moved around the console and motioned for Winn to change places. Instinctively, Winn knew Lars would be better at negotiating the difficulties that lie ahead, so he slipped out of the van's driver's seat as Lars slid in. A second or two later they were cruising 20 mph faster, and the tires squealed as Lars turned sharply on 19th Ave, heading north.

"The freeway is just up ahead, so why are you turning here?"

"The floaters will have the freeway blocked off. We may be able to get onto it, but we won't be able to get off. We've got to get through the city and then pick up the freeway. This is the most direct route."

From Van Buren up to Greenway, they traveled without incident. Sheltered in Norma's basement for weeks, Winn was shocked at the disintegration of order since he was last outside. It wasn't that some stoplights were out and blinking red; all the lamps were dead at every intersection. Garbage, filth, and human waste littered the streets so heavily it became difficult to navigate a path through it. The grim body count stood at four so far, and those were badly decomposed.

They passed two cars traveling in the opposite direction. One was an ambulance whose lights had been torn off the top of the roof, and the other was a Jeep that someone converted into a kind of assault vehicle. An iron fireplace grate was welded onto the front bumper and spiked rods stuck out from the frame on all sides. Thick steel bars were welded over the front window. As they passed, the driver slowly raised a handgun from his seat and looked over at Lars with malice, but they passed without incident.

The floaters had thinned out considerably since Winn last encountered them. No doubt the harsh conditions, coupled with a lack of food, water and medicine, had taken their toll. In a classic Darwinian survival of the fittest scenario, the floaters that remained were stronger, resistant to disease and extremely vicious.

At Northern Avenue, he noticed a single floater standing by the side of the road leaning against an inoperable streetlamp. A light rain had begun to fall, and the man's wet hand covered a lesion on the side of his face. His eyes were riveted on the van as it passed, and he held out his free hand in a desperate plea for help.

Winn looked at the stranger and cursed himself for such a lack of empathy. This same scene repeated itself so many times since the Chicago bomb exploded he had grown numb to the suffering. His companions all shared the same look of indifference. If there was any hope for humanity, he wondered where it resided.

The floater's expression hardened as the vehicle passed, and his eyes narrowed into a squint as he dropped his hand to his side. No one spoke as they continued moving on, and Lars gave Winn a thumbs up as they approached Bell Road. "I think we're past the worst of it," he said.

Two blocks later, he realized he spoke too soon. Simultaneously, two large commercial dumpsters rolled out from a side street into the middle of the street from either side, effectively blocking the van from moving forward. Shortly thereafter, a group of floaters emerged from the shadows wielding a variety of homemade weapons. Deep lines of desperation sunk into their haggard faces conveyed an explosive anger. They approached cautiously from all sides, weapons at the ready. Winn raised his handgun, and from the back, he could hear Nicholas loading the shotgun.

"Not unless we have to," cautioned Lars as he slowed and rolled down the window. One of the women stepped forward, a tire iron raised head high.

"Don't come any closer," Lars said. "Tell me what you want."

She opened her mouth to reveal teeth blackened and rotted from decay. Her skin was covered with oil and dirt that had morphed into a thick layer of grease. Only her red, active sores remained exposed. Her companions were at least as filthy, and some were even worse.

"You had a chance to give Jimmy a small donation back at Northern. He'd a taken anything, pretty much. Just something to help us get through the night. Now we're gonna take whatever you got, so I'd give us something good."

"We have guns," said Lars, and Winn brandished the handgun for effect.

The woman laughed. "You think we give a fuck about guns? We're not gonna let you get out, and it'll sure be hard to shoot us through the windshield."

Winn turned to the back of the van. "What's that sound? I hear something splashing." The words weren't out of his mouth when the strong smell of gasoline invaded the cab. He looked over at Lars who already knew what was happening.

"You gun that engine," the woman said, "and we'll burn you out. Gas is like gold, so you know we mean business."

"What is it you want?" said Lars.

"Get out of the van, slow. Leave the guns inside. I see one gun and the van goes up with you in it; I swear."

Winn looked at Lars, who shook his head and sighed. "No choice. They've got us." He nodded slowly before opening his door. Following his lead, Winn laid the gun on the center console and stepped out on the passenger's side. The side door slid open, and the rest of the group moved out into the street with their arms raised.

Instantly, two floaters jumped inside the van. Like a well-oiled machine, they split up with one retrieving the weapons and the other grabbing the supplies.

"Look, Marta, look a di tuff," said a slumped shouldered, gnarly looking man who appeared to be in his late 20s. "Dey got waher, foo, cothes and a bunch of udder tuff."

"Good, Smiley, bring it here."

"Three guns, Marta. Not much ammo, though. Only six shots for each one," said the other man.

"We'll take it." The lanky man jumped out of the van and handed the guns to Marta who checked the magazine and then pointed the handgun at the others.

"We're gonna take your van, so start walkin' away and maybe we won't kill ya."

"You don't understand," said Bahati. "We just got out of a dungeon where we were tortured. We need that van."

Marta laughed and Smiley raised the shotgun. "Can I toot dem, Marta? Pease?"

"Not if we don't have to, Smiley," Marta answered. "I don't want to waste the amo." Then turning to Lars, she said, "I'd get yur ass walkin' before I change my mind."

Winn glanced at Lars and then motioned for the group to follow as they started slowly down 19th Ave. None of them saw Smiley level the shotgun and prepare to pick one of them off with Marta's blessing.

A loud crack pierced the air and Winn whirled around just as Smiley fell over backwards with a clean hole through his forehead. Quickly thereafter, two more precision shots rang out in succession as Marta and Tex collapsed to the pavement. The remaining floaters ran for cover as the harsh sound of automatic weapons fire sounded all around them.

Winn looked in every direction, certain he would see a squad of skankers emerging from the shadows. Getting saved by skankers was like crawling out of the frying pan into the fire. They would be apprehended and interrogated, and eventually, someone in the Corporate Elite Guard would connect them to Norma's death. In the end, they would right back where they started.

He turned to retrieve the weapons, but Lars reached out and grabbed his arm. When Winn turned around, he saw a group of five men in jeans and hunting coats approaching with assault weapons drawn. Whoever they were, at least they weren't skankers.

"You looked like you could use some help," said the man at the point. "Name's Jeff Larsen, and these are my friends. None of you have the look of a floater, am I right?"

"No, we . . ." Winn winced as Lars elbowed him in the gut.

"We're Corporates," said Lars, "and we're on our way to a new housing project they're building in Los Angeles. I'm an electrical engineer. My friends are engineers as well."

The one named Jeff smiled, and his weapon dropped to the side. "Ah, that's what I thought." He turned to one of his friends in the group. "See, Chas, I told you they were one of us."

"Maybe," said the one named Chas, "but they're sure dressed like floaters.

"Give 'em a break, Chas. It's rough out on the road." He looked back at Lars. "We run one of the newest Corporate housing projects in Scottsdale. We come down here to pick up floaters and bring them back to the compound for training and then we put 'em to work. Nothing like seeing a floater sweating at the pumps or cooking the meals. It makes you think things are getting back to where they should be. By the way, which corporation do you work for?"

"We're all part of Gehenna," said Lars. "I can show you credentials if you would like."

"Naw," said Jeff. "We're with Amrosia ourselves. But hell, we're all part of the same thing with this HUGE conglomerate merger deal." He paused and briefly glanced at his friends. "Hey, why don't you come back to Scottsdale with us? We'll feed you and get you some fresh supplies and clean clothes. L.A. is a long way away, and it's the worst cesspool in the whole country right now."

"We'd like to," said Winn, "but we really need to get on the road."

"Nonsense," said Lars as he picked up immediately after Winn finished. "We'd loved to take advantage of your hospitality."

"Excellent," Jeff's smile widened. "Just follow us. We'll plow the road."

Lars nodded, and they walked back to the van, picking up their scattered supplies and the guns. Once they were back inside, he started the engine and put the van in drive.

"What the fuck, Lars. Why did you do that? The last thing we need is a long delay."

"Listen to me, Winn. We either go to their compound, or they'll shoot us. Trust me on this."

Winn recognized conviction in Lars' expression. "What about running?"

"Not a chance. Look at that Humvee. I'll bet they have multiple patrols north of Bell Road."

Winn nodded. "Okay, I'm starting to understand."

"Good. We have about a twenty-minute ride to get our stories straight because if there is any sort of slip up, they'll kill us on the spot. Let's start with Bahati. You're an H1 visa immigrant who arrived a year before the bombs went off . . ."

***

Wanda offered the Corporate regional manager a seat inside her tent, and she opened a second foldable chair and set it across from him. "So, what is it you would like to discuss?" she asked.

Cameron Wintz looked around at the sparse décor with an almost imperceptible look of disgust. "Well, I just want to see how we can work together to improve the lot of your people down here. At HUGE, the welfare of our global citizens is paramount, and we know those in this area are especially vulnerable. That is why I'm here to offer our help."

"I see. And exactly what does that mean? What kind of 'help' did you have in mind?"

"Obviously, based on the physical appearance of the people here, you are all undernourished. What is your protein porridge allotment?"

"We get one barrel of gruel a week, but we have to feed 75 people. That's less than two cups per person per day."

"And water?"

"Two 55-gallon drums per week. That's a third of a gallon per person per day. Barely enough to survive on. Lately, we haven't even been receiving our full allotment of either food or water. We're scrounging for canned goods and drinking water from the Los Angeles River."

"Hmmm . . . I see." The Corporate man reached into his pocket and pulled out a tablet computer. He made several swipes and clicks on the screen before turning his attention back to Wanda. "What if I was able to increase your allotment to three drums of protein porridge and four barrels of water per week and guaranteed delivery?"

Wanda regarded him carefully. "Assuming you have the authority to make that commitment, what are the conditions? I imagine you want something in return."

"Not really," he said while shrugging casually. "Of course, I would assume that if your people are properly fed, there would be no need to continue with your agricultural activities."

"Ah," said Wanda as she leaned back in her chair. "So, in order for us to get more food and water, we have to give up our quest for self-sufficiency."

The Corporate man regarded her for a moment and leaned forward. "No, I wouldn't put it that way at all. We want to take care of our citizens, and I'm promising you that everyone within four city blocks will have enough food to eat and water to drink. In fact," he paused for a moment, "I'll tell you what. I'll even make sure everyone gets a fresh set of Corporate uniforms."

Wanda smiled. Over time, and with training at the facility, she had become adept at identifying a ruse. "I will relay your offer to the people, but frankly, I'm going to recommend against it. We are very close to feeding ourselves with our own fresh food, not the unhealthy toxic slop you put in those barrels. With rainwater collection and purifying river water, soon we won't even need your deliveries." She rose and pulled back the tent flap, inviting the Corporate man to leave. "Thank you for coming by, and I will let you know what we decide."

Wintz's smile instantly disappeared, and he stood up slowly. "You understand this is a onetime offer. I must remind you that growing your own food violates the HUGE Bylaws: Item 12, section six, paragraph 14. If you choose not to cooperate, your situation could . . . worsen considerably. You have gained the attention of those in the highest echelons of upper management. Even the Board of Directors is aware of your activities.

"Good day, Mr. Wintz," said Wanda as she pulled the flap even farther back. Slowly, the Corporate manager ducked down through the opening, straightened his jacket and began walking back to his waiting vehicle.

"What was that all about," asked Sam as he leaned into her tent.

"He tried to bribe us, Sam. He wants to give us more water and gruel if we give up growing our own food and harvesting our own water."

"That would rob these people of their purpose and dignity," he said.

"I know. Still, I can't hide the offer. Go spread the word and get everyone together after work. Anyone who is part of our effort will get to vote."

Sam nodded and left the tent while Wanda started looking at the daily handwritten reports that kept track of water reserves, seed inventories and harvest projections. As the day passed, she noticed the residents looking at her more closely than usual as she walked the neighborhood, which now extended all the way over to Maple and south to 8th street. She watched as the people toiled with a sense of pride they lacked before she and the others from

338

Sedona arrived. As the days turned into weeks and eventually months, the purpose of her training became clear.

The gift of enhanced perception she shared with her companions lifted the spirits of the people around her and gave them hope. The results of hard work served as a restorative balm that enhanced their self-confidence and self-esteem. Helping people gave Wanda a kind of spiritual fulfillment far beyond anything she had experienced before.

After a full day of hauling dirt and planting tomatoes while standing shoulder to shoulder with her neighbors, she set down the makeshift wheel barrel, wiped her brow and looked at her watch. It read 5:28 pm, which meant the crew had already worked half an hour longer than planned. She gave the signal to wrap it up and started to make her way back to the center of their makeshift village.

Just past 7th St. on San Julian, she saw a number of people had already gathered for supper. Thanks to Papa Grande, they would go to bed less hungry tonight.

When she got closer, she saw that someone had arranged several old milk crates and placed a sheet of plywood on top to serve as a platform. Talie was the first to greet her when she got to the center of the camp.

"Look, Wanda," she said with a smile and a sparkle in her eyes. Talie held up the most beautiful, lush, red radish Wanda could remember seeing. As she looked around, she noticed several people had a cup of gruel in one hand and a radish in another.

"We harvested two full baskets of radishes today. We'll probably pick twice that many tomorrow." Wanda nodded as she continued to stare at the radish. Slowly she made her way over to the platform and stepped up on it.

"My friends," she said, "this is a milestone. Tonight, some of you are eating fresh produce for the first time in years." She held up the radish for everyone to see. "Isn't it beautiful?" Applause, cheers and whistles followed.

"You did this," she continued. "Your hard work has created self-sufficiency." She stopped and lowered the radish to her side. "Still, I need to tell you about a meeting I had today with a Corporate regional manager. It's only fair you know they offered more than double our weekly allotment of gruel and water, and he said the shipments are guaranteed. In return, we would have to cease all efforts to grow our own food."

"But that would make us dependent on the Corporates again," said someone from the crowd.

"Yes, but everyone would have enough food and water to live. Self-sufficiency carries risks."

The neighbors talked among themselves before Iris stood up. "I don't want anything to do with those corporate bastards. They lie, and they are only offering this because we represent a threat. What if everyone starts growing their own food? Who would need them? I say no!"

"I say, *hell* no!" Papa Grande stepped forward. "There is no future with the Corporates. We're better off on our own."

The background murmur grew in volume until Wanda quieted them down. "We must vote; it's the only fair way. All in favor of taking the Corporate offer?" She waited for several seconds but not a single hand was raised. "Well then, we have our answer. We go it alone." Except for a few claps and whistles, the neighbors went back to their dinner and the evening conversation. Without saying it,

340

each person knew the probable consequences of their decision.

***

The next morning, the sound of multiple loud engines revving in front of her tent woke Wanda. The streets were essentially blocked off and used for housing now, so she knew something was very wrong. Quickly clearing the cobwebs out of her mind, she grabbed her clothes and ducked outside her tent. She surveyed a chaotic scene and tried to process it. Several people lay in the streets, deliberately struck by one of five military-style SUVS that drove aggressively into camp. As the doors opened, twenty large, well-muscled corporate goons got out and took a position in front of the vehicles, striking poses that clearly conveyed hostility.

From the opposite end of San Julian, Papa Grande, and his Pocks approached menacingly with clubs and whatever other weapons they were able to gather at such short notice.

Quickly, Wanda waved them off and quickly covered the distance between her and the Corporate thugs. "What are you doing here? You've injured several residents for no reason. You might have killed someone."

The door of the last SUV in the line opened, and a tall, thin woman stepped out. Her arms, neck and upper torso were covered in tattoos depicting horrific scenes of death, debauchery and mutilation. She walked slowly toward Wanda with an air of extreme confidence and stopped about six feet away.

"Who are you, and why are you here," asked Wanda.

The woman slowly removed a pair of dark, wraparound sunglasses. She stared at Wanda for a moment, and her expression hardened. "I am Sandra Bentenhouse, and I am the Corporate Director of Security for the HUGE conglomerate. I had to come all the way from Detroit because of the trouble you're causing, and I hate Los Angeles." She walked up close to Wanda. "Enough kissing your ass, hon. You have five minutes to disperse before we knock this whole shithole neighborhood down."

As Wanda looked behind Bentenhouse, she saw a group of about 50 or more people approaching. As they grew closer, she noticed their arms bore the same markings Arturo had. The Crege were joining the confrontation.

Chapter Twenty-Seven

The yellow glow of the two orbs enveloped Zach in a light so bright he barely saw the outline of Sasha's body. He wondered what was partially drowning out her shrieking until he realized it was his own screaming. The energy from the orb invaded every cell in his body, injecting a potent dose of malevolence and altering his DNA in a way that affected his synaptic pathways and changed his body chemistry.

Slowly, the light began to ebb and recede until his vision cleared. He looked over at Sasha, and for a moment, he thought he would lose consciousness. Staggering backwards, he pointed a finger and said, "*Sarah?* You . . . Why?"

She met his gaze, but she looked different in a way he couldn't explain. Her soft, attractive features were harder, chiseled and more masculine, and her expression was one of smoldering hatred. The anger in her eyes was extremely unsettling, and they darted back and forth looking small and beady. As she glared at him, Zach wondered if she saw him in the same way. At that moment, he realized his eyesight had been completely restored, but the ability to see aura was gone.

"I wasn't going to let you do this without me," she said finally. "My hatred for Cox runs deeper than

343

anyone else, and whatever abilities Sasha has are no match for my loathing. I have a sickness inside of me. My thoughts are so dark, and my emotions are twisted. I—I want to kill someone. Inflicting pain and suffering appeals to me. There is no way I can control this or live this way. After I kill Cox, I will kill others, probably you first."

Zach walked closer to her. "My anger for what you have done is so overwhelming I feel like killing you where you stand. I am warning you, I can barely contain my contempt. My natural abilities have returned, and I am much more powerful than you." He approached her with malice but stopped before wrapping his hands around her neck. She crouched low and balled her fists as her eyes swept the area, searching for a weapon.

Zach took several deep breaths and fought to control his rage. "We must remember the goal is to destroy the monster," he said. "When we are finished with that task, I'll deal with you. However, if you can't control your own emotions, I won't hesitate to kill you instantly."

She sneered at the challenge, and Zach felt the impact of a stream of toxic energy that flowed through her orb in his direction. He parried it and gathered a lethal combination of his own putrid telepathic soup augmented by the extraordinary power of the orb. His body shook, and he gritted his teeth so hard he thought they would break and crumble. "Control it, Sarah. Control it or die."

Her breathing grew very rapid as she closed her eyes, leaned over and vomited. She remained in that position for nearly a minute before standing back up. "I'm not sure I can, Zach, I have marginal control over this extraordinary power. I'm managing it . . .

barely. So, where are we, and what are we supposed to do here? I heard Marshall say the name 'Sixtus Maras', and the date February, 13, 2364. That's what I focused on when I pulled the orb from Sasha's hands."

Zach turned and looked around. The temperature was frigid, and the few trees he could see were in winter dormancy. At least Sarah was smart enough to have worn a jacket, although it was not sufficiently thick to mute the chill. "Put the orb in your pocket. We need a place to keep them. The intensity is too much, and I can feel the extreme energy coursing through me even now."

They were in an older neighborhood, which looked remarkably similar to the big cities from his time. There was nothing particularly unusual about anything he saw around him except the absence of people and technology. The first hint they had actually traveled to the future was the electric hum of an air car as it passed overhead, but he expected the skies and roadways to be packed with vehicles. The lack of traffic was surprising and unsettling.

A woman turned the corner pushing a cart that carried two or three partially filled bags. She was bundled in a heavy coat that covered a thick body, and a scarf wrapped around her head hid her face. To Zach, she looked more like someone out of the mid-20th century than a 24th century inhabitant.

She paused for a moment as she regarded the pair. Zach reached out and accessed her active thoughts rather than just her memories, and he listened while she debated whether their cleanliness conveyed decency, or their lack of winter wraps signaled danger. Slowly, she came forward with her head down, obviously looking to avoid interaction.

"Excuse me," said Zach as she stopped and stiffened. "I was wondering if you might tell me where we are?"

She pulled the scarf down off her face and looked at him uncomfortably. "You are at Park and Adams," she said cautiously.

Zach felt the rage bubbling up inside of him. He wanted to reach out and strangle her. Inflicting pain with his hands would be even more satisfying than causing mental agony. "You moron," he said. "What goddamn city are we in."

"Detroit!" she said with alarm and immediately started pushing her cart at a pace so rapid it toppled over, and the contents of her bags scattered on the pavement. "Oh my," she said in angst as she started gathering up the apples, tomatoes and head of lettuce that dropped out. Unable to resist the temptation, Zach walked over and began stomping on the produce until it lay in one semi-gelatinous mess.

The woman dropped to her knees and began to cry. "Why would you do that?" she looked up through tears and asked. "That was my allotment for this week."

Zach looked down and watched as the melancholy sadness with hints of anger drifted up off her body. He inhaled scent and experienced a rush of adrenaline that felt like a cocaine-fueled orgasm. "What year is it?"

She looked at him like he was a madman. "2364. Now please, can I leave?"

"Get the fuck out of here before I break your neck," he replied.

"Yeah," said Sarah as she charged forward and used her foot to knock the woman back down. "Listen to him, or we kill you."

Now whimpering, she started crawling away, leaving her cart and spoiled groceries behind.

"Wait!" Zach reached down and grabbed her arm. He could sense her fear, and it was intoxicating. "We need to find someone. Sixtus Maras is the name. Do you know who that is?"

The woman shook her head. "No. Detroit is a big city. I . . ."

"How do we locate him?" asked Sarah.

"The Ministry of Information. It used to be the Corporate Directory. Just go down Adams," she said while pointing to the east. "Make a left on Woodward. You can walk there. It is about two miles." She took Zach's hand off her arm. "Now, please, let me go." She crawled away still sobbing and mumbling to herself.

"Did you feel that, Zach," said Sarah as she moved up close. "Her fear, anger and frustration. It's like I'm on fire. If there was a place we could go, I'd fuck you right now." Zach looked at her and grabbed her tight. Her hand aggressively grabbed at his crotch. The temptation to take her into the alley just up ahead was almost overwhelming, but he knew he must not lose sight of the goal, so he pushed her away gruffly.

"Not now. We need to get to the information center or whatever they call it. The orb took us to Detroit but not his headquarters. Marshall told us we must find Sixtus Maras." He thrust his hands in his pocket and began walking down Adams with Sarah trailing.

"What if Maras isn't in Detroit? He might be anywhere in the world," she said while double stepping to keep pace.

"The orb brought us to Detroit for a reason. It can't be a coincidence this is where Cox established his headquarters. If Maras isn't here, we'll hunt him down, but I have a hunch he is here." When they reached Woodward, Zach saw a man standing inside an entryway with walls that extended outward to provide shelter from the elements. He had a blanket wrapped around him, but Zach could see he was also wearing a long, thick coat of some kind.

"Take your jacket off, I need it," he said while closing the distance.

The man looked up. His face was creased with age, but they were the soft lines of wisdom and character. "Who are you, friend?" he asked. "Detroit is a free city now. There is no more looting. If you need a coat, you can get one from a pavilion. There is one just down the street."

"I don't know what you're talking about," said Zach. "I just want your goddamn coat."

"Alright, if you need it that badly . . ." The man stopped talking mid-sentence and went rigid. He stiffly unwrapped the blanket and began unbuttoning the coat while staring absently into space. When he finished with the last button, he took it off and handed it to Zach, who brushed it off. While it wasn't attractive, the garment was well made and would provide adequate protection from the elements. Once he put the coat on, he gave the man control over his own thoughts again.

"How—why did you do that? You—you hijacked my mind . . ." Silence followed as he started grabbing at his throat as though he was being choked. Stumbling around in distress, he made a series of gurgling noises before falling to the concrete as his body convulsed and fought for breath. Zach looked back and saw Sarah smile and lick her lips as a stream of blood ran down the porch onto the steps.

"Delicious," she said.

Centuries ago, the Ministry of Information once served as the central library, and it appeared it was in the process of being transformed back to its original purpose. They walked into the interior of the building, which was massive and eerily quiet. Their footsteps echoed across the worn marble floor as they approached a large circular counter set in the center of the room. Several people in similar smart attire worked behind it, filling in ledgers by hand. Zach didn't see a computer terminal anywhere.

"Excuse me," he said impatiently. "I need information."

"Well," said a perky young woman in her twenties, "you have come to the right place." She looked into his eyes for a moment, and her smile faded instantly, almost as though she sensed his wickedness.

"I'm looking for someone. His name is Sixtus Maras. I need an address."

She leaned back. The look on her face became increasingly serious. Sensing something unusual was evolving, her coworkers stopped mid-task and looked over. At that instant, Zach realized he was dealing with people of heightened perception.

"You... You used a contraction. I encountered them in one of the old books." The girl seemed confused but wary.

"Yes, yes. Maras. I need to know how to contact Maras."

"I am sorry," she said cautiously. "I cannot reveal personal information like that. As you know, there are still Corporate rogue agents out there, and we have to guard against unwarranted attacks. Hopefully, someday soon we will live in a society where there are no secrets, and we can share personal information freely."

Zach regarded her carefully. "If this place isn't run by Corporates, who do you represent?"

She shrugged and a hint of her smile returned. "I represent myself, of course. I joined with many others to open the old library back up. People of like mind uniting for the betterment of all. It is that simple."

"Where are the computers?"

She tilted her head and paused for a moment. "Your questions are so odd. 'Computer' is such an ancient term. We have no need for processed information from artificial intelligence if that is what you meant. They just create stress and a sense of urgency and lessen our joy by interrupting our thought patterns. We have learned the very old ways of categorizing books works best."

Zach frowned. "How do you communicate over distance?"

"You are not from the city, are you?" She looked over her shoulder and nodded at a console with a headset on the counter. "We have a communications device available for emergencies. For the most part, we remain attached to our collective. Traveling distance is frivolous and wastes valuable resources."

Something felt familiar about all of this, but he couldn't quite figure out why. "I imagine there are others like you?"

"Why, yes," she said. "All around the city and all around the world. We realize that every positive action begins . . ."

" . . . with a conscious choice." He finished her sentence.

"Yes," she said with delight. "You do understand!"

"Tell me," he said casually, "is there a founder of this movement?"

"There are many people who have contributed to bring us to this enlightenment. Far too many to mention. However, most people attribute the initial impetus of the movement to Marshall and Wanda Beiner along with Sasha Simone. You must know of them."

Zach nodded. "But the Corporates. I—I thought they were in charge here."

She looked at him oddly. "You really have been away for a long time. The Corporate structure was a failure built on the defective pillars of oppression and repression. They are now mostly confined to the southern part of the African continent. Our experts think they will disappear completely in less than a decade."

Zach stumbled backward until he ran into Sarah. When he turned around and looked at her, he saw she was experiencing the same degree of shock and surprise.

"Sarah, we prevailed," he said. "The Corporate tyranny was destroyed and replaced by enlightenment. Marshall, Wanda and Sasha did it."

She slipped her hand into his. "Yes, after all we endured, we succeeded."

The instant passed as quickly as it came as the black waters rose up and submerged his sense of happiness and accomplishment. Sarah's expression hardened at the same instant, and Zach turned back toward the girl at the counter.

"Maras. I need to know where he lives." He locked his eyes on hers. "You do understand I can force you to do it if you resist."

"Yes," she replied. "I realized the instant you walked in the door you were different. I will get you the information you want." She stood up and walked to an ancient wooden drawer and opened it. Row after row of tightly packed 3x5 index cards were placed between dividers with sequential letters of the alphabet. She rifled through cards in the "M" section with speed born of repetition. Finally, she stopped and eyed a card for a second before pulling it out and walking back over to the counter.

"There is no one named 'Sixtus Maras' in our files, but that does not mean they do not exist. We are still trying to get our census up to date. However, I have found a Laxtus Maras. I do not know if they are related." She took a piece of paper and wrote down the address and handed it to him.

Zach reached over and looked down at her scribbling. 3215 Norman Ave. "I have no idea where this is."

"It is in sector 14, about 12 minutes by ground crawler." She turned and looked at the old analog wall clock. "You only have to wait about ten minutes before the next one arrives."

Zach nodded and took Sarah off to the side. "We need to find a place to hide the orbs. The energy is so extreme I had all I could do to not sink my teeth into her throat and rip out her esophagus," he said.

Sarah's irises were tinged with red. "I know . . . I can hardly control my urge to hurt these people."

With a nod, Zach started walking toward a sign that identified the washrooms and a fire exit off the main floor. Past the restrooms, he pushed the metal bar on the door leading to a set of steel stairs that went down to the basement. After moving through the lower levels, Zach opened the basement door and walked inside with Sarah following closely behind. In the relative darkness, the yellow glow in their pockets was more pronounced as the orbs pulsed with fetid energy.

Looking around at ancient tools and equipment covered in dust, it appeared this place was rarely visited if ever. He went over to a darkened far corner where he spotted a rusted chilled water pump with a broken flange with its connecting pipe twisted off to the side. The pump opening was large enough to accommodate the orbs, and the thick iron would keep most of the energy from escaping. He removed the orb from his pocket and placed it inside the pump housing.

Without looking back, he reached his hand out toward Sarah, but she hesitated and backed up. "Don't do this," he said as she drew his attention. "Give me the orb."

"No," she said. "I'm the same as the rest of you now, and I like the feeling of power."

"Sarah, think this through. We're here to stop Cox. The orb comes from a spoiled source of evil. If you let it consume you, you'll never return from the abyss."

"I—I don't want to give it up."

"Then, do it for me, Sarah. Please." Once again he held out his hand. Slowly, she approached and reached inside her pocket and handed him the orb, but her reluctance was palpable. He set hers inside the housing next to the other and realigned the pipe with the pump so they looked like they were still connected.

"C'mon," he said, "the transportation the librarian talked about should be here in a couple minutes."

The public transport ground crawler arrived exactly on the hour. Zach gave the address to the driver, who traced a path along a laminated paper map attached to the flat console next to him. Zach and Sarah waited impatiently for several minutes until it was apparent no one else was boarding. The driver flipped the vehicle around and started north until he reached an intersection that led them to a much wider road. Zach thought it must have been a freeway at some point, but most of the land was undergoing conversion into parks and natural habitat. They traveled at a very slow speed to avoid the construction equipment.

"I cannot wait until they have the hyper-loop running again. I hear the council approved the new plan now that it meets their environmental enhancement guidelines. Traveling will become much more efficient when it is completed."

"Uh huh," Zach replied. "How close are we?"

"Just a few more minutes." The driver got off the old freeway and back onto surface streets. Nearly ten minutes later, he pulled up in front of an old Greystone that sat alone on a deserted cul-de-sac. All the other homes must have been demolished at some point since the adjacent area was covered with grass and trees all at about the same growth stage. Since it was winter, everything had the same dull look of dormancy.

For some unknown reason, just this one house had survived despite the boarded up windows and crumbling exterior facade. Cautiously, Zach and Sarah exited the ground crawler and started toward the porch, climbing up the five worn cement steps until they reached the front door. There was no bell, so Zach closed his fist to knock, but the door opened before he could strike it. An old woman in a large green pullover and a kind of blue sweatpant stood in the doorway looking at him and then Sarah alternately. Her thinning hair was pulled back in a bun, which tended to accentuate her plump face.

"Well, what is it?" she said finally.

"I'm sorry to intrude," said Zach to ease the awkwardness of the moment. "We're looking for Sixtus Maras.

The woman jerked her head backwards. "Who? There is no one here by that name. You have the wrong place, my friend."

Zach grunted and hung his head. "Look, we've come a long way . . ."

From another room, a middle-aged man emerged and walked toward the door, his steps causing the wooden floorboards to squeak. He was tall, lean and fit, and Zach thought he might have been considered handsome except for outsized ears that were large to the point of distraction.

"Who is it, Mother? What do they want?"

"They have the wrong address. They are looking for someone named Sixtus Maras."

The man stopped for a moment, and then came quickly to the door. He paused and stared at Zach to the point where it became uncomfortable. "I don't believe it. You must be — Marshall Beiner."

Chapter Twenty-Eight

With fresh supplies and a cache of weapons, Winn waved goodbye to the Corporates as he pulled out onto Camelback heading west. Their stronghold was impressive, like an oasis in the desert. They had electricity, running water, meat, vegetables and housing that brought back memories of a time when nearly everyone felt comfortable and secure.

Bordered by East Bell, North Scottsdale Road, Pinnacle Peak, and the McDowell mountains, the area inhabitants built a 20-foot high wall that spanned the full 15 miles around the perimeter. While they ate ribs and baked beans and sat out on the veranda of the Wingate Ranch, Jeff bragged.

"Used those goddamn floaters to build the wall. Sons of bitches aren't good for much, but they do make pretty good servants. But you have to pick the right kind, and you get to a point where you can tell if they're right for working or not. You don't want the ones with hate in their eyes. The ones who look like they've given up don't work either. They just want to die. But there are some of thos sons-a-bitches who still have hope. Like, the dumb asses still think there's a chance things will get better."

At that moment, a severely malnourished woman walked up and refilled their glasses with an '89 Bordeaux. "See, like this one," said Jeff. "Look in her eyes. She still has hope."

Winn, Lars and the others were able to keep their stories straight enough that they didn't raise suspicions that might have caused a delay or worse. Throughout dinner, Winn continued to emphasize the need to get back on the road. After enjoying an after dinner drink and dessert, Jeff took them on a tour of the area, showing off the various projects that were finished or under construction. Once the excursion was complete, without saying it directly, he gave them permission to leave.

"You're good people," he said. "This new world we're building needs good people like you. The big corporations were always in a better position to govern, anyway. The corporate culture is far more efficient than government. And you don't have those damned elections to get in the way."

Winn nodded enthusiastically as Nicholas clapped Jeff on the back. "Damn shame we have to leave this place," said Lars, "but we need to bring this type of order to L.A. They need us."

Jeff nodded. "Yeah, I understand. Well, you travel safe. It's still a jungle out there."

As Jeff said his goodbyes, several other corporate employees moved off to other tasks as Winn led his group back to the van. No one said anything as they pulled out and drove through the iron gates while a group of Corporates waved and smiled. Once they were clear of the compound and back on the road, Nicholas said, "What the fuck was that all about?"

"You've just seen the future," said Lars. "The Corporates are sequestering themselves behind high walls in every part of the world. If they don't have the talent they need, they go outside and kidnap it."

The ride up I-17 was silent and empty, almost as though the floaters had cleared a pathway. In reality, humanity was reaching a tipping point, and the population was thinning at an alarming rate. Winn had to drive with the windows up to avoid the ever-present smell of rotting human flesh. Cars were scattered to either side of the road, with bodies in and around the vehicles. Some decayed naturally while others displayed huge holes where meat and flesh were ripped out and eaten by animals.

Around Rimrock, Winn heard Bahati say, "I'm cold."

"Sure, Bahati, I'll turn on the heat." Winn flipped on the heater switch and turned the thermostat up.

"What?" said Bahati. "I said nothing. But it's odd because I was thinking about wanting to turn the heat up."

Bhati's always cold. In Norma's basement she always complained about it.

"I did not always complain about it, Nicholas," said Bahati.

"What are you talking about, I didn't utter a word." Nicholas pointed a finger at himself, and his face showed surprise and denial.

"I heard it too," said Winn.

"Yeah, so did I," said Felicia.

"But I swear I didn't say anything." Nicholas now took a defensive tone.

They drove several miles more looking at each other suspiciously.

Can any of you hear this?

"Yes."

"I do."

"Me too." Felicia, Nicholas and Bahati answered in succession. Only Lars remained silent.

Where are we heading to?

"Sedona," they said out loud in near unison.

"There's something strange is going on here. My body is energized like I just popped a handful of white cross. My mind is razor sharp, and I think I'm reading your thoughts."

"Yes, I feel the same way. A growing confidence and abilities that I can't describe."

"Yes," said Lars quietly. "I sense it too . . ."

They drove for several miles without further discussion as Winn tried to process what was happening. *Nicholas, if you can hear this, answer through your thoughts. Say nothing out loud.*

Several seconds elapsed before there was a clear reply. *Yes, I hear you, but I don't know how. Your words just pop into my mind. First as a thought bubble that unfolds into sentences.*

I'm getting better at recognizing your thoughts. I think if we focus only on ourselves, we exclude the others. Let's bring Felicia in. In the same instant, both Winn and Nicholas opened their minds and summoned Felicia into the conversation.

Felicia, you're now connected to Nicholas and me.

She jerked her head around as if some unidentifiable person was talking to her.

I'm not talking to you; I'm projecting my thoughts. It will be important to learn the difference.

She looked over at Winn and nodded. *I understand. This is incredible. It must be the reason why we were targeted by the skankers and Norma. Or, are we this way because of what Norma did to us.*

I'm not sure, but I'm going to bring Bahati and Lars into the bubble. Winn reached out to the other two and invited them in. Bahati jumped as though someone pricked her with a pin before she realized they were communicating with here telepathically. For his part, Lars remained stationary. He looked at them suspiciously but said nothing.

After the 4-way connection was firmly established, Winn said, *Lars isn't hearing us.*

You're right, said Nicholas. *He's not tuned in . . . What does that mean?*

I'm not sure. Maybe Felicia is right and we have this ability because of the drugs Norma pumped us full of, but I don't think so. Lars just doesn't have the gift.

Then . . . Then why is he here? asked Nicholas, but no one responded.

Winn turned off on 179 as the strength of the new pheromone grew in intensity with each passing mile. He never wavered or required directions as his hands seemed to turn the wheel on their own accord. In his conscious mind, he had no idea where he was going, but somehow, he did know. By the time he reached the juncture 89A and Dry Creek Road, there was no doubt he was being led by someone or something.

At the same time, a new phenomenon was creeping into his mind. Images of multiple suicides fought to draw him into their horror, and he struggled to keep the encroaching visions at bay. As he looked at Felicia sobbing, Nicholas rubbing his temples and Bahati bent over with her head in her hands, he realized they were dealing with the same issues. Only Lars continued to be unaffected. His steely gaze hardened as they drew closer to their destination.

On Vultee Arch, several miles past Devil's Bridge, Winn turned down a dirt road that eventually ran out and ended near the shear walls of a large red mountain. Without words, he stopped the SUV and everyone got out, walking directly east in the same direction. For a moment, Lars remained behind, and when he caught up, Winn noticed he had the shotgun at his side and the pistol in his waistband.

"What are you doing?" Winn asked him as he stopped and turned toward Lars. "No guns are necessary here. This is not a place for guns."

"I'm bringing them. Who the hell knows what this place will be like."

"Lars, please," said Nicholas.

"Just shut up, Nicholas. I'm bringing the guns." Lars raised the barrel from the ground slightly in an intimidating way, and Winn shook his head and started walking back toward the force that was drawing them closer.

They moved through an area where the vegetation was sparse, and Winn stopped suddenly. He looked around, but there was only the mountain to his right and dead brush, prickly pears, yuccas and agaves.

"This is it," said Winn as he turned to the group. "I can feel it. There is a convergence of harmonics right here at this place."

Nicholas nodded. "I can sense it to, but I don't see anything."

Lars looked at them and raised an eyebrow. "There's nothing here. We must be in the wrong place."

At that moment, Winn, looked directly behind Lars at the approaching form of a smallish man flanked on one side by a slight, attractive young woman and on the other by a well-dressed middle–aged man. Behind them, what appeared to be a 3-person security detail followed closely.

Greetings, the words pulsed through Winn's mind with extraordinary command and power. *My name is*

Sasha Simone. We welcome you to the Sanctuary. Your arrival is a most unexpected and incredible event. The abilities you are discovering are a gift, and we will help you learn to better control and perfect them.

The small man spoke. "Welcome, Overseers Ryan, Okeke, Cruz and Wright. My name is Juan Gustavo Ricardo Pena, and I am the care taker of the facility."

Winn could see Lars face as his rage grew. He began to tremble and his grip on the weapon tightened. He whirled around with the shotgun pointed at Sasah and her companions.

"Delgado!" Lars screamed the name with contempt. "What the fuck are you doing here?"

"Lars," said Delgado while nodding his head and shrugging. "Where was I to go after I was dismissed from Gehenna? Fortunately, I found a place here, and I have a new purpose. With my help, Alan Ziminski will file a lawsuit on Monday to establish his right as the sole heir to Mr. Cox. I saw you approach from one of the security monitors and warned Pena. It's over, Lars."

"The Suicide Society lair. I found it. I finally found it!" Lars brought the shotgun up to his shoulder, but that's as far as he got. He grunted and sputtered as spittle flew out of his mouth. His muscles bulged, and his hand started to shake as his finger rested on the trigger.

"You have caused great hardship for the Suicide Society," said Sasha. "You killed Speaker Anston, and you forced us to go underground into hiding. But it is over, Lars. You will no longer be a threat to anyone."

Sasha entered Lars mind, and with laser-like precision, started to shave small slices off his brain at the cellular level, removing diseased portions and disrupting the deeply established thought patterns that lie at the core of Lars' sociopathic behavior. The gun dropped to the ground and Lars began to writhe and shudder while muttering expletives and alternately laughing in blood curdling shrieks.

Winn stood in stunned silence as the energy that emanated from the one named Sasha penetrated every cell in his body with an indescribable force and power. Could she kill someone with thought? Winn wondered.

Yes, I can. Winn heard the thought clearly. *But the gift must be used wisely and with great discretion. Your education begins today, Winn.* Expanding her reach to the entire group, she said, *Welcome home, and my warmest welcome to the next generation of the Suicide Society.*

Winn looked at the others and then at Lars who was now sitting up with the grin of an idiot. Pena's attendants helped him to his feet, and together, they walked to a nondescript portion of a sheer rock face that looked identical to every other part of the mountain that was visible.

Pena pushed back a bush to reveal a small keypad, and he punched in a code. A huge, seamless slab retracted and slowly slid open. When Winn walked inside, he knew that Sasha was right. He was overwhelmed by a surge of energy so full of love, that he realized he had finally come home.

***

"Is there a problem here?" asked Papa Grande as he walked up with his contingent of Pocks to join Wanda. She reached out her hand and grabbed onto his arm, shaking her head slowly as he looked her way.

363

"Yes, there is a problem," said Sandra as she shook her dark, black hair so more of her face was revealed. Wanda saw multiple tattoos that crawled up from either side of her neck and met in the middle of her forehead. A large skull covered her exposed breastbone, and the interlocking tattoos around it depicted snakes, spiders and other venomous creatures in aggressive poses. "You are violating Corporate global law. Obviously, we can't have that. It represents a threat to the well-being of the people."

"Threat?" said Wanda with incredulity. "They were starving. The water and gruel shipments were cut off. We grew our own food out of necessity."

"And yet, when you were offered increased rations of water and protein porridge, you turned them down. This suggests you have plans and intentions that go beyond this area." She took several steps forward as more people filled in behind her. "Whoever you are, you are very persuasive, and it appears that a number of movements similar to this one are springing up in various cities across the globe. I want to know who you represent."

"I represent myself and no one else," said Wanda without hesitation. "Everyone here represents themselves. If they join together to help each other, that is their choice."

"And yet, you are clearly their leader." Sandra looked away as if she was in deep thought. "We will take you in for questioning, along with the other four with you. The people here will be moved into other neighborhoods, and this area will be sanitized so it can be inhabited by others."

From a distance, Wanda could hear the sound of helicopters approaching. Instinctively, she looked up. "Oh yes, just in case you have the urge to resist, those approaching helicopters are armed."

Wanda sighed, and for just a moment, her shoulders slumped. When she drew her next breath, she raised her head and spoke with conviction. "You can apprehend us, and we will go peaceably. You can destroy what we have built and drive these people away, but it won't matter. They understand what is important, and it isn't control or external power. They will simply disperse and organize in another area, and the movement will grow. No matter what you do, you will not be able to stop it."

"Really?" said Sandra. "Well, let's find out." She turned and looked over her right shoulder at a large man with a crooked nose and one eyebrow. "Kill the loudmouth and those five other Pocks standing next to him," she said.

Instantly, several rounds of automatic weapons fire erupted, and the people standing near Wanda scattered as she dove for cover. Bullets sprayed everywhere, and the shock of the moment was so deep, she didn't realize a slug had grazed her calf until she felt a warm trickle of blood run down her leg.

In the chaos that unfolded as if in slow motion, Wanda realized Papa Grande was no longer standing either. As she looked to her right, she saw him lying on the ground gasping and grabbing at his abdomen. Around him, four other Pocks had fallen. Three were dead, and one was screaming in pain.

Wanda crawled over to Papa Grande and took his hand.

"I did it, Wanda," he said between gasps for breath. "I believe in you. This body is temporary and was given to me to gain experience." He coughed up a chunk of bloody lung tissue and spit it out before continuing. "I have done so many horrible things. May I be forgiven? I—I hope I have learned the lessons you've taught me."

Wanda's eyes spilled over, and the tears splashed down on Papa Grande's blood-soaked shirt. "You have been an excellent pupil," she said. "You've grown so much in such a short time. I'm certain you are going to graduate from the Earth School, Tomas."

He smiled and revealed teeth coated with blood. "Don't let them destroy what we have built . . . Too important . . . Sometimes you have to . . ." She felt the pressure of his grip lessen as he exhaled a long, ragged breath. His eyes glazed over until they were lifeless.

Wanda turned back to Sandra, and with great effort got to her knees. With a final push and a grunt, she stood back up and looked at her antagonist with defiance. "You can kill all of us, but it won't matter. Ultimately, no one can defy the rules of the universe."

Sandra sighed and rolled her eyes as the sound of the helicopters grew closer. She looked in toward the group with the semi-automatic weapons and said, "This bitch bores me. Take the other four. One of them will tell us what we want to know. This one probably wouldn't talk anyway. Go ahead and kill her."

Wanda's sense of perception slowed considerably as she watched the one-eyed assassin raise and shoulder his automatic weapon. He pointed it at her, and she could see every detail of the gun, his face and hand as though everything was magnified 100 times. A small bead of sweat formed on his brow and traced a path down wrinkles in his forehead. Unexpectedly, he grimaced slightly and let out a small yelp. She watched as he re-gripped the weapon several times. The small muscles in his finger trigger began to spasm.

Wanda knew she had only a few seconds to live, but they were unfolding slowly as each second felt like a long chapter in a seemingly endless span of time. She couldn't understand why he wouldn't just shoot. As she stared at him, another ball of sweat rolled down his forehead and then a third. Why was he flushing with color and trembling? When a vessel in his eye burst and flooded the sclera with blood, she realized something was wrong.

Suddenly, he turned the weapon on Sandra, and people on both sides of the conflict gasped. The Corporate's Director of Security opened her eyes wide as she looked at him. "Call off the helicopters," he said. "Call them off right now."

Sandra regarded him for a moment. "What are you doing, Clog? You know you're a dead man, right?"

"I—I don't care. Just call off the helicopters, or I will shoot you."

The barrels of two dozen weapons pointed at the rogue Corporate soldier, but he didn't seem to care. Studying him for a moment, Sandra must have sensed his deep-seated determination because she grabbed a radio from her pocket and pressed the send stud. "This is Director Sandra Bentenhouse. The situation here is under control. Turn the choppers back to Edwards."

Sandra put the transceiver back in her pocket and turned to the rogue soldier. "Now what?" she asked.

"We leave, and we don't come back here. Because if we do . . ." He stopped talking but kept the gun trained on her.

"Because if we do, what?" she asked in a tone that displayed her disdain.

"I don't think you want to find out." A voice came from behind Wanda. A voice so familiar she didn't need to see the face. Without turning around, she smiled for a moment and wiped away the tears that rolled down her cheeks.

"Who the fuck are you?" Sandra had no sooner asked the question when her body lurched forward as she expelled a thick stream of yellow vomit. She bent over and wiped her mouth as the rogue soldier lowered his weapon and looked around at his comrades with an expression of terror and confusion. Sandra fell to her knees and as her body shuddered as her entire neuromuscular system seized up.

Marshall walked forward and briefly squeezed Wanda's arm. "I want all of you to watch this," he said loudly as he looked at those on the other side. "This is what you are dealing with. I am not the only one with the capacity to inflict this kind of pain and damage. If you come back here with ill intent, I promise no one will make it to the border of Skid Row." As he finished speaking, Sandra let out a squeal that caused everyone to grimace. She wiped blood from her nose and began to babble incoherently between loud wails and deep moans.

When she had thoroughly humiliated herself and permanently tarnished the veneer of invincibility and toughness, Marshall stopped aggravating her pain centers and withdrew partially, allowing her to rise. She looked around at

368

her people as they turned away to avoid eye content. Then, with Marshall still telepathically controlling her thoughts, she said, "We are going to leave. None of you represent any threat to the HUGE conglomerate. Till your silly fields and tote your river water, that's just more protein porridge for the others." She turned and began walking away as the Crege and skankers followed while the distinctive sound of the helicopter blades faded in the distance.

Marshall turned back and looked at Wanda. "You came," she said as two tears fell from her brimming lower eyelids. "You came for me."

He smiled. "Of course. This was a critical moment; one that could have disrupted everything. The overseers will not intervene often, but this was—a special case. Besides, there was no way I could stand by and watch someone harm you. I love you, Wanda."

She rushed to him and fell into his waiting arms. The neighbors, who watched the scene unfold, burst into spontaneous applause.

***

Later, inside her tent with the flap zipped up, Marshall lay with Wanda on her cot. She snuggled deeper into his chest as though she wanted to crawl inside him. "What happens next, Marshall?"

"You leave tomorrow for a new settlement in Chicago."

She leaned up and looked at him, scowling. "I can't leave here. There is so much more work to be done."

He nodded. "Yes, but Talie and Jerry can take it from here. You, Sam and Aisha must go to Chicago and start the same process there. You have proven that people can come together and work for a common good. Every

369

day, more of the facility's students are leaving the sanctuary and organizing these communities that have been left for dead. At this point, you're the best we've got, Wanda."

"And you, Marshall. What will you be doing?"

"Until Speaker Randall comes back, I will assume the role of Speaker. Yesterday, four new overseers arrived in Sedona . There may be more out there. I will have much to do, but don't worry, I have a hunch I'll also have a lot of work to do in Chicago."

She leaned down, smiled, and kissed her husband.

Chapter Twenty-Nine

Seated in the small living area of the apartment, Zach sipped at his beverage. It had a bland taste that was not unpleasant but lacked flavor. His expression must have conveyed his impression of the drink.

"Doscious tea," said the man sitting across from him. "A plant constructed in a lab that got into the food chain and killed thousands of native tea species. It is almost tasteless, but it contains an abundance of essential nutrients."

"You sound like a commercial," said Zach.

"A 'commercial'? I am unfamiliar with that term."

"Never mind," said Zach waving him off. "Let's get to the matter at hand. You are Sixtus Maras."

The man sipped his tea before shaking his head. "No, I am not. My name is Laxtus Maras. I never met my brother, Sixtus. In this reality, he never existed. However, I am aware that he traveled back. As the timeline cycles through its repetitive progressions, his fetus is aborted, which, as you know, was standard Corporate policy for Time Sculptors."

"But then, how could Sixtus have traveled back in time when he was never born?" asked Sarah.

"That was a quantum physics dilemma finally solved by Ruthenstein in 2298. In essence, the first run of space-time is, for lack of a better term, 'pristine'. The person who initially pierces the continuum exists outside of the constructs of time. Even if they are killed in an altered cycle, the original event still stands no matter what happens in subsequent loops. The NIN system was wired directly to each Time Sculptor, so detailed records gave local officials the information they needed to ensure the fetuses were aborted as each loop completed itself."

"If Sixtus Maras was killed before he was born, how could you know we would be coming?" asked Zach.

Laxtus reached into his back pocket and extracted a folded piece of paper and handed it over. My brother hid this in an edition of an old book by an author he knew I would someday read avidly. The library in Old Metropolis has books that sat on shelves undisturbed for centuries. One day, when I was 13, I opened a volume by Storm Davis, and in between the third and fourth pages from the end, I found that note.

Carefully, Zach unfolded the brittle paper and started reading:

Laxtus Maras, I am your brother Sixtus. I was sent back to the past through the Time Sculptor program, and since the timeline is now contaminated, you will not remember me. I have an important decision to make, but if I choose incorrectly, it may have dire consequences. Mr. Cox is the one I do not trust. I wonder if he is also a time traveler. If the Corporates assume control of global governance, you will know I have failed.

Zach passed the note to Sarah, who took it gently and began reading while Zach spoke. "I—don't understand. An old man visited us in the past and gave us a warning. If that was not Sixtus Maras, then who was it?"

"I assume it was me," said Laxtus. "I imagine you are going to ask me to travel back to the past and give Marshall Beiner these time coordinates."

"But, how would we know to do that?"

"Obviously, as Sixtus mentioned, this is not pristine time. This could be the second pass in the loop or the millionth. There is no way to know for sure. Perhaps in the first reality we met randomly. Again, who knows?"

"Wait," said Sarah, "why are you in Detroit to begin with?"

Laxtus reached into his pocket and pulled out a second note and once again handed it to Zach.

On February 13, 2364, you must be in Detroit at 3215 Norman Ave. A man named Marshall Beiner will approach you. Follow all of his instructions and accompany him to the library. You must go back and warn them.

"Is this also from Sixtus?"

"No, that is my handwriting. The note was in the same book where I found the other. Apparently, I sent it to myself so I would know to be here at this place and time to meet you. Still, it is odd that I didn't mention the woman," he said as he nodded at Sarah.

"So, you came back to warn us because we told you to."

Laxtus shook his head. "Yes, of course my brother had something to do with it as well."

Zach scratched his head. "We may have big problems. You see, I'm not Marshall Beiner, although I know him well. My name is Zach Randall, and this is Sarah Johansen."

Laxtus sat back and looked at Zach for several seconds. "Then, this version of time has been altered yet again. It seems the fabric of space-time is becoming increasingly unstable."

"Yes, I agree. How do we know Mr. Cox is even here?"

Laxtus got up and walked to a table where he rifled through several papers. When he found the one he was looking for, he returned to the living area. "Global media, or what's left of it, has followed the exploits of a rebel who apparently has recently overthrown Amrosia and re-established control over remnants of the HUGE conglomerate. Some are saying Amrosia has disappeared completely, and many assume they used hidden Kerr Ring apparatuses to travel to another time."

"So, they may contaminate the time line even further."

"Perhaps they already have, which would explain why you are here and not Marshall Beiner,." said Laxtus. "Amrosia expunged the history of the Corporates and replaced it with their own revisionist version, but enough authentic evidence remains to verify that a mysterious figure known as 'Mr. Cox' played a critical role in the establishment of HUGE in the 21st century. Word has spread quickly that he planned to return to Detroit, and I am certain today is the day of his arrival."

"Gehenna headquarters. Of course," said Zach.

"Yes, and because the world is now one of pacifism and accommodation, no one is really in charge over there. He will easily take over the complex. It is a housing facility now; very low security.

Zach looked at Sarah. "We need to get back to the library." He turned and looked at Laxtus. "It appears we need to take you with us," he said.

Laxtus nodded. "Yes, if I am to go to the past and warn you, I will need access to a time travel mechanism. I spent years tracking down machinery I am certain is mothballed in the library basement. They've preserved it as historical. Hopefully, it's a Kerr Ring setup. If I have to go back through Einstein Rosen Bridge, I will die shortly after I arrive."

Zach glanced at Sarah but refused to meet Maras's gaze. "Is the device functional?"

Laxtus shrugged. "Probably not. Time travel requires a great deal of power, and the pacifists only generate as much as is necessary to keep people comfortable in their homes."

"Alright, let's go. We'll figure it out when we get there." Zach rose from the chair and walked to the door. Sarah got up to join him as Laxtus called out, "Mother, I'm going to the library with my friends."

"Remain safe, Laxtus," she yelled from the bedroom.

The trip back to the library took longer than expected since there wasn't a connecting public ground crawler. The walk down Woodward Avenue was brutal as the wind kicked up, which drove the adjusted temperature down into the teens. Zach pulled up the tattered lapels on his jacket as Sarah leaned into the wind and thrust her hands into her pockets. Laxtus walked as though it was a spring day.

Halfway down Woodward, a ground crawler pulled over and picked them up. Zach was grateful for the warmth inside the cab, but the driver still shivered and rubbed his hands together. The pacifists did not believe in autonomous vehicles, and although developing and implementing artificial intelligence systems wasn't illegal, the horrid history of advanced technology made it unattractive. The few motorized vehicles that existed were operated by humans and designed only to help move people over distance when necessary.

As they reached the steps of the library, Zach turned towards Laxtus. "This is a huge place, and the basement runs the entire length of the building. How would we find a time mechanism if one even existed?"

"I have a general idea where it is, but as I said earlier, we have no way to power it."

"Let us worry about that," said Zach as they entered the building and walked to the fire escape corridor that also served as the entrance to the basement, Carefully surveying the area, he noted there was no surveillance whatsoever. No cameras or security guards anywhere in the building. Zach found the lack of suspicion and implicit trust disarming. The friendliness of these people didn't lessen his desire to hurt them, but it was clear this society lacked the hatred, depression and rudeness that was so prevalent in his time.

For a brief moment, Zach paused, and through the turbulence and boiling stew of orb's dark energy, a momentary feeling of gratitude ran through him. The Suicide Society's plan to sow the seeds of kindness, generosity, equality, and cooperation throughout the world had taken root after all. Major cities now functioned in a way that would have been considered a utopian fantasy in his time. According to Maras, the Corporates were disappearing and losing control everywhere. The only force with the capacity to disrupt the natural evolution of society was Mr. Cox. Zach ground his teeth, and his level of animus toward the time traveling psychopath made it difficult to breathe.

"Here, this is where we need to go," said Zach as he pushed open the door to the basement and descended the stairs with Maras and Sarah following close behind.

When they reached the lower floor, Laxtus pointed to a corridor up ahead. "The time travel apparatus is down that hallway."

"Wait for us outside the room. We need to make a stop first."

"I will accompany you . . ."

Zach shook his head. "No. We'll catch up to you." The tone must have sounded authoritative enough that Maras paused before nodding and starting off toward the intersection up ahead. Zach waited until he turned the corner before ducking inside the mechanical room to retrieve the orbs.

Crackling with raw power, Zach felt a new wave of hatred wash over him as he picked up his orb. Somehow, it had the capacity to unlock the vault that stored his repressed telekinetic and telepathic abilities, and the effect was proving almost too toxic to control. He wanted to kill someone, and Sarah was standing right next to him. *What did I ever see in her? She murdered my friends and almost destroyed the Suicide Society.* A mass of lethal energy formed inside him.

***

All through the space plane journey to Detroit, Mr. Cox remained unsettled. Something was undeniably wrong with the flow, but he couldn't pinpoint the origin. The presence of one, no perhaps two, dark energy masses occupied space in the psychokinetic sphere, but there was something odd and different about them. No matter how much he tried to dismiss his thoughts as irrational, he couldn't shake the feeling that something threatening lurked just ahead.

The craft descended through the clouds and landed vertically on top of the Gehenna Center's Building 1. In preparation, rebel corporate loyalists had forced their way into the facility, which was now used as a housing complex.

As he walked to the stairs from the roof and traveled down a floor to his old penthouse, Mr. Cox shook his head in dismay at the transformation of the building. Once a bastion of lavish opulence, these cretins had turned it into basic functional living space. Gone were the expensive crafted lighting fixtures, replaced by unshaded LPD emitters. The ornate hand-textured walls he commissioned from Spanish craftsmen were painted over in a mono-shade of beige. The drab color even covered the handmade oak doors imported from Italy.

Perhaps more depressing was the renovation to the penthouse. The spacious living area was now divided into eight separate efficiency cubicles each containing a bed, chair and dresser. His old bedroom was partitioned to provide four additional sleeping spaces. Inside the bathroom, there were multiple sets of identical towels and washcloths, and 12 baskets sat out on the lengthy vanity filled with toiletries, including razors, shave cream, toothbrush, and toothpaste.

Walking through the penthouse, Mr. Cox looked with disdain at his surroundings. Then, turning to Minkus Term, he said, "Where are the people who occupy these beds?"

"Out working," replied Term. "The pacifists encourage work as they believe it serves as spiritual balm for the soul."

"So, they won't be back for several hours?"

"Yes, sir. I imagine they won't be back until after dark."

"Good. That will give you time to tear out all these beds and disinfect the place. There is an offensive odor of humanity here. It smells of rot."

"Well, sir, the building is very old . . ."

Mr. Cox snapped his head around. "I don't care how old it is. I want it restored to the exact state and floorplan when I occupied it in the 21st century."

Term shuddered and bowed. "Of course, Prevus Coxnotus. Of course."

"We must let the world know that HUGE is open for business, and the Gehenna Corporation is back in charge. A global broadcast to rally our forces."

He stopped talking, but all of his aides hung their heads, and no one replied.

"Well, what is it?"

"Benefactor," said Term in the absence of anyone else speaking, "there are no 'global broadcasting' capabilities. The pacifists have changed the bandwidth assignments and transmission wattage so broadcasts only reach local residents. They believe in communities making rules for themselves rather than a central government. You might reach greater Detroit, but no farther."

Mr. Cox looked up to the sky and shook his fists. "This is all unbelievable to me. A nightmare, really." His hand fell to his sides, and he slump slightly. "Fine. Then let us make a broadcast to Detroit to raise an army. We'll use persuasion to win over the local populace as we did in Nzoni. We will need to recruit these people to perform the unpleasant tasks."

"Sir," said Hismus Malconus, "you do not seem to understand. Detroit and all the other large cities were converted by the pacifists. No one here supports the Corporates. They won't stop us if we wish to make a broadcast, but it is highly unlikely we will find converts."

Ignoring the lingering smell of the person who recently slept in the nearest bed, Mr. Cox sat down. The room swirled, and he became lightheaded as the reality of the situation came into clear focus.

He could not have envisioned a place and time more unpleasant than this one. Pacifists? How could such a movement have gained traction in a world tightly controlled by Xavier Watts, Sandra Bentenhouse and the deep infrastructure he created? The Benefactor again felt a pain near his heart where the voodoo priests had plunged needles into their dolls. A sudden pang of doubt erupted near the site of the discomfort that traveled through his body to its furthermost extremities. What is this, doubt? I do not ever feel doubt.

He rose from the bed and turned toward his contingent. "In this reality, where are the deranged and mentally disturbed housed? Before I left, those people were altered at birth, but I imagine the pacifists would find that behavior barbaric and inhumane."

Term nodded. "Indeed. Now, those people are taken in by the numerous communal cells throughout the city where they cared for are nurtured."

"So, they are not in a facility?"

"No. Institutions are not encouraged although they are not outlawed. There is no need for them."

"How would we find the Satanists, murderers, psychopaths and other miscreants?"

Term looked back at the others, but no one spoke up. "No one in this time fits that description anymore. Those with challenges are taken in the community at large and given a great deal of attention."

Mr. Cox began breathing rapidly, and he fingered the jeweled box that held the orb. "This is utterly horrible. It cannot be true." He looked up at Term with just a hint of desperation in his eyes. "Are you saying the only place that is safe for us is in the small area of Africa that these pacifists have yet to spoil?"

Term nodded. "Yes, we tried to tell you that. It is all that is left of our world, and it continues to shrink. Although recruitment efforts here will not be obstructed, no one will join us. Once the pacifists absorb an area, it remains contaminated forever. You have shown us that containing the contagion is possible, but we must focus on the few remaining areas that have not yet converted."

"Get me to a Kerr Ring arrangement and make preparation for a Casimir Vacuum," said Mr. Cox with the slightest hint of panic in his voice. "I must get away from here . . . I must."

"It is unlikely there is a functioning Kerr Ring arrangement anywhere in the world now that the Amrosians have destroyed those that remained. Since they are easier to assemble and require less energy, we might be able to locate an Einstein-Rosen Bridge mechanism."

"You fool!" bellowed Mr. Cox. "I don't want to travel back to the past just to die from radiation sickness." He hung his head. "So, the only real alternative is to return to some backwards part of Africa in the stifling heat and try to hold the pacifists at bay. This cannot be . . . It simply cannot be."

"If you would like," said Term with a sense of empathy, "we can try and make a broadcast to find Corporate sympathizers here in Detroit. As I said, no one will stop us, but I am afraid our efforts will be fruitless."

Mr. Cox got up and walked towards the door. "We will find a convert. The next person we encounter will be a convert."

Outside in the hallway, he went down to the elevator with his entourage following. His finger pressed the down button repeatedly before the cab finally arrived. Once inside, they started toward the lobby, but the elevator only traveled ten floors before it stopped. The doors opened and a woman got in. She was tanned youthful, wearing the type of cotton jumpsuit that seemed so prevalent around the city. She smiled politely as she checked to see the lobby button was already pressed.

As the car began moving, Mr. Cox turned to Term and said, "Our first convert." He projected solid tendrils of pitch-black energy directly into her cerebellum. The effect was instantaneous, and she stumbled up against the side of the elevator and began moaning as her eyes rolled up and showed only white. Probing deeply and with little regard for her health or safety, the Benefactor tore into her amygdala, digging into the woman's emotional centers and focusing on raising her fear and anger.

The probe darted back and forth and through the temporal lobe, but it was like trying to hold onto a Teflon sphere soaked with oil. It kept slipping off the surface of the amygdala, unable to rewire the circuitry. This enraged Mr. Cox as he yelled out and increased the intensity of the incursion, yet, it was to no avail. Something was physiologically different about these people, and they seemed impervious to any effort to change their constitution.

He could manipulate her appendages, which he did, and she began to strangle herself. After stimulating her pain centers to the point where she panted and begged to die, Mr. Cox granted her wish and sent a lethal dose of his most potent telepathic poison into her mind. Although his companions could only see the trickles of blood rolling out of her nose and ears, he knew that inside her skull, her brains were bubbling in a brew of liquefied jelly.

No one said a word as the elevator reached the ground floor. They stepped outside, and Mr. Cox stood for a moment, watching people scurrying around to their various appointments. He probed them gently and found the same brain symmetry as the woman he so recently killed. They were uniformly monotone, and while they might be influenced, they couldn't be corrupted.

With his shoulders slumped, the Benefactor turned to Minkus Term. "Let us go to the space plane and return to Jaunde. This battle will be much longer and more difficult than I ever imagined, but I will prevail." He spoke in a low tone, and for the first time since he arrived in the future, he convinced no one.

Mr. Cox turned back to the elevator and pressed the button to go up to the roof when he heard a voice from behind.

"Turn and face me, you son of a bitch."

His back stiffened just a bit, but then a small smile slowly spread across the Benefactor's lips as he turned around. "Just like your mother. You can't get enough of me, can you, Sarah?"

Chapter Thirty

Laxtus Maras pulled the cover off the Einstein-Rosen Bridge apparatus and stared at it with a look of resignation. He walked up and ran his hand along one of the titanium fins while shaking his head and sighing. Sarah and Zach walked in and drew his attention.

"It won't work," said Maras. "This thing has been decommissioned for a half a century. The pacifists draw power from solar arrays in low orbit, but they only generate enough electricity to provide basic needs. An Einstein-Rosen Bridge is a relatively simple device, so it might still work, but if we try to power it up, we would probably blow every circuit in the city.

Zach pointed at the machine. "Stand wherever you would as if you were preparing to make the journey."

"Why? I . . ."

"Just shut the fuck up and do it." Zach's expression was dark and menacing, and Laxtus walked over and opened the phars shell bubble and stepped inside. The targeting computer was dead. In fact, the whole machine was dead.

"When the operating system is finished rebooting, enter your coordinates quickly. I'm not sure how much time you'll have. When you arrive in the past, you know exactly what you must do, correct?"

"Yes, I've been rehearsing this for years. When I get there, I leave the note to myself alongside my brother's note. Then I travel to Portales to warn Marshall, the young one, and give him the date. Hopefully, radiation sickness won't have killed me by then. But there is no way to get this machine to function so . . ."

"Just remember what you're supposed to do," said Zach. He looked at Sarah and nodded, and together, they took the orbs out of their pockets at the exact same moment. They lowered their heads and held the orbs out in front of them as a soft yellow light pulsed inside the sphere. Laxtus looked at them with curiosity as the output of the orbs began to intensify until he was forced to cover his eyes. At that moment, both Zach and Sarah looked up, and Laxtus shuddered as he was drawn into the infinite depths of blackness that occupied the sockets where their eyes were supposed to be.

Shortly thereafter, the glow turned deep red, and a low-pitched hum shook the basement until the heavy overhead pipes began to sway. Zach reached over and took Sarah's hand, and in that instant, two thick, sludge-like streams of energy surged out from the orbs and merged, hitting the Einstein–Rosen Bridge as a shower of sparks covered Laxtus. He opened his eyes as the screens lit up. Shortly thereafter, the software rebooted and the spherical fins began to spin.

Laxtus stumbled and blinked before regaining his senses. He looked at the terminal and started to enter coordinates as the fusion reaction began forming the temporal bubble that would transport him back in time. Zach made eye contact as Laxtus' finger hovered above an icon on the touch screen.

He nodded at Zach and then stabbed it forcefully. For a moment, everything remained static, but the machine's output ramped up even higher, and the turbine-style fins rotated rapidly, which created an ear shattering high-pitched whine. Laxtus' composition began to break down into its molecular components until his physical body shattered into wisps of vapor, and his essence disappeared entirely. The screens on the apparatus flickered a few moments and then died out, but the steady, low hum of the orbs continued for some time until the red color receded, and the intensity of the light lessened. Finally, the deep yellow fluorescence signaled they had returned to their dormant state.

"I could rip your clothes off and fuck you in this room right now," said Zach as he looked at Sarah. He was panting, and a slick layer of sweat covered his body. She held his gaze with unbridled lust, and her eyes smoldered a deep red.

"Go ahead and do it you dirty bastard," she said. "I want you to. Right here on the floor. I—I need it."

Zach could barely restrain himself, and he closed his eyes to fight against a spontaneous orgasm. In any other circumstance, he would be on top of her clawing at her naked flesh, biting and drawing blood, perhaps ending the primal episode by killing her. Yet, from somewhere deep inside, he grasped onto the last remaining vestige of his soul and looked past the surging raw malevolence.

"Sarah, it's about Cox. Focus your hatred on him because he is all that matters. We must control these emotions, or they will destroy us."

She continued to look at him as her eyes glowed and spittle leaked from the corners of her mouth. Finally, her breathing slowed, and color returned to her cheeks. "I don't know if I want to fuck you or kill you," she said while still panting, "but you're right. My rage is reserved for that son of a bitch, Cox. Let's go."

They made their way back up the stairs to the ground floor. The people in the library were standing in place and looking around, trying to make sense out of the shaking and trembling they just experienced. Over at the counter, the perky receptionist was talking on the landline telephone. "It felt like an earthquake," she said with a hint of panic in her voice. "You had to feel it, did you not? I—I can't explain . . . No, it has stopped, but we all thought building was going to fall apart."

As Zach and Sarah made their way to the door, she put the phone down and said, "Excuse me. Do you know what just happened?"

Zach turned and said, "We created an Einstein-Rosen Bridge to send someone back to the past. But don't worry, it's over now."

Her eyes widened, but then she smiled. "That is sarcastic humor, is it not? Your words have a double meaning. Everyone knows that machine is a museum piece. Besides, time travel is one of the ten prohibited actions."

"I wouldn't worry about it. The building was probably settling. Everything is good," said Zach as he walked through the door and out to the street with Sarah next to him.

Finding a public ground crawler wasn't difficult once you understood the scheduling, and the trip to the Gehenna Center took less than ten minutes. As they walked through the revolving door, Zach was stunned at the transformation from what he remembered of the building when he and Marshall confronted Xavier Watts in the past.

"What if he doesn't show up?" said Sarah.

"We may have to wait, but Laxtus told us he would be here today. Patience . . ." It was at that moment that his eyes traveled over to the elevator bank. There was a small entourage that partially blocked his view, but through the gaps between the people, Zach recognized him immediately. The small frame and jet-black hair were clues, but it was the strands of dark energy wafting off his body that removed any doubt.

"Sarah." He pointed, and she followed his finger until her line of sight reached the elevator.

"Cox," she hissed and stormed in his direction with Zach closely following.

***

"Turn around and face me you son of a bitch." Sarah stood about five feet away and pointed towards the elevator. She noticed Cox' back stiffen slightly, but he said nothing.

Then slowly, he smiled and turned. On a primal level, the Benefactor understood he was in a grave situation, but something triggered another emotion he couldn't quite describe. *Could I actually be pleased to see people from the past even if they are here to destroy me?*

"Just like your mother," he said. "You can't get enough of me, can you, Sarah?" He heard the subsonic buzz of temporal energy gathering, but before he could make sense of it, Sarah unleashed a mass of telekinetic plasma that hit Mr. Cox with such force it propelled him backward, and his head hit the elevator door with a loud smack. Slowly, he recovered from the shock of the collision and faced her, the jeweled box that held the orb still in both hands.

389

Almost instantly, Genera Cron and Zietra X charged forward, but they stopped in mid-step and looked as though they were trudging through quicksand. Zietra X grunted and shook her head, but she no longer had control of her limbs. She fell to the floor with her hands curled and seized up like someone suffering from an epileptic seizure. Across from her, Cron lay still, looking unconscious or dead. The way their companions were so thoroughly neutralized seemed to affect the others, and they remained motionless standing next to the Benefactor.

Mr. Cox opened the jeweled box and sneered as high intensity yellow light leapt out and bathed the area in the familiar dark shade of yellow. "I should have killed you when that bitch of a mother killed herself," he said. For a moment, an expression of extreme confidence crossed his face, but when Sarah pulled her orb from a jacket pocket, he gasped and stepped back.

"How — how could you have . . ."

Sarah used his momentary confusion to strike again, and her enormous hurt, pain and hatred manifested itself in a mass of concentrated telepathic poison amplified by the power of the orb. She struck with blind fury on behalf of her mother, her aunt and uncle. The intensity of her attack escalated until it became an unhinged frenzy that purged the stain of every murder she committed while under Cox's control and every rape she endured while under his control.

The orb in her hand pulsed, and the color was so rich and red it overwhelmed the projections from Cox' own orb. Sarah's hands and fingers began to burn, and the flesh on her palm bubbled and blistered, but she didn't let go of the sphere. Just as Cox regained his wits and desperately tried to amplify his foul energy through the orb, he felt another jolt of black thought plasma. This one was even more powerful and concentrated. He used a small part of his consciousness to focus on the new assault and saw Randall holding a different orb.

The room started to spin, and everyone inside the lobby collectively covered their ears while stumbling around and screaming. The force of the dueling orbs was so powerful it sucked the oxygen from the center of the room. Mr. Cox, already losing the battle with Sarah, succumbed to the hopelessness of his situation as the assault from Randall overwhelmed him.

He reached out telepathically and desperately tried to negotiate.

"Please, let me live. I will give up the orb; I will give up my power. You can banish me to a remote area in an ancient time. I won't fight you."

"Too late," Zach sent back. "Your crimes are too severe. You must never be allowed to hurt anyone again."

Zach plunged through Mr. Cox' weakened shielding and drove deep into his brain with a telepathic explosive that detonated upon contact. Inside his head, Cox' brain burst against the interior of his skull. He dropped the jeweled box, and the orb rolled across the floor and stopped at Zach's feet. Mr. Cox fell backwards into the elevator door and slid down, a bloody smear tracing his path as he slumped over to the side, quite dead.

Sarah continued to project her darkest energy, and his flesh began to smoke and stink as it smoldered.

"Sarah, enough!" said Zach, but she continued her assault. Two small flames shot out of Cox' eye sockets, and his hair combusted shortly thereafter.

"Listen to me, Sarah!" Zach yelled again, and this time he grabbed her shoulder and shook her hard. For a moment, she curled her lip back and readied to attack. At the last instant, she seemed to regain a small sense of sanity, and it took hold as the seconds passed. Finally, she slumped over and began crying, reaching out and handing the orb to Zach.

The sound of the orbs lessened as the light energy dissipated. A few of the people lying on the floor began to stir, massaging their temples while trying to process what they just experienced. Most of them were bleeding from their ears, and a few wiped blood from eyes that were swollen and red from burst vessels.

Sarah and Zach continued to stare at Mr. Cox' body as it lay on the floor. By now, the flames had ignited his clothing, and as he reached flash point, a small fireball rose up and consumed him.

"Is it over? Is he finally dead, Zach?" said Sarah in a low whisper.

"Yes, he's gone. I experience nothing but emptiness when I reach out to him. His life force has been extinguished."

She nodded and said, "Now what? It feels like my entire life has revolved around this—thing. I have a deep sense of emptiness."

"I understand," said Zach. "The quest to stop him has crowded out everything else. I wonder how we can ever return to a cosmopolitan life again."

They looked at each other, and slowly, their hands clasped together. At that moment, Zach's mind, body and emotional core completed the reconnection process. As the last of the psychological bilge was swept away, his flood of emotions returned. The foremost and strongest was his love for Sarah, and he squeezed her hand tightly. He vowed that this time, he would never let her go.

As they stood staring blankly at the burning corpse, Zach's attention was distracted by the chiming of the elevator bell. He looked over just as the door slid open. An androgynous figure in a long robe and hood stepped out and looked down at the charred body, slowly shaking her head. He carried a bright metal box with six separate compartments. Without moving, she suddenly stood directly in front of Zach and Sarah.

"I will take the orbs now," he said while setting the box on the floor and lifting the lids of three compartments.

"Who — who are you?" asked Zach. "Why would we entrust you with something so powerful and evil?"

She stared deeply into his eyes and removed the hood, revealing skin that was a shade of ebony so deep Zach assumed it was genetically enhanced. His eyes were human but had a hint of feline in them. There were small, fleshy appendages surrounding her ear canals, and his perfectly spherical head was devoid of a single hair follicle.

"Of course, after all you have endured, you deserve an explanation," she said in a voice that sounded so soothing and pitch perfect Zach assumed it was artificial. "I am from a time in the distant future. Before we constructed a space-time Extron field, a firewall so to speak, the time traveling disruptions caused by those in previous centuries were very damaging to us and to the multi-dimensional structure of the galaxy. We should have been more diligent. Fortunately, your act of

393

terminating this individual," she said as he swept a hand behind her towards the dead body of Mr. Cox, "closed a catastrophic loop in space-time. The chapter is complete now, and the cataclysm averted. The future and past are reconnected and secure due primarily to your actions."

"I—I don't fully understand. The Corporates still need to be stopped," said Zach.

"You only need to look around yourself in this city to see the healing that has taken place. The effort you started in the 21st century has continued to grow and bear fruit. Your friend, Marshall Beiner, was at the forefront of a movement that usurped the Corporate Empire and laid the groundwork for the advanced utopian society from where I come. No one wants; no one needs."

"What about us?" said Sarah. "How can we go back to our time?"

The being shook her head and a look of sadness crossed his face. "As I said, the loop is now closed and quarantined. No one must ever pierce it as this would only create further instability."

"So, what will become of us?" said Zach.

The being tilted its head and looked away. "Both of you will join me, and you will be put into stasis. Your physical embodiments will be isolated so you cannot affect our timeline. However, you will never know you are unconscious inside the stasis tube. Instead, you will believe you are living out a full and complete life in your time. There will be no distinction. You will make decisions and control your destiny, and you will never suspect you are in an artificial reality."

Zach looked at Sarah. "I don't like it any more than you do, but we're long past the point where our own well-being matters. If I can be with you in any reality, that's good enough for me."

Sarah leaned down and picked up her orb. "Here, get these hideous things away from us."

The being nodded and took the orb and placed it into the first compartment of the container. The lid made a slight whooshing sound as it sealed, and the drone in the room decreased by a third. Zach handed her the other two orbs, and he packaged them similarly. By the time the third compartment closed, the room was completely silent except for the groaning of those on the floor.

"There are three other compartments in your case. Do you have the other orbs?" said Zach.

"Do not worry. The responsibility for the orbs is our burden now. Your task has been completed."

The being beckoned for them to follow, and Zach stepped over the bodies of Zietra X, Minkus Term, Ignasus Cron and the others, but the entity seemed to move through them. The elevator door opened, and she took a place near the rear of the cabin as Zach and Sarah followed. Zach remembered hearing the door shut and the bell chime . . .

***

On a bright day filled with sunshine, Zach adjusted the beach umbrella and moved his chair. The island remained deserted except for the locals and a few tourists who stayed past September. Hurricane season was fast approaching, but for some reason, he just knew the island would not be in the path of a hurricane this year.

He sipped his Mai Tai, leaned over, and kissed Sarah full on the lips. She was sleeping but had never looked so beautiful.

THE END